LIBRARIES NI
WITHDRAWN FROM STOCK

Somewhere Inside of Happy

Anna McPartlin

TRANSWORLD IRELAND

TRANSWORLD IRELAND PUBLISHERS
28 Lower Leeson Street, Dublin 2, Ireland
www.transworldireland.ie

Transworld Ireland is part of the Penguin Random House group of companies
whose addresses can be found at global.penguinrandomhouse.com

First published in the UK and Ireland in 2015
by Transworld Ireland/Doubleday Ireland
an imprint of Transworld Publishers

Copyright © Anna McPartlin 2015

Anna McPartlin has asserted her right under the Copyright,
Designs and Patents Act 1988 to be identified as the author of this work.

This book is a work of fiction and, except in the case of historical fact,
any resemblance to actual persons, living or dead, is purely coincidental.

A CIP catalogue record for this book
is available from the British Library.

ISBN 9781848271951

Typeset in 11½/15pt Sabon by Kestrel Data, Exeter, Devon.
Printed and bound in Grat Britain by Clays Ltd, Bungay, Suffolk.

Penguin Random House is committed to a sustainable
future for our business, our readers and our planet. This book
is made from Forest Stewardship Council® certified paper.

1 3 5 7 9 10 8 6 4 2

To my husband, Donal. I'd be lost without you.
(You're a bit like GPS that way . . .)

Prologue

Introducing Maisie Bean Brennan

The room was silent, but for the sound of shuffling, an un-identifiable clicking and Maisie's own heartbeat. Shuffle, click, boom, shuffle, click, boom. *Calm down, ya silly old cow. It'll be OK.*

She could feel her husband's hands on her shoulders. He was standing right behind her, at the side of the stage, and she could hear him talking in her head. *It's all good, lady, you're doing fine. Forget the sweats. Just smile.* She watched her daughter Valerie limp in and lean against her stepfather, then pull off her shoe and shake out a piece of gravel.

Her face and head were on fire: her latest hot flush had drenched her scalp, frizzing her lovely blow-dry at the roots. She tried to smile but her lips stuck to her upper teeth. *Oh, brilliant. Now I'll look mental.*

The distinguished, learned man introducing her to the stage had been talking for several minutes; clearly he liked the sound of his own voice. It was a nice voice, to be fair, posh and plummy, and he was so softly spoken it had a lulling effect as you listened.

Maisie was busy scanning the crowd and immediately spotted Deirdre, in an immaculate and expensive dark suit. Just behind her, Mitch and Jonno sat together. Mitch was eating a large ham roll, dropping half its contents on to Jonno's lap. *Years*

pass by . . . Everything changes, yet everything stays the same.
She looked for Dave: he'd promised he'd be there if he could, but
he toured a lot and his girlfriend had just given birth to twins.
That's no joke, Dave. She smiled to herself as she spotted him
moving across the aisle to push a gawky teenager out of his seat
so that he could sit with his old mate. John elbowed him and
grinned, then tickled the back of Lynn's neck, earning himself a
shake of one of her knitting needles.

Now Maisie focused on Lynn, who had been knitting since
she took her seat, lost in one-plain, one-purl. Over the years
Lynn had grown more and more nervous of crowds, but she
had been determined to be there for her best pal, and knitting
calmed her. Everyone who had contributed to the book was
there to support her. Even after all these years they stood by
one another. Her heart swelled. *The gang's all here.*

It would be the first and possibly last – depending on how
badly she ballsed it up – college lecture she'd give. Barely
educated Maisie Bean Brennan lecturing a bunch of academics?
It didn't feel real, but there she was, waiting in the wings a
few feet away from a large glossy poster of her book: *Jeremy's
Spoken: A Recollection of Love and Misunderstanding.* It was
a larger-than-life photo of her sixteen-year-old son Jeremy and
his best friend Rave, both glistening, fresh-faced and beaming.
She'd been looking at that photo for twenty years and it still
made her well up.

The plummy-accented academic looked her way. It was time.

'Ladies and gentleman, I now take great pleasure in introducing you to Maisie Bean Brennan.' The audience clapped
and Maisie felt her husband nudge her gently on to the stage.

'Go get 'em, Ma'sie,' Valerie whispered.

What am I doing here?

The clapping died down. She stood behind the lectern. The
room returned to silence, save for the murmur of youthful rest-
lessness.

Shuffle, click, boom, shuffle, click, boom.

Maisie cleared her throat, took a sip of water and separated her teeth from her lip. All eyes were on her. Theirs had been a story a long time in the making and it was time to tell it. She closed her eyes and inhaled deeply, opened them and began.

'My name is Maisie. My husband calls me Mai and me children call me Ma'sie but yous can call me what you like.'

There was a little laughter. Maisie wasn't sure if it was because of her opening line or accent. It didn't really matter, so she forged on.

'Me first-born, Jeremy, was conceived in violence and he died in violence, but while he was alive he was the light of me life.' Maisie's voice hitched slightly. *My sweet, lovely Jeremy.* 'I'm here to talk about him and the things our short time together taught me, if yous'll bear with me for just a little while.'

The students stopped shuffling, whispering and giggling. The fancy mahogany wood-clad hall disappeared. The shuffle, click, boom, shuffle, click, boom slowly quietened.

As Maisie continued, she was back in her small cottage in Tallaght, twenty years ago. It was the morning of 1 January 1995, the day her life had changed irrevocably, and the day her son's had ended.

'It started with my sixteen-year-old boy Jeremy waltzing his granny Bridie around the kitchen table . . .'

SUNDAY,
1 JANUARY 1995

Chapter One

'Jeremy'
Pearl Jam, 1992

Maisie

SEVENTY-EIGHT-YEAR-OLD BRIDIE BEAN was gliding around the room, her grandson Jeremy leading her in an old-time waltz. As Maisie looked on, Bridie counted to three, then pivoted. It was beautiful to watch and it seemed as though the old woman hadn't a care in the world. Maisie had spent most of her early morning bathing her mother, then dressing her in a crisp white shirt, a soft grey cardigan and her favourite tweed skirt, which came to just above the knee, then pinning her long white hair neatly into a smooth bun. Bridie liked to look nice so her daughter made sure that she was always pristine. It was the least she could do for her: despite her advanced age and mental condition, Bridie still enjoyed an innocent flirt and was full of fun. She was what the locals would refer to as a 'game old bird' and everybody loved her. As she twirled, her skirt lifted to reveal her twig-like legs moving in time to the music. She had no trouble keeping pace with sixteen-year-old Jeremy, and even though her mind was cluttered and foggy, ex-army nurse Bridie Bean was as fit as a flea. Vera Lynn's 'We'll Meet Again' played and she hummed along.

'Ah, it's just like the old days, Arthur – you, me and a bottle of rum.' She giggled to herself.

'Grammy, it's me, Jeremy!' Jeremy said. The last time he'd allowed her to think he was her long-lost husband, she'd mentioned how much she missed his manhood – and when the word 'vagina' fell out of her mouth Maisie's first-born complained of battling a combination of nausea and light-headedness. It was clear to Maisie that he wasn't willing to go through that trauma again. She smiled to herself when he stopped dancing and pointed to himself. 'Jeremy, your grand-son, so don't be mentioning your bits.'

'I know who you are, sunshine,' Bridie said. 'Just talking to your auld gramps in the sky.' She held out her right hand and he clasped it in his left. 'Once more around the table for luck.'

'All right, but then I'm off. It's me last day of holidays and I have a life, ya know.'

'Oh, I know,' Bridie whispered. 'Very exotic, filled with girls and secrets.' She tapped her nose with her index finger. 'I have a few secrets of me own.'

'Ah, Jesus,' he said, shaking his head, 'please don't start.'

'All right, love.'

Jeremy often feigned exhaustion, because it entertained his gran. It was a game Maisie often watched them play, a role reversal: he was the adult and she the bold child. She smiled at him and pushed his sandy hair away from his eyes. She didn't speak, just sighed contentedly, then tapped him on the shoulder.

'Good boy,' she said. She raised a finger in the air, turned slowly and pointed to the large sticker with the word 'Fridge' on it. She went towards it purposefully and opened the door. 'I would like cheese.'

Jeremy grinned at his mother. The old lady was having a good day.

Maisie intercepted her: 'Cheese gives you wind, Ma.'

'Well, it's a good thing I don't give a shite about wind.' Bridie laughed.

'Ah, let her, Ma'sie. Go on, Grammy, you only live once.'

'Ah, Jeremy loves me enough to let me pop off in peace.' Bridie's head was firmly stuck in the fridge as she rummaged around.

'Jeremy is a teenage boy. He finds your noisy arse hilarious,' Maisie remonstrated, as Jeremy grinned.

Bridie emerged from the fridge with a block of Cheddar. 'Ah, cheese,' she said, and Maisie watched her son's grin widen. If there was one thing you could say about Jeremy Bean, it would be that he loved his grammy. 'One thin slice. I'm cooking breakfast,' Maisie said firmly, and Bridie nodded, unwrapped the cheese and sank her teeth into it.

It was the first day of a new year and the last day of the Christmas school holidays so Maisie had made a large fry-up to celebrate both. Jeremy and Bridie were both tucking into theirs when she opened twelve-year-old Valerie's bedroom door to tell her to come and eat. Valerie was lying on her bed singing along, painfully loudly, to East 17's 'Stay Another Day'.

'I've been shoutin' "Breakfast!" at the top of me lungs for the past five minutes, Valerie Bean.'

'I'm not hungry yet, Ma'sie,' Valerie said.

'Get your skinny arse into the kitchen before I murder ya. Not hungry yet? Where do you think you are, the bleedin' Ritz?'

'As if! Bleedin' Holiday Inn is as far as we'd get.'

'Don't say "bleedin'" and move it,' Maisie warned.

Valerie huffed as she got to her feet.

Valerie was a tween before anyone had put a name to it. She liked loud pop music, black clothes, her room and little else. When she had turned eleven she had packed away all her dolls and cuddly animals, and a few weeks later she'd handed them to a gypsy woman, who had called to the door begging for old clothes. She had kept just a small pink Care Bear that her daddy had given her on the one and only occasion he'd visited after the separation. She had hidden it in the bottom of her wardrobe in a shoebox with her unused diary and a piece of sticky rock presented to her by her best and only friend, Noleen Byrne, following a family holiday in Blackpool. Valerie had licked it, then announced that it tasted like shite and rewrapped it.

Over Christmas, Maisie had introduced a swear jar to encourage her daughter to stop saying her two favourite words, 'bleedin'' and 'shite', but it simply served to highlight her own bad language. She had tried to change her ways after she was hauled into the school principal's office to discuss her daughter's use of the word 'shitebag'.

'To be fair, Principal Young, the lad was painting her hair with white Tippex.'

'That is not the point, Ms Bean.'

'I respectfully disagree.'

'Valerie is learning this kind of language somewhere and it's not in this school. We have strict rules about cursing here.' Principal Young handed Maisie a list of banned words. She surveyed the list, most of which Maisie uttered on a daily basis. 'I don't see "shitebag" here,' she said, in an attempt to lighten the mood.

Principal Young wasn't amused. 'Perhaps not, but you do see "shit", and "shite" is simply "shit" with an *e* on the end. We have no problem with "bag".'

Principal Young was being snotty. Maisie tolerated a lot but snottiness really got under her skin. It was her trigger, the thing that switched her gear from amenable to dogmatic. Normally she would have put that middle-class college-educated woman with the posh accent and bad attitude back in her box because Maisie did not react well to being looked down on. However, in this instance, her cheeks had flared red and she'd bitten her lip because the arrogant bitch was right. Valerie had picked up her cursing from herself and her mother, and although Maisie defended her right to express herself as she saw fit, little kids cursing was offputting. In that moment she resolved to set a better example for her children – after all, how hard could it be?

It turned out that it was very hard not to swear when you were a single mother of two and your mother was in the middle stages of dementia, you had a part-time job in a dental surgery during the week and cleaned a factory at weekends. By now the jar was overflowing. Maisie dreaded her next meeting with Principal Young.

When Bridie had still been well, she had often commented that Valerie would be the death of Maisie. 'I love the bones of her but she's hard raring, that child,' she'd say. She'd often smile as she said it, as though the notion pleased her. 'She'll come good, though. I see my mother in her – she'd have picked a fight with Jesus on the cross – and when the chips are down, Maisie, that's when our Valerie will come into her own.'

In contrast, Jeremy was the golden boy. He minded his grandmother, his mother and even his little sister when she'd allow him. Aside from his fondness for the word 'Jesus' (Bridie always maintained that it was used more as a prayer than a curse), he never swore, at least not in front of adults. He helped his ma carry the shopping and he always made sure the doors were locked and the fireguard was in front of the fire. He was the man of the house and he took his role seriously. Of course, he wasn't a saint: he had a very annoying habit of lecturing his mother.

'Jesus, Ma'sie, how many times do we have to talk about the dangers of hanging tights on the fireguard?'

'Sorry, son.'

'Seriously, Ma'sie.'

'You're right. Sorry.'

'Don't let me see it again.'

'You're crossing the line, buddy.'

'Sorry, Ma'sie – but tights off the fireguard.'

Sometimes Maisie dreamed of shoving a pair of tights into her son's mouth. He was mad for closing doors, too. He spent half his life shouting at people to shut them. It was especially annoying when the person he was roaring at was still walking through the door in question. Even Bridie had a pain in her face with it. 'Ah, for God's sake, child, let me get through the fucker first,' she had once hollered. Everyone got out of Bridie's way when she shouted.

Gentle, sweet, lovely Bridie had never shown any signs of aggression before she'd started to lose her marbles. The doctor explained that anger and lashing out were symptoms of her condition. It was understandable but every now and then, when she lost her temper, it terrified Maisie. Bridie had pushed Jeremy into a wall one day when he'd annoyed her over a door. He was shocked but pretended he was fine, even though he'd banged his elbow against the frame. Bridie breezed past as though nothing had happened but Maisie saw the tears in Jeremy's eyes. Her heart had sunk. *Oh, no.* It was only a small incident, no real harm done, but it had upset her and, more importantly, it had upset her son. Maisie had removed her children from one violent home and she didn't fancy having to do it a second time.

Since then, she had made sure that she took the brunt of her mother's outbursts. She'd been kicked, pushed, pinched and bitten, mostly when she was dressing or washing Bridie. It was nothing on the scale of what Maisie was used to – she batted her mother away easily, without suffering any real damage. She told herself that Bridie didn't know what she was doing, that she just had to keep it all under control, away from the kids, and everything would be all right. It made life more stressful, but she wouldn't abandon her mother when she needed her most.

Maisie left Valerie's room and took a moment to fix a photo of Bridie, Jeremy and Valerie on the hall wall. Bridie was front and centre and her grandchildren were climbing all over her. Even though it was raining and their hair was stuck to their heads they were laughing and happy. She wished she'd been in the photo too. At the time Bridie had told her to hand her camera to a passer-by – 'Maisie, get that spiky-haired young fella to take the picture' – but Maisie had thought the spiky-haired young fella looked like he'd have no problem taking off with it. It had been expensive, and if she lost it, she couldn't afford to replace it.

'You have trust issues,' Bridie had told her.

Maybe she did. The boy had been wearing runners. *I'd never catch him*, she'd thought, glancing down at her squelchy flip-flops. If she'd known then that, just a few short months later, her mother would display signs of dementia, she'd have risked it.

When the photo was straight, she returned to her mother and son in the kitchen. Bridie and Jeremy were finishing their breakfast when Valerie eventually joined them at the table.

'Well, it's about time, Maisie Bean,' Bridie said to Valerie.

'I'm Valerie.'

Bridie stared at her, trying to find some meaning. Valerie just ate her breakfast, pretending to ignore the mist that had descended behind the old woman's eyes.

Jeremy was patient and he seemed to know instinctively how best to handle Bridie when she was having a moment. Now he took her hand in his and hummed 'We'll Meet Again'. After a moment or two Bridie joined in, leaning on her grandson's shoulder, beating time to the music she could hear in her head.

'I think you need a rest, Grammy,' Jeremy said softly to her.

'And I think you're right, son.'

Maisie watched them walk down to Bridie's bedroom. He opened the door for her and she stepped through, turning to say, 'Nighty, night,' even though she had just had breakfast.

'Nighty, night, Grammy. Remember, Jeremy Bean loves you.' He always said that: it was a ritual.

Bridie blew him a kiss as he pulled the door to. She wouldn't remember it, but that was the last time Bridie saw her grandson alive.

*

19

Jeremy stayed in the house, babysitting his sleeping grand-mother, while Maisie spent an hour in the supermarket, curs-ing because the entire lay-out of the shop had changed.

'Why? Why would they do that?' Maisie ranted.

Valerie shrugged her shoulders. 'Maybe they knew it would make you mental, Ma'sie.'

Maisie skipped from the dairy aisle to the detergents. 'It was here, right? There were fridges right here with pre-packed meat in them last time we came, right?'

'Right.'

Maisie spun around. 'Who puts the dairy aisle next to de-tergents?'

'It's bleedin' unsanitary,' Valerie mumbled.

'Ten pence in the jar.' Maisie stalked off towards what would turn out to be the biscuit aisle. As she turned into Jams and Canned Goods for the third time, she spotted her daughter emerging from the next aisle.

'Dog food,' Valerie said.

'Right, back to Pizzas and Frozen Veg – it has to be some-where near there.'

'Jesus, Mas'ie, we've done that one three times already.'

Maisie was trying hard not to lose it but supermarket shop-ping was her least favourite occupation, even when the super-market powers that be weren't trying to mess with her mind. *I'm going to write a letter of complaint. Dear Bastards . . .*

It was hot and stuffy and Maisie's head hurt from too much wine. *Stupid New Year's Eve.* She had spent it alone. Her mother had gone to bed at just after seven p.m., her son had been with his friends and Valerie was holed up in her bedroom. *Still, at least she's not doing drugs . . . yet.* Maisie was terrified of drugs. She had read every pamphlet imaginable on the subject and watched her children, like a hawk, waiting for the signs, paying particular attention to her twelve-year-old daughter. Each day she performed a mental check on Valerie: *Appearance? Unchanged. Good. Eating habits? Unchanged.*

Good. Change in interests? No. Good. Rude or rebellious attitude? Always has been rude and rebellious so no change there. Good. Change in friends' line-up? No, still just one friend. Although that does concern me – Jeremy's so popular . . . Moody? She was born moody . . . Left to her own devices, Maisie had opened a bottle of wine and drunk it in front of Jools Holland. A few fireworks had gone off at midnight, setting off Vera Malone's dog, Jake. His howls were punctuated by Vera roaring, 'You didn't do that when the house was being burgled. It's a wonder ya didn't make those lads a cup of fuckin' tea!' Through the wall, she couldn't tell if the dog had quietened due to shame or fatigue.

Maisie wasn't used to drinking. She had stumbled to bed, stubbed her toe on the night-stand, and when she'd lain down the room had been spinning. She had felt fine when she woke but now, walking around the seventh circle of Hell, her head hurt, her toe pounded, sweat was emanating from every pore and she felt nauseous.

She stopped, sighed, and turned around slowly, taking in the shampoo and moisturizers on the shelves. 'All I need is a fucking chicken.'

'That's another ten pence in the jar. So, with "arse", "bleedin" and "fuckin" you're thirty pence poorer and it's not even midday,' Valerie pointed out smugly.

'I didn't say "arse",' Maisie said, and set off in the direction of the deli counter.

'You did so. You told me to get my skinny arse into the kitchen first thing this morning.'

Maisie remembered and sighed. *Bollocks*, she thought, as she reached the new butchery area, which was close to the deli. A boy in a white, slightly bloodied apron and a paper hat he'd pinned to the crown of his head stood leaning on the counter, one leg stretched in front of him. 'Could you please tell me where on earth the frozen chickens are?' She was trying not to sound aggravated but she was failing.

The young fella, with a faceful of spots and a thick fringe glued together with gel, eyed her. 'They're in the freezer.'

She gritted her teeth. 'But where is the freezer?'

'Behind me.' He gestured over his shoulder.

She looked past him to a wall with a heavy stainless-steel door in its centre. 'Why?'

'Because this is the butcher's.'

'I know it is, but the frozen meat has always been on the aisle, not in the butcher part.'

'Well, me ma says a change is as good as a rest.' He shrugged.

'Does she now?' Maisie pictured herself wringing his neck. 'Well, may I suggest that you put some signs up to direct customers around this ridiculous new system?'

The young fella looked from Maisie to Valerie and threw his eyes to Heaven. Valerie gave him the finger. 'Making eyes about my ma! The state of ya.'

Valerie might indeed have been hard raring but she was loyal. Aside from the hand gesture, Maisie felt proud.

'Am I talking to myself?' Maisie asked.

'Look, missus, do ya want a frozen chicken or do ya want to rant some more?'

Maisie parked her tongue in her right cheek. She leaned into the counter, ready to let him have it.

'There ya are, Maisie! Happy New Year.' Fred Brennan was holding out his hand to shake hers.

Oh, Jesus. She was caught rotten. The young fella grinned and walked away.

'Garda Brennan, hello! What do you have to do to get a chicken around here?' She pretended to laugh. *Oh, God, I'm pathetic.*

'Whatever you do, don't hold the place up, at least not until I leave.'

Together they moved away from the butcher's counter and into the centre of the aisle.

'How are you, Maisie?' The question was weighted with his concern.

Maisie's cheeks flashed red. 'I'm fine, really, good, even.' He was nodding along but he was clearly waiting for more. 'Er, great, yeah, great, and thanks again for everything you did for us, Garda Brennan.'

'You never have to thank me, Maisie, and how many times do I have to tell you to call me Fred?'

'Sorry, Fred.'

'So you've never heard anything from him, Maisie?'

Fred always asked about Maisie's ex-husband. It had been years since Danny had disappeared without a trace, and part of her wished he'd stop asking.

'No. Nothing. He's gone for sure.' *Now let it go, will ya?*

Fred turned to Valerie, looming over her. At six foot six Fred looked down on most people. 'And how are you, Valerie?'

She shrugged – it was the best answer he was going to get. Maisie's kids were not comfortable around grown men. To be honest, Maisie wasn't either.

He moved on quickly. 'How's Jeremy and your ma?'

'Grand, thanks.'

'And work?' Fred had set Maisie up with the job in the dental surgery. The dentist was a friend of his from his golf club.

'Lovely, thanks again.'

'Will you stop thanking me? I just got you an interview, you did the rest. And, just so you know, you're doing a great job there. How's the cleaning going? Are you still at it?'

'Ah, yeah . . . It's handy money.' Once the young, wide-eyed Maisie had had big dreams. Then she'd met her ex-husband. The snob in Maisie hated admitting how she supplemented her income.

'If they were all like you, Maisie Bean, women would rule the world.'

Valerie made a puking sound and Maisie shot her younger child a filthy look.

'You're a great woman, Maisie.'

She didn't know how to respond to that. Silence followed, and it slowly dawned on her that he seemed uncomfortable. He was a nice-looking man but right now he appeared rather too warm and slightly sweaty. 'A great woman,' he repeated. She wondered if his cheeks were red because he, too, was battling a hangover or whether he'd picked up the bug that had struck down half her road. *Please don't sneeze on me. I don't have time to be sick.* 'It's very hot in here, isn't it?' she said.

'Roasting.' Fred's eyes darted around the aisle. He pulled at his beard and rubbed his nose vigorously.

'Well, I should get on.' She was wondering how to make a quick getaway.

He nodded and smiled but he looked as if he might just burst into tears. As she passed him, he took hold of her arm – not viciously like Danny used to, but gently – with both hands. It felt warm, cosy and nice. His face was now the colour of beetroot. 'I'd love to take you out for a meal,' he said, the words racing out of his mouth. He redirected his gaze to the floor, let go of her arm and rubbed his chin.

Maisie was a little shocked. 'I'm sorry?' She looked from Fred to Valerie, whose mouth hung wide open.

'Anytime you're free.'

'Right.' Maisie wasn't sure what to say. A thousand thoughts spun in her head. *Is this a joke? Why me? Nah, I didn't hear him right, did I? I'm losing it. What if . . . ? Jesus, I can't! I couldn't. He is lovely-looking under that bleedin' beard, though. But I have two kids! He knows too much. Still, he's very kind. No, it's not right. I've nothing to wear! Although Ma's red silk dress fits and it's a classic . . .*

'Maisie?' His voice sounded small after what seemed an eternity of silence.

'Yes?'

'Any chance of an answer?'

'Yes,' she said.

'Great, fantastic,' he breathed.

Maisie froze. *Oh, Jesus! I just meant yes I would answer the question, not yes I'll go out with ya!*

'How about tonight?'

'Tonight?' Maisie looked at her daughter, who stared back at her, mouth still wide open, eyes bulging.

'Come on, please say yes.' He wasn't exactly begging but at the same time the hope in his voice made it impossible to say no.

'All right. Yes.'

'Great. Seven o'clock. I'll pick you up,' he said. 'Fantastic!'

'OK.' Maisie nodded.

He clapped his hands and rubbed them briskly together. Then he tipped an invisible hat, winked and was gone.

She felt rooted to the floor, bewildered, wondering what the hell had just happened – and how she was going to get out of it.

Her daughter crossed her arms over her chest. 'I'm telling Jeremy and Grammy on you.'

Maisie felt a little ill and started to walk away.

'What about the chicken?' Valerie asked.

'We'll have pizza. At least we know where it bleedin' is.'

'Forty pence,' Valerie called, running after her mother, who was racing up the aisle.

Valerie

Valerie was silent most of the way home. She liked Fred, always had, but the idea of him taking her ma out did not sit well with her.

She didn't share Jeremy's vivid memories of the years spent with their father. At the time, she couldn't make sense of her fear: she was too young to grasp the terrible reality that her father regularly beat the living shit out of her mother. She woke to muffled screams behind closed doors; she noticed make-up covering bruises; she watched her mother clean blood from walls and surfaces while listening to silly excuses about broken heels, swinging doors and, once, the ridiculous 'Sure that's just some jam!' She was only five when Maisie had spent three weeks in hospital with extensive injuries. Her memories were foggy and confused, filled with blanks and questions. Her mother never spoke about the past and, although Valerie didn't know a lot, she knew enough not to ask. Her dad was someone she'd buried deep, and with each day that passed, he drifted further and further away. On the very rare occasions he crept into her mind, she pictured him as charming and funny – he had swung her around, raising her high in the air, laughing when she squealed – but beneath that vision of the ideal dad she had a fuzzy recollection of a loud, scary man.

It had been a full seven years since her parents' marriage had ended and her father had vanished. Her mother hadn't dated anyone in that time. Aside from Jeremy (and Jeremy didn't count), their home was man-free, just the way Valerie liked it. Valerie knew Fred as a man in uniform who swooped in and sorted out trouble: he turned up when everyone was crying and left when they had stopped. Her most vivid memory was of waking in his arms when he was carrying her from her bedroom to his car. She was wearing a pink nightdress, patterned with white bunnies. It smelt of soap and he smelt of cigarettes mixed with spicy cologne. He'd wrapped her in a blanket and held her close to his chest. When she had woken she had been scared, as any child would have been, to find a giant with a black beard holding her tight, and she'd cried. He'd smiled at her, wiped away the tears with his free hand, told her she was safe and that he was minding her mammy. 'Do you love your mammy?' he asked her.

She'd nodded.

'Well, she needs you to be strong,' he said, 'and I promise I'll keep you all safe.' Five-year-old Valerie wasn't sure what was happening but in that moment she felt safer than she ever had before.

She knew that Fred was a good man but even the good ones couldn't be trusted – she'd heard her ma say so. Now the thought of where this one date might lead sent her into a silent panic. Her heart raced as she envisaged the wedding, Jeremy walking Maisie down the aisle, all smiles, and she'd be following behind, wearing some stupid bile-yellow or vomit-green dress, with poxy flowers in her hair and a face like thunder. Life would never be the same again. She felt herself welling up, and the back of her nose, just below her eyes, burned. She rubbed it with her closed fist and faced forward, holding it together even though she was now imagining a baby – it looked like a monkey – cradled in her mammy's arms. *Can me ma even have kids any more?*

She sensed her mother wanted to talk but she had nothing to say, so she just stared ahead and fumed.

Maisie

Maisie sneaked glances at Valerie all the way home. She tried to make a little conversation when they were on their second tour of the roundabout. Maisie didn't do roundabouts. She could never work out which lane she was supposed to be in to avoid collisions, aggravated beeping and/or profane hand gestures so she drove round and round until theirs was the only car left on the road, then turned as quickly as she could, darting across lanes and hoping there wasn't a cop car anywhere in the vicinity. It drove Jeremy mad but Valerie never seemed to notice.

'Are you looking forward to going back to school tomorrow, Monkey?' Maisie asked, desperate to break the silence.

'Don't call me Monkey. In fact can we put that word into the swear jar?'

'No.'

'Unfair.' Unfair was Valerie's third favourite word behind 'bleedin'' and 'shite'.

'OK,' Maisie said. 'You can put "monkey" in if I can put in "unfair".'

Valerie huffed, but at least she didn't look like she was about to burst into tears. That was something.

When they were finally off the roundabout Maisie made one last attempt to connect in some kind of meaningful way. 'Why don't we have a girls' day next Saturday?'

Valerie eyed her. 'Can we buy things?'

'What kind of things?'

'There's a hole in me schoolbag and me tracksuit's so small it's up around me knees. It's bad enough doing PE without having your teacher ask why you're wearing shorts in winter.' It wasn't often that Valerie was embarrassed, but Maisie could see the tell-tale pink in her cheeks.

'Done.' *What kind of a mother am I?* Maisie spent her life second-guessing herself. She burdened herself with blame and shame. Without a father it was up to her to do everything right so that her kids didn't grow up to be the 'product of a broken home'. She'd read a lot about it, and the theory that a broken home meant broken kids was widely agreed upon. As far as middle-class academics were concerned, her kids were far more likely to end up pregnant, on drugs and/or in jail than those with two parents. She felt like crying but didn't allow it to show.

'And can we have McDonald's?'

'As if we'd have a girls' day without McDonald's,' Maisie said lightly.

Valerie smiled. 'All right, then.'

'Great.' *Calm down, Maisie.* Fred had blindsided her and she felt overwhelmed. It was a feeling she had experienced often but it didn't make it easier to cope with. She didn't consider herself an anxious person, she only worried when she had something to worry about. Fred Brennan was an attractive, kind, caring man, who deserved better than being stood up. *How can I let him down without hurting him?* Fred had been so good to

Maisie. He had pretty much saved her, and she felt obligated to him even after all the years that had passed. Fred still cared for her and her kids. She didn't want to ruin that.

Maisie started opening and closing her free hand as it hovered over the gear stick, earning herself a suspicious eyeing-up from Valerie. 'Cramp,' she lied. She was making a fist and letting it go, just like Lynn always told her to do. She wasn't sure if it worked but there was no harm in giving it a go.

Valerie was silent for another second, then sniffed and rubbed her nose again. 'Well, if you think a trip to McDonald's means I'm happy about you dating the copper, it doesn't.'

'Didn't think that for a second,' Maisie said. *No one in this car is happy about that, love.*

'And Jeremy's going to lose it,' Valerie warned.

'I've no doubt.'

The last time he had thought Maisie was dating was when her American cousin had called without warning. Jeremy had slammed the door in Matt's face, then shouted through the letterbox, 'She's not seeing anybody. She's not able for it.' He was merely repeating what he'd heard his mother tell well-meaning friends on the phone. Then he had closed the letterbox, walked down the hall and slammed the kitchen door, leaving a bemused Matt standing outside.

Maisie had been in the back garden, hanging clothes out to dry and only discovered what her son had done when Matt phoned later that evening. She was terribly apologetic and he was very understanding, but although he'd promised to call again before he left for home, he hadn't attempted a second visit.

Valerie was spot on. Five years had passed since Matt's arrival but Maisie was more worried about Jeremy's reaction to the idea of her on a date than she was about Valerie's. Jeremy had terrible memories of what they had gone through with his father. That night, when an ambulance had collected his mother, with head injuries, and his sister had been carried out of the house in her nightdress, Jeremy had also been in hospital, having his arm plastered, because his dad had flung him across the room. He had dared to stand in front of his mammy, crying and begging his dad to stop banging her head against a wall. Jeremy's broken arm and tortured screams had distracted his father from killing his mother, and those screams had been the last straw for Maisie. After that there was no going back. From that night they were on their own: no one really gets over that level of violence and betrayal.

Jeremy's not going to like this. I can't just spring it on him. And who in hell asks a woman out in a supermarket? When did I last shave my legs? Do I even have a razor? Maisie's stomach filled with butterflies as they pulled into the driveway. Valerie's seatbelt was unbuckled and she was out of the car, barging through the front door and calling her brother before Maisie had parked and switched off the engine.

She took a moment to gather herself, gripping the steering-wheel. Then she got out, grabbed the shopping bags from the boot, slammed it shut and went into the house.

Valerie was hollering her brother's name as he emerged from the toilet.

'Keep it down, Shortstuff. Grammy's still sleeping.' He always called her Shortstuff, even though she was taller than most of the girls in her class.

Nobody wanted Bridie to wake until at least lunchtime: when she was rested she was less agitated, even when she became confused. She often walked at night, up and down the narrow bungalow hallway, for hours at a time, shuffling along the wooden floor. It was no good trying to coax her into bed when she was in walking mode: she'd fight for her right to lose herself in her own hallway. She'd whisper to herself, or sing softly, and sometimes she was silent, her eyes disappearing behind a fog. They all made sure to double-lock the doors and Maisie had even had the windows secured with fancy keys to ensure Bridie didn't make it outside. Jeremy's window key had gone missing so he locked his door from the inside to ensure Grammy couldn't pass him during the night and hop out of the window. It was a fire hazard but Maisie had put a wrench under every bed so they could all break their windows to escape if they had to. It also served as a tool to batter any would-be rapist or psycho killer who saw women and kids in a bungalow as an easy target. To date, Bridie hadn't tried to escape the house in the wee hours and the wrenches were still in their wrappers.

'You're not going to believe what's after happening,' Valerie said to Jeremy, who was relieving his mother of two of the four bags she was laden with.

'Wha'?' His tone suggested he wasn't very interested.

'Flintstone asked me ma out.' The kids had been calling him Flintstone since the day, two years previously, when he had told them to call him Fred, rather than Garda Brennan. Big mistake.

'Do not call him Flintstone,' Maisie said, heading for the kitchen.

'Yeah, right.' Jeremy laughed a little. He followed his mother, Valerie trailing behind.

'He did, I swear.'

'Are you messin'?'

Valerie shook her head and folded her arms. Jeremy looked from his sister to his mother. 'Seriously?'

Maisie sighed. She'd made a decision in the car. If she was going to let Fred down she'd have to do it gently over dinner. It was the least she could do under the circumstances. *Anyway, he'll probably see sense halfway through and realize I'm not for him.*

'It's just dinner,' Maisie said. *I can't believe I'm saying this.*

'And a drink. Dinner always means drinks,' Valerie said.

Jeremy sat himself on the stool as though his legs had suddenly lost the strength to hold him upright. 'Jesus, Ma, you're not going through with it, are ya?'

'I am.'

'Why?'

I can't stand the man up, son. Even if Maisie hadn't been caught on the hop, she would probably have said yes: Fred had been so kind for so many years, going above and beyond for her and her kids. He'd been a friend to her when she needed one most. How could she say no to a man who wouldn't dream of saying no to her? Still, in that moment it occurred to her that the inability to say no was what had got her pregnant and married the first time around. Look how that had ended.

'Ma, answer me.'

'It's dinner, Jeremy, that's all.'

'And a drink,' Valerie repeated.

'And why not?' she heard herself ask. *Have you lost your mind, woman?*

'Why not?' Jeremy echoed, as though he couldn't believe he'd heard her correctly. '*Why not?*' He shook his head. 'You know why not.' His voice had an edge to it.

'He's not your da, Jeremy. He's a nice man.'

'You don't know that,' he said sharply, but there was more fear than anger in the words.

'I do.'

'No, you don't, not for sure! You thought me da was lovely and look what happened.'

Maisie didn't argue. It would have broken Jeremy's heart to know the real story behind her marriage to his father.

Danny Fox had asked her out one evening and because she was polite she had agreed – even though she didn't have much time for him. In fact, despite his good looks, he wasn't even on her radar: he was vain and boastful, even though he had little to boast about. Saying yes had been easier than saying no, and what harm would it do? At the end of the evening, he'd kissed her and it was an OK kiss, a little too frantic but not the worst she'd ever had. But when she tried to walk away he had grabbed her. She'd still had half a bag of chips in her hand when Danny Fox had forced her up against the wall. It had taken her a minute or two to realize they were having sex.

She'd tried to push him away but he'd responded by pressing her head against the wall, then banged it hard, once, twice, three times, as he came. Her stomach twisted.

'That was superb – I knew it would be.' He grinned, grabbing a chip.

Maisie was stunned. Her head hurt and her knickers felt wet. She touched the back of her head, and when he saw blood on her fingers, he asked her what had happened.

'You banged me head against the wall,' she'd said, in shock. Tears stung her eyes and her chest felt like it was about to burst. *What happened? We were just kissing and then . . . and then . . .* Maisie was confused and angry. She wanted to throw her chips in his face, kick him in the shin and run but he was smiling at her and holding her hand.

'Ah, Jesus,' he said, examining her head, and he seemed genuinely sorry. 'I must have lost the run of meself.' He held her hand all the way home and told her how beautiful she was. Maisie felt sick and uneasy. She kept wondering what she'd done wrong. She worried that her dress was too short but she knew it wasn't. She thought about where she'd rested her hands on him when he kissed her. Had she kissed him too deep or given him any kind of signal? She just didn't understand, and decided to put the whole thing to the back of her mind. There was no point in crying over spilled milk. She'd just be more careful. She'd learn from her mistakes.

It wasn't until ten years later, when she read an article in a magazine, that she realized she had been date-raped, so when Danny arrived the next day with a box of chocolates and introduced himself to Bridie as Maisie's boyfriend she didn't scream or call the guards. Instead she worried that if she told him to leave he'd spread rumours about her. *I'll give him a month and then I'll break it off, no harm done. There'd be nothing worse than being branded some kind of whore.* A month passed and she spent much of the time avoiding being alone with him, using her friends or her mother as excuses not to see him. If he suspected she was avoiding intimacy with him he didn't say. He behaved like a gentleman, relatively speaking. He didn't open doors or pull out her chair for her but he didn't slip his mickey into her while she wasn't looking either.

She wanted to break it off on the fourth Sunday: it seemed an appropriate day to end things. She had it all worked out but then he'd phoned her on the Friday, all excited because he was going away for a week.

'Great news,' he'd said. 'My da's brother's had a stroke so there's a free space on their golfing trip.'

'Oh! When are ya off?' Her heart had dropped to her stomach.

'Sunday morning.'

Ah shite.

She had no option but to wait and by then they would be going out for six weeks, which was a totally respectable amount of time to end things. But by the time he'd returned home, everything had changed. There was no escape.

No mother ever wants to explain to her child that on the night they met his father had shoved himself into her without asking, banged her head so hard that she'd needed it stitched and got her pregnant before her chips had gone cold. Even now she never referred to the incident as rape, not even in her own head. She couldn't bear it. She'd always let Jeremy believe that his da had played nice at first, but the truth was that Maisie Bean never could tolerate Danny Fox. Maisie didn't know much about men but it was clear to her that gentle giant Fred Brennan was a very different man from her husband.

She also knew that Jeremy was waiting for her to say she would tell Fred Brennan to go away, but the longer he waited the clearer her mind became. *He's a good man, a kind man. He's not Danny. It's just a night out, and I'm a grown woman, for God's sake.* Suddenly Maisie felt the knot in her stomach unfurl. She eyeballed her two kids.

'I'm going out on a date with Fred Brennan tonight. Nothing bad is going to happen. I might even have a good time. No arguments.' She watched Jeremy process the news. He craned his neck and pulled his left arm towards the floor with his right. He did this whenever he was stressed. When Bridie was well enough to notice her grandson's idiosyncrasies she used to laugh and say it looked like he was trying to pull it off.

'Right, then. I'm going for a run,' he said eventually, bolting for the door.

'What?' Valerie punched her brother's arm as he passed her. 'Is that it?'

'Jesus, Shortstuff, what do you want from me?' he said, hands in the air, then turned away, walked out of the house and closed the door behind him, leaving Valerie and Maisie to face off.

'Flintstone's a plonker,' Valerie grumbled.

'You may not like me spending time with Fred but, Valerie Bean, if I ever hear you bad-mouth that man again, you can pack your bags!' Maisie said, allowing her temper to get the better of her. It took her by surprise. It was the first time she had ever threatened to kick out her child. Immediately she felt guilty. She turned away from her startled daughter and started to put away the shopping.

'I'm only twelve,' Valerie mumbled, as she headed for the door.

'Yeah, well, no more from you, madam,' Maisie said, tears stinging her eyes. *That was too harsh. I'm sorry, love.* She would have never said that to Jeremy. Valerie had a way of bringing out the worst in her. *I'll make her a cup of hot chocolate later. Two marshmallows and extra love.* She pulled herself together, glanced at her watch and caught a glimpse of her reflection in the window. Five hours to the date and her hair was a mess. When she frowned, her eyebrows met in the middle, and she had a small strawberry blotch on her left cheek. *I look like seven shades of shite.* Was she making a huge mistake?

An hour later, Maisie was hovering in front of a boiling kettle. It was the third time she'd boiled it. Each time she'd walked off to wash dishes, wipe cupboards or sweep a floor. Each time she'd forgotten to make herself the cup of tea she told herself she needed. She was filled with guilt about her handling of Valerie's outburst, and dreaded eating a meal with a lovely man only to let him down, when Jeremy appeared behind her.

'Ma?'

'Yeah, son?' She turned to greet him just as the kettle reached the boil.

'You should go out. Everything's going to be all right.'

'Ya think?' He'd shocked her.

'I know.'

He wasn't going to give her a hard time. It made her both happy and sad. 'When did you get so grown-up?'

He smiled at her. 'It crept up on me, Ma.'

As he walked away she could feel the tiniest pain dart across her heart.

Chapter Two

'Sunday Sunday'
Blur, 1993

Maisie

BRIDIE SPENT THE AFTERNOON watching *Blockbusters* on TV. She loved all game shows but she described *Blockbusters* as her 'very, very favourite'. When Maisie asked her mother if she wanted anything, Bridie thought for a second and said, 'I'll have a T, please, Bob,' just like one of the contestants on the show, 'and make that T with two sugars.' They laughed. The sleep had done her good.

Maisie laid her hand on her mother's head. 'A T with two esses comin' up.'

'Yeah.' Bridie giggled. 'Two esses.'

Jeremy had gone out with his friends to play soccer and Valerie was in her room, listening to music and sulking. It was raining, and as Maisie made her way into the kitchen she lamented that her son hadn't put on a coat.

'He's a big boy now,' Bridie said.

'I know, Ma, but he'll be a big boy dyin' of pneumonia if he's out in a bleedin' hurricane in a tracksuit top.' She heard her mother tutting at the TV.

'If you don't know that the MS that accompanies a lamb

37

dinner is mint sauce, you've no bleedin' business being there, son.'

Bridie had watched that particular episode at least twenty-five times. After eleven series the show had ended, and all they had was a videotape of twenty programmes that Bridie watched over and over again. Maisie squeezed the teabag: her mother liked her tea strong. She reviewed the colour, not deep enough. She swirled it around the cup and squeezed again.

There had been a time when she would have confided in her mother about the date – she might even have shared a smidgen of the excitement that was quietly building, despite her reservations and her determination to end things before they began. She wondered what her ma might have said when she still had her faculties. Bridie had liked Fred: she'd described him as a good man. She'd always had a smile for him and insisted he never left her house without a slice of cake to take away. 'A man like him shouldn't be alone,' she'd said once, but she hadn't expanded. Bridie had never shown an interest in finding a man to replace Arthur, even though she'd only just celebrated her thirty-fifth birthday when he'd died of a massive heart attack in his own bed.

In the first few years after her separation Maisie had been so raw and scarred that she couldn't bring herself even to think about being with another man, and by the time the wounds had healed, Bridie was acting a little strangely. Within a short space of time, Maisie's greatest support had become another burden. Maisie worked hard to keep everything together but she was struggling to keep her head above water. She was exhausted most of the time, stretched so thinly in a constant battle to compensate whichever family member she felt she'd let down. She hated second-guessing herself and she had tried to stop but it was like asking a bee to stop buzzing. Impossible. It wasn't just Danny who had sown the seeds of self-doubt in her: she did it to herself. Her mother used to tell her, 'Maisie Bean, you're your own worst enemy. Nobody's perfect. Do your best, that's all you can do and it's good enough.'

But often it wasn't. It wasn't good enough that her daughter was wearing tracksuit bottoms so small they looked like shorts or that she cursed like a trooper because it was all she heard at home. It wasn't good enough that she'd let Jeremy outside without a coat in a bleedin' rainstorm, and it certainly wasn't good enough that if he did get ill she didn't know where she'd find the money for a doctor, even though she'd promised her little girl McDonald's and a shopping trip just a week after she'd borrowed money from Lynn to get them all through Christmas. She worried about paying her back. *It won't be till February at least.* Every time she shouted at or lost patience with her mother, she regretted it, and every bruise her mother received from fighting her and slamming herself off walls was Maisie's fault. She saw how Lynn's ma was with her: she never fought Lynn or, at least, not with the same aggression. Lynn carried herself with authority so no one messed with her. Everyone messed with Maisie.

As she squeezed the teabag, she lurched from feelings of intense anxiety (*Oh, God, what have I agreed to?*) to excitement (*I like him. I've always liked him*), guilt (*I have no business going out on a date*) and back to anxiety (*Oh, God, how do I let him down?*). She poured in a drop of milk, then stirred in two sugars and brought in the tea, with a plate of biscuits, to her mother, who was still staring at the TV screen. 'Here you go, Ma, nice and strong just the way you like it.'

Bridie smiled and nodded. Maisie sat quietly next to her, her head bursting with questions. *What if?* Bridie sipped her tea. *If you could think straight, Ma, what would you say? I wish I knew. I wish you could tell me what to do.*

Bridie went to bed at seven and it was usually well after midnight before she'd start wearing a hole in the floor. Maisie was planning to be home by eleven at the latest. Bridie didn't have to know anything about her date with Fred Brennan. She'd only worry, then forget anyway. Maisie and Bridie had never spoken about men: it just wasn't something her mother was comfortable with.

Back in 1977, five weeks after that fateful date with Danny, Maisie had complained of feeling ill, and after losing Arthur so tragically Bridie was not about to take any chances with her daughter. She had marched Maisie straight to the doctor. Even though Maisie was eighteen it hadn't occurred to anyone in the room that Bridie should wait outside – after all, Dr Brown had been Bridie's GP since before Maisie was born. By the time he'd grasped that a totally clueless Maisie was pregnant, it was too late to ask her mother to step outside.

Bridie had needed a chair, a glass of water and a Disprin to thin her blood and prevent a stroke. Forgotten, Maisie was left standing there, head spinning, with a terrible urge to vomit on Dr Brown's pale green rug. Following what would later be referred to as 'the incident in Doc Brown's', it wasn't so much decided as expected that Maisie would marry Danny, especially after her mother had spoken to Father Benton: he had made clear to her that neither she nor her daughter would be welcome in his church if the matter wasn't handled one way or the other. Maisie would marry Danny and raise the child or go to the nuns and give it up. It was that simple.

In the years that had followed, her mother, along with the rest of the country, had become a little more educated and the Church had slowly lost control of people's sex and family lives. Since then, Bridie had often apologized to her for the 'great mistake', starting when Maisie had had brain surgery – Danny's final beating had left her with extensive injuries, including a major blood clot. She'd opened her eyes to find Bridie holding her hand and smiling through tears. 'There she is. Do you know who I am? I'm your mammy,' she had said slowly and loudly.

Maisie knew who her mammy was but she couldn't answer as her jaw was wired shut.

'I love ya, Maisie, and I'm sorry I made ya marry that man.

You and the kids are coming home with me. If God's mean-spirited enough to send us to Hell, well, we'll go together, love, you and me and a bottle of rum.'

So Maisie finally found the courage, strength and support to leave her husband. The kids had originally been called Bean-Fox because Maisie had insisted on keeping her name and Danny had agreed they could have both names: being a gobshite he'd thought Bean-Fox made them sound upper-class. It made it much easier after they split, as she immediately dropped Fox and it was as though Danny had never existed, at least for Maisie and Jeremy. For two lovely years afterwards Bridie had been Maisie's partner and friend. They were happy, and once the kids had settled in, they felt secure for the first time in their lives. Maisie worked her two jobs, and Bridie helped with the kids. Things were good until Bridie started losing her reason and Maisie lost her rock. Every day Maisie felt her mother drifting away from her, little by little, piece by piece . . .

'Oh, God, I miss you, Ma,' she said now. It had just slipped out, and her hand went up to cover her mouth.

Bridie peered at her daughter through watery eyes, and Maisie's heart threatened to stop. 'I'll have a T, please, Bob.' Bridie raised her mug. 'A T and a . . .' She picked up a biscuit from the plate and stared at it intently, then dipped it into her tea, as though Maisie hadn't uttered a word.

'Sorry, Ma. I'm just feelin' sorry for meself. It's stupid. I'll work it out. I love ya. Don't you worry about a thing,' Maisie said. She held out her hand but Bridie didn't reach for it. She was just a human mound on a chair, eyes fixed on the TV, impenetrable and unreachable. Wounded, Maisie stood up and went to sit on the windowsill, looking out at the rain. Her mind moved on to more pressing matters. *Hair up, not down, not in the rain. I've got a Revlon lipstick somewhere. Wide-legged black trousers—* Her thoughts were interrupted when Bridie forgot she was holding her mug, dropped it and soaked herself. She cried out and Maisie was on her feet.

'Ah, no! I don't know why I keep messing up,' Bridie said, upset – she hated any fuss.

'It's OK, Ma. We'll sort it out.'

'I didn't drink me tea.' In an instant Bridie was crying tears of frustration.

'I'll make you a new one.'

'I'm covered in it! I'm filthy – look at me!' Bridie pulled at her wet clothes, pointing at bits of biscuit on her otherwise pristine cardigan.

'OK, Ma, calm down. I'll put you in the bath.'

Bridie liked a bath so she calmed a little. 'Silly me,' she said, patting one hand with the other.

'Silly you.' Maisie gave her a big bright smile, letting her know everything was OK and nobody was in trouble.

Bridie grabbed her daughter's hand and looked her in the eye. 'I'm so very sorry, love.'

She did hear me! Maisie's eyes burned. 'Don't be sorry, Ma. Never be sorry.' She raised her mother's hand to her lips and kissed it.

Bridie nodded and turned to look out of the window at the rain pouring down. 'Where's my Arthur, Maisie? He'll get soaked in this weather.' She let go of Maisie and knotted her hands in her wet lap. 'Come on home now, love.'

Bridie

Bridie heard herself humming but wasn't sure which song it was. It might have been something from the radio or something she'd made up. She didn't know. She felt wet. She was in a bath. The water prickled her skin. She felt hands on her. She was naked. *What's this? What's happening?* She tried to cover herself. She looked up at a stranger rubbing her bare skin with a facecloth. There was something she wanted to say. The words were on the tip of her tongue but she couldn't form a sentence so instead she hit out. She slapped the stranger but they were too strong for her. She thrashed in the water and banged her arm on the hard bath.

The stranger tried to soothe her. 'Come on, Ma, don't be like that. Please.' She stared at the woman calling her 'Ma'. *The bleedin' neck of ya. I don't know you. Why am I here? What are you doing to me?*

'Just calm down now, Ma.'

'Stop, stop, stop.' She'd finally found a word she was look-ing for. She looked at the shampoo bottle branded Timotei, grabbed it and squirted it right in the stranger's eye. 'Take that.'

The stranger let her go. 'Jesus Christ, Ma. Me eyes!'

Bridie hugged herself. 'Go . . .' *What's the word? Go . . . what? Go where? Go away. That's it.* 'Go away!'

'It'll be over in a minute.'

'Please, leave me be,' she begged the stranger. It was then Bri-die noticed her hands, how wrinkled they were. They seemed like they belonged to someone else. *I'm dreaming. It's a bad dream. Wake up, wake up, wake up . . . What's me name? Wake up who? Wake up . . . Who?* 'What's happenin'? What's happenin'?' She held her face in her hands and sobbed.

The woman took pity on her. 'We're done now, and you're good as new. You had a little accident but it's fine. Everything's all right now.'

Bridie took her hands from her eyes and stared at the woman standing in front of her. She was a mess. She looked like she'd been through the wars. She was soaked and she had a roar-ing red pinch mark on her left arm. *Did I do that?* Now the woman seemed familiar. She was trying her best to smile but Bridie could tell her heart wasn't in it.

'D'you want to get out now, Ma?'

I wish she'd stop calling me that.

Bridie felt the softness of her bedsheets beneath her. She was in her dressing-gown. She looked up at her daughter, who was brushing her hair for her.

'I love my dressing-gown, Maisie.'

'I know ya do, Ma.'

'That and . . .' She thought about it for a second. She could see a picture in her head of a rollneck but she couldn't think of the word. She put her hand to her neck. 'That and . . .'

'Jammies?' Maisie enquired.

'No,' she said, her hands still hovering around her neck. 'That and . . .'

'Oh, the butterfly nightdress?' Maisie said.

'No. No. No.' She felt frustrated: she could see the picture so clearly in her head. 'The one that goes up around your neck.'

'A rollneck?' Maisie said.

'That's it! I love a rollneck, Maisie. But not on a nightdress. That wouldn't work at all.'

Maisie smiled at her and Bridie smiled back. 'Your daddy loves me in a rollneck,' she said, slapping her thigh and laughing.

Valerie

Valerie was sketching a picture of an eagle at the kitchen table when Jeremy walked in. He was drenched. 'Ma's going to have an eppo if she sees you in that state,' she said, without looking up from her drawing.

He sloshed around the kitchen, grabbing a drink of milk from the fridge. 'I'll be grand,' he said. 'Rain never killed anybody.'

'I'm not sure that's true,' Valerie said.

Jeremy had been going to the gym religiously for the past year and Valerie could see it was making a big difference. He was growing into himself: he wasn't the skinny kid he used to be. He was becoming a man. She was still a skinny kid. She wondered if she would fill out.

'What are ya lookin' at?' he said, conscious that she was staring.

'Nothing.' For a moment she thought about going to the gym one day when she was old enough, but if she did, she'd have to work out and Valerie didn't like doing anything that involved vigorous movement, all sweating and aching. *Life is hard enough.* He walked out of the room, leaving her to flex her skinny arms and look at her reflection in the door of the microwave. She often thought about the day Jeremy would leave home. He had only two years left of school. She couldn't imagine the house or her life without him. He was the buffer between her and her mother. He was the one who knew how to handle Bridie, and he was good company when he wasn't being bossy. She hoped he'd go to university: then he'd have to live at home and maybe she'd get to leave first. There was no way she could cope alone with their mother and grandmother. She finished her sketch, made a paper aeroplane with it, opened the window and sailed it high into the air, watching it drift into the middle of the road and land on the Ryans' car.

It was Jeremy's turn to make dinner: omelette and chips night. Maisie often worked late – the dentist offered late-evening appointments from Monday to Thursday so that he could take Fridays off to play golf. After Bridie had nearly burned down the house for the second time in a month, Maisie had spent a long weekend teaching them how to make an omelette, spaghetti bolognese, chicken casserole and fish pie. It was a short menu but the techniques they had learned through making bolognese and fish pie extended to shepherd's and cottage pie and they varied the omelette fillings. Valerie liked ham and mushroom, while Jeremy was a spinach and cheese man.

When Jeremy returned, she asked what he was intending to cook.

'Spinach and cheese.'

'Ah, come on, Jeremy.'

'It's my night.'

'But I don't like spinach and cheese.' Valerie opened the drawer to get out the knives and forks.

'Better than ham and poxy mushrooms.'

'Matter of opinion, shitebag.'

He grinned at her, then told her to grow up.

'Me ma threatened to pack me bags if I called Flintstone a tosser again,' she said, hoping for his guidance on the matter.

'Look, it was bound to happen sometime. She's still young – well, youngish – and the lads, well, they say she's a good-looking woman.'

'Me ma's good-looking? No way, the back of her head gets so fluffy it looks like the neighbours' cat's arse most of the time.'

'Rave says she's the best-looking ma out there.'

'And what would he know, the state of him?'

'Rave's cool,' he said, a little too defensively.

'Rave's cool!' she said, mimicking him. 'You sound like a girl.'

Jeremy turned away from her to focus on his omelette.

'Valerie, why do you always have to be such a bitch?'

She thought about it for a minute. 'Dunno. Maybe I'm like me da.'

'Don't say that.'

'Why not?' she said, pushing.

'Stop it, Valerie.'

But she couldn't stop. It was one thing living without her father; it was quite another allowing a new man to replace him. She'd seen it happen with kids in her class, in fairy tales and on the TV, and it never worked out well – at least not for kids like her. She was like her daddy – everyone used to say so. She was the head cut off him, according to Nanna Fox's best friend Hilda. The first time Valerie was introduced to her Hilda accused her of robbing her daddy's eyes right out of his head. She said it with a smile and handed Valerie a fiver but it was still scary. Valerie didn't really remember his eyes but she could still hear his laugh. He definitely had a really nice laugh. No matter what bad things Jeremy said about him. She remembered that one good thing.

'I bet I am. I bet I'm just like him.'

'I said stop it.'

'Why? Because he's so evil? I bet that's just shite talk. I bet he's lovely. I bet me ma just drove him out. Noleen's da says he was the best postman in Tallaght and he was brilliant at playing cards. I bet he was brilliant at loads of things.'

Jeremy looked shaken. Valerie never spoke of their father – no one in the house did. 'Stop it.'

But Valerie was on a roll now. All the thoughts and feelings that had been building up inside her spilled out.

'I'm gonna talk to Nanna Fox. I'm gonna ask her to put me in touch with him. If me ma can have new friends, so can I.' *He's me da, after all!*

Valerie watched Jeremy's eyes settle on something behind her. He looked as if his heart was in his mouth. She turned to see her wet and slightly frazzled mother standing in the doorway. She was pale, and when she put her hand up to her face it was trembling. 'Don't you dare, Valerie Bean.' Her voice was trembling too.

'I'll do what I like, Ma'sie. He's my fucking da.' Valerie was shaken. She hadn't meant her mother to overhear but her default position was attack. She couldn't help it, and besides, Danny Fox *was* her da. She didn't know him and it made her really sad.

'Go to your room!' Maisie roared.

'No.'

'Do not test me, Valerie.'

'Why? 'Cause you'll throw me out? Fine. I'll go to me da's.'

'You don't know what you're talking about, little girl,' Maisie said evenly.

'Valerie, just stop it.' Jeremy warned.

When Valerie got sad she got angry.

'No. You can be cool all ya want, Jeremy, but I'm sayin' me piece. If there's no room for me da then there's no room for that big fat hairy auld fella!'

'Go to your room, Valerie,' Maisie hissed, and before Jeremy could insert himself between them, his mother had his sister by the arm and was dragging her out of the kitchen.

'But dinner's ready.' Valerie pulled against her mother.

'You don't get dinner.'

'But I didn't have lunch!' Valerie disentangled herself from Maisie. She stepped back but Maisie wasn't letting her get away.

'Tough.'

Valerie was nearly pinned to the wall. She faltered. 'I'm starving, Ma'sie.'

'Go to bed, Valerie!' Maisie yelled. Drenched and red-eyed, she looked and sounded like a mad woman.

'I was only joking.'

'Go to fuckin' bed, Valerie.'

Valerie glanced at Jeremy. He shook his head. She wasn't going to win this one. She didn't know what to do so she stamped her foot before storming out of the room, slamming the door behind her. She made sounds as though she was walking down the corridor but stayed where she was to listen to what her mother would say about her.

'Do you want some omelette, Ma?' Jeremy asked.

'No thanks, love.' She sighed.

'She'll forget about it tomorrow. You know what she's like,' Jeremy said, which really stung Valerie. *What am I like? Like him? Is that what I'm like?* The way he said it cut deep, as though he thought little or nothing of her.

'Yeah.' Her ma said, her voice quiet and small.

'She'd never call him, Ma'sie. It's just talk.'

'I know, love.'

'She couldn't call him even if she wanted to anyways. Right, Ma'sie? Even Nanna Fox doesn't know where he is.'

'That's right,' she said, but Valerie guessed her mother was lying. If Nanna Fox didn't know where her dad was, why wasn't she looking for him? *She might hate me ma, she mightn't like me and Jeremy, but she loves me da.*

'I need to get ready,' Maisie said, and Valerie scampered down the hallway. She heard the kitchen door open and close, then her mother's bedroom door. She thought about going back to Jeremy, giving him a piece of her mind and grabbing some dinner before her mother could catch her, but instead she lay on her bed, working herself into a temper and listening to her stomach grumble.

An hour passed and still Valerie lay on her bed, face down, her pillow covering her head. The room was unusually silent but her temper was always noisy. She could feel and hear it pounding in her head.

She wasn't sure where her outburst had come from. Of course she knew that she didn't want Fred Brennan as a new dad but she hadn't been prepared for what had come out of her mouth. *It's not my fault. Me ma doesn't have a clue. She's so selfish. No one ever asks me what I think. So I miss him sometimes. So what? Doesn't mean I'm wrong. Noleen's da likes him. He says he's a great fella and maybe he is. Maybe me ma is a liar.* But she knew her mother wasn't a liar: she had nearly died at Danny Fox's hands. She knew that Jeremy's fear of his father was based on reality. She knew he was a bad man. She just didn't want him to be. Even if he was bad, seven years was long enough for him to have changed. Everyone was redeemable, weren't they? It's not like she dreamed of the day her parents would reunite. She knew it wasn't likely and that was fine. She knew deep down they were all better off without him . . . but Fred Brennan? That was the thing that haunted her: in an instant in a supermarket aisle a man she had always known had come along and changed everything. Her ma had said yes. She felt sick. *Everything's changing again. I know it.* In the past, change had meant confusion, pain and suffering. *I'm sorry, Ma'sie. Please don't hate me.*

Now the mattress was wet from her streaming eyes but she didn't mind lying in damp – she even liked it. The tears cooled her face. After a while she relaxed her hands and drifted into a light sleep. She was spent. She needed to get her head together for what was to come.

Maisie

Maisie sat on her bed, crying, for at least ten minutes before she dusted herself off and opened her wardrobe. Her daughter had frightened her. The very idea of Danny reappearing in their lives . . . *It's never going to happen, Maisie. He's gone. He's never coming back. Just relax.*

She decided against the wide-legged black trousers when she found a hole in the left knee. She had nothing else that didn't make her look like a waitress or a cleaner so she sat on her bed, feeling sorry for herself, for another four minutes as a wave of nausea rolled over her. Then she stood up, dried her eyes, headed for the bathroom, stripped off and got on with the business of showering. She drenched herself in hot water, washing away every ache and pain. Her arm hurt and her eyes burned; her mother had been particularly vicious. Her daughter had been particularly vicious too. She sighed, inhaled some soap and spat it out. She thought about how she was going to let Fred down. *I've had a lovely time, Fred, but, as you know, I'm a very busy woman.* Or *I've had a lovely time, Fred, but I have to think of the kids.* Or even *I've had a lovely time, Fred, but I just can't.*

That was the real truth. That was how she felt. She couldn't explain why because to do so would be to reveal what a terrible mess she was in. *I just can't.* She hoped the night would go terribly. That way she wouldn't even have to say anything. He'd just drop her home and thank her politely and they could both move on. That would be best. Still, she couldn't deny that, despite the drama which had just unfolded, she felt slightly giddy.

She returned to her room, blow-dried her hair, slapped on some make-up and returned to the business of dressing. Once she'd tried on and discarded everything she had in her own wardrobe she slipped into her mother's room. Bridie lay on her bed, still swaddled in her dressing-gown. She watched quite happily as her daughter put on the old red silk dress.

'Ah, you're lovely,' she said sweetly. 'I remember when I was that shape and not this old bag of bones. I remember it like it was yesterday. Beautiful, beautiful girl.'

Maisie wasn't sure which of them her mother was talking about but it didn't matter: at least she was smiling and calm. The dress fitted perfectly, and her short wavy brunette hair felt fresh and smelt of coconut. Her eye make-up was a little smudged but it was as good as she was going to get it, and when she looked in the mirror she liked what she saw. *That'll do.*

'I'd forgotten you could be so pretty,' Bridie said.

'Thanks, Ma.' Maisie laughed.

'You're . . .' Bridie could get no further. Instead she pulled her close for a hug.

When it was time to sleep Bridie took off her dressing-gown but she didn't want to put on her nightdress. She was too hot after her bath. Maisie didn't have the energy for another fight. She insisted on putting a second duvet on top of the first and Bridie had no problem with that. She kicked around in the bed and raised her skinny arms in the air. 'I love to be free, Maisie, free as a flying thing.' She giggled.

Maisie wasn't sure it would be so funny when her mother was walking the hall butt naked at two a.m. but she resolved to deal with that then. She closed Bridie's door and headed for her room, where she sat quietly veering between mentally cancelling her date – *I just can't do it* – and having long conversations with Fred in her head – *I'm very sorry but . . .* She tried to stop herself thinking about Valerie starving. She wanted to call her out of her room, give her a big hug and feed her, but she also needed to show some backbone – at least, that was what Lynn said.

'The child needs to know who's in charge,' Lynn would say. She was all about following through. 'You don't back down – once the little bastards smell weakness you're done for.'

Maisie heard Jeremy's soft knock before he walked in. She hadn't the energy to remind him that he had to wait to be invited. He was too busy closing the door behind him, double-checking it was shut tight, to see her wipe the tears from her eyes. He sat down on the floor beside her bed. 'You all right, Ma?'

'Grand,' she lied.

'You're not,' Jeremy said.

'No.'

'You don't have to go.'

'I know.'

'So don't go if you don't want to.'

'I'm scared, Jeremy,' she whispered.

'Why?'

'What if the only thing in my life that changes is you?'

'What do you mean, Ma?'

'In two years you're going to be the age I was having you.'

'I won't get a young one pregnant, Ma, I promise.'

She knew he meant it: he'd once told her that just the thought of it made him bilious, but he was only twelve at the time. 'What if you all leave me?'

'No one is going anywhere, Ma.'

'The years pass by in the blink of an eye, son,' she said, 'and as suddenly as I felt you growing in my tummy, you'll be gone, living your own life, and I'll be alone.'

'So Flintstone is your Plan B, is he, Ma?'

'His name is Fred, and I don't know what he is.'

'It doesn't have to be him. You'll have plenty more chances and, anyway, I'm never going to leave you.' He grinned. 'You're stuck with me.'

She smiled. 'I hope not, love.' She stood up and gave him her hand, hauling him up so that they were standing facing one another.

'I'm going to go on my second date in seventeen years,' she said and, despite the crippling anxiety and all the flip-flopping, her mind was set. *I'm not backing out.*

'In that case, Ma, fix your make-up – it's bad enough when birds cry at the end of a date, never mind at the start of it.'

She dabbed at her eyes with a tissue. 'You'll stay at home and watch your grammy and Valerie?'

'Yeah. It's lashing out there anyway.'

'And as soon as I'm out the door bring Valerie in a plate of food. Don't tell her I know about it.'

He laughed a little. 'I'll say nothing.'

Maisie fed her naked mother in bed. Bridie was asleep after eight bites, and those eight bites were hard won. Maisie was reminded of the kind of cajoling she'd engaged in when Jeremy was little. Back then he had been a bad eater, unlike Valerie. She had been such an easy baby, always smiling and happy to bounce in her chair. She didn't cry much, and when she did, she stopped as soon as she'd got what she wanted. Maisie missed Valerie's smile and often wondered if she'd ever see it again.

The thing that bothered Maisie most about Valerie's out-burst was that Valerie had been her daddy's little girl. She had gravitated towards him from the day she was born. He was the apple of her eye. He was the one to elicit her first smile, giggle and hearty laugh. Baby Valerie didn't see a monster: she saw someone captivating and wonderful. The toddler loved her daddy even as she became more cautious. The little girl feared him but, oh, when he smiled at her, Valerie Bean-Fox couldn't help but light up. After the break-up, when Danny had disappeared, Valerie's light had dimmed to darkness and, of course, Maisie blamed herself. *I'm sorry I couldn't make it work love.*

Jeremy was definitely a mammy's boy, and it had been mutual love at first sight. She'd sing to him and he'd clap, she'd talk to him and he'd whistle, beep and gurgle back. He was a crier unless he was safe and warm, tucked up in the crook of his mammy's arm, listening to her breathe. As a toddler he would find a corner in a room, usually behind some furniture, place a cushion on the floor, put his head on it, as though he was about to do a headstand, then tuck his knees to his chest and roll into a ball. Maisie would come looking for him: 'Jeremy Bean-Fox, where in hell are ya?' she'd call, moving from room to room. 'Jeremy Bean-Fox, come on out, wherever you are!'

Eventually she'd move furniture and find him, then pull him to his feet. 'I was calling you, asking you where you were!'

'You know where I was, Ma.'

'And where was that?'

'Somewhere inside of happy,' he'd say, before he pottered off to play or draw large orange dogs.

When Maisie thought about her children's childhood she'd think about Valerie giggling at her daddy and Jeremy curled up somewhere inside of happy.

Valerie was pretending to be asleep and Jeremy was listening to music in his room when Fred knocked at the door. Maisie didn't want to make a fuss about leaving so she was standing in the hall with her coat and hat on, umbrella in hand. He'd barely had time to knock before she answered. He was wearing a suit and holding up a large black golf umbrella as he stood outside. 'Me lady,' he said, and she put her umbrella back into the closet and stepped under his. They looked out into the dirty grey drizzling night. It was an ominous start to the evening. A combination of dread and hope twisted Maisie's stomach into a tight knot.

'I'll race you to the car,' he said, and they ran together, avoiding puddles. When their hands touched, like magnets, they immediately clasped. She exhaled and her stomach relaxed. *Oh, my.*

8 p.m. to 9 p.m., 1 January 1995

Jeremy

Jeremy was lying on his bed, hands behind his head, staring at the ceiling and thinking about John Travolta in *Pulp Fiction*. *He's so cool. Wish I was cool.* Mitch's da's brother had written and directed a film that had won a few big international prizes. There were benefits to having a celebrated director in the family and one was that Mitch's da got his hands on video-tapes of films that weren't even out in the cinema yet. The lads had watched *Pulp Fiction* the night before in Mitch's da's den. It was so good that when it had finished they watched it straight through again. Mitch's parents weren't fazed by the 18 certificate.

'What's two years?' Mitch's da, Frank, said. 'I was working and raising Len by the time I was fifteen. You're not afraid of a few guns and a pair of tits, are ya, boys?'

'No, Mr Carberry.'

'You aren't going to run off, do drugs and diddle someone up the jacksey, are ya, fellas?'

'Jesus, no, Mr Carberry.'

'Good lads.' He'd left them to it.

Sometimes Jeremy envied Mitch his two parents and big house. They had movie nights and parties. They didn't have to worry about paying bills or locking themselves down so that one of them didn't set the place on fire or disappear down the avenue halfway through the night. Mitch didn't have nightmares about his da killing his ma. He didn't have an ache in his arm whenever it rained, and it rained loads. When Jeremy saw Frank Carberry, he saw a giant. He wanted to be him. At sixteen Jeremy didn't really have any great ambitions, and the closest thing he had to a dream was his desire to be

Frank Carberry. He fantasized about taking care of his ma and Valerie, about living in a big house, surrounded by nice things, and about getting a live-in nurse for Grammy. Frank Carberry was cool, like John Travolta, and Jeremy wouldn't mind if he turned out even a little bit like either man, even if John Travolta did a bit too much dancing for comfort.

Jeremy heard the door close behind his mother. *It's just a date*, he told himself. *Nothing is going to change.* He wasn't as relaxed about his mother's date as he'd pretended to be, but he wanted to be fair to her and let her be who she wanted to be. She hardly ever smiled or laughed, these days, and when she'd walked in from the supermarket she'd been all flushed and happy. Besides, he'd enough to stress out about. His Christmas exams had been way harder than he'd expected and he wasn't sure he'd done as well as he should, especially in French, which he hated. The teacher refused to speak much English, and how are you supposed to learn French if your teacher won't translate? She just stood at the top of the class speaking to herself without anyone following a word she was saying. It stressed him out.

He wanted to change to German but his year head had said it was too late. *I should have done German. I only did French 'cause Rave was doing it. Stupid, stupid, stupid.* He needed good marks if he wanted choices and a good life. That was what his ma had said, and she was right. He'd seen first-hand what having no choices was like and it wasn't good. He worried that the Christmas exam results would set him back. Deirdre would ace all hers. If he wasn't careful she'd leave him in the dust. He had only a year and a half till he was leaving school. He needed to do better.

Rave kept telling him to chill out, but he was worried about Rave, too. His friend was hiding how bad things were at home. Jeremy kept asking him about it, but every time he did, Rave would shut down. He always said he was fine but Jeremy knew better: as close as they were, Rave hid lots of things from him. He got angry if Jeremy pushed him to reveal his secrets so he never did. He didn't mind. He hid lots from Rave too. It was just the way things were. He worried a lot about what would happen when the truth came out. *Will I lose him?* He was absolutely sure he'd never recover if he did, and the truth always came out – or so his ma said. It was only a matter of time and he dreaded it.

A rush of sadness came over him and crept into his bones. *I'm so tired.* Jeremy spent a lot of his time preoccupied. He worried about his mother: she worked too hard and ate too little. He worried about his grandmother: she was getting worse. He kept picturing her in her coffin and it made his eyes sting. He worried about Valerie. He hoped his mother wouldn't kill her. He worried about his grandmother hitting his mother. She pretended it wasn't happening often, and he let her, but if it got worse, if his grammy continued to bite and pull his mother's hair . . . It wasn't right. His mother deserved better. Most of the time he pretended he didn't notice when she cried, because the embarrassment would kill her, and maybe him too.

He was getting a headache – he always did when he was stressed, right behind his left eye. Brick by brick the pain built until it formed a wall that leaned against his eyeball, threatening to push it out of his head. Sometimes a wank helped ease the tension. He looked around the room for an old sock and some hand cream. He liked the smell of the hand cream, which moisturized his knob and made it smell nice. For eight full minutes he was transported out of himself and his room to a place where one face and one body dominated his thoughts: they belonged to someone he could never have, someone he loved and who terrified him all at once.

As soon as he was done the guilt set in. *There's something wrong with you. You'll never be the same as everyone else. You'll never fit in. You're going to hell.* He was so used to pain that he was nearly numb to it, and just about tired enough to push his fear and disgust to the back of his mind. He often ended a wank with a cry but not tonight: he was sick of crying. Instead he washed himself in the sink, pulled up his jocks and his tracksuit bottoms and threw his soon-to-be-crusty sock into the laundry bin. He returned to his bed and lay prostrate, breathing in and out slowly until his eyelids were heavy.

Seconds later he heard a loud knocking. He shot up and saw Rave's face pressed against the window. His heart skipped a beat and he nearly threw up with fright. *He could have seen me pulling me knob! Less than two minutes ago! From now on close the curtains, Jeremy! Jesus, what's wrong with you?*

Rave rapped on the window more urgently and Jeremy hurried to open it.

'Jaysus, Beany, what were you just standing there for? It's raining frogs out here.'

'Sorry,' Jeremy said, and helped him climb in through the window.

'Why'd ya close it?' Rave asked.

'Because it's raining frogs!'

'Is your grammy asleep?'

'Yeah.'

'Is Maisie in the sitting room?'

'She's out.'

'Really?' Rave lit up. 'Fuckin' great, let's go.'

'Go where?' Jeremy said. 'It's lashing.'

'It's not acid rain, Numbnuts.' Rave took several small bottles of booze out of his pockets: two from the front of his jeans, two from the back and four from his jacket.

'Jesus, where you'd get all that?'

'Don't ask. Here giz a lend of your schoolbag, will you? It's a bitch to cycle with glass bottles bulging against me knob.'

Jeremy handed it over and Rave emptied it of books, but instead of just dumping them on the bed he put them carefully in the wardrobe, neatly stacked. Jeremy smiled. He liked that about Rave: he was precise, clean and cool, not like the other dirty tossers they hung around with.

Rave filled the bag and put it down. 'Much better. Any food lying around?'

'What?' Jeremy asked.

'Biscuits, leftovers – you know, food!'

'Your da not feeding you again?' Jeremy asked.

'Nah, I take care of meself. Come on, get some grub, and later, when the others go off home, I want to show you something.'

'Jesus, Rave, I promised me ma I'd watch the girls.'

'Don't call your granny a girl.'

'Why?'

'It's creepy.'

'Sorry.'

'Just come on, man, will ya? Don't let me down.'

Jeremy was caught between a rock and a hard place. His ma needed him to do the right thing, but Grammy and Valerie would be fine until after midnight, and, although his friend would never admit it, Rave needed him more. *What can go wrong?*

'I could make up a few sandwiches to go with some biscuits, and me ma's just done a shop so I can throw in a few bars of chocolate.'

'Nice one.' Rave grinned. 'I love you, man, you're a rock star, Beany.'

Jeremy laughed. Suddenly he was wide awake and his previously dreary night seemed filled with possibility.

'And hurry up! The girls are waiting in the park.'

He was on his way back from the kitchen when he heard Valerie calling him. *Crap.* He rested the schoolbag by her door, carefully so that the bottles didn't clink, and opened it just a crack. 'Hey, Shortstuff.'

Valerie was sleepy. 'Is she gone?'

'Yeah.'

'She thinks I'm like him. That's why she hates me, isn't it?'

His heart sank. He walked into her room and closed the door behind him, taking a seat on the floor next to her bed.

'You're not like him, Valerie. You could never be like him, not in a million years.'

'So why does she hate me?'

'She doesn't, ya mad lunatic. She loves you.'

'You don't bleedin' starve the people you love,' Valerie said, and Jeremy laughed.

'There's a kitchen full of food out there, if you're hungry.'

'No, screw that, I'm on hunger strike.'

'You know who you are just like?'

'Who?'

'Me ma.'

'Jaysus, no wonder she hates me.'

'You didn't mean it about finding him, did ya, Valerie?'

'No, course not.'

'Sure?'

'Yeah.'

'I couldn't face it.'

'I know. I'm sorry.'

'All right.'

He got back on his feet, walked over to the door and was just about to open it when he heard his sister say something very quietly behind him. 'Wish I was a bit more like you, Jeremy. Then life would be so much easier for all of us.'

'Don't say that. Don't ever wish to be like me.'

'What's wrong with you?'

'Nothing,' he snapped.

'I know you. Spit it out.'

'Just leave it!' he shouted.

Jeremy rarely shouted: he didn't have Valerie's temper. Tears filled her eyes and he felt bad. *You just don't know what you're talking about, Valerie, that's all.* 'Goodnight, Valerie,' he said softly, then left the room, closing the door, before his sister could say another word.

He grabbed his old duffel coat and followed Rave out of his bedroom window.

Rave had a slick black Raleigh bike, whereas Jeremy's was an ancient yellow Triumph Twenty that once belonged to Bridie. He had been slagged off about it so often by their mates that he refused to ride it any more. Instead he went everywhere on the back of Rave's bike, his arms folded across his chest. Even if the ride got rocky, and it often did, he'd never grab Rave's saddle or his waist to steady himself. That was what girls did. Jeremy would rather he and Rave just fell off than be seen to grab on to his best mate.

Jonno and Mitch caught up to them just outside the park, cycling like the clappers. Jonno's ma insisted he wear a helmet, which made him look like a fucking queer – that was what Mitch and Dave said every time he wore it. The only reason he continued to wear it was because she threatened that if she or anyone else saw him on the bike without it he'd never cycle again. Jonno's ma worked for the council and she was like a spy. It made him the butt of every joke but he weathered it as well as he could. Jeremy really admired him for that.

'All right, lads,' Jonno said to Jeremy and Rave.

'Still driving Miss Daisy?' Mitch said, referring to Rave giving Jeremy a backer.

'The old ones are the best, eh?' Rave said, and took off at speed. Even with Jeremy on the back he was faster than the others. They caught up when he hit the park and slowed down, and when Jeremy jumped off, the lads followed suit. Dave sauntered into view, wearing a black waxed coat to his ankles, clearly too big for him. It was rolled up at the sleeves. As he emerged from the mist he looked like a miniature Van Helsing. He parked his bike by the tree and blew hot air into his cold hands. 'Just in time, I see.' He pushed in between Jonno and Mitch. Grabbing the bottle from Jonno, who had just received it from Jeremy, he opened it and took a slug. 'What a poxy day. Happy New Year, me hole.'

'What are you wearing?' Rave said.

'Me grandad's coat.' He pushed the sleeves up his arms. 'Cool, isn't it?'

'If looking like a prick is cool,' Mitch grunted.

'I like it,' Rave said.

'Yeah, well, me nanna was going to bury him in it. I put a bleedin' stop to that.'

'You took the coat off his dead body?' Jeremy was appalled.

'Don't be stupid, Beany. I had me ma do it. Who gets buried in a bleedin' coat? It's ridiculous.'

'True,' Rave said.

Dave took another gulp of vodka. 'And, besides, he had a top-notch suit on him . . . so I know where to go if I ever need it,' he joked. Dave was always joking, even about a recently deceased grandparent.

Rave laughed and everyone joined in.

The three girls were waiting for them under the Hanging Tree, which provided the only cover from the rain. Mel was smoking a cigarette, looking nonchalantly past the boys as though something in the far distance was of greater interest. Casey appeared really pissed off; Deirdre just looked happy to see Jeremy. He felt a tiny bit sick in his stomach when she grinned, but he smiled back.

'We've been standing here for a fuckin' hour,' Casey moaned.

'Sorry, we got held up.' Rave took her hand and pulled her into him. When he kissed her neck she giggled and pushed him off but he pulled her back and wrapped her in his arms again. She relaxed against his chest. They were a beautiful couple: she was blonde, he was jet black; her eyes were green and his were grey. They were both pale but it was winter. They were poster-campaign gorgeous. Jeremy psyched himself up to move towards Deirdre. She wasn't as pretty as Casey but he wasn't as handsome as Rave. She had the best smile, though, the kind that made him smile back even if he didn't feel like it. 'That's a gift,' he'd told her once.

'Shut yer face.' She'd gone red but was still smiling that smile.

'Seriously, it's a gift.'

Sometimes his face hurt from smiling when he was around her. She didn't smile as much as she used to, though. He hoped it was just a winter phenomenon.

They all sat in a circle on the damp ground sheltered by the tree, Rave in the centre. Jeremy often wondered how he managed to do that, but people just gravitated to him. When Rave talked, everyone listened. He was the glue that held the group together. Jeremy and Rave had been best friends since they were four years old. Jeremy couldn't remember a time without Rave.

Dave had joined them for sixth class in primary school. He had just moved and no one really wanted to talk to him because once they did he forgot to shut his mouth. He liked to joke around, play pranks. Sometimes his ma was called in. He was suspended once for covering the boys' toilet pans with cellophane. Some of the lads splashed themselves and laughed about it, but Spots Farrelly appeared in class crying his eyes out and covered with shite: Dave had been suspended for a week. Rave liked him. Most of the time, he laughed at him but when Dave went too far he was always the first to tell him. Dave listened to Rave: he respected him. Jeremy had put up with Dave initially but only because Rave asked him to.

'But why?' Jeremy moaned.

'Because he's funny.'

'He's a prick.'

'Only because he thinks he has to be. He'll work it out.'

Jeremy had no idea what Rave meant.

'It means he's cool, Jeremy.'

Jeremy disagreed but he never brought it up again.

When they'd moved to secondary school, Rave and Jeremy had joined the soccer team, and that was where they'd met Jonno and Mitch. Jonno was slim and fast. Mitch was tall and built like a brick shit-house. They were both good players. Rave was good too. Jeremy was OK but he loved the game. Mitch made it clear from day one that he wanted to be friends with

Rave. He made no bones about it. With Mitch came Jonno, and Mitch accepted that if he and Rave were to be friends, Jeremy and Dave were part of the package, but he was unsure about Dave. Rave didn't care. Dave was in or Rave was out, so Dave was in. It was fine. Jeremy had got used to him by then.

Jeremy sat to one side of Rave and Casey was on the other. Deirdre was on Jeremy's other side, holding his hand. *Her hands are so hot even in the freezin' cold . . . and here come the sweats. Crap.*

Rave fished the bottles of vodka out of Jeremy's bag and threw one to Mitch, who caught it easily. 'Share with Mel,' Rave said, and Mitch nodded.

Rave threw another to Jonno. Jeremy was slow to take a drink from his bottle. He was worrying about being away from home. *I should be there.* The lads didn't notice at first. He let them all drink away and share stories of their Christmases with the girls.

'Me ma nearly burned the house down, I swear. We were smoked out of it. The cat's still got a black face – she looks like the bleedin' chimney sweep in *Mary Poppins*,' Dave joked.

'I loved that,' Jonno said.

'Course ya did, ya big homo.' Dave elbowed him in the ribs.

'Me da wants to go away to the sun next Christmas,' Mitch said.

Jonno shook his head. 'Lucky bastard.'

'I bleedin' hate the sun in summer, never mind at Christmas.'

'Me heart bleeds for ya.' Dave raised his eyes to Heaven. 'Try eating a fire-damaged turkey for the third year in a row. It's a wonder I have any fuckin' teeth left.'

Mel laughed at him.

'Alright, fatso, wanna get fingered?'

'You're such a pig, Dave,' Mel spat at him. 'You make me wanna puke.'

'Yeah, that's not what your Ma said last night,' Dave laughed to himself.

'Not funny.' Rave's voice was low and warning. Dave stopped laughing immediately. 'He doesn't mean it, Mel. He fell on his head when he was a kid.'

'Well, when Rave says fell he means his Ma landed him on it.' Jeremy felt a need to break the tension. Mel was upset and he liked Mel.

Mel smiled. 'I don't blame her.'

'They say he was an even bigger thick before . . .' Rave made quote marks with his fingers, 'the fall.'

Mitch and Jonno laughed. 'Explains a lot,' Jonno said.

'Yeah alrigh', ha ha.' Dave went pink at being the butt of their jokes. It needed to stop.

'I was only messin'. Sorry, Mel.'

'It's OK, you can't help being a thick.'

'Exactly,' Dave said and he made a face, talked slowly and banged the side of his head. Everyone laughed. Jeremy just felt relief – this was normal.

Evidently Rave had had enough of the banter: he put his arm around Casey and turned to Jeremy and Deirdre. 'Are yous coming?'

Deirdre tightened her grip on Jeremy's sweaty hand. Jeremy nodded. It was time.

Rave clicked his fingers. 'Let's go.'

They left Jonno, Mitch, Dave and Mel sitting under the tree, sharing the vodka while Mel passed around cigarettes. Mitch was the only one who didn't smoke: his granddad had died a few months back of emphysema.

'He's literally drowning in his own phlegm in me ma's sitting room,' he'd say, when the lads lit up. 'Yous are mad. If you'd seen what I'd seen, you'd shove your knob in a blender quicker.'

The lovebirds found a spot in the bushes where they drank a little more of Rave's vodka before going their separate ways. Casey was always giggly after a few sips. Deirdre drank a tiny bit but Rave downed it like it was water.

'What about you, Beany?' he asked, handing him the bottle.

'I've had enough,' Jeremy said, after just two sips.

'Sure?' Rave asked.

Jeremy looked from his friend to the bottle, then grabbed it and downed some more. It made him feel sick, but it took the edge off the anxiety that was raging in him.

Rave took back the vodka and finished it, along with a ham and cheese sandwich that he fished out of the rucksack.

Jeremy was preoccupied with his sweaty hand. He tried to loosen Deirdre's grip but she was having none of it.

'How's Maisie?' Rave asked Jeremy. He always liked a little small-talk before they all got down to business.

'She's on a date,' Jeremy said.

'No way!'

'Yeah.' Jeremy sighed, giving away a little of his despair.

'Jesus,' Casey said. 'I hope she doesn't get pregnant.'

Rave and Deirdre laughed. Jeremy's face was set in stone.

'So who's she dating?' Rave asked.

'The copper.'

'What copper?'

'Flintstone.'

Rave sat forward. 'No way! Fuckin' told ya he was after her,' he said, looking to the girls. 'He's a cool—'

'Yeah, he's great.' Jeremy cut him off. He didn't want to talk about it. The calm he'd felt earlier about his ma going on a date had slipped away and instead there was just worry: worry that he wasn't at home while she was out, worry that she'd have a bad time, worry that she'd have a good time . . .

'Jesus! Maisie and Flintstone, that's one for the books,' Rave said.

Casey leaned back against Rave's chest while he finished off the sandwich. 'My ma said if my da died she'd never love again.'

'That's romantic.' Deirdre played wistfully with a strand of her hair.

'I know,' Casey said, 'and comforting. I mean, who wants to

deal with that?' She looked over at Jeremy. 'Sorry, Beany.'

He raised his shoulders. *It is what it is.* Deirdre squeezed his sweaty hand in solidarity.

When Rave had drained the bottle and finished eating he gave Jeremy the signal. It was just a simple tilt of his head to the left, but it meant 'Clear off: it's time for business.'

Jeremy and Deirdre had read it and stood up.

'There's a spot over there.' Rave gestured as he slung his arm around Casey's neck. She caught his hand and kissed it. Jeremy's stomach knotted. He could feel the vodka climbing back up his throat. He and Deirdre moved just far enough away and under enough cover to have some privacy. She lay down and he sat in beside her, squeezing himself into the tight space under the big bush. It was easier to lie under it but he insisted on sitting, even though he had to pull stray leaves out of his hair every few moments.

Deirdre seemed glad to be alone. 'I missed you earlier.'

'Yeah, sorry, I had to go.'

'You always have to be somewhere.'

'Busy man, me.'

'You should slow down. You'll do yourself an injury with all that rushing around.'

'Maybe someday.'

'Are you going to lie down with me?' she asked.

His stomach lurched. He lay down and propped himself on his elbow. He was going to talk about *Pulp Fiction*, how cool John Travolta was, when she leaned in and kissed him. *OK, then. Time to put on a show.* He kissed her back. *One, two, three, four, roll your tongue, Jeremy, five, six, seven, pull it out, eight, nine, ten, kiss her lips, eleven, twelve. OK, that's her tongue again. Just go with it. Next step, it's bra time.* He lifted her top at the back and wrestled to undo her bra strap. He heard a snap, then rubbed her back for a minute or two while he steeled himself. Then he gingerly moved his hands to her front where he felt her warm breasts. They were doughy, clammy and a little damp. *Push through, just push through . . . Play with the right, then the left, tickle and massage and hold and . . .*

Deirdre stopped kissing him and pulled away a little, Jeremy still cupping her breasts. She was trying to look him in the eye but he found it hard to face her. It was all a bit awkward.

'Is everything all right?' she asked.

'It's fine.'

'Well, you're kneading me tits as though you're about to bake bread, and did you know you were humming when you kissed me?'

'Sorry. I'll stop.'

'Just relax.' It was clear that Deirdre had way more experience than Jeremy. She had spent every summer since she was eight down the country with her cousins on a farm so she was bound to. Country girls were horny as, everyone knew that.

Jeremy fought his embarrassment. 'Sorry, Dee, I'm just . . .'

'You're great!' Suddenly she was flustered and looked as if she was about to cry. Jeremy didn't know what to do so he kissed her with every bit of passion he had in him, like Butch kissed Fabienne in *Pulp Fiction. Be a man, Jeremy, be Butch . . .* It seemed to work.

She kissed him again, then lifted up her top, and Jeremy wasn't quite sure what was happening until their lips parted and he felt light pressure on his head. *She wants me to lick her tits. Ah no, ah no, ah no . . . and now I'm licking tits. Don't gag – do not gag. Calm down, relax. This is fine, it's no big deal.* Her hands moved to his trousers and he felt his zip opening. He was really regretting the wank he'd had earlier – at least if he'd arrived with a full load he'd have some hope.

She stopped and pulled her top down. 'What's wrong?'

'Nothing.'

'You're really stressing.'

'Don't know what you're talking about.' He tried his best to sound relaxed.

'I tried to open your jeans and you slapped my hand back.'

Jeremy feel his face redden. 'I'm sorry,' he said. 'I took a kick to the balls at soccer practice.'

'Oh, poor Beany,' she said. 'I could kiss it better!'

It was a joke, and he knew it, but Jeremy nearly started to cry. 'It's really sore, that's all.'

'If you didn't like me you'd tell me, wouldn't you?'

'You know I do.' He hesitated. 'I'm just . . .'

'Just what?'

'I'm . . .'

'What?' she said urgently.

'. . . just bad at this stuff.'

'You're not.' She smiled at him, a warm smile, the one that made her look so pretty and was so ridiculously catching and then they were kissing again and he resumed counting in his head. *If only, Deirdre . . . You're the one I want to like.*

They emerged from the bushes first, but Rave was always last, no matter which girl he was with. The rain had stopped and the night sky was peppered with tiny stars. Mel and Dave were sharing the last cigarette and passing a bottle between them. Mitch hung upside down from the tree and Jonno was feeding him the last of the vodka.

Mel offered Deirdre a swig of whiskey.

'Me da will smell that on me breath from a mile off.'

'It's good for the cold,' Mel said.

'Nah, I'm going home.' Deirdre shrugged. 'You coming?'

Mel thought about it. 'I'll hang on awhile. Me da's brother is still visiting – he's a freak.'

Deirdre nodded. 'OK, take it easy.' She turned to Jeremy. 'Will you walk me home?'

'Yeah,' he said, 'of course.' His ma had raised him never to leave a girl to get home on her own. It wasn't gentlemanly.

'See yis,' Deirdre said. Mel waved and the two lads grunted.

Jeremy rubbed his hand on his jeans furiously before she grabbed it. 'Tell Rave I won't be long,' he called back to them.

'Will you bring some chips?' Jonno said, from under the tree where he was making what looked like a daisy chain with sticks.

'With loads of salt and vinegar!' Dave hollered.

Jeremy nodded. 'All right.'

As he and Deirdre left the park, hand in hand, he looked up at the sky. It was black and threatening to turn nasty. For a moment he thought about dropping her off and going home to his warm room, his wild sister and his mad, sweet grammy. He ached for it. But he'd made a promise, and he couldn't let his best friend down.

MONDAY,
2 JANUARY 1995

Chapter Three

'You Are The World'
Live, 1991

Maisie

MAISIE WOKE AT THREE A.M. to the sound of heavy rain pounding on the roof and Bridie shuffling along the corridor, singing to herself, 'She'll be coming round the mountain when she comes . . .' She stopped and continued to shuffle. A lot of Bridie's thoughts, feelings, ideas and sentences just fell off proverbial cliffs. It had driven Maisie mad in the beginning, but she was used to it now. She lay still, listening to her mother's slippers dragging along the floor, reliving the night she'd just spent with Fred Brennan.

It had been the perfect date. He was a gentleman who had treated her like a lady but, more than that, he had made her feel like a real woman for the first time in years, possibly ever. They had been to an expensive steak house, but even wearing her mother's best dress Maisie had felt uneasy. A young man in a black suit and white tie had been playing a black baby grand piano in the corner, and when they were seated the waiter had handed them each a large menu, leather-bound and heavier than a brick. She had forgotten to eat that day so she was starving. She feared her stomach would rumble – and it was quiet enough in the restaurant for him to hear it if it did. *Stupid woman, you could have made yourself a slice of toast at least.* She scanned the menu, her eyes catching on the prices. *Twenty pounds for a steak! At least he's ordered the house red. Thank God for that.*

'Best steaks in town, Maisie,' Fred said.

'Great.' *They'd bleedin' want to be.*

She ordered the cheapest, smallest steak on the menu and a side salad.

'Are you sure that's all, Maisie?'

'Ah, yes, thanks, Fred.'

'God, that's very little.'

'I don't have a big appetite.' *If me stomach rumbles now I'll die.*

'Whatever you want.'

I could feed the kids for a week on the price of that piece of meat alone. Yis are a bunch of well-dressed bandits in this place. She smiled and handed back the menu to the waiter, whose mind was clearly somewhere else. His eyes kept drifting towards the man playing the piano, even as he answered Fred's question about what dauphinoise potatoes and julienned mixed vegetables were.

'Garlic potatoes and vegetables cut into strips?' Fred repeated.

The waiter nodded, still eyeing the pianist, who was laughing with another young waiter. 'Yeah,' he said. 'The spuds are good, though, not too garlicky, real light, and the chef glazes the veg. It's so skinny it melts in your mouth.'

'Sounds good.' Fred handed the waiter his menu, but the lad was rooted to the spot and didn't notice. 'Hello?' Fred said. 'Earth calling Orson, come in, Orson.'

Maisie smiled. She'd been a fan of *Mork and Mindy* back in the day. *Something in common, maybe?*

'Sorry,' the waiter said. Fred followed his gaze. The piano player looked up. The waiter averted his eyes. 'So what can I get you?' he said, as though Fred hadn't already decided.

'The well-done steak, garlic spuds and veg that I just ordered two seconds ago.'

'Excellent choice. How well done would you like the steak?'

'If in doubt, burn it.'

'Right.' He placed the menus under his arm and walked past the piano player with his nose in the air. The man's eyes followed him to the kitchen.

Fred leaned in. 'It looks like the queer fellas are having some sort of spat.'

Maisie laughed. 'Dinner and drama.'

'My gut says the piano fella was caught with his pants down by our lad.'

'Oh, don't! I don't want to think about it!'

He grinned. 'Yeah, it's toe-curling enough. Still, live and let live.'

Initially their conversation was stilted. It was difficult to know what to say. Maisie kept thinking of topics, anything other than gay sex, and they'd exhausted *Mork and Mindy* after a minute or so when they both realized the only thing they really remembered about it was 'Mork calling Orson, come in, Orson,' and you can repeat that only so many times without coming across as slightly simple. *Gardening? No, he doesn't look like a gardener. Besides, I don't know a flower from a weed. Music? I haven't a clue. Books? Yeah, right, I've got time to read. Oh God, I have nothing to say. Why am I here? Don't panic, Maisie. It's just dinner. It'll be over soon and then you can tell him . . . I just can't do this.*

Fred didn't seem to notice the silence, or if he did, it didn't bother him as it did Maisie. He was soon busy digging into his dinner. 'He wasn't wrong – the veg really does just melt in your mouth. Are ya sure that salad's enough for you? That's a very small bit of meat.'

'It's good.' She wanted to expand, so she added, 'The dressing is melt-in-your-mouth too.'

The second it was out of her mouth she regretted it. *How could dressing melt in your mouth? God, I'm a thick.* She had no appetite, and her mouth was so dry she couldn't even taste the meat she was picking at, even though it looked delicious. *I wonder if it would be rude to ask for a doggy bag. Throw some ketchup on it and Jeremy would hammer into it.*

He watched her move her food around her plate. 'Is that meat done OK for ya?'

'It's lovely.'

'Are you sure?'

'It's great.'

'Really?'

'Seriously.'

'It's just that I've seen you eat more than that with your jaw wired shut.'

The words landed between them, awkward and heavy. *I can't believe he said that. I don't belong here. I want to go home.* Maisie put down her knife and fork and pursed her lips.

Fred had paled. 'I'm so sorry. That just slipped out. I don't know what to be saying. I'm no good in these places. Fancy food and fruity waiters, piano playing and foreign menus – it puts me on edge, and when I'm on edge I say stupid things.'

He looked like he was about to cry. He held up his hand. 'Hello, my name is Fred Brennan and I'm an eejit.'

The daft look on his face relaxed her and she exhaled. He'd just admitted everything she was feeling. 'Me too.'

'You're far from an eejit.'

'No, but I'm on edge too, and for the record, the salad dressing does not melt in my mouth.'

He laughed and then he reached for her, and the brush of his hand against hers woke Maisie up. She felt alert, bright, buzzing, twitchy in places she hadn't felt twitchy in for years. *Oh, Jesus, I'm not able for this . . .* She escaped to the loo to calm herself.

When she returned Fred had ordered a second bottle of wine and poured her a glass. Her stomach was still dodgy from the previous night but she drank it as if it was medicine.

'Tell me one thing about you that I don't know,' he said.

She thought for a second. She knew he wasn't looking for something personal – he knew everything there was to know about her personally, every little dark secret. *I don't know.* She wanted to run, but then he rested his hand on hers and looked into her eyes, and when he smiled at her the corners of his eyes crinkled. 'Anything at all.'

Maisie exhaled. 'I trained to be a hairdresser. I didn't finish but I loved it.'

'I knew that.'

'Oh.'

'You told me that while I was keeping you company one night.'

He didn't elaborate. He didn't need to. They both knew it was one of the many times they'd waited together for an ambulance, him stemming the flow of blood from her latest wound. She felt a little sick again.

'Right,' she said. *This isn't going to work.*

'You should go back and finish, if that's what you want.'

She laughed. 'Because I have that kind of time.'

'Someday soon you will. You're still a young woman.'

'I don't feel young.'

He gazed into her eyes. It wasn't romantic – there was no chance of him leaning in for a kiss: he was just looking at her, or into her, she wasn't sure which. It should have felt awkward but for the first time all evening she was calm. She held his gaze.

'Tell me something else, something nobody in this whole world knows about you.'

'Wow, Jaysus, that's a tall order.' She thought for a moment. There was only one thing about Maisie that no one else in the world knew. *Should I? If I want to put him off me, I should.*

It'll make letting him down easier and, anyway, it's the truth and he asked.

'I thought about killing Danny once.' She waited for Fred's look of horror, followed by a swift gesture to the fruity waiter for the bill.

Instead, he broke into a grin. 'Oh, yeah? How would you have done it?' He leaned in, still with that grin.

She was relieved – so relieved that she laughed and shook her head as she admitted, 'I was thinking rat poison in his dinner.'

'Appropriate.' He nodded. 'But not as effective as you'd think.'

'No?'

'No.' He shook his head. 'Besides, a fella like him deserves something a lot more painful.'

'I did think about backing into him in the driveway once and pinning him to the garage door, maybe throwing a few darts at him as he took his final breaths.'

'Much better.'

She laughed, then fell silent. *It's not funny, though. I wanted to kill him.* She shrugged her shoulders. 'I even bought the poison.'

'And what did you do with it?'

'I flushed it down the loo as soon as I got home. You probably think I'm a mad woman.' *I know I do.*

'Maisie, I'd think you were a mad woman if you hadn't imagined killing that animal. Thinking isn't the same as doing.' He averted his eyes. 'Not the same at all.' His mood changed and, for a fleeting moment, he was sombre. Something bothered him but Maisie was smart enough to notice and smarter still not to push him about it. The good news was that he didn't think she was psychotic, and as a guard he was qualified to know. It was reassuring.

'And what about you? I don't know a thing about you, other than that you bought your ma's house from your brother when she died, you like two sugars in your tea and the odd cake, but you're not a biscuit man.'

He smiled. 'Sorriest thing I ever did was buy that house. The fuckin' electrics alone cost a fortune and the pipes – Jaysus, don't talk to me about the pipes.' He put down his cutlery. She waited.

'I was engaged once.'

Maisie's mouth fell open, just like Valerie's had earlier that day. 'What happened?'

'She was in the force, on foot patrol. There was a fire in a shop on Store Street. A woman and two children were stuck in the dressing room. Joy radioed it in and then she ran in against orders. By the time the Fire Brigade got there it was too late.'

'Jesus, Fred, I'm so sorry. Were you there?'

'I heard the call and got over there as quick as I could but by then the roof had collapsed. She was gone.'

'When?'

'It will be the ten-year anniversary in March.'

'You must still miss her?'

'No, I don't, if I'm honest.'

Maisie hadn't expected that.

'It was a long time ago now.' He smiled. 'Now I just miss missing her.'

'Oh,' she said. *God, he's lovely.* Maisie had loved the ghost of her dad long enough to understand. Now he was just a collection of happy memories and nothing more tangible than that. 'I am sorry.'

He smiled at her and patted her hand. 'There's a time for all things, Maisie,' he said, with a quiet emotion, and although she wasn't absolutely sure what he meant, she knew he was allowing her into the darkest corners of his soul.

'You deserve better.' She meant it.

'Back at ya, lady.'

After that, they couldn't shut up. He talked about working for the guards and how he'd moved up the ranks, how he felt about his job and the difficulties he faced. He loved it, though. When he talked about it and the people he worked with he spoke with passion. 'There's a lot of heartache out there, a lot of fucked-up people, but there are the good and the great too, like you,' he said, over dessert.

She blushed tomato red. She wished she knew what he saw in her.

The first half-hour of their night had felt like a lifetime, but the next three and a half flew by. When they stepped out into the night air, Maisie didn't feel the cold at all. She was all aglow, high on wine, adult conversation and attraction.

Fred

'Watch your step there, me lady. It's a night for black ice.' He took her hand as they left the restaurant, the evening coming to an end all too soon.

They had talked about everything from his job to burping babies to fishing to dental hygiene to politics. Fred particularly enjoyed any story that featured Valerie. He had a soft spot for the child: she was strong and had attitude, a force to be reckoned with. Every time she'd encountered him she'd sized him up, even as a toddler. She'd always had her eye on him. *Good for you, love.* When she was younger she'd been more open, easier to reach, but that was OK: she was growing up, learning, finding out about life, and when you're a young one growing up in a city, it's good to be guarded.

Jeremy was softer but that didn't make him weak. He was a brave boy with a big heart. He was always polite to Fred but he was more closed off than his sister. It was hard to know what the boy was thinking half the time. A person knew where they were with Valerie, but even as a small boy Jeremy had been more of an enigma. Fred didn't have much time for kids. He didn't know many. His only brother had settled in Australia fifteen years previously. He had two kids but Fred had only met them twice. Most of the kids he met through work were either victims or deeply troubled, and Maisie's – despite her circumstances – were neither. They were just kids, getting by, doing their best. He admired her for that, especially after what he'd witnessed them all go through.

He loved the story about Valerie finding the neighbours' cat Pebbles dead in the road. The Joyce clan was on holiday so she'd grabbed one of Bridie's merino-wool cardigans from the washing line, wrapped the dead cat in it and placed the bundle carefully inside the freezer between a bag of ice lollies and a packet of four lamb chops. She didn't bother communicating her grisly find so when Jeremy fancied an ice lolly, reached in and pulled out a wide-eyed, stiffened Pebbles, he did what any normal kid would do: he spewed his guts up and cried for his mammy. The fact that he was fourteen and his best friend Rave was doubled over laughing with his baby sister didn't help.

'He took a while to get over that one. He wouldn't even walk past the freezer for a month,' Maisie said.

'Ah, she was only doing her best for the Joyces.' Fred chuckled.

'Yeah,' Maisie agreed, 'if you consider charging them a fiver for storage as doing her best.'

Although he'd spent years mooning over her, the scene in the supermarket had been totally spur-of-the-moment, and he had immediately worried as to whether or not he was doing the right thing. He knew how damaged she was, but there was something about Maisie that made it worth the risk. He believed that if they gave each other a chance they'd fit like two pieces of a jigsaw puzzle and, despite the awkward start to the evening, they did.

'I'd like to call you Mai,' he announced in the car on their way home.

'You can call me what you like, Garda Brennan,' she said, attempting to flirt and instantly feeling uncomfortable. 'Sorry, that sounded weird.' She was tipsy and Fred had only drunk two glasses of wine. *Oh no.*

He laughed. 'How about from here on in you call me Fred and I'll call you Mai?'

Maisie bit her lip, but her smile travelled across her face. 'That's a deal, Fred.'

Fred liked the sound of 'Mai': it tripped off his tongue. She looked more like a Mai to him. Plop a blonde wig on her and she'd look like May Britt in *Murder Inc.* It was one of Fred's favourite films, because it was the only film he'd ever seen in a cinema with his dad. His father had always been an outdoorsman – he'd liked fishing, golf and doing the garden in that order. Other than that he'd sold insurance door to door and hadn't had time for much else. It was hard to talk him into going to see the film but Fred had been determined. It was his father's birthday, and a day out together was Fred's present to him.

'That was magic, son,' he had murmured, as he'd wandered from the dark theatre into the dim light of the evening, disoriented but elated. 'Just magic.'

Two days later he was dead. He'd suffered a massive heart attack at a woman's doorway while selling her life insurance. Years later the family would joke that he'd do anything to make a sale. It still made Fred chuckle. His dad would have enjoyed it too.

Whenever Fred looked at Maisie he saw May Britt, and in his head he heard his da's words. *Magic, son. Just magic.* It wasn't that he didn't like the name 'Maisie', but he could still hear Danny spitting it with such venom. It brought back too many memories of her terrified and bleeding in a doorway, hidden in a locked room or passed out on a wooden floor. Fred Brennan had attended fourteen calls to the Bean-Fox household in the space of two years. His colleagues had attended eight more. It was a miracle Danny Fox hadn't killed his wife and it wasn't for the lack of trying. No, 'Mai' had a ring to it and it gave them both a clean slate and a fresh start. *It's time to let go of all that, Mai, for both of us. If you'll only let us.*

Fred sensed that Maisie was there out of a sense of obligation; he knew that she was probably planning to let him down gently but he hoped he could change her mind. *A second chance. We all deserve that, don't we?* Fred carried his own guilt, shame and scars about Danny Fox but he didn't like to dwell on that. He wondered how Bridie would react to him romancing her daughter. It could go either way. He shared a secret with Bridie, one that could ruin his burgeoning relationship with Maisie, not to mention the only stability he had in life: his career. He had used his power as a member of the force to go outside the law and ensure Danny Fox was never seen or heard of again. If Fred Brennan was really honest, it was the only thing that had kept him at arm's length from Maisie for so long.

Lost in his thoughts, his eyes glazed over. Frank Sinatra was singing from the tape deck that lit up the dashboard.

'What are you thinking?' Maisie asked.

Fred's eyes met hers. 'Just about the rain.' It was true: he was thinking about the rain. He was thinking about one specific wet wintry night when he had crossed the line. *Never again, Mai, I promise, never again.*

They were in a warm bubble, the rain teeming down from the heavy clouds that blanketed the sky. It was a miserable night, yet Fred didn't feel miserable. They had been alone together on so many occasions and in such difficult circumstances. It was nice now just to be. 'I think I might have to celebrate the rain from here on in.'

'That'll be a lot of celebrating.' She grinned and blushed again, so brightly that her neck and face matched her dress.

'You light up the place, Mai, and that's a fact.'

She looked as though she was biting back tears. She turned away from him and stared out of the window. He'd seen her battle emotion before, under much worse circumstances than receiving a compliment. He was yet to see that woman break. 'Is that too much to say on a first date?' he asked.

She covered her face with her free hand and shook her head. 'No.' And then she gave him a genuine bright smile and he relaxed.

She likes me. Of course she does, an old devil like me. Still got it, Brennan, still got it. 'Good. I'm way too old to play it cool.' He slowed the car to a stop in front of her house.

He'd left the umbrella in the stand at the restaurant so he got out, opened the door, took off his jacket and held it over their heads with one hand, his other arm around her waist, and they ran up the driveway together. At the doorway they faced one another, their faces inches apart. They'd been that close so many times before, times when he was talking to her and look-ing her right in the eyes while murmuring comforting things, like 'Hold on, love, you're going to be all right.' He reached out now to touch her face but this time it wasn't to wipe away blood or bring down a swelling. Her skin felt soft. He traced the scar just above her eye with his finger, and she pressed her hand against his. He could see she was embarrassed by it but there was nothing to be embarrassed about. He remembered the night she'd got that scar as though it was yesterday.

She'd met him at the door holding a tea-towel up to it. Danny had run as soon as he'd heard the sirens. 'It's not bad,' she'd said, as she put on the kettle. He was happy she was still on her feet but he wasn't going without assessing the damage.

He removed the tea-towel from her head and blood began pouring down her temple. 'Not bad, eh? Rocky took less of a blow than that and lost the bleedin' fight.'

'To be fair it was a split decision,' she'd said, and he laughed. Not only was she a *Rocky* fan, she'd retained her sense of humour even after a beating – which took guts. That night she wasn't bad enough for an ambulance so he'd put the kids into the car and driven her to the hospital himself. The cut had taken sixteen stitches. It was a mess but had healed well and faded to a faint line. *Sixteen stitches and she took the time to buy me a sandwich from the vending machine when she went to the loo.* Now, before he even realized it, he had leaned in and kissed her, just above her eye. 'There's no one quite like you, Mai Bean.' He cupped her face with his big hands, and she looked up at him with watery eyes. He leaned down again and kissed her gently. Her mouth parted and he tasted her sweetness as she kissed him back. His heart raced and lifted, and in his head he started dancing. He hadn't felt this way for a long time, not since Joy. He hugged her tightly, kissed her cheek and let her go.

'Goodnight, Mai.'

'Goodnight, Fred.'

'I'd love to see you tomorrow, if that's not too much too soon?' he said, and she smiled.

'Come for your tea,' she told him, and he backed away before sense overruled her.

'Looking forward to it already.' He got into his car. She seemed lighter, giddy even. It was beautiful to witness. She waved at him as she slid her key into the lock. He waited for her to walk through the door and close it safely behind her, then thought of how much he had to lose if she ever found out what he had done.

Maisie

Maisie lay on her bed as her mother shuffled up and down the hall. She relived Fred's tender kiss, then twice more, before she remembered her mother was probably naked. *Jesus, she'll catch her death.* She jumped up and steered her mother, dressed only in a pair of black socks and slippers, back into her room. Where on earth had the black socks come from? Sometimes Bridie fought Maisie off but not that night. She seemed absent, as though she was robotic, incapable of rest or peace. She was stuck somewhere in a half-life, shuffling to nowhere and back. She emerged from her stupor just as Maisie tucked her in.

'It never rains but it pours,' she said to her daughter.

'But then the sun comes out and if you're lucky a rainbow appears.' Maisie was caught up in the romance of her evening.

Bridie snorted. 'Bloody rainbows, never did see what all the fuss was about. Give me a red sky at night, Maisie. There's a lot more promise in that.'

Maisie lay down beside her mother and gently rubbed her head. 'I suppose you're right, Ma.'

'Although I did see a lovely one at your daddy's graveside. No pot of gold, of course, just that headstone with the wrong spelling on it. Arthur Beam! Who the fuck is Arthur Beam? They fixed it, didn't they, love?'

The next time Maisie woke it was with a start and to the radio blaring. Her mother wasn't beside her. She lifted herself out of bed and went to the kitchen. When she opened the door Valerie was eating a large bowl of cornflakes and pointed to two slices of bread toasting. 'I hope you don't mind me eating today, or would you rather I starved to death?'

'Have what you like, love,' Maisie said, her spirits high after her perfect evening. She wasn't going to ruin it with worry and doubt. She was too happy. Bridie was also sitting in front of a bowl of cornflakes. Maisie leaned down and kissed her mother's forehead. 'You all right, Ma?' she said.

'I'd like a bowl of cornflakes,' Bridie said.

'You've got one, Grammy,' Valerie said.

Bridie looked down. 'Oh.' She started eating.

Maisie gave Valerie her toast, put two more slices of bread into the toaster for herself and re-boiled the kettle even though it was still hot.

'Did ya hear, Maisie? That murderer Fred Brennan hung himself last night,' Bridie said.

Maisie gasped. '*What?*'

Valerie laughed. 'Fred *West*, Grammy!'

My nerves!

'It's all over the gramophone. He hung himself in his cell, if ya can believe that.'

'I'm glad he's dead,' Valerie said.

'The world is better off without Fred Brennan,' Bridie said.

'Fred West, Ma,' Maisie said.

Valerie laughed again. 'I agree, Grammy. Who needs Fred Brennan anyway?'

Bridie nodded. 'No one, love.'

'Now you're just being mean, Valerie. Your grammy is confused enough.'

'Sorry,' Valerie said.

'You can't trust a dangerous man,' Bridie said, shaking her head.

'Fred *West* was a bleedin' scumbag.' Valerie made an attempt to compensate.

'Please stop cursing, Valerie Bean.'

'Sorry.'

'I just can't face that principal again.'

'I know, Ma'sie. I'll try.'

'OK.' *At least she's making an effort. Maybe I should starve her more often.* 'Go and put your uniform on and call your brother. He'll want a shower before I wash your grammy.'

'I can wash myself, thank you,' Bridie said.

'I know, Ma. It's just that I'd rather you didn't drown yourself or the bathroom,' Maisie said, as she buttered her toast. She took a bite and sat down opposite her mother, who was now staring suspiciously at her soggy cornflakes. 'Here,' she said. She broke off some toast and popped it into her mother's mouth. 'Nice.'

She heard Valerie banging at her brother's door. 'Get up, Jeremy. Snooze and lose.'

Bridie laughed. 'Snooze and lose.'

Maisie shared her toast with her mother, feeding her small pieces while drinking coffee and listening to the radio DJ talk to a leading criminal psychologist about Fred West's mental state. Valerie appeared, dressed in her school uniform.

'Where's your brother?' Maisie said.

'Probably still in the shower.' She shrugged.

Maisie wondered why Valerie hadn't interrogated her about her date with Fred. Perhaps she was waiting for Jeremy. Two against one. *I can't believe I asked him here for dinner. I've lost the run of myself. 1995: the year Maisie Bean went loco.*

'Jeremy, would you move it? Come on!' Maisie shouted down the hallway. She looked at the clock. It was after eight thirty and it was unlike Jeremy to run late: he hated rushing. God forbid his hair wasn't ruffled and moussed or gelled to within an inch of its life. He had the messy just-out-of-bed look perfectly honed. His loose sandy curls were sculpted to look unsculpted. He spent a lot more time in front of the mirror than his younger sister, for two reasons: one, she had her daddy's straight thick hair that she could just wash and leave, no styling required; and, two, she was too young to bother with make-up, and clothes existed to keep her warm. Jeremy wasn't vain – in fact, Maisie worried that he didn't rate himself highly enough. 'You're beautiful, son, inside and out,' she would tell him. But Jeremy had always been a perfectionist. Everything had to be right, because if it wasn't it was wrong, and the difference between right and wrong meant something to Jeremy Bean.

'Let's go, Jeremy. Ten minutes and counting,' Maisie called, as she popped two more slices of bread into the toaster. He could eat them on the way. There was no need for her to knock on his door: she was sure he was awake and engaging in his morning rituals. He was the only one in the house with a sink in his room – it was avocado green and came away from the wall slightly. He didn't like to be disturbed, especially when he was shaving the wispy bum fluff that had recently appeared just over the left side of his lip. Maisie had walked in on him once and he'd cut his lip.

Maisie handed Valerie her lunch money, then went to knock on Jeremy's door and hand his over. Bridie followed her down the hallway. 'I need the loo,' she said.

'I'll be with you in a minute, Ma.'

'I'm perfectly able to go to the toilet myself, Maisie. I'll just say a quick hello before I go.'

Maisie knocked on Jeremy's door. 'Jeremy, it's me. Can I come in?' When she didn't hear a response, she cracked open the door to find his room empty and his bed already made.

'Where's Jeremy?' Bridie said.

'Jeremy?' Maisie called, walking out of his room and into the sitting room. The bathroom door was open and Valerie was alone in the kitchen. Maisie dropped the money on to the counter and opened the back door. 'Jeremy?' *Stupid, why would he be in the garden?* She turned back to Bridie, who was staring at her wide-eyed.

'Where's Jeremy?' Bridie asked again.

'I dunno, Ma. Maybe he's in Valerie's room.'

She checked it, then her own and Bridie's. He was nowhere.

'Jeremy? It's your grammy, love. Where are ya? Jeremy?' Bridie was walking around, pushing doors and wringing her hands.

'Calm down, Ma. We'll find him,' Maisie said. She wasn't panicked, like her mother, just curious. It didn't dawn on her that anything could be wrong.

Bridie

Bridie followed Maisie to where Valerie was sitting at the kitchen counter. She was listening to a woman crying on the radio and talking about what the Wests had done to her. 'Rose West should hang herself too,' she remarked.

'Turn off the radio, Valerie. It's not suitable,' Maisie said.

'It's the radio! How is that not suitable?' Valerie huffed.

'Did Jeremy tell you he'd be leaving early?' Maisie said.

'No.'

Jeremy, Jeremy, Jeremy. Where is he? Where are ya, love? Oh, you could be in my room, looking for me. I'll find ya. Bridie turned on her heel to go searching again. Valerie stopped her by standing in her way.

'They say he was depressed. I didn't think psycho killers

got depressed. I thought they felt nothing at all, didn't you, Grammy?'

But Bridie was focused on Jeremy. 'Have you seen Jeremy, love?'

'No, Grammy.'

He's upped and left us. He's gone. Oh, no.

'Are you sure?' Maisie switched off the radio. 'Did he say anything at all?'

'I'm positive he didn't.'

'Where is he, then?' Bridie felt scared, her skin flushing hot all of a sudden.

Where was I going? What was I doing? Something about Jeremy . . . Why are you just standing there, child?

'There'll be a simple explanation, Ma,' Maisie told her, guiding her to a kitchen chair.

Oh that's right, he's missing in action!

'I don't like it, Maisie. He wouldn't leave without saying goodbye to his grammy.'

'Well, he's taken his lunchbox and half the bloody cupboard with him,' Maisie said.

Supplies, they won't last long out there.

'Guess he doesn't need that fiver, then.' Valerie grabbed her bag, threw it over her shoulder and left.

We need to send out the troops! Bridie stood up and brushed herself off. She had a mission. *Find Jeremy.*

'Jeremy!' Bridie shouted walking down the hall. 'Where are ya, love?' She felt something trickle down her legs. 'Oh, no.' *Silly woman. Dirty old woman. What would Arthur say? What would Jeremy say? What about Jeremy? Something . . .* She looked at the puddle on the floor.

'Let's get you cleaned up, Ma.' Her daughter had appeared at her side.

He's missing!

'No, Maisie, we need to find Jeremy,' Bridie said, stepping out of the puddle she'd made and heading for Jeremy's room.

She needed to focus and remember her mission, she was losing the details, she could feel it. 'Jeremy, love?'

Maisie followed her. 'Look, Ma, his schoolbag is gone. Jeremy went in early, that's all.'

'He wouldn't go without saying goodbye to me.' Tears filled her eyes and she couldn't see properly. She couldn't see.

'Well, maybe he did. Maybe you forgot.'

'I wouldn't forget that.' *I know I forget a lot, but not that. Something's wrong.*

'Ma . . .'

'I wouldn't, Maisie.' The tears tipped on to her cheeks. *What's wrong? Everything's wrong. Nothing makes sense. Where am I?*

'Ma, he's not a baby any more. He just left early.'

Who left early? No matter how hard she had tried to hold on, Jeremy and all that concerned her about his disappearance was gone.

'Come on,' Maisie said and Bridie felt herself being herded towards the bathroom.

'God almighty, let me go.' Bridie pulled away from her daughter. *Who in the blazes does she think she is?*

'You're drenched, Ma!' Maisie was half dragging and half pushing her into the bathroom now.

'Let me go, you bitch.' She raised her hand to slap Maisie, who caught it in time. *I won't be rough-housed. I'm a nurse – I've been to war, young lady. It would take more than you to bully me!* She fought valiantly. *You won't take me!*

'Stop it, Ma.' Her clothes were being pulled off roughly, so she grabbed her daughter's arm and pinched her as hard as she could.

Maisie yelped. 'Ouch! Jesus Christ, Ma!'

She struggled when Maisie lifted her into the shower. She hit out and slammed her shoulder against the shower, then screamed in pain. 'Why are you doing this to me?'

'Oh, Ma, Ma, Ma, I'm so sorry . . .'

Once Bridie was naked and standing in the shower, her energy spent, she looked down at herself, and instead of seeing the young strong woman she thought she was she saw a tiny, skinny, bony old woman, hunched over, hugging herself, and she heard herself crying softly. *What's happening to me?*

'Leave me alone,' she begged, trying to cover herself. 'Just leave me be.'

Maisie stood back.

Bridie sobbed quietly until her head emptied and then allowed her daughter to wash her. Afterwards, when her thoughts were more ordered, Maisie wrapped a big fluffy towel around her and hugged her tight. *Ah, there you are, Maisie. My sweet girl.* 'I'd like some cornflakes, love.'

'All right, Ma,' Maisie said. 'And afterwards why don't we fill your prescription and have a coffee in Jingles?'

'And a bun.' Bridie smiled at the thought while her daughter rubbed her vigorously with the towel.

'Might as well. I'm back to work tomorrow and there'll be no time for buns after that.'

Bridie sighed contentedly. 'They love me in Jingles.' She felt warm and secure in her daughter's care.

When Maisie tried to get her to put on some tights, horrible scratchy things, Bridie pushed her fingers through the thin fabric, ruining them. After three pairs were in the bin, Maisie gave up. 'No tights today, Ma. We'll think of something else shall we?'

Who was that fella hung himself like that Fred Brennan? He did it with a pair of his ma's tights. She was a big woman, Mary something, or was it Margaret? He was a small man but he weighed a ton, I remember that. They don't make tights like they used to . . . she thought as she sat rocking gently to and fro.

Maisie

They pulled up at the pharmacy and Maisie handed in her mother's prescription. Barbara Cline was a friendly woman who always had a kind word for Bridie.

'There you are, June,' Bridie said happily. 'All well with you, love?'

June had retired five years previously. Barbara smiled. 'Keeping on keeping on, Bridie, and a happy new year to you.'

'Happy new year, Barbara. Sorry,' Maisie murmured. 'We had a bad start to the day.'

'And how are you keeping?' Barbara asked.

'Great,' Maisie said, and, for once, she meant it.

'Keep smiling like that and 1995 could be your year.' Barbara winked.

'How was your Christmas?' Maisie asked.

'Glad we all got through it in one piece. The bloody cat got cystitis and she's ruined the place, and my mother-in-law swore she'd never darken the door again, so I suppose something good came out of it.' She smiled.

'A vet's bill – that's all you need,' Maisie said sympathetically.

'Tell me about it. If I had cystitis it would have cost me thirty-five quid to visit the GP and twelve for the antibiotics. The vet charged me eighty – I nearly fell through the floor.'

'I'd have taken the brush to him,' Bridie said.

Barbara laughed. 'I'll bear that in mind for next time.'

Maisie sat down beside her mother while Barbara made up the prescription.

'I had cystitis back in the day, an awful dose. The poor cat,' Bridie said.

'Is that the one where you feel like you're weeing broken glass?' Maisie wondered.

'The very one. It's a killer.' Bridie was knotting her skirt so that it rose above her knee, revealing a pair of Jeremy's long soccer socks.

'That's very fashionable, Bridie.' Barbara pointed to the socks.

'She wanted to put tights on me, June, hot, stuffy, tight tights. I wanted to put two pencil marks down the back of my legs and be done with it, but she wouldn't hear of it.' Bridie tutted and continued fiddling with her skirt, which rose even higher.

Maisie pulled it down. 'I couldn't let you out in just a skirt and a pair of knickers, Ma,' she said, for Barbara's benefit.

'She's right, Bridie. You'd be the talk of the town.'

'Not for the first time, love.' Bridie smiled at an old memory. Whatever was amusing her, Maisie prayed she'd keep it to herself.

Barbara handed the prescription to Maisie. 'Oh, I'd say not.'

In Jingles, Lynn was waiting for them with coffee and buns.

'Happy new year. Did ya miss me, Bridie?' Lynn asked. She was a much bigger woman than Maisie, and even with a bad heart, she could handle Bridie without breaking a sweat. Like Bridie, she'd been a nurse but angina had put an end to her career. They were comrades in arms. Bridie respected her authority and her experience made a difference.

'Oh, I did.' Bridie pointed to Maisie. 'I'll look forward to her going back to work so we can get back to normal.'

Lynn took care of Bridie in her own home during the day from Monday to Thursday while Maisie worked at the dental surgery. Jeremy took over at the weekend evenings so that Maisie could clean the factory. He'd made a fuss initially. 'I have a life you know, Ma!' But she was always home by nine and had agreed he could stay out till midnight on Fridays and Saturdays to make up for it. Maisie paid Lynn as much as she could but Lynn didn't do it for the money. Her husband worked and her two kids were in college. She didn't like to venture out too far on account of her heart problems so taking care of Bridie gave her purpose and helped to fill her days.

The three women sat by the window, which overlooked the busy street.

'I hate January,' Lynn said.

'Worst month of the year.' Maisie was wrestling with her ma to get the rock bun out of her mouth. 'Not all at once, Ma.'

Bridie was determined to stuff it in.

Lynn raised her eyes. 'Bridie, bun out, now.'

Bridie dropped it. 'She's very strict,' she said to Maisie, 'but it's for my own good.'

Lynn grinned at Maisie. 'And that's how it's done.'

'If only it were that easy for me.' She broke the bun into small pieces and handed one to her mother.

'I'm not a child, Maisie.' Bridie tittered.

'What did you want to tell me?' Lynn asked, when she was sure that Bridie was lost in her own head, singing softly, picking crumbs off her skirt and staring out of the window.

'I went on a date with Fred.'

'The copper!'

'What copper?' Bridie whipped round to look at them.

'Nothing, Ma.' Maisie was nodding vigorously.

'Well, it's about time.' Lynn set her cup in its saucer. 'Ah, don't look so shocked – he's been after you for years.'

'Who's after you?' Bridie said, concerned.

'No one, Ma.'

'It's all right, Bridie, I was only playing with her.' Lynn grinned, then cupped her mouth with her hands. 'Any good?'

'As if,' Maisie whispered. 'What kind of woman do you take me for?'

'A woman who hasn't been laid since the boy they called Jesus made a frigging sandcastle. Maisie, take it from me – life is too short.'

'You have angina. You're not dying.'

'Easy for you to say. When are you seeing him again?'

'Whispering is rude,' Bridie piped up. 'You weren't reared to whisper, Maisie Bean.'

'Sorry, Ma.' She raised her voice. 'He's going to nip in for his tea later.'

'Who is?' Bridie asked.

'Fred Brennan, Ma.'

'The fella who hung himself?' She looked as confused as she sounded.

'No, Ma, Detective Brennan, remember?'

'Oh.' Bridie screwed up her face. 'I don't like that man.'

'Yes, you do,' Maisie said. 'You've always liked him.'

'I do not, young lady,' Bridie said.

'She thought he was the bee's knees,' Maisie told Lynn.

'It's just the disease. It can do that. She doesn't mean it.' Lynn patted Bridie's hand.

'It is not,' Bridie said, clasping Lynn's fingers. 'He's trouble. Just stay away from him.'

'Maybe this is a bad idea. It's too soon. I got carried away,' Maisie said. *What was I thinking about, inviting him to the house?*

Lynn moved her hand from Bridie's to Maisie's. 'Listen to me. Fred Brennan is a good man who has taken care of you for years. You like him, I know you do, and if this is your idea of fast I'd hate to hear your version of slow.'

'What about the kids?'

'They'll be happy because their ma will be happy. Don't be a bleedin' martyr, Maisie. It doesn't suit you.'

Maisie could always count on Lynn to cut through the bull-shit and say it how it was. She felt a rush of affection for her friend. 'Life's too short.'

'Exactly. Life is for the living.'

'Right, then. I'd better get Ma home for a nap.'

'I'll see you tomorrow.' Lynn kissed Bridie's cheek. To Maisie she added, 'You'd better phone me later tonight. I want every last detail.'

'We'll see.'

'Delighted. That's made my day. Finally, a bit of action!'

She was so genuinely pleased for her that just before Maisie left she leaned down to Lynn and whispered, 'Best kiss ever.'

When Maisie answered the door to Fred he was holding flowers. He handed them to her and kissed her cheek. 'Hello, beautiful.'

'You shouldn't have,' Maisie said, feeling slightly awkward. She wasn't used to receiving gifts.

'They're only from the garage. I needed petrol anyway.' Fred followed her down the hall.

'They're lovely.'

Bridie was sitting in the kitchen and looked up warily at Fred as his broad frame filled the room.

'Hello, Bridie,' he said a little nervously.

'I told you not to come back here.' She looked from the top of Fred's head to the tips of his toes, disdain written on her face. 'I won't stay in a room with him.' She stood up and went into the sitting room.

Maisie was appalled. 'I'm so sorry, Fred, I just don't know what's got into her.'

'It's fine, honestly,' Fred said, but he seemed a little shaken.

'Just give me a minute with her.'

'Please, Mai, just leave it.'

'I will not.' She followed her mother into the sitting room. 'What are you doing, Ma?'

'I'm watching the . . .' she pointed at the TV '. . . the box thing.'

'Why did you talk to Fred like that?'

'Because of something bad.'

'You'll have to be a little more specific than that, Ma.'

'I can't,' she said. 'But something.'

'Ah, Ma.' Maisie sighed. 'Please, for my sake, be nice to him.' She left Bridie to her own muddled thoughts and returned to Fred in the kitchen, closing the double doors behind her. 'She gets confused.'

'I understand.' He looked around the kitchen. Maisie watched him read all the signs on the cupboards: 'Cups', 'Glasses', 'Plates', 'Pots'. Above the oven in large writing: 'Oven, Hot and Do Not Touch!!!' It was odd to see her kitchen through Fred's eyes because she and the kids didn't notice the signs any more.

'It's hard on you,' he said.

'Some days are better than others.'

She moved to the kettle, which had 'Do Not Touch' painted on it in Tippex. She filled it and flicked the switch.

He sat at the counter and took his mobile phone out of his inside jacket pocket, placing it in front of him.

'Fancy.' Maisie didn't know anyone else with one.

'Annoying. You can never get a minute off when you have one of these, Mai. They'll be responsible for the end of the bleedin' world, mark my words.'

'Wouldn't know what a day off was,' she said.

He grinned. 'Fair point.'

She set a cup of coffee in front of him and sat next to him. He took her hand and squeezed it a little before letting go.

'The kids will be home soon. Jeremy has soccer practice and Valerie is in the local drama group.' She was nervous.

'It's nice just to spend some time with you.'

She blushed. *Jesus, Maisie, grow up.* 'I've got a stew in the oven.' It struck her that not everyone liked stew. 'Do you even like it?'

'Love it.'

Maisie sighed with relief.

'And even if I didn't I'd eat shite for you, Mai.' Suddenly he pulled her into him and kissed her, with her ma only a room away. The room seemed to spin a little. It was all happening too fast but it felt really good, too good to be wholesome. Torn, she pulled away, she bit her lip and covered her mouth, flustered. She wanted to keep kissing him, but . . .

'Am I coming on too strong, Mai?' he asked gently.

'No. Not at all. I just feel foolish.'

'Why?'

'It's all so unexpected and . . .'

'Good?' he said hopefully.

'Yeah.' She nodded. 'And weird.'

He pulled her in close to him, his beard against her cheek.

That's the only thing I'd change. Beards are unhygienic, no getting away from it.

'I'd never let anything happen to you, Mai. You'll never have to fear me.'

'I know that, Fred.'

He took her face in his hands and she put her arms around him, losing herself in the kiss. *Yeah, that beard will have to go.*

'And that's how you get yourself pregnant, young lady,' Bridie said from the doorway. Then she pointed at Fred. 'And you get out before I take the brush to you.' She turned back to Maisie, her hands on her hips. 'Into your room, Maisie Bean.'

'Ma, Fred is my guest.' Her voice held a warning note.

'And this is my house,' Bridie said, as Valerie walked in with her bag on her back and a face like thunder.

Valerie

Valerie threw her bag on to the floor and kicked it into the corner. 'What's he doing here?' she asked, scowling.

'I invited Fred for tea.'

Valerie eyed the flowers still sitting in the sink. 'Jaysus, Ma, you pair need to calm down.'

'Don't be cheeky, Valerie.'

'How are you, Valerie?' Fred sipped his coffee, holding Bridie's gaze.

'I *was* grand.' She eyed him suspiciously before turning to her grandmother, who was staring at Fred with murderous intent. 'You all right, Grammy?'

'I feel slightly sick, truth be told,' Bridie said, and walked out of the room.

Valerie's mother rounded on her. 'Where's your brother?'

'Dunno.'

'Did you see him at school?'

'To see him I'd have to go and look for him. Why would I do that?'

Her mother looked at her watch. 'He's probably at Mitch Carberry's. They're never out of the place lately.' Maisie glanced at the oven, then at the table, set for five people. 'We may as well eat.' She went to fetch Bridie.

Valerie watched Grammy stare at Fred for the entire meal. She was silent throughout, and when he spoke to her she ignored him. Valerie had never seen her grandmother behave like that before. It was quite entertaining. 'What's going on, Grammy?'

'I dunno, love. Maybe he brings bad luck.' Grammy pointed at Fred. Her mother just put her head into her hands.

'Like old Ted Duffy's black cat,' Valerie said.

'Exactly. You see that cat you'd better watch out.' Bridie shook a finger sternly.

'I had a cat when I was a kid – a cat, two dogs, a parrot and a few fish I won at carnivals. Although not all at the same time,' Fred said.

'I bet none of them survived you,' Bridie said.

'Ma!'

Valerie laughed – her mother's face was a picture.

'Well, no, animals don't tend to live that long, Bridie.'

Valerie could tell Fred was embarrassed but he recovered quickly.

'Ma, apologize to Fred.'

'I will not.'

'Right. That's your last trip to Jingles. No more rock buns for you.'

'You can't do that!' Bridie said.

'Apologize.'

Bridie looked like she'd been punched. She turned to Valerie in disbelief. 'I love Jingles.'

'Uncool, Ma,' Valerie said.

'Apologize.'

'I apologize,' Bridie said, to the wall over Fred's head.

'No problem, Bridie,' Fred said brightly.

He was a hard man to put down, Valerie had to give him that. Her grandmother and she remained quiet while Fred and Maisie talked together for a minute or so until Fred attempted to engage Bridie once more. 'So, Bridie, you told me once you were a nurse in the war.'

Bridie belched in his face. Valerie laughed and slapped the table.

'I've had enough. Fred, get your coat,' Maisie said.

'Where are we going?' he asked.

'Away from these two.' She turned to her daughter. 'Tell your brother there's stew in the oven and mind your grandmother.' She picked up her and Fred's half-eaten dinner and dumped the plates in the sink, then disappeared into the hallway while Fred put on his coat.

'Oh, that's lovely.' Valerie turned to her grandmother. 'She's starves me last night and abandons me tonight. He's a great bleedin' influence.'

Bridie took her granddaughter's hand. 'He's trouble.'

'Goodbye, Bridie,' Fred said, but when Bridie refused to look at him he turned to Valerie. 'Goodnight, kiddo.' He smiled at her, then left the room.

'I don't want him here,' Bridie said.

'That makes two of us,' Valerie agreed.

Bridie left her food on the table and walked into the sitting room. Valerie picked up her plate and followed her. She went to the window and watched as her ma and Fred walked down the path, their hands clasped, only breaking apart to get into the car.

'There's a storm coming,' Bridie muttered. 'Batten down the hatches, Maisie. Is the dog in?'

'I'm Valerie and the dog died two years ago.' She was watching Fred's car move off.

'I remember now. I'll have a W, please, Bob.'

'All right,' Valerie said and she put on the *Blockbusters* videotape. Grammy immediately disappeared into the show.

Valerie sat beside her and ate her stew. *Where the fuck are you, Jeremy? You'd better get back before Ma does.* Neither Jeremy nor Rave had turned up at school, which she knew for sure because Dave and Mitch had accosted her at lunchtime, looking for them. At first she'd felt excited that Jeremy, the good boy, had finally done something bad, but that had been hours ago. It was just after six when Valerie began to worry.

Fred

Fred turned on the car radio. REM's 'Let Me In' was playing. He turned it down but left it on. The police car had a clean leather interior and a green pine-smelling cardboard tree hanging from the mirror. 'I just had her cleaned,' he said.

'Sorry?'

'The car.'

'Oh, it's lovely. Mine is a mess.'

'That's kids for you.'

'It's me and Valerie, to be honest. It drives Jeremy mad – that and the fact that I can't use roundabouts.'

He smiled to himself.

She looked out of the window as the rain fell. He could tell that she was wound up by Bridie and Valerie's behaviour because her hands were all twitchy. He was glad to be out of there.

'So, where to, me lady?'

'Well, we didn't exactly get to eat our tea, so how about the chipper?'

'A woman after my own heart. I know just the place.'

He drove her to Dun Laoghaire to a small chipper over-looking the sea. They sat opposite one another by the window sharing a large cod and chips.

'Sorry about my mother and Valerie.'

'Stop apologizing. It's fine.'

'And I don't know what's going on with Jeremy. He never just leaves me in it like that.'

'He's a teenage boy. He's off doing his own thing.'

'I know you're right. It's just not like him, is all.'

When they'd finished their tea, they took a walk together by the pier. It was cold and raining but, arm in arm, neither minded. In fact, it brought them closer – gave them a reason to hold on to one another a little tighter.

'Did you ever want kids?' she asked.

'Oh, yeah,' he said. 'I wanted a football team.'

'And now?' She was slightly alarmed.

'And now I don't make plans.' He squeezed her. 'But you never know what tomorrow will bring.'

'You're telling me.' She chuckled but she seemed distracted, staring out at the sea.

'I can take you home, if you like, Mai.'

'I just wish I knew if Jeremy was back. Valerie isn't the best with Ma.'

'I'm sure he is. I know I wouldn't miss a meal at his age.'

'True. He never does.'

'There you go.'

They walked on.

'What's the worst thing you ever did to your ma?' she asked, out of nowhere.

He thought for a minute. 'So many to choose from.'

She laughed. 'I'm sure you can pick one.'

'I ran away with a girl when I was Jeremy's age.'

'You did not.'

'Lucinda O'Brien. She was eighteen.'

'Ah, no.'

'I left a note saying, "Goodbye, Mammy, I'm in love", and we took a train to Galway.'

'Was that all you said?'

'That's it.'

'I'd have murdered you.'

'If she could have, she would have.'

'How long did you stay?'

'I lasted about two weeks before I rang home and asked me old man to collect me. Lucinda O'Brien was a bit of a nutter, I'm afraid, and what was initially exotic and quirky became dark very quickly.'

She bit her lip.

Maisie knew all about that as Fred was aware. Although Danny had never been exotic, he was most definitely dark.

'Did you ever see her again?' she asked.

'Nah. When a woman threatens to stick a knife in herself because she thinks you have a thing for her ma, it's best to leave well enough alone.'

'And did you have a thing for her ma?' she asked.

'I'd never even met the woman.'

She laughed.

The rain kept coming down, and by the time they got to the car they were soaked through. He turned on the heater, which blew warm air into their damp faces.

'I'm sorry I dragged you out into the rain,' she said.

He smiled at her. 'I'd go anywhere with you, Mai.' He took his chance, leaned over and kissed her. Suddenly they were making out like two teenagers on a deserted road in a storm. Eventually Fred came up for air. 'I have a proposition.'

'OK?'

'There's a hotel around the corner. No pressure, absolutely none at all. I'm only saying. Your choice, Mai.'

She smiled at him, a proper smile that reached her eyes. 'What are you waiting for?'

He kissed her full on the mouth. 'Remember this date because from now on, Mai Bean, this is my new birthday.' He put the car into gear and tore off around the corner like a Formula 1 driver at Silverstone.

Chapter Four

'Welcome To Paradise'
Green Day, 1994

Maisie

FRED AND MAISIE LAY in one another's arms, naked and warm on a large double bed in a clean but sparse room on the third floor of a hotel she hadn't even noticed the name of. *Slut.* She giggled in her head. 'I can't believe I just did that.'

'You're not sorry, are you, Mai?'

'No.' She shook her head. 'It was lovely.' Suddenly she was crying. *Where did that come from? Stop it, Maisie, stop right now.* She'd never cried in front of Fred before, no matter how much she'd wanted to.

'I'm so sorry, Fred.' She snivelled. *Attractive.* 'I don't know what's got into me.'

He kissed her forehead. 'You just have a cry, love.' So she snuggled in and bawled her eyes out.

Forty minutes had passed since they'd stood together in the lift, both soaked to the skin, hands barely touching, skin buzzing. Maisie had thought the door would never open, and when it did, they clasped hands and ran to the bedroom, like two kids in a silly romance novel.

Once it had closed behind them, Maisie and Fred had

106

stripped each other in a matter of seconds. Fred was frantic but at the same time he was careful, not like Danny who had been so rough she'd nearly lost a nipple when he wrenched off her bra. Fred was strong yet gentle. Maisie was terrified but she was also exhilarated. For once she wasn't thinking about the kids or the jobs she had to do. She wasn't wishing the time away or singing in her head, *Fuck off, please fuck off and die in a flaming wreck* just to keep from punching him on the side of the head. She wasn't screaming silently, *I don't like that!* With Fred, she got lost in the moment, no fantasizing about being somewhere else. Instead she was feeling something good. *Jesus, they're not lying. Sex is really lovely!* Maisie Bean had finally let herself go.

When she finally stopped crying he handed her a tissue from the complimentary box on the bedside locker and she blew her nose. 'I'm done.'

'Feel better?'

'You've no idea.' She smiled. Wrapped in Fred's arms she felt warm and tingly, bright and full of life. She even felt sexy.

'That felt like my first time,' Maisie said honestly.

Fred couldn't hide the fact that he was chuffed to bits. He stroked his beard happily. 'Ah, they don't call me Stud Brennan for nothin'.'

'They don't call you that, do they?'

'No. But if you wanted to spread any rumours I'd be fine with it.'

She laughed at him, *eejit*. She realized she'd laughed more in the previous twenty-four hours then she had in years. *Jesus*.

'I believe I fell for you the first time I laid eyes on you, Mai,' Fred said softly. 'I shouldn't admit that, but I did.'

'Why? How, even?' She remembered that terrible night. Mrs Nugent next door had banged on the wall ten times to warn Danny that enough was enough, but the more she banged the louder he roared. The argument had started over a stew. She had spent half the day making it and he'd said it tasted like pigshite. He had kicked and slapped her before but that was the first time he'd used his fists. When the bell rang she was lying in a pool of blood on the floor. She heard him open the door and argue with someone as he was pushed to the floor. She couldn't move so she lay there trying to work out what was happening. For a second she'd thought they were being robbed, but then she saw Fred's kind face and his uniform. He was on his knees, looking down on her. 'Don't move. We've got you, love. Is that ambulance on its way, Dempsey?' he shouted to the other guard, who was holding Danny.

'Get the fuck off me,' Danny shouted, 'yis fucking toerags.'

Fred had placed a blanket on Maisie and held a clean tissue to her bleeding nose, mouth and eye. 'Take him to the car,' he'd called, and Maisie heard the other guard wrestle him outside.

'I'm sorry,' she said.

'Why?'

'I know you're busy.' As the shock and numbness subsided, she realized he was holding her hand.

He had pushed her dark curls off her bleeding forehead with his other hand. 'Never too busy.'

'I'm Maisie.'

'Fred.'

'I made a big mistake, Fred.' Before he could respond the paramedics had arrived and taken over. She'd waved at him as they loaded her into the ambulance. He'd waved back.

'How could you fall for that?' she asked now.

'You were so lovely,' he said, 'but I think it was the wave that did it. You had such dignity, Mai, even during the worst of it. It was like the world was going mad around you but you never let it change you.'

Oh, I changed. 'I got harder.'

'You got tougher. It's different.'

'That was the first time I was away from my kids. Mrs Nugent took them, do you remember?'

'Remember? I had to give her twenty quid out of my own pocket to do it.'

'No way!'

'She was a hard auld bitch.' He chuckled.

'Yeah, but I'd be dead without her,' she said, 'and I'd be dead without you.'

Fred stroked her arm. 'I would never have acted on it, of course, and I was a bit of a mess myself back then. I was still mourning Joy, but I want you to know that for me it was love at first sight.'

Maisie took a moment to let that settle in. 'Seven years is a long time to get around to asking me out.'

'Yeah, well, once you were safe I had to let go. It was only right. Then I kept seeing you around the place, looking happy and beautiful, and I thought about it, especially after the promotion, but you'd been through so much.'

'What changed?' She was intrigued.

'I got lonely.' He couldn't look her in the eye. She guessed it was hard for Fred to admit weakness – she could understand that – but she knew him as a man who valued honesty.

'Me too,' she admitted.

'You, Mai?' He seemed surprised.

She nodded. 'I didn't know how lonely I was.' She turned to the window. He wrapped his arms around her stomach and chest and they lay there, spooning.

'I worried I'd missed my chance. The way you looked at me yesterday when I asked you out . . .'

'It was a shock.'

'It wasn't planned. It was the first day of a new year and there you were in a supermarket, and I thought, *This is the day, Fred. Now or never.*'

Maisie smiled and bit her lip. *If he can be honest I can too.* 'It was one week after I came out of the coma,' she said.

'What was?'

'The first time I thought about you like that. You walked into my hospital room and I thought, *God, I wish he was mine.*' A stray tear trickled down her face.

He squeezed her around the middle gently. 'I'd say you'd have settled for running away with a gypsy's donkey back then.'

'True.'

'And now here we are, Mai.' He kissed her neck.

'I tell you, Fred, if this is a dream, I'll be gutted.'

He laughed and pulled her closer.

And she thought, *To hell with the world*, and they made love again.

It was just after eight when she rang home.

Valerie answered the phone. 'What?'

'Don't answer the phone like that.' Maisie sighed.

'Oh, pardon me, Ma. Hello, this is the Bean household. Can I be of bleedin' service?'

'Valerie, swear jar!'

'I forgot, sorry.'

'Put your brother on the phone.'

There was silence for the briefest moment. 'He's gone out again, Ma.'

'You're joking! Where?'

'I didn't ask him.'

'What the hell's got into him? Did he eat his dinner?'

'Yeah, Ma. He said it was the nicest stew he ever ate,' Valerie said sarcastically.

'How's your grammy?'

'Mental.'

'But she's fine?'

'Well, she's alive. So are you coming home or what?'

'I'll be there in half an hour.' Maisie hung up and turned to Fred. 'Jeremy came home for his tea and decided to go AWOL again. I have to go.'

'He's sixteen, Maisie, just acting his age,' he reassured her.

'I know. I just wish he could have picked any day of the year

I sit in on my own to do a disappearing act.' She got out of bed and hunted about for her knickers.

'One more hour.'

'I've already pushed it, Fred.'

'Just one more,' he pleaded.

Say no. Stand your ground. The rain pelted against the window, the room was cold, the bed warm and inviting. She'd never wanted to sink into a man before. *I should go.*

'What's the worst that could happen?' he asked.

A million things raced through her mind including, but not limited to, fire, flood, famine and pestilence, but Valerie could handle all of them.

She nodded. 'One more hour.'

He grinned. 'Maybe two.'

Don't get cocky, mister. She slipped back into the bed, wrapped her arms around him and laid her head against his chest, the sound of his heartbeat in her ear.

Valerie

Valerie put down the phone to her mother and bit the only nail she had left. *What are you up to, Jeremy?* She worried that if her mother came home before Jeremy she wouldn't be able to give him the heads-up on her lie. She could have ratted that he'd bunked off school and still hadn't come home but, as much fun as seeing the golden boy get into trouble would be, the cons far outweighed the pros. Her ma would freak out, leg it home and start calling around. She'd be questioned like a criminal and ultimately – as always – her ma would find a way to fight with Valerie about it. *Everything's always my fault.* On the upside Valerie wasn't an eejit: she knew if she covered for him he'd owe her, and she needed all the favours she could get.

She sauntered down the hallway and knocked at the bathroom door. 'Are you all right, Grammy?' It had been a testing few hours. Grammy hadn't stopped getting up and down, walking in and out, wanting this and that. She was exhausting, and Valerie was tired of running around after her. This was her third time in the loo in an hour, and whatever else they helped Grammy with, Valerie and Jeremy did not do bathroom stuff with her. There are some things you can never unsee, and both children had made it very clear to their mother that she was on her own when it came to naked Grammy.

'I'd choke on me own puke,' Valerie had said.

'I'd never be right again, Ma,' had been Jeremy's stand on the matter.

Their mother hadn't needed much convincing. She'd admitted that it was hard enough on her, and she was an adult who had seen her share of horror.

Valerie knocked again. 'What's happening? Wait! Jaysus, don't tell me. Just say, "Finished."'

'Finished.'

'Great. Are you decent?'

'Oh, yeah,' Grammy said.

'Brill. I'm opening the door then.'

Grammy was standing there with her skirt up around her chest and her knickers around the ankles of Jeremy's soccer socks.

Valerie immediately covered her eyes and turned her back on her grandmother. 'What's wrong with you?'

'I'm air-drying, love. There's no toilet roll in this place,' Bridie said. 'Oooh . . .'

'What?'

'I feel dizzy, love.'

'Ah, shite.' Valerie sighed. 'Stay where you are. I'll deal with this.' Mercifully her grandmother had dropped her skirt. She went to her, grabbed her knickers and whipped them up as far as her knees. 'Take it from there, Grammy. Come on, pull, pull, pull.'

She did as she was told. 'Easy.'

'Nice one, Grammy.'

When Valerie went to flush the toilet she saw a full fresh toilet roll in the bowl. She thought about putting on a pair of gloves and retrieving it. *Nah. Me ma will get it.* If Jeremy was home he'd have put Bridie to bed, but she wouldn't go anywhere for Valerie, even though she was tired.

When they were back in the sitting room, in front of the TV, Bridie became slightly agitated and Valerie sensed something was brewing. *Oh, no.*

'Where's Jeremy?' she asked.

'He's at soccer practice.' It was better to keep on lying, Valerie decided.

'It's too late for that,' Bridie said, looking out into the darkness.

'They have them inside now, Grammy. It's real posh.'

'But where is he?'

'He's on his way, Grammy.'

'I want him home now.' Tears welled in Bridie's eyes.

'You're not alone.' Valerie looked out into the darkness beyond the window, as if Jeremy might suddenly appear and make everything OK. 'I'll make you a cup of tea, if you like, and some of those biscuits you can dunk for half an hour without breaking.'

'OK, love.' She sounded fine but the tears kept streaming from her eyes. Then, all of a sudden, she had that weird wild look about her – the one that told Valerie she was lost in her head. 'I'm looking for me family,' Bridie mumbled. 'Have ya seen them? Can ya help me?'

She's bleedin' gone now. Bridie clutched at Valerie's hand, but Valerie shook her off and moved to the kitchen, leaving her to sob alone. 'Those biscuits are comin', Grammy,' she shouted, as though her grandmother had a clue what was going on. 'Any minute now.'

She stayed where she was, listening to her grandmother's cries until it was safe. It was the best thing to do. When Grammy disappeared into the past or became confused, agitated or sad,

Valerie shut down and pretended it wasn't happening. *I mean, what am I supposed to do? No one can help her, she's gone. My grammy is gone.*

She waited there until her grandmother dozed off, then covered her with a blanket and headed to her bedroom.

Maisie

Maisie arrived home just after midnight. She couldn't believe she'd allowed herself to fall asleep. She felt a mad desperation just to get home, be inside, see her kids. As the car pulled into the driveway she could just make out Bridie asleep on the sofa through the front window. *That's not right.* She put her hand on the car's door handle. She really needed to get inside. Guilt was weighing her down. The afterglow had dimmed and reality was setting in. *I walked out on my mother and child to have sex with a man I've had one date with. What kind of a person does that?*

As soon as the car stopped, she opened the door. 'I have to go.'

He took her hand and stilled her. She couldn't make herself face him, not in the driveway of her mother's house.

'I'm not going to push myself into your life, Mai. I know you have kids and a mother to take care of. We'll take it at whatever pace you want but I can't let you push me away either. OK?'

She took a breath and faced him. 'It's midnight, Fred. I need to get in to me family now.'

'OK.' He handed her a card. 'Here's my new mobile number. Use it, please.'

She took it. 'I can never do something like this again.'

'I understand, Mai.' He was so kind and had been so apologetic when she'd woken just after eleven thirty. He'd half killed himself getting her home as quickly as he had.

'Thank you.' She smiled as she got out, then ran up the

driveway and didn't look back before she entered the house. She heard the car drive off as soon as she was inside. She made her way down the hallway towards Valerie's room where music was seeping through the closed door. When she opened it she found her daughter fully dressed and passed out on her bed, one foot on the floor. She turned off the music, took Valerie's shoes off and covered her with a blanket. Then she went quickly to the sitting room. Bridie was in her chair, fast asleep with a blanket thrown over her. *It's unlike Jeremy not to be able to sweet-talk her to bed.* She began the process of waking her mother slowly, and practically carried her to bed. She stripped her and managed to put a nightdress over her head. Bridie was exhausted, way too tired to fight or to even try to help. She was a dead weight, eyes half open and glassy.

'Where did you go to, Maisie?' she asked drowsily.

'Work, Ma.'

'You're a good girl. Don't forget to leave the dog out.'

'I will, Ma. Go to sleep now.'

She checked Jeremy's room last. She opened the door, looked in and saw an empty bed. She was already automatically closing the door before it truly registered that she had been looking at an empty bed. She stopped and allowed the door to swing open again. Her eyes darted around the room. *No Jeremy?*

'Jeremy?' She turned on the light. He was definitely not there. *He's not here? He wasn't here this morning and he's not here now? It's after midnight and he's not in his bed. I'll kill him.* She moved into the hallway and walked through the house in the darkness, checking her bedroom, the bathroom and then the kitchen for him.

She sat at the kitchen table, waiting for the sound of his key in the door and trying to figure out what to do. *I can't call his friends – it's too late. Should I wake Valerie? No, I'll wait a while before I do that. He might come home.* She battled to hold off the dread that ebbed and flowed. At one moment she believed something was truly wrong; at the next she was convinced he was punishing her for going out with Fred. Maybe he was staying at Mitch's and had left a note.

She tore the kitchen apart. There was no note. It was after two. Her head buzzed, her stomach flipped and her knees threatened to buckle. *I should have been here. If I'd been here I'd know where my son is.* That night it was Maisie pacing the hallway, not Bridie, until she fell asleep with her head in her hands at the kitchen table just before the clock struck five.

9 p.m. to 10 p.m., 1 January 1995

Jeremy

Jeremy and Deirdre held hands as they walked home, his favourite part of the time he spent with Deirdre. The dreaded deed was done so he could relax, and when she wasn't all over him like a rash, Deirdre was great company. She knew exactly who she was, and he envied that. Aside from Rave, Deirdre was Jeremy's best friend. He dreaded the day he'd lose her and he knew he would. *She'll hate me one day.* It was inevitable. The thought gave him stomach cramp.

The lads were jealous of him and Rave having girlfriends. Dave pretended he didn't care but it bugged him.

'What the fuck does Deirdre see in a curly-haired muppet like you, Beany?' he'd asked on more than one occasion. 'I mean, Rave's cool, but you? You're a fluff-faced mammy's boy.' Dave had a point. Jeremy had no idea what Deirdre was doing with him: every time they were together he disappointed her.

Jonno was terrified of girls. He still thought of them as the enemy.

Mitch Carberry was a different kettle of fish. He was desperate to hook up with somebody, anybody, but, to his chagrin, their response was always a variation of no. 'What's wrong with me?' he'd lament. 'I thought women liked money. I have money.'

As entertaining as Mitch's predicament was, none of the lads really knew why Mitch couldn't get himself a girlfriend. Mitch would have given his right testicle to be with Deirdre. Jeremy felt guilty about that but not enough to break it off with her. He'd worked too hard at being with her to give up. He'd asked Deirdre once why girls didn't go for Mitch. 'He's totally desperate. Nothing worse than desperate, except maybe being an utter prick, which he is, too. You know he offered Jean Foley a tenner to let him shove his tongue down her throat?'

'He did not?' Jeremy was totally shocked. His horror made her giggle a little.

'He did and I'm not going to tell you how much he offered her for a blow-job.'

'Jesus, there's no excuse for that.'

'He said he was only asking because she kept calling to his house offering her services.'

'Ah, stop.' Jeremy was aghast.

'The thing is, Jean Foley's not a prostitute – she's a Jehovah's Witness.'

'I don't think they do blow-jobs.'

'Probably not. I'd say Jehovah wouldn't entertain any of that messing.'

'A bit like God.' Jeremy often used religion and fear of God's reprisal for not engaging in the most minor sexual act, but he wasn't lying about his fear. It was just that it wasn't rooted in anything he did with Deirdre.

She thought about it. 'Maybe, but God's not as strict as Jehovah – at least He doesn't have us knocking on doors.'

It was nice to be part of a couple. It was normal and expected. Jeremy's life had been abnormal for such a long time. He craved the ordinary. All Jeremy Bean had ever wanted was to fit in and live an easy life. He was determined to do whatever it took to achieve that aim. *If I wish hard enough. If I believe. If I just try my very best, I'll be like the other lads. It just takes time and patience. I can change. It's not too late.* When his ma had insisted that he went to counselling after they'd left his da, he'd discovered how easy it was to hide behind lies. He was only nine but by then he had learned to put on a happy face and bury the bad stuff. It was a muscle he exercised often, a learned behaviour, a difficult habit to break because burying bad things had become natural to him. Taking out a shovel and digging for trouble was wholly unnatural, and that was what Mr Derek Bond, clinical psychologist specializing in traumatized children, was expecting him to do. Jeremy had learned early on to maintain eye contact. He wasn't sure why but the more intently he stared at nosy-parkers like Mr Bond the more they averted their gaze. It gave him a semblance of control.

'Do you miss your father?' Mr Bond had asked, in their first session.

'No.'

'Why not?'

'Because he's an awful man,' Jeremy said, with great authority. He had heard his grandmother say that to neighbours and friends who called to sympathize with his ma on the end of her marriage.

'Why is he awful?'

'He just is. He doesn't mean to be. He's made that way. That's what me ma says. Grammy says that some people are born rotten, and when you're born rotten, you either try to be the best you can be or you give in to it.' His voice had shaken a little. It was unnerving when Mr Bond scribbled something down.

'And did your daddy give in to it?'

Jeremy nodded.

'Does that upset you?'

'Nah. I'm just happy he's gone. Me, Ma, Grammy and Valerie, we're just fine without him. It's nice.' He smiled, and it didn't matter how many questions the man asked after that, he had held that smile for three long sessions. Jeremy's mantra was a simple one. *I'm not scared. I'm OK. Everything is great.*

Sometimes now he'd lie awake, look back to that time and wonder why he'd lied, why he hadn't told Mr Bond that he had nightmares about his da coming to get him, that his arm ached and he felt sick all the time. He guessed it might be because he was so desperate to be normal because, even at nine years old, he'd known he never would be. So what was the point? It didn't matter why he had lied so successfully, hiding his pain and fear. What mattered was that he could. Whenever Jeremy doubted himself, he recalled that experience because it told him he could pretend to be whatever he wanted to be. He certainly didn't have to be his real self.

Still, it was getting harder to be the good boy, the one who could be relied upon, and harder still to please everyone: his ma, Grammy, Rave, the lads and Deirdre – especially Deirdre. He was trying his best with her but his mickey and his gag reflex were letting him down.

'Rave looks thin,' Deirdre said, and as they walked she leaned into him.

He put his arm around her and held her close, like Rave did with Casey. 'He's all right.'

'Is he?'

'Yeah, he's grand – you know Rave.'

'My ma says she saw his da the other day. He was on the street making a show of himself.'

'What's new?' Jeremy said.

'It's terrible. He used to be such a nice man.'

'Well, not any more,' he said, with a hint of bitterness. Rave's predicament worried his best friend – Jeremy worried about him all the time.

'Don't give out to me,' she said. 'Promise?'

'Go on, I promise.'

'I know you don't like talking about it but my ma said Rave's ma's been in the nuthouse all this time.'

'For four years! They wouldn't keep that auld dragon in for longer than four minutes,' Jeremy said. Jeremy didn't hate many people but he hated that woman as much if not more than his own dad. She'd never been warm, loving or kind like his own mother. She'd never even pretended to be. She was removed, strict and obsessed with rules – ironic, seeing as she couldn't seem to follow the most basic natural law. *Take care of your young!*

'So where is she, then?'

'I'm telling you, Deirdre, I don't know. She ran off, is all.'

'It's weird. Who does that?'

'Well, Da did.'

'That's different.'

'Is it?'

'Yeah, your ma left him and, anyways, mothers are different.'

'I suppose they are.'

They walked on for a short while. Deirdre was humming to Pearl Jam's 'Jeremy' – she liked to sing that song to him, mostly because it annoyed him and she said he was cute when he was annoyed.

'Speaking of cults, Dave reckons Rave's ma joined the Moonies,' he said.

'Oh, well, then, it must be true.' She laughed.

'He's not the only one saying it. Ma heard it in the dentist's.'

'Jesus,' she said. 'The Moonies! Poor Rave.'

Jeremy sniffed. 'I suppose they're a bit like the Jehovah's Witnesses.'

'Yeah, but even more fucked up. At least the Jehovah's Witnesses live in their own houses, not in some bleedin' commune, like animals.'

'That's harsh. I'm sure they're not so bad.'

'Harsh? They're brainwashers.' She spoke with absolute authority. She'd been warned about the Moonies, she'd told Jeremy, when her ma had become obsessed with them after watching a documentary on the BBC. 'If a Moonie approaches you, what do you do?' her mother had asked her.

'Run.'

'Like you've never run before – and while you're running?'

'Pray to Jesus in me head.'

'That's right, and why do you do that?'

'Because Jesus will save me.'

'Good girl.'

Between the ages of ten and twelve, Deirdre had spent a lot of time running away from friendly strangers, even some kids (because they can be Moonies too). She hadn't taken any chances, Jeremy knew.

'A Moonie,' she repeated. 'Poor Rave.'

'I think his da is worse but Rave wants to take care of himself now.'

'Talk to him.'

'Can't. He goes mad. I wish he'd just let Ma help. He knows she would.'

'What does your ma say?'

'Every time she sees him she tells him, "We're here for you, Rave, anytime, son," and he just nods and says, "Ta, Maisie," and that's it.'

'At least he knows.'

'Yeah. He won't let me say anything to her about his da, though. If she knew, she'd go mad.'

'Maybe he's not that bad.'

'He hasn't let me in the house since last June.'

'Jesus.'

'Still, though, he's grand. We'll take care of him.'

'Course we will. It's sad, though. He always looks so lonely.'

'He's not lonely, he's cool,' Jeremy said.

'"Cool" – what age are you?' She laughed. 'Ya big goon.'

'He's not lonely.' He pulled away from her.

'All right, sorry.'

He hated the idea of his best friend being lonely or feeling bad in any way. *But how could he not feel bad? His ma walked out on him. His da's in bits.* He wished he could tell his ma how bad things had got but Rave had warned him off. 'They'll take me away, Beany,' he'd said, and the fear in his eyes had made Jeremy promise he wouldn't say a word. He loved his ma but he couldn't trust her with this so he did his best to feed his friend, care for him and be there whenever he needed him. *You have me, Rave. You'll always have me.*

When they got to Deirdre's house, the light was on in the porch. 'Da's looking out the window,' she said.

He always was. *Nice one.* Jeremy waved to him. He didn't wave so much as raise his hand, as though he wanted to slap something.

'I'd better go,' Jeremy said.

'Right,' Deirdre said, and turned away. He started to walk down the road but she turned back. 'You do really like me, Jeremy, don't you?'

'I think you're brilliant, Deirdre,' Jeremy said, and he meant it – but it wasn't enough.

'Goodnight,' she said.

He blew her a kiss.

'Gobshite.' She walked away – but he'd heard it in her voice: she was thrilled.

On the way back he stopped at the van for chips. He bought three bags with the tenner his grammy had given him the day before. 'Say nothing, son. Happy new year. It's between you and me.' He was happy to take it: between buying Deirdre's Christmas present of CK1 and a smiley-face scarf, and Rave tapping him for a few quid every few days, he was nearly broke. He told Della to wrap them twice and ran all the way to the park with the chips under his coat. Nothing worse than cold chips.

The lads were sitting around the Hanging Tree when he got there, a little drunker than when he'd last seen them. The rain had stopped but the tree was so dense it would be hard to get wet under it anyway. Rave was sitting on the ground leaning against the trunk. Jeremy reached into his coat and pulled out a bag of chips for him and handed the other two bags to Mitch to share with Dave and Jonno either side of him. 'Where are the girls?' he asked.

'Gone home.' Jonno grinned.

'How come he gets a full bag?' Dave pointed at Rave.

'Shut your mouth, Dave. I'm sharing with Jeremy.' Rave sounded a little too defensive.

Jeremy sat next to Rave but he didn't touch them. Rave needed chips more than he did.

Mitch handed him a bottle with some vodka in it. 'Nah, I'm grand,' he said.

'Go on, mammy's boy, have a drink,' Dave said.

'I said no, Dave.' Jeremy was always careful to drink enough not to seem a square but never too much. He couldn't afford to lose control.

'Thanks for the chips, Beany,' Jonno said, his mouth full.

'Can't believe it's 1995,' Rave said, when Dave handed him the bottle. He examined it before he drank. 'Nineteen-fuckin'-ninety-five.'

'Let's play a game. 1994 was the year that . . .' Mitch said.

'What? Like 1994 was the year I stuck me knob between Melissa Granger's tits?' Dave said.

'Nice one, Dave, exactly like that,' Mitch said. Dave never had a problem getting a girl. His problem lay in keeping them longer than five minutes. If you knew Dave, then at some point or other you were going to find yourself the butt of a joke, which didn't go down well with the girls.

'1994 was the year I broke me leg in three places,' Jonno said.

'Boring.'

'Screw you, Dave – I had iron bars sticking out of it for weeks, never mind a pipe up me knob. I was like Robocop. Ma said if I wasn't wearing me helmet I'd have had a brain injury.'

'You do have a brain injury. It's called your personality,' Dave quipped.

Mitch laughed, grabbed the bottle from Rave and drank. 'Go again, Jonno.'

'OK. 1994 was the year me ma made me wear a cycling helmet and made me look like a headcase.'

'Still boring but better.' Mitch handed Jonno the bottle.

'1994 was the year Kurt Cobain died,' Jeremy said.

'Yeah. Shite!' Rave said, and for a moment he looked like he was about to cry. He grabbed the bottle from Jonno. '1994 was the year Da started injecting heroin.' He drank, then raised the bottle high. 'Here's to Kurt and my da, two selfish pricks, one dead and one dying to meet him.' He forced a laugh, then drained the bottle. Everyone was silent. No one knew what to say. Dave and Jonno looked to Jeremy for guidance but even he had no idea. *Say nothin'. Just leave him. He'll be OK. Come on, Rave.* Rave gulped and Jeremy wondered if he was going to laugh or cry. He waited. Rave's face broke into a grin and Jeremy exhaled. 'It was the year I did it with Casey.'

Oh, no way.

Instantly the general mood lifted.

'No fucking way!' Dave said. 'You really did it? Like seriously DID IT?' He was shoving his finger into a circle he'd made with his thumb and index finger.

Rave laughed.

'Full details. Now, Rave,' Mitch demanded.

'What's there to say?'

'Everything,' Dave said.

'When?' Mitch said suspiciously.

'Before Christmas.'

'Where?' asked Dave.

'In her room when her parents were away.'

'Did you know about this?' Mitch said to Jeremy.

He shook his head. *Of course not. Why would he tell me something as important as that? I only spend every day of me life with him. I only take care of him and worry about him. I'm only the one he talks to when there's nobody else. Why would he tell me?* His face and neck felt hot even though the rest of his body was really cold. He hugged his hands under his arms and kept his eyes on the ground in front of him, even when he could feel Rave staring at him. He knew he wasn't reacting right, that he should be joining in with the questioning, but he couldn't find it in himself to fake it this time.

'I have a question,' Dave said. 'Does it feel better than a wank?'

'Jesus, Dave,' Jeremy said. *Please, please, stop.*

'No, no, no,' Mitch said. 'That's a good question.'

Rave smiled. He pulled yet another bottle from the inside pocket of his jacket, opened it and took a slug. All eyes were on him.

'Well?' Dave said.

'About a million times better.'

'Bollocks,' Mitch said. 'If it was a million times better your bleedin' head would be blown off.'

'You'll see,' Rave said condescendingly.

Jeremy grabbed the bottle from Rave and drank it down in several deep swigs.

'You all right?' Rave asked.

'Yeah, grand. Just getting cold sitting around,' Jeremy lied. He wasn't grand at all. Jesus, no wonder Deirdre was putting the pressure on. He felt like crying. *Whatever you do, don't cry. It was always gonna happen. It's not like it changes anything. Get your act together. Why the hell are you so upset? If Casey's done it, Deirdre'll want to do it too. That's why my chest feels like it's gonna explode.*

'Go on, Rave.' Jonno sounded fascinated, if a little scared. 'What was it like?'

Rave thought about it. 'It was like sticking your knob into the softest but tightest thing.'

'Like a pipe full of pudding?' Mitch said helpfully.

'A bit.'

Mitch nodded thoughtfully.

'I love pudding,' Jonno said, and the lads laughed, but Jeremy wasn't in the mood to join in. He was cold, tired and a little emotional. *I just want to go home. Please, Rave, let me go home.*

Jonno looked at his watch and stood up. 'It's nearly ten. I'd better go before Ma releases the hounds.' He put his helmet on and secured the strap.

Mitch laughed. 'The state of you.'

'See yis.' Jonno picked up his bike and cycled off. He was a little rocky at first but once he got going he was fine.

'If he doesn't sober up, his ma will kill him.' Mitch snorted.

'He'll be grand,' Rave said.

Jeremy remained silent, relieved that now one of them had gone home the others would probably follow soon enough.

Mitch took another slug of the vodka, then handed it to a subdued Dave. 'If I head now my da will be snoozing in the chair. Ma can't smell booze but Da can from the bleedin' path.' He got up and grabbed his bike. 'See yis.'

Two down, one still to go.

He pedalled off with his arms in the air. 'Goodnight, Dublin, I love you,' he shouted.

'Rock on, Mitch,' Dave shouted, then looked at Jeremy and Rave. 'What now?'

'You're goin' home,' Rave said.

'Yeah, we've got something to do, Dave.' Jeremy was desperate to get out of the park, find out what Rave wanted to show him, then go home. If they were quick, he'd make it before his ma got back.

'Oh, yeah, Beany! Ya big knob-jockey, do you want some quality time with Rave? He's never gonna go for it, you know,' Dave said. Jeremy's heart threatened to fall into his stomach. He couldn't speak or move or do anything, and then he heard Rave's anger.

'What did you say?' Rave got to his feet a little unsteadily, but once he was up, he was in Dave's face.

'Nothing.'

'Come on, what are you trying to say?'

'I was only messin',' Dave said nervously.

'Rave, it's fine.' Jeremy took his arm and tried to pull him back.

'It's not fuckin' fine.' Rave shrugged him off and gave Dave's shoulder a shove. 'You can do what you want with everyone else, Dave, but you don't ever fuckin' call him names. All right?'

'Right, sorry, Rave. Sorry.'

Jeremy put himself between them. 'Just go, Dave. It's fine.'

Dave picked up his bike and cycled off. Rave watched him go.

Jeremy sat down again and waited for Rave to relax. It took a few minutes before Rave would look at him. Eventually he flopped beside his best friend.

'Sorry, man. I was out of line there, I know I was.'

'He was only messin'.'

'Yeah, well he sounded like he meant it and shite sticks, Jeremy.' Rave took another drink.

'You scared him,' Jeremy said.

'I'd never have hit him. You know that, don't ya?'

'Yeah.'

'OK, then. It's time to show you . . .' Rave was picking up the last of the bottles lying around the tree and placing them in Jeremy's backpack.

'Show me what?' Jeremy got to his feet and brushed himself down.

'It's a place.'

'Where?'

'Past the reservoir into the mountains.'

'Jesus, Rave, it's the middle of the night.'

'Please,' Rave said. 'Your ma won't be home for ages.'

Jeremy thought about it. Grammy and Valerie were probably still alone. His ma would go mad if she found out.

'Come on, please.'

'I dunno.'

'I need you to see it.'

Shite. 'Right, screw it, I'll go. But get a shift on before it starts pissing down again.'

'I knew I could count on you, Beany.' He got on the bike and waited for Jeremy. 'Well?'

Jeremy hopped on to the back. 'Don't kill me.'

'As if.'

They took off down the dirt path that would lead them out of Dodder Park just as the rain began to pour from the sky.

TUESDAY,
3 JANUARY 1995

Chapter Five

'Come As You Are'
Nirvana, 1992

Maisie

THE FIRST TIME MAISIE went to a battered women's support group she had no real idea what she was letting herself in for. She went because everyone around her told her it was the best thing to do. She wasn't sure, but at the time she wasn't sure about anything. She faced an uncertain future, and starting as a single mother filled her with a new kind of terror that was laced with hope. It was Fred who had motivated her to go. He had called in at her mother's house the afternoon after she had been discharged from hospital to check how she and the kids were settling in. She was still recovering from her injuries so Bridie had let him in and greeted him warmly.

'There you are,' she'd said. 'I'm going to hug you now.'

Maisie could just about hear their voices softly floating down the hallway.

'It's lovely to see you too, Mrs Bean.'

'Call me Bridie.'

'Bridie it is.'

'Good man, come on in. She's in the sitting room.'

Maisie was too weak, frail and battered to stand. She was

sitting in the armchair with a cup of tea. Her mother had tucked a blanket around her. Fred's eyes widened when he saw her.

She had left her vicious husband and her old life behind, and although she was fragile, she had never let him break her. Her physical state was a whole other story – she knew she was a sight to behold, even for a seasoned veteran such as Fred, so she attempted a smile for him.

'There you are,' he said.

'She can't seem to get warm. I've the heat on all day and night but she's still freezing. I think it's those blood thinners they gave her. Cup of tea?' she asked.

'Coffee, if you have it, thanks. Milk, two sugars,' he said.

She made for the kitchen.

'I hope you don't mind me calling in,' he said.

'No.'

He sat down. 'How are you feeling?'

'Free.' She tried to maintain her smile but her jaw hurt too much.

'Good.' He nodded. 'That's good.'

She didn't know him well but she could see he had something on his mind. 'You have something to say?' she asked.

He sighed. 'You're right.'

'Spit it out.'

'He'll leave you alone to heal, then start knocking.'

'I know.'

'He's the kind that won't give up. But you can't let him back in.'

'I won't.'

'And we'll help, if he comes anywhere near you.'

'I'll call.'

'That's all I wanted to hear.'

Bridie brought in the coffee and some cake. 'It's me own. I made it fresh this morning.' She waited for him to take a bite.

'Delicious.' It was clear that he meant it.

'That's me special ingredient.'

'Love?' He gave a light laugh.

'Booze.' She winked. 'I'll leave you two alone.'

'She's great,' he'd said, when she'd walked out of the door.

'I'm lucky.' Despite everything she felt that was true.

'Look, I want to give you this.' He handed her a flyer for a battered-wives group.

'Thanks.'

'Don't just thank me. I want you to go.'

'You and everyone else.' She was dribbling and pressed a tissue to her lips.

'It'd be good for you to talk to those other women.'

'Not really in the form for chat.'

'So listen. It's important.'

'I'm not going back,' she said. 'He broke my son's arm.'

Fred nodded. 'They have cake,' he raised Bridie's, 'maybe not as good as this one but it's free.'

She pulled out some forms and handed them to him. 'I asked Ma to pick them up.'

He ran his eyes over them. 'Deed poll.'

'I'm dropping the Fox from our names.' She attempted another crooked smile. 'I'm not going back.'

Fred put the flyer into her hand and held it there. 'All the more reason.'

In the end, after many sleepless nights and a lecture from Lynn, Maisie had done as she was told.

The thing about most battered women was that they loved their husbands, she learned that first night. It was a strange revelation. *How?* The group was made up of five and a counsellor, who happened to have been battered too. Maisie didn't talk but everyone could tell that she was still recovering. A woman called Beatrice spoke about her husband, Paul. She was short, a little pudgy, and wore her red hair in a high ponytail on top of her head, even though she was forty-seven and a little too old for it, in Maisie's opinion. *Then again, who am I to judge? The back of my head looks like I've been through a bush backwards.* Beatrice talked about their courtship and how he used to make her laugh. He was handsome, accomplished, a bank manager with a number of degrees in things Maisie had never heard of. She talked about him as if he was something special to be proud of instead of the man who had broken her nose, eye socket and three teeth.

'The thing I'll miss is his warmth when it was good,' Beatrice said. She didn't talk about the abuse, even though it was a battered-wives' meeting: she'd rather talk about how great he was. Maisie felt a little sick. *Sorry, Fred, this isn't for me.* She got up to leave.

'Don't go yet,' Julia, the counsellor, said.

'I've left the kids with my mother.'

'Just stay the hour.'

Maisie didn't like to make a fuss so she sat and all eyes were now on her.

'Tell us what you'll miss most, Maisie,' Julia said.

'Nothing.'

'Nothing at all?' Julia asked. But that was all Maisie would say that night. After another woman talked about finally having had enough and bashing her husband's skull in with a frying-pan (he'd survived but suffered a serious concussion and ringing in his left ear), she felt a little better about the group and returned on and off for a year. She knew everyone there by the time she confessed to hating her husband from first sight. She even mentioned the article she'd read on date-rape and admitted that that was what had happened with Danny.

The room was silent until Beatrice mumbled, 'Sweet suffering Jesus.'

'Ah, no,' someone said. She wasn't sure who had spoken because she was staring at her shoes at the time. She immediately worried that she'd said too much but it had felt good to get it out. She couldn't talk about sex with her ma, and back then, aside from Lynn, she'd had no real friends left. Danny had seen to that. She'd never told Lynn about the rape – not because she didn't trust her but because she feared that Lynn would never understand how Maisie had walked into a marriage with a rapist. She didn't understand it herself.

Julia and the group were instrumental in giving Maisie back some confidence. That first night Julia shook Maisie's hand and congratulated her.

'For what?' Maisie said.

'Having the courage to get out.'

'I should have done it a long time ago.'

'You've done it now, and you'll never have to experience that dread again.'

Maisie smiled at her. 'That would be nice.' She knew the dread Julia meant: she'd felt it every time her husband had put his key in the door. Even after she'd escaped she felt it – that time she'd seen him on the street or when he'd walked up her mother's driveway to bang on the door and she'd thought he'd break in and kill them all. Then, one day out of nowhere, he'd packed up his job and left. It was three months before she stopped holding her breath and the dread lifted. In the years since she had almost forgotten how intense and crippling it was.

That morning, Maisie woke from a fitful sleep at 6.05 a.m. Her neck was stiff, her back hurt, and even through the fog, she acknowledged a hint of a headache. When she opened her eyes and realized she was sitting at the kitchen table, she shot to her feet. *Jeremy.* She limped to his room, straightening herself and gathering pace with each step she took. It was empty. She stood there, looking at his pristine bed, exactly as it had been in the middle of the night. *This is all wrong.* Her heart hammered and her hands shook. She stood up and, although she felt like she was walking through treacle, she walked down the hall until she reached Valerie's room. She opened the door and leaned on the frame to steady her jellied legs.

Valerie was stretched out like a cat under a hot sun. *My son should be in his bed.* Maisie's chest constricted and she had to work hard to breathe normally. Her old friend Dread was unfurling inside her with every step she took. She dropped heavily on to Valerie's bed but Valerie just groaned and turned over so that Maisie was facing her back. 'Valerie,' she whispered, and rested her hand on her daughter's shoulder. 'Valerie.' She shook her gently. *Something's very wrong.* She knew it in her heart. She knew it in her soul. 'Valerie!' she shouted, crying now.

Valerie opened her eyes. 'What's wrong?'

'Valerie, promise to tell me the truth, OK?'

Usually Valerie would point out how incredibly unfair and mentally scarring it was that her mother felt the need to solicit sworn testimony from her before asking a stupid question. She'd never do that to Jeremy. But this morning was different. Something terrible was happening: she didn't know what it was but it scared her.

'Did Jeremy come home for his dinner last night?'

Valerie shook her head.

Maisie was almost afraid to ask her next question because she knew the answer. 'Was he in school yesterday?'

Valerie gulped and shook her head.

Maisie let out something between a moan and a groan. 'When did you see him last?' Her voice was shaking.

'Sunday night,' Valerie said, tears welling in her eyes.

Maisie's heart froze. She took a huge breath, then exhaled in a stuttery way.

'Ma'sie?'

No one has seen him since the night before last. Oh, God. Maisie was up and walking across Valerie's room. Her hand was on the door when Valerie's raspy voice stopped her. 'Where's Jeremy?'

Maisie stopped but she kept her back to her daughter because she didn't want her to see she was still crying. 'I don't know, love, but we'll find him.' She walked on to the kitchen, talking herself down as she always did when trouble found her.

It's OK, everything's fine. He's just on a jolly with the lads or with that Deirdre. He's making me pay for dating Fred. He's in big trouble with his mother but he's safe. She tried to believe herself but her gut was screaming, *Get help, get help, get help.* She closed the kitchen door and rooted through her bag for Fred's mobile number. She picked up her house phone and dialled it. He answered on the fifth ring.

'Detective Brennan.'

'It's Maisie.' Her voice sounded foreign and far away.

'Mai?' She registered alarm in his voice. 'What's wrong?'

She could hear him struggling to sit upright in the bed. 'It's Jeremy. He's missing.' The words rang in her ears.

'How long?'

'He didn't come home last night, no one saw him at school, he wasn't there yesterday morning. It was Sunday night!' She spoke in a rushed, hushed manner, as though she couldn't believe what she was saying, guilt dripping from every word.

'It's all right, do you hear me, Mai? It'll be all right.'

'I don't think it is. Something's really wrong, Fred.' She wouldn't allow herself to become hysterical. *Breathe, just breathe, you silly cow. Hysterical never got anything done.*

'I'm on my way.'

'Thank you.'

'Put on the kettle.'

'OK.'

'And, Mai . . .'

'Yeah?'

'We will find him.'

She put down the phone and she switched on the kettle robotically, just like in the bad old days when all she felt was fear and pain.

Fred

Fred arrived before Bridie had stirred. Valerie let him in and led him through to the kitchen. She was fully dressed in her school uniform, subdued, not eating the cereal placed in front of her. She just stared at it as though the concept of breakfast had lost all meaning. He hugged Maisie. 'I'm on the case,' he said lightly. 'You've got the best in the business here.'

She was pale and exhausted, a completely different woman from the one he'd bedded the night before. He put his arm around her shoulders and sat her down beside Valerie, then took a seat opposite them. She didn't offer him coffee or tea, clearly too anxious for that, so instead he got straight to business, taking out his notepad and pen.

'So, Sunday was the last time either of you saw Jeremy?' he said.

They nodded.

'What time?'

'It was maybe half an hour before our . . .' she faltered '. . . date.'

'So, about seven thirty?'

She nodded again. That sounded about right.

'Valerie?'

'Maybe ten past or a quarter past eight.'

Fred scribbled on his notepad. 'And he didn't say he was going anywhere?' Fred directed his question to Valerie.

'No.'

'Does he often leave you and your grandmother alone?'

'No, never.'

'He wouldn't have left them alone,' Maisie said.

Fred sat back and looked her in the eye. 'There's a first time for everything, Mai. He's sixteen. I'm going to raise the alert from the time he was last seen. That's approximately eight fifteen on Sunday, the first of January. OK?'

Maisie looked mortified. 'Sunday, Fred. It's Tuesday! What kind of a mother—'

'Rave wasn't in school either,' Valerie interrupted, as though it had just dawned on her. 'The lads were looking for both of them. Dave was really pissed off that they'd bunked off school without him.'

'That's a good sign, believe it or not. Does your brother bunk off school often?'

Fred caught Valerie glancing at her mother. 'This isn't about getting Jeremy in trouble,' he reassured her.

'He never bunks off. That's why the lads came looking. Rave does sometimes but not Jeremy.'

'Good, Valerie. I'm going to the school to catch up with some of those lads – see what they have to say.' He was calm: for Fred this was something and nothing. The missing-persons unit saw this kind of thing all the time. *Nine times out of ten, teenagers come home.* He wondered if Jeremy was punishing his mother for dating him or maybe he was up to no good. He hoped that wasn't the case: it would make life awkward. The boys were probably off chasing some young ones. Maybe there was a concert or festival on somewhere, although in the first week of January it was unlikely. He made a mental note to check it out. He looked at his watch. It was still too early for school.

'Try and eat,' he said to Valerie. She pushed her bowl away. He ignored the small act of defiance. *You'll be all right, love.*

'And you, Mai, how about some toast?'

'It would choke me. But thanks.' Then she thought about it. 'Sorry, Fred, you must be hungry.'

She stood up but he was on his feet in a flash, put his hands on her shoulders and guided her back to her chair. 'I'm fine. I'll grab something later at the station.'

'Are you sure?'

'Positive. Besides, I've enough meat on me to keep me going for a day or two at least.' He patted his belly.

Valerie rolled her eyes, then excused herself. 'I need to get my schoolbag.'

'Sure you can travel with me,' Fred said. Her expression suggested she'd get into a car quicker with an armed robber. 'So we can talk.'

'I don't have anything to say.'

'And I'll bet you're still great company.' She looked at him strangely. He smiled at her. 'It's going to be all right, love.'

Her eyes welled and she walked out, leaving Fred with a dazed, dishevelled Maisie in a room full of creeping anxiety.

Maisie

Maisie was quiet, lost in the fear that was bubbling in her head. *He's been kidnapped by some psycho. He's fallen into the river. He's run away because I went on a date with Fred. He's hurt somewhere and can't get home. Oh, Jaysus, his da has him!*

Fred pulled Valerie's chair to face Maisie and sat down. 'Is there anywhere you can think of that he and his friend might go?'

'They like the beach and Bray Head.' She used to take the boys to Brittis Bay and Bray Head when they were younger. They would spend hours together playing in the dunes or running in and out of the water, their skin goose-pimpled and their hair thick with sand. Even Valerie didn't complain at the beach. At Bray Head the boys liked the bumper cars and the ghost train. They'd eat sticky blue candyfloss and play on the video games until the few quid Bridie had given them had run out. Valerie didn't like bumpers, candyfloss or video games so she'd buy a bag of chips with Bridie's money and climb into the car, eat them looking out at the sea, then lie down on the back seat and fall asleep. Maisie and Bridie had spent many a happy time sitting on a bench drinking takeaway coffee and watching over the sleeping child.

The summer that stayed in Maisie's mind was the second after Danny had disappeared, before Bridie's dementia had started to steal her away, and they were all living happily in Cypress Road. Jeremy and Rave were eleven going on twelve and Valerie was seven. Bridie loved the sea. Her father had been a fisherman and she'd grown up in Bray. The love of a soldier had taken her inland to Tallaght. 'This is the best of life, Maisie,' she'd say, gazing at the blue sky turning pink. 'Right here and right now.'

It was true: those precious days logged in Maisie's memory were the absolute best of times. Maisie wondered if her mother remembered a single day from that summer.

'Mai,' Fred said gently, bringing her back into the moment.

She tried to smile and took his hand in hers. 'I'm here.'

'Anywhere else?'

'The thing is, Jeremy wouldn't just go off somewhere.' Tears scalded her eyes. 'He just wouldn't.'

Fred sighed. 'I'm phoning this in, Mai, and I need you to find me a good clear photo of the two boys, just in case we need it.'

'OK,' Maisie said. The tears spilled down her cheeks. *This is it, the jumping-off point.* The moment when everything good turned bad, the jumping-off point was the place of no return. It had once involved a look in her husband's eye, his raised voice, the sound he made when he moved to strike her. It didn't matter what happened after the jumping-off point – there was no way to stop, rewind or reset: the only way was down. Now she felt the familiar drowning sensation. *Just hang in there, Maisie. Let it play out. Stay alive. Don't let go.*

Valerie

Valerie was dragging her schoolbag along the floor behind her when Fred passed her in the hallway, taking his phone out of his pocket and giving her a slight nod. She stopped just short of the open kitchen door, transfixed by the sight of her mother.

She didn't move, just watched Maisie: she was sitting at the table, staring into space, like her grammy did when she disappeared.

'Listen, Tom, I'm reporting a sixteen-year-old boy missing, last seen by family members at approximately eight fifteen on Sunday, the first of January. Jeremy Bean. Thirty-four Cypress Road. No history of running away, no argument with the family. I'm with them now, so I'll get the information necessary to start the ball rolling, if that's all right with you . . . Great. Oh and, Tom, I need your full attention on this . . . Yeah. Will do. Thanks.'

This is all my fault.

He hung up and she heard him approach her, then felt his hands on her shoulders as he guided her back to a kitchen chair. 'Now, young lady, I'm going to put on some toast and tea, and then we're going to sit down together and you're going to tell me everything you know and supply me with the names of everyone Jeremy knows. OK, Valerie?'

Valerie nodded. *I shouldn't have lied. We could have been looking for him yesterday. Why did I lie?*

'Maisie, you go and look for that photo, one of the two boys, just in case he's gone off somewhere with his friend.'

She dragged herself upright and left the room.

The signage around the kitchen helped him find what he needed without having to ask. 'Jesus, I should do this in me own house. It's fierce handy.'

'No, it's not, it's weird,' Valerie mumbled. *You don't know what you're talking about.*

He put a plate of buttered toast in front of her, then sat opposite. She didn't touch it.

'So, the last time you saw your brother was just after eight p.m.' He took out his notepad again.

Valerie nodded.

'Was he agitated? Did he say anything to suggest he was going somewhere or that something was wrong?'

'No,' Valerie said. 'He just told me if I was hungry to eat something.'

'Why?'

'Ma went mental and sent me to bed without dinner because I called you a tosser, and then I said I was like my da.'

'Oh.' He smiled at her. 'You were going for gold there. And then what?'

She shrugged. 'We talked.'

'About what?'

'I dunno, stupid stuff. It was only for a minute.'

'And he said nothing at all out of the ordinary?'

'No.' *Well . . . No. He was just grumpy. Everyone gets grumpy, even Jeremy.*

'OK. Now, how about we list off all his friends.'

'Can't we just do this in the car?' Valerie wanted to leave. *Grammy will be awake soon and when she finds out she's going to go mental. I need to get outta here.*

Fred looked at the clock on the wall. 'It's still too early and, besides, we're not going anywhere until you have at least one slice of toast.'

'You have one.'

'Don't mind if I do.' He picked one up and shoved it into his mouth in one go. 'Yum.' He wiped some butter off his beard, then pushed the plate towards her. She picked up the toast and took a bite. He grinned at her with his mouth full. It looked pretty disgusting but, hard as she tried, she couldn't hide a hint of a smile. *He's a headcase.*

'He hangs out with four lads including Rave, some girls too.'

'Good girl.'

Maisie appeared, laden with boxes and old albums. She placed them on the table.

'And can you find his passport for me?' Fred said to Maisie.

'Passport?'

'Just in case he decided to take a trip.'

'Oh, God.'

'No need for panic, this is just procedure. OK?'

'It's always in the drawer of my locker.' She left the room in a daze.

Fred took down all the names of Jeremy's friends, Deirdre's too. Valerie pulled out her mother's book with their parents' phone numbers and read them out while he noted them down. Maisie appeared with the passport, and as Valerie rattled off addresses and phone numbers of everyone close to Jeremy, Maisie delved through smiling family photographs. Valerie noticed that Fred kept an eye on her mother while she worked, glancing at the pictures she discarded one by one in a pile on the table. *Me da isn't in any, if that's what you're looking at.*

Maisie found a recent school photo of Jeremy pretty quickly. He was standing straight, shoulders back, in his navy uniform, against a blue backdrop, his hair moussed to within an inch of its life. He wore a noncommittal smile and focused fiercely to the left of the camera lens. Her ma dusted it off and carefully placed it on the table to one side of the others. Then she made a new pile of photos of Jeremy and Rave together. There was one of their first day at secondary school, the two boys linking each other by the neck as though they intended to wrestle as soon as the photo had been taken. Then a picture taken in the summer – they couldn't have been more than thirteen, both in their swimming shorts, Jeremy flushed and strawberry-coloured, Rave pushing his fringe from his eyes, both glistening and holding up fishing rods.

Valerie remembered that day. She was only small but she could picture the boys sitting on a rock wall together, fishing in a shallow river for hours. *Where were we?* Maisie put it to the side with the others and Valerie picked up a picture of Rave sideways on, sitting in the window playing a battered guitar, his brow slightly furrowed. He was about twelve, a little plumper back then than he was now, his hair growing out. *He only looks a little bit like himself. He's different now.*

Fred picked up the small pile of carefully selected photos and looked at them. 'Nothin' more current?' he asked.

'Not so far.'

'Well, we'll leave you to it. You ready, Valerie?' She was standing up with her bag on her back before he'd finished his sentence. She could hear her grammy stirring. *Come on, let's go.*

He threw his car keys at her. 'Heads up.'

She caught them easily.

'I'll meet you in the car.'

She couldn't bring herself to say goodbye to her mother but it was OK because her mother didn't seem to notice she was leaving. She was still thumbing through old photographs as though her life depended on it. *I'm sorry, Ma. I'm really very sorry.*

Bridie

Bridie woke up to the sound of birds. At least, she thought she did, but she quickly realized the chatter was human. *Who's there?* She recognized a male voice. *Arthur? Ah, Arthur, you've come home.* She jumped out of bed as quickly as her old body would allow and scurried into the hallway to see a hairy man on his phone. *You are not Arthur Bean!* It was so disappointing she felt like hitting out at him. *Who are you?*

'I have to go,' he said into the phone, averted his eyes and held his hand up, as if to stop her approaching.

'Bridie.' He turned his head.

He looked familiar but she couldn't place him. *Why won't he look me in the eye? Never trust a man who can't look you in the eye.* 'What are you doing here?' she shouted. 'You have no business here.' Her dressing-gown was swinging behind her. The heating hadn't warmed up yet and the air in the hallway was lovely and cool on her naked skin.

'Sorry Bridie,' he said to the wall. 'Eh, Maisie, could you come out here, please.'

As soon as he said her daughter's name, something clicked in her head. *Fred Brennan, he's a wrong one. He did something. What did he do? I know he did something . . . She could almost remember. He scared me, but why?* 'You can't even face me and do you know why? I know what you did. I know!' she lied. Fred leaned on the wall and swallowed hard. *He's a guilty man, all right. What did he do, what did he do, what did he do?* It was as though the memory was in an inflated balloon, floating off into the sky; she kept grabbing for it but it was just out of reach.

'Bridie, please.'

She could hear Maisie moving towards the door.

'If I did something wrong, Bridie, it was because you asked me to,' he said, low enough for only her to hear him.

Me? What did I do? She stepped back.

'God almighty, Ma.' Maisie was reaching for her and the ties of her dressing-gown. Bridie allowed Maisie to cover her. *I don't understand.*

'I'm so sorry, Fred, she gets too hot.'

'It's no trouble at all,' Fred said to the wall.

'You should go now,' Maisie said, and it was an order not a request.

'Maisie?' He moved to touch her but she pulled away.

'Just go, please, Fred.' There was an unfamiliar edge to her voice.

She doesn't want you here either, Fred Brennan.

'OK. I'll be in touch,' he said, and Bridie could detect his hurt and concern. She stayed quiet, busy thinking, digging deep. *What happened? It's there, hiding somewhere. I can see its shadow. What did I do? What did he do?*

Fred

Fred left the house with a heavy heart. *I'm losing her. She's slipping away. Come on, Jeremy, don't do this to me, fella.* Valerie was sitting in the front seat of the car. Most kids would have sat in the back but not Valerie: she was a front-seat kind of kid. *Good for you, love.*

They were both silent, minds adrift, and out of the estate before she talked again.

'Ma looks weird.'

'She's just got a fright, that's all.'

'Jeremy's too much of a Goody Two Shoes to do something wrong,' she said, as though she wasn't sure if that was a good or bad thing.

'What about you?' Fred said.

'Me grammy said I'll end in jail somewhere. She says she hopes it's somewhere exotic 'cause even if the food's shite at least the weather'll be nice. Ma'sie says not to mind her. I can be whatever I want to be.'

'Your ma is right.'

'I think I'd be a good criminal.'

Fred's lips curled into a smile. 'Well, then, they're both right,' he replied, without missing a beat.

They pulled up to the school. Kids were buzzing here and there, talking, laughing and shouting to one another. Valerie stayed seated, watching everyone live their lives.

'You don't have to stay here if you don't want to. I can take you home,' he said.

'My ma doesn't want me there.'

'That's not true.'

'I don't blame her.'

'Valerie, tell me, why did you lie?'

''Cause I'm a thick.' She got out of the car. 'Noleen!'

Her friend turned and walked back to meet her. She looked into the car. 'Who's yer man?' she asked.

Fred just caught her response, 'No one,' before she slammed the car door and they walked off together, leaving him alone. He waited till all the kids were inside and the class bell had rung, then pocketed his notepad and pen. He stepped out of the car and went to work.

Maisie

Maisie sat on the stairs and rang her work.

'Hello, the Village Dental Surgery, can I help you?'

It was Lorraine. She thought about hanging up but she couldn't just let them down. She needed to keep her job. 'Hiya, Lorraine. I'm sorry but I can't come in today.'

'Ah, Maisie, we've a full house here. I've more young fellas with broken teeth booked in than you'd believe.'

'Sorry, Lorraine, I can't.'

'What's wrong with you?'

'It's Jeremy. He's missing,' Maisie said. It was a battle but she maintained her composure and succeeded in sounding disturbingly emotionless. Lorraine was an awful gossip: she wouldn't tell her more than she had to.

'Ah, no, that's terrible. Of course we can manage. I'll let Perry know. I don't know what to say. Jesus, that's desperate.'

'Thanks,' Maisie said.

'All right, God love ya, Maisie. Keep us posted, yeah?'

Maisie hung up. She imagined Lorraine belting out of Reception and up the stairs to the office to tell anyone who would listen. Gossiping about 'poor Maisie' would make up for having to repeat 'Happy new year' to everyone all day.

Bridie emerged from her room, dressed in a crisp white blouse, a grey cardigan and a pair of black slacks. She hadn't bothered with shoes or socks and one button on the blouse wasn't done up, but other than that she looked perfect.

'I should have showered you,' Maisie said.

'Nonsense. I'm clean. People shower too much, these days. It's bad for the skin.'

She wrapped her arms around her mother, who eagerly squeezed her back. She smelt good, a mixture of fresh linen, washing liquid and roses.

'You could do my hair, though, Lynn,' Bridie said, which reminded Maisie about her friend. She'd forgotten about her. She obliged her mother and combed it into a ponytail, then pinned it up in a tight bun.

When the phone started ringing, Maisie ran like she was on fire and nearly broke a finger picking up the receiver. 'Jeremy?'

'What? Where are you?' Lynn said.

'Oh, Lynn, I'm sorry.' Maisie walked her mother to her bedroom. 'Back in a minute, Ma.' She closed the door on her.

'No phone call last night and now you stand me up. One kiss has changed you, Maisie Bean.'

Maisie slid on to the floor and leaned against the door. It was so surreal: the last time she had spoken to Lynn, life had been exciting and things were looking up but even then, when she was gossiping in Jingles, her son had been missing. *How did I not know? I abandoned my family to have sex with Fred. I didn't notice my own son was missing for over thirty hours.* How could she tell Lynn? How could she face her or anyone? She didn't deserve to be a mother.

'Oh, Lynn.' She pressed the top of her head with her free hand. *My brain just might burst. Maybe it'd best if it did – anything is better than this.* The guilt tasted like metal. Her disgust for what she and Fred had done weighed heavy in her chest. She wanted to throw up but she was empty. She wanted to hurt herself but she was numb.

'What's going on?' Lynn said, and her tone had changed. She was instantly serious.

'Jeremy's missing,' Maisie whispered.

She could hear her mother in her room, riffling through the presses. 'I know it's here somewhere,' Bridie said.

'Since when?' Lynn said.

'Sunday night.'

'Sunday!'

'I thought he'd left for school early – his schoolbag was gone and he'd taken enough lunch to feed an army. He didn't come home last night. And Valerie said . . . I was so busy with Fred . . . I . . .'

151

'No, no, no. Don't you dare do that! I won't have it,' Lynn said, and paused. 'He's sixteen, Maisie. Take it from me, sixteen-year-olds act the bollocks at every available opportunity.'

'Not Jeremy.'

'Listen, do me a favour and give up that auld St Jeremy business. It gives me a fuckin' migraine. Teenage boys are capable of anything, even the best of them.'

'That's hardly comforting,' Maisie muttered.

'Well, he's big and bold enough to look after himself and you've done nothing wrong here. Do you hear me?'

'He wouldn't just go off.'

'Oh, but he did – because I can assure you, no matter how mad it gets around here, there's no boogie-man running around Cypress Road lifting teenage boys out of their beds at night.'

'Rave's missing too,' Maisie said.

'Good. Point proved. They've gone off somewhere to act the bollocks, mark my words.'

It was possible, of course it was, but still something clawed at her, whispering that something was very wrong.

'Have you told the police?'

'Fred's taking care of it.'

'He's great,' Lynn said.

Maisie snorted. *Great? He kept me out half the night when my child was missing.*

'Jeremy'll be back in no time, and when he does get home, you need to put the foot down.' Lynn was clearly convinced that this was nothing more than silliness.

'OK.' Maisie wished with everything in her that her friend was right.

'What about Bridie?'

'I'm staying home, by the phone.'

'Of course you are. Look I'll come and get her – better she's not upset by this.'

'That would be great.'

'I'll be there in a jiffy.' Lynn hung up.

Maisie stood up and opened her mother's door. Bridie was standing in the middle of her bedroom, bewildered. Maisie took her hand and walked her into the sitting room. Bridie went to the window and gazed at the rain tumbling down. 'It seems like it never stops,' she said, then spotted Kenny, the postman, attempting to get past Vera Malone's dog, Jake. Maisie made her mother a cup of tea and joined her to watch the stand-off between man and dog.

'When Kenny moves left Jake moves left. When Kenny moves right Jake moves right. It's funny.' Bridie grinned. Jake kept his head low, and even with the window closed they could hear his low, threatening growl. 'The dog really hates that man.'

Kenny cupped his mouth and shouted over the dog: 'Vera! Hello, Vera! It's Kenny. I have some post here and the bleedin' mutt won't let me pass.'

'I suppose you should put him out of his misery,' Bridie said to her daughter.

'Yeah.' Maisie went to the front door and opened it in time to see Kenny approach gingerly.

'He's getting worse, Maisie, and I'll tell ya something. If he bites me it's over for him, I'm tellin' ya now. Do ya have any idea how many tetanus jabs I've had over the years?' He handed her a few letters for Vera. 'And these are for you.' He handed her two bills with the word 'overdue' stamped in red. 'Sorry. Fuckin' hate January, poxiest month of the year.'

'Yeah.' She sighed.

'Thanks.' He started to walk back to his van. Jake was still snarling, hunched low behind the bush that separated Bridie's driveway from Vera's.

'Kenny, you didn't see Jeremy on your rounds by any chance, did you?' Maisie said.

Kenny stopped and turned to face her. 'No. Everything all right, Maisie?'

'Yes, I'm sure it is. But in case you do see him, can I give you my phone number?'

He nodded and immediately looked perturbed. 'Of course. I have some paper in the van.' She followed him to it and he opened the door, rummaged, then handed her a pen and paper. 'Kids.'

She scribbled down her number and handed it to him. 'If you see him . . .'

'I'll radio it in and Mary in the depot will buzz you.'

She nodded. 'And if you can catch him, tell him his ma wants him home.' She was trying not to cry.

'If I can catch him, trust me, I'll bring him home meself.'

'Thanks, Kenny.'

'What did Kenny want?' Bridie asked, when Maisie stepped back into the house.

Maisie was impressed, she seemed a little sharper than she had in days. 'Nothing.'

'So what were you talking to him about?' Bridie said.

'I was trying to talk him out of murdering Jake,' Maisie said.

Bridie giggled. 'I've never known a dog to like a postman like your Danny, Jesus, they hated him but then again didn't we all?'

It had been a long while since Bridie had mentioned Danny. The doctor had said she was trying a new tablet on her, but as Maisie had filled the prescription only the previous day, she felt it wasn't possible that it could have had such a profound effect in less than twenty-four hours. Still, Bridie did seem more like her old self.

'That was Fred Brennan here this morning,' Bridie said.

Maisie was shocked she remembered. 'It was, Ma.'

'I don't like him here, Maisie.'

'Don't worry, Ma, he won't be coming around for long,' Maisie said, and a little piece of her ached. *I can never take my eye off the kids again. I'm all they have.*

'Did I miss Jeremy again, Maisie?'

'Yes, Ma. He's very busy in school.'

'It's unlike him not to say goodbye to his grammy.'

'I didn't want him to wake you.'

'I miss him,' she said. 'You'll tell him that, won't you, Maisie?'

'Yeah, Ma. I'll tell him.'

'Just in case I forget. Am I going to Lynn's, love?'

'She's picking you up any minute, Ma.'

'Good. You look like you need a bit of peace, love,' Bridie said.

Maisie felt as if she'd been thumped. She led Bridie to her chair, then made an excuse to leave the room and went into the kitchen to wait for Lynn, trying to make sense of this new crazy world, a world in which her mother made sense and her son was nowhere to be found.

Dave

The first time Dave had laid eyes on Rave he was on his back, fighting off punches from Bush Farrelly and her best mate Josie. He had just turned eleven. Bush was fourteen and the hairiest girl Dave had ever seen. She had wild curly hair that was so thick it came out as far as her shoulders. *How does she even carry that weight on her head?* She even had a hint of a moustache over her top lip. Her given name was Hayley but Dave thought it was funny to call her Bush. He had been sitting on his wall listening to music on his Walkman when the two girls passed. Bush was bouncing a basketball and they were laughing about something Dave wasn't a party to.

He was new to the area and didn't have any friends, although he hadn't had friends back in Finglas either. He didn't really understand why. His mother Marie said it was because he'd never learned to share properly. Ray, his father, maintained it was because he was a smartarse. 'Nobody likes a smartarse, son,' his dad would say, and ruffle Dave's hair, but when they were at the dinner table and his father was giving out about someone he didn't like (and Ray hated everyone), Dave would say something smart and his da would guffaw and hold his stomach with laughter. 'Did you hear that Marie? That's hilarious. Good boy, good boy,' his father would say, wiping tears away. 'Ah, Jesus, the lads will love that one.'

Dave received a lot of mixed messages when he was a kid. One second he was heralded as a little star, the next he was in the doghouse.

'What on earth made you think it was funny to paint the word "bomb" on the fuckin' dog?' his father had roared at him. The dog was an American White Shepherd called Barry, after Barry McGuigan, Ray's favourite boxer, and the animal was his pride and joy. No matter what his mother did she couldn't remove what Dave later discovered was permanent marker. They had to shave the dog, and because it snowed, and they couldn't afford a fancy dog coat, he was forced to go around Tallaght with an old furry purple car-seat cover taped around him.

'It's humiliating, and not just for me, for the fuckin' dog. Look at him! He's traumatized. Ya little bastard,' were Ray's final words on the matter.

Dave was called names a lot. He pretended it didn't hurt but it did. *I just thought it would be funny.* His da didn't speak to him for a long time after that particular incident.

'He'll get over it, son,' his ma promised. 'But you know what he's like.'

Dave's da could hold a grudge, all right, so Dave backed off and disappeared into his room for three months until the dog's hair grew back and the car-seat cover could be binned. He'd really missed his da when he wasn't talking to him, but more than that he missed his laughter. It was confusing. All Dave wanted to do was entertain. He didn't mean to hurt anyone. He liked Bush Farrelly. Although she was hairy she was pretty cool: she was an amazing basketball player and she had a great laugh, one you could hear for miles. When he heard a hearty, contagious laugh, it lit him up and gave him a reason to be. He just wanted some attention, maybe to talk to the girls for a while. The boys didn't really talk to him: he hated sports and his sense of humour confused them. Girls put up with him for a little longer but, ultimately, everyone turned their backs on Dave, until the day Rave had found him being beaten up by Bush and Josie.

Rave had been cycling home when he'd come upon them. 'All right, Hayley, Josie. What's going on here, then?'

'They're boxing the head off me, that's what,' Dave screamed, covering his face and stomach.

Hayley stopped. 'Just dealin' with this dickhead.'

'What'd he do?'

Josie was still kicking him and Dave was shouting for her to leave off. The dog was sitting in the garden but he couldn't be relied upon to defend his owner. Since the permanent-marker incident, even the dog had turned his back on Dave.

'He's a name caller,' she said.

'Nobody likes that but, to be fair, I think he's had enough, Josie.'

Josie stopped kicking Dave. 'Never let me hear you call my mate Bush again,' she said, and even through eyes full of tears Dave saw the smallest smile creep across Rave's face.

'Are yous going to youth club on Friday?' Rave asked.

'Yeah,' the girls said.

'Cool, see yous there.'

'OK,' they said, and Dave watched them turn from animals into gooey girls. *Giggly bitches.*

When they had walked on, Rave gave Dave a hand up. 'You OK?'

'Yeah, grand,' Dave said, wiping away his tears. He picked up his Walkman. The earphones were broken and he felt like crying again. 'Bleedin' man-arms is after breakin' me head-phones.' He sat on his wall.

Rave smiled again and sat beside him. 'So ya christened Hayley "Bush".' Rave was no longer concealing his amusement.

Dave grinned. 'I thought Hairy was a bit obvious.'

Rave laughed. 'I like Hairy too but I see what you mean. "Bush" has punch.'

'Exactly,' Dave said, getting excited. 'That's exactly it.'

'So you're new here.'

'Yeah.'

'I'm Rave.'

'I know. I've been in your class for a month. I'm Dave. Dave and Rave sounds a bit shite, doesn't it?'

'Good thing we're not going out.'

'Yeah, Rave is a cool name though.'

'It's cause of me black hair. John became Raven and Raven became Rave.'

'Fuck, that's even cooler.' Dave had been purposely keeping his head down because his ma had warned him that the first month in a new school was the hardest. 'Don't make it harder on yourself, son,' she'd said, which was code for 'Shut your mouth.'

'D'you want to hang out with me and my mate Jeremy?'

'Are you messin'?' Dave felt like he was going to cry again.

'No, course not.'

'Cool! Great! I'd love that.'

After that day, two things happened. Dave had friends for the first time in his life, and somehow Hayley Farrelly became affectionately known as Bush by all of Tallaght.

Dave secretly thought that Jeremy had never really warmed to him the way Rave had. He was nice to him, he put up with him, he even laughed at him, but they didn't have a particularly close relationship. They never spent any time alone together, and that was all right. He wasn't that pushed as long as Rave liked him, and no matter what Dave did or said, even if it pissed him off, Rave was always quick to forgive.

He knew he'd really angered Rave on Sunday night and wanted badly to make it up to him. It had been a blow when he hadn't turned up to school. He wanted to say sorry, but more than that, he just wanted Rave to say everything was cool. *Jesus, Rave, I'm so sorry.* Without Rave he felt he was the most expendable member of the group. Rave and Jeremy were thick as thieves; Mitch and Jonno lived in one another's pockets. He was the spare but at least he was there. He'd die if he lost his friends. It would kill him to be alone again. Mitch didn't mind him so much – he laughed at him more than the others did – and they hung out alone together when Jonno's mother had grounded him for some stupid reason. Jonno had probably hated him for a while because, to be fair, he was the butt of most of Dave's jokes, but when he needed someone to time his sprints at the crack of dawn three times a week, Rave had suggested Dave do it.

'Fuck that!' Dave had said at the time.

'He'd really appreciate it.'

'Five o'clock in the morning? In the freezing cold? Why doesn't Mitch do it?'

''Cause Mitch has breakfast in bed at eight. He's a lazy bastard and he doesn't make Jonno want to punch him in the face every day of his life.'

'Right, yeah, I see your point.'

'It would be good for you two to hang out together.'

'OK, I'll do it.'

He'd been timing and cycling after Jonno for six months now. Initially it had been painful, but now he'd really got into it. Jonno was seriously fast, and it was cool to be a part of something. He wasn't a bad motivator either, and even though he still annoyed the heart and soul out of Jonno, they were closer. Rave had been right. Still, it always felt weird when Rave wasn't around.

Dave, Mitch, Jonno, Deirdre, Mel and Casey were called out of class almost as soon as it started. They sat outside the principal's office trying to make sense of why they were there.

'Someone saw us drinkin' in the park,' Jonno said, sounding petrified. 'Me fuckin' ma is going to burst me.'

Mitch wasn't sure. 'Nah, it's not that.'

'Why?'

'Because they don't bring in coppers for teenage drinking,' Dave said.

'What?' Casey said. 'What copper?'

'The one talking to Principal Young.' He could see the man through the glass window, even though it was frosted.

'What makes you think he's a copper?' Deirdre whispered.

'Look at the fuckin' size of him. He's a copper, all right.'

'Oh, Jesus,' Mel whispered. 'My da's on parole.'

Mitch wasn't impressed. 'He could be a bleedin' circus ringmaster, for all this clown knows.'

Principal Young appeared in the doorway and addressed the six pale-faced kids.

'I don't know if you're aware of this, but Jeremy Bean and Rave Murphy have been missing since Sunday night, and we're hoping you might help with the inquiry. I've informed your parents that Detective Brennan will be talking to each of you and assured them that, in their absence, I will be there with you.' She looked at Jonno. 'Your mother is on her way in.'

He slapped his head. 'Shite,' he whispered.

'Just give us a minute or two and then we'll be calling the first one in.' She closed the door and the stunned kids looked at one another.

'Missing since Sunday?' Casey said, red in the face.

'They're just bunking off,' Mitch said.

'Jeremy doesn't do that,' Deirdre said quietly.

'Balls. They're grand,' Dave said, 'and at least it gets us out of class. I say relax and say nothin'.'

'Well, my ma is going to bleedin' murder me so I hope wherever they are they're fuckin' happy,' Jonno said.

'Look, calm down. We were in the park, talking, nothing else. Don't land us in it and definitely don't land Rave in it,' Dave said. *He'll bleedin' kill us.*

'What if something's happened to them?' Mel said.

'As if! We're not in South Central LA,' Dave said, and Mitch nodded.

'He's right, say nothing.'

Mitch was the first to go in. He came out fifteen minutes later, shaking his head and whispering, 'Sorry, lads,' as he passed by, under the watchful gaze of Principal Young.

'Ya thick,' Dave mumbled.

'What was that, David?' Principal Young said.

'Nothin', miss.'

'That's what I thought. Mel, you're next up.'

One by one they all went in. Casey was only in there for five minutes but she came out in tears. Deirdre was there for ten. She came out dry-eyed but worried-looking. When Jonno's ma arrived they were taken straight in, and when they came out half an hour later she was busy clipping him round the ear. 'You're dead,' she said, as she frog-marched him out of the waiting area.

Dave was last in. *Lightweights, I won't leave you down, lads.* Holding his own against the copper was the least he could do after calling Jeremy a knob-jockey. He'd only been messing but he'd never seen Rave angry with him like that.

He sat down on the chair opposite the guard and heard the door close behind him. *Show no fear.*

'David,' Principal Young said, 'this is Detective Brennan. He has a few questions for you about Jeremy and Rave. I expect you to answer him openly and honestly.'

The copper asked him a series of questions, but Dave refused to answer. 'I can't answer that,' he said, for the fifth time in a row.

'Why's that?' Brennan said.

'On the grounds that I may incriminate meself.'

'We don't care about the drink, son. We just want to get to the bottom of what happened to those two boys. Were you the last one of the group to see them Sunday night?'

So someone had spilled their guts about the booze. Dave nodded reluctantly. 'Yeah.'

'Did they say where they were going?'

'No.'

'Do you think Rave was drunk?'

Yes, he was high as a kite. 'Talk to my solicitor.'

Dave later learned that Jonno had pretty much gone through the entire night moment by moment, including telling the copper that Rave said riding a girl was like sticking your mickey in a pipe full of pudding. *Gobshite.*

'Fine. I think the others have given us enough.' The copper tucked his notepad away in his jacket pocket.

Dave got up to leave.

'One last thing, son. When you headed off, were they anywhere near the tank?'

Dave stopped in his tracks. 'At the Old Bawn Bridge?'

'Yes.'

Dave gulped. *Ah, no. They're not in the bleedin' tank!* 'We spent the night mostly under the Hanging Tree so, yeah, near it but not – not near enough to . . . I mean, they'd have no reason to go near the water. It was dark and raining . . .'

'OK. I just have to ask. It doesn't mean anything, son,' the copper said, putting a hand on Dave's shoulder. 'You can go for now.'

Dave moved to leave but turned back when he got to the door. 'I've seen Rave way worse and he's cycled home just fine.'

'That's good to know. Thanks, Dave.'

Principal Young escorted him outside.

'They're not in the tank,' he said again, needing her to believe him.

Principal Young nodded. 'Go back to class, David.'

He didn't go back to class. Instead he went into the boys' toilets and sat there for ages on his own just thinking, hoping and convincing himself everything was going to be all right.

Fred

Fred sat in the front seat of his car and phoned the station. Linda answered. 'I heard,' she said.

'Nightmare.'

'Unlucky, but we'll find them. Glad you finally pulled the trigger, though.'

Linda had been his friend for a long time. He'd admitted his feelings for Maisie to her while drunk on two separate occasions but he hadn't mentioned going out on the date in case it went badly. 'Tom told you about me and Maisie?'

'It's all over the station.'

'Jesus.'

'Now what can I do?'

'Take this down, will you?' He rattled off his notes, including everything that was important, a description of what the kids were wearing, their last-known whereabouts, the make and model of the bike they were on.

'I'll pass it on.'

Deirdre Mahoney had said something interesting during her interview, he recalled. She had been cautious but insightful. 'If you ask me, they've run off,' she'd said.

'Why's that?'

'Because Rave's da is a junkie and he makes a show of him.'

'If that's true, why would Jeremy follow him?'

'Because Jeremy would follow Rave to the moon.'

'Where do you think they'd go?'

'Dunno. England . . . or maybe they'd look for Rave's ma. She's been on the missing list for years.'

He gave Linda Sid Murphy's details and the address of the house.

'Hold on, Tom's here,' she said, and put Tom on. It was clear he was scanning the notes Linda had taken while talking to Fred.

'We'll put all this over the radio and get it to national and local press. In the meantime I'll meet you at Sid Murphy's house, if you're up for it. You're strictly a bystander, mind.'

'Do you think he'll know something?'

'Probably not, but it's as good a place to start as any,' Tom said.

'And what about the tank?'

'I'll have some lads walk the river and do a little recon. It's too early to call in the Sub-aqua Unit.'

'OK.'

Uneasy, Fred hung up and sat quietly for a minute, staring absently out at the empty schoolyard, biting the skin at the top of his thumb. *Where are you, boys?* He kept picturing the tank. He pictured Sunday night. While he was holding his jacket over Maisie as the rain came down, where was Jeremy? He pictured the park: he knew the Hanging Tree well. He saw the boys drinking and talking, the girls huddled and cold. He imagined them walking or cycling away one by one until it was just Jeremy and Rave. *Where did you go?* He saw Rave pick up the bike and Jeremy sitting on the saddle, Rave a little worse for wear, the bike swerving, Jeremy trying to steady him. *Maybe he cycled too close to the water. It was dark, muddy and slippy. Was the water high that night after all the rain?* He pictured the tank, saw the boys silently floating in the dark. *No. No way.*

He cast his mind to the hotel room and lying in bed with Maisie. It seemed like a lifetime ago.

Chapter Six

'Everybody Hurts'
REM, 1992

Maisie

THE MURPHY HOUSE WAS run down. It hadn't been painted in years and the garden was overgrown with bits of cars and bikes strewn across an overgrown lawn. Maisie was banging on the door when a police car pulled up. 'Sid Murphy, I know you're in there so open this bleedin' door.'

She turned to see two men step out of the car. The one she didn't recognize must be Detective Tom Doran. He had called her earlier to introduce himself and to set out what would happen over the course of his investigation until the boys were found. He was calm and practical, but everything he had said terrified her. She couldn't bring herself to look Fred in the eyes so she avoided his gaze. 'There's someone in there – I can hear them.' She turned back to the door and resuming banging. 'Open this door.'

'Ms Bean, I'm Tom Doran. We spoke on the phone.'

He looked to Maisie to be in his early fifties, a handsome man, short fair hair, tall but not as tall as Fred. 'Hello.' She shook his hand. It was the polite thing to do, after all.

'You OK, Mai? What are you doing here?' Fred said.

She wasn't sure if he was concerned or annoyed. He had told her to stay at home by the phone. She didn't care what he'd said: she couldn't just sit there when Sid Murphy might know where her child was. 'His phone is dead.' She kept her back to him while she hammered on the door again.

'I understand,' he said, placing his hand on her lower back. 'But you need to allow Tom to do his job.'

She pulled away from him. She didn't have to look him in the face to know he was hurt.

'We'll take it from here,' Tom said gently.

'By all means, but I'm going nowhere.'

Fred sighed.

Tom nodded. 'Fine.' He bent down to the letterbox and opened it. They could plainly hear someone crashing around inside. 'Mr Murphy, it's Detectives Tom Doran and Fred Brennan here. Open the door and we'll ask a few questions. If you leave or stay hiding, we'll kick the door down and raid the place. You decide.'

Maisie waited and watched. She'd been banging at that door for five minutes solid. She just wanted to know where her boy was and she couldn't understand why Sid would allow her to stand there, begging for help. *Please just help us.*

Tom knocked again. 'Don't make me break this door down, Mr Murphy.'

Finally they heard shuffling, the door opened and Sid Murphy peered out. He looked like hell, eyes sunken and skin blotchy. His dirty clothes hung off his bony body and, most striking of all, his shaved head was covered with scabs. The smell that came from him was inhuman. Maisie's shock was profound. *What happened to you?* Maisie's eyes watered and she couldn't help but hold her nose and cover her mouth. He looked past the two men to her. 'Maisie?' He seemed half asleep and a little confused. 'Is that you, Maisie Bean?'

She dropped her hand from her nose. 'Hello, Sid,' she said, in a much friendlier tone than the one she had employed just moments earlier. 'Sorry to disturb.'

Sid leaned on the door heavily, his eyes half closed. 'Nah, it's grand. I always have time for you, Maisie.'

Don't throw up! God almighty, what is that smell?

'Can we come in?' Fred asked.

Sid looked from Fred to Tom, then back to Fred. 'I don't know yous.'

'That's OK, we know you.' Tom pushed the door in and Sid stumbled backwards.

'Oh, me foot! Mind me bleedin' foot!' he shrieked.

'Ah, Fred, there's no need—' Maisie said.

'Let Tom do his job, Mai.'

She followed the men inside but was stopped in her tracks by the smell in the house. And then another wave hit her. 'Oh, sweet Jesus.' She raised her hand to cover her nose and mouth again.

Fred and Tom seemed unfazed. They followed Sid, who was limping badly. He wasn't wearing shoes but one foot was covered with tea-towels and a black plastic bag, all held together with tape and a rubber band. He moved slowly and held on to the wall as he made his way through the dingy hallway, passing the broken public telephone that was practically hanging from its bracket. The receiver was lying on the floor beside it, its cord cut or pulled out of the wall.

The men went with Sid into the sitting room. Maisie regained her composure and followed them in time to witness Sid throwing a filthy blanket over the coffee-table. He pointed to it. 'That's none of your business.' He was unsteady, unsure, but determined. Maisie was aghast at the living conditions her son's best friend endured. *I had no idea. Why didn't I know about this? What else have I missed? Why didn't Jeremy tell me? Oh, Rave, lovey, I've let you down. I'm so sorry.* The room was filthy. Empty cans and half-full bottles littered the floor, and takeaway containers lay everywhere she looked, some with congealed sauce, others with dried-up bits of pizza, cigarettes stubbed into the dough and wet ash streaking the boxes. *There has to be rats*, Maisie thought, and suddenly her legs felt itchy and she wanted to hop. She had read that stamping frightens rats away. *Or is that snakes?*

Sid slumped on to the grimy, torn, burned, possibly infested sofa and put his scabby head into his dirty hands. 'You brought these coppers here, Maisie?' He looked as if he was about to cry.

'I didn't.'

'They're standin' right in fuckin' front of me, Maisie.' He pointed a long, thin finger at Fred. Fred waved at him.

'We're just looking for Jeremy,' she said. 'Have you seen Jeremy?'

'Jeremy doesn't come here any more, Maisie.'

I can see why.

'Where's your son, Sid?' Tom was standing over the man with his arms folded. Fred stayed back, as if he was giving Tom the space to conduct his interview.

'I don't know. He comes and goes.'

'When did he come and go last?'

'Dunno. He lives in that room of his. I can't get up there with this fuckin' foot.'

'Well, did you see him yesterday, the day before, the day before that?' Tom asked.

Sid didn't answer but pulled himself up off the sofa and balanced himself before he gingerly limped to the door. 'He could be up there now for all I know. Rave?' he shouted. He steadied himself by holding on to the door, then went into the hall and made his way towards the stairs. 'Rave!' he said, tripping. 'Rave, if you're there, shout down.' He turned to the three adults behind him. 'Maybe he's in school. It's a school day, isn't it?'

'He's not,' Maisie said. 'Neither is Jeremy. He hasn't been home since Sunday, Sid.'

Sid faced the stairs again. 'Fuck,' he mumbled. 'Come on,

will ya, Rave?' He started to climb the stairs but it looked too painful, too difficult, and he gave up halfway and sat on the step. 'It's me diabetes.' He pointed to his foot.

'Pull the other one,' Fred muttered.

'He locks himself in his room. Go up there if you want. Be me guest.'

Fred and Tom passed him on the stairs. 'Which room?' Tom said.

'The one with the "No Junkies" sign on it.'

The men disappeared, leaving Maisie frozen at the bottom of the stairs with the shell of a man she'd once respected crouched on a step facing her. He was sniffing and itching. 'It's been hard without his ma,' Sid said, in an attempt, she guessed, to explain away the state in which she had found him and his child's home.

'She's been gone a long time, Sid. It's no excuse.'

'I know, Maisie, I know. I'm sorry. I tried. I really did.'

She couldn't deal with his self-pity. *You did this to yourself. How could you, Sid? You're all he has.*

'Any sign?' she shouted up the stairs.

Fred leaned over the banister and shook his head. 'No, Maisie, they're not here.' He disappeared back into Rave's bedroom.

'The kids are missing, Sid,' Maisie said. 'Do you understand?'

'They'll be grand. They're big boys now. They can take care of themselves.'

'When did you see Rave last? Please think.'

'I dunno . . . Last week sometime.'

'Last week!'

'In case you haven't noticed I'm outta me fuckin' mind here, Maisie.' He rubbed his head and a scab flew into the air.

Maisie's stomach lurched. 'This is no good, Sid.'

'Don't judge me, Maisie.'

'Can't help it, Sid. I'm sorry, but there's no excuse. You're a grown man. You knew what heroin does to a body. You knew what you were doing.'

He sniffed and rubbed his nose. 'You never did beat around the bush, did ya, Maisie?'

'No, Sid.'

'Is that why he hit you?' He looked up at her for her reaction.

'You were always a loser, Sid, but you were kind once so I'm going to put that piece of nastiness down to drugs and let it go.' His words had struck a chord and, for just a second, she'd let her temper get the better of her.

His eyes filled with tears. 'I'm sorry. I'm very sorry.' He buried his head in his hands. 'I could do with a few quid, Maisie.'

She couldn't spend another second in his company. 'You're getting nothing from me,' she said, stepping by him and heading up the stairs.

Maisie came to Rave's room and pushed the door open to reveal a space in stark contrast to the rest of the house. It was all in perfect order: the window was opened a crack to let in fresh air, every item of clothing was neatly stacked, folded, hung; the comb and hairbrush were lined up perfectly on the dresser. Nothing was out of place; everything was pristine. The carpet was worn. The curtains were tattered. The bed's headboard was broken and had been repaired with gaffer tape. The sheets were frayed and clearly not washed in a while but the bed was made with hospital corners. Maisie closed the door behind her so that the smell from the rest of the house didn't leak into the child's sanctuary.

Tom stood by the window, examining something on the wall, and Fred was by the boy's dresser; the attached mirror was tarnished, cloudy and peppered with photographs stuck on with tape. In one corner tucked into the frame there was one of Rave and Jeremy. Fred pulled it out and straightened it between his fingers, and Maisie went to stand next to him for a closer look. It had to be less than a year old: the two boys were facing forward, both wearing shorts. Rave was leaning against a surfboard and his arm was casually slung around Jeremy. They were wet and smiling. Rave was cool and confident, looking straight down the lens; Jeremy's smile was goofy and he was giving the photographer the thumbs-up. Her heart soared. *There you are, love.* Then reality returned, so quickly that she needed to sit down on Rave's perfectly made bed.

'Here's our photo,' Fred murmured.

Maisie allowed a single tear to roll down her cheek. 'Rave trusted me once. What happened?' she said aloud to herself, as she looked around the boy's sparse prison. 'When did I forget about him?'

'Maisie . . .' Fred said.

'Don't.'

Tom pulled his head in from the window. 'No wonder his father hasn't seen him come and go. He climbs a rope to enter and leave the house.' Tom lifted up a thick rope that had been expertly knotted to a thick metal wall plug. 'It would be a workout but doable for a strong young fella like Rave.'

'At least we have a reason for the kid to go on the run,' Fred said. 'I'd fuck off if I lived here.'

'Yeah,' Tom said, catching Maisie's eye, 'but what about Jeremy?'

'Word on the street is, where Rave goes Jeremy goes,' Fred said.

Maisie knew that much was true, and this was a desperate house. She could so clearly picture Rave using a rope to climb to and from his second-floor window. She could picture him locked into this room, dreaming of something better and brighter. She could feel his frustration and his desire to get out. She could picture him running. A new year a new start . . . But could she picture Jeremy not just following but actually leaving his own home without a word? It just didn't make sense. Maybe at first he'd tried to talk Rave out of it. Maybe he'd even tried to talk him into coming to Maisie . . . Maybe they had tried and she hadn't listened, hadn't seen or just wasn't there enough. *What if Rave had come for help when she was with Fred? What if he was so desperate that Jeremy felt he had no choice but to go with him in her absence? Why didn't I just say no? I could have been there. I could have helped.* She was running away with herself now, guilt consuming her. *This is my fault.*

'The kid doesn't have a lot of clothes. He could have packed some,' Tom said, looking at the photograph. 'They're about the same size and weight.'

'They could definitely share clothes if they left in a hurry,' Fred agreed.

'So what are you saying? That they've run away but they're safe?' Maisie asked, with hope in her voice.

There was a beat of silence before Tom answered: 'All we can safely say at this stage is that the boys are officially missing.'

'Maisie,' Fred said gently, taking her arm, 'we'll put out an alert and canvass the locals for any more sightings. Everything is in hand. We're doing everything we can.' She didn't pull away this time but she didn't lean in either. He was trying his best but she was too busy keeping her growing anger at bay to placate him. *What's the worst that can happen, Fred? Look around.*

'I'll call this in, get the wheels in motion,' Tom said.

Fred steered her out and away from the room that looked nothing like a teenage boy's should. At the top of the stairs Maisie paused. She wasn't sure if Sid was just asleep or if he'd died right then and there: he was slumped over and still. She noticed some pint glasses filled with a dark brown substance under the broken telephone box and by the door. *Is that urine? Oh, God. It is.* She felt hot and dizzy. She wanted to be sick. She breathed in and out, shallow breaths, with her sleeve jammed against her nose. Fred walked down before her and nudged Sid as he passed.

'Where's your missus, Sid?'

Sid stirred and Fred knelt in front of him. 'Dunno. Don't care,' he said.

'You've no idea?'

'She just dropped off the planet.'

'Does she have any family?'

'Yeah.'

'And you, Sid, do you have family?'

'None of them talk to me.'

'I'm going to need their names and numbers anyway.'

'Ah, man, I don't know . . . I can't be fuckin' dealin' . . .'

'Let's get you straight, then,' Fred said.

'Ah, no, fuck off, will you?'

'What about kids? Rave your only child?'

'The only one left,' Sid said, and instantly seemed sadder.

'What's that supposed to mean?' Fred said.

Sid's eyes filled. His hands shook as he wiped the liquid snot from his nose.

'Jason, Rave's brother, died on the football field five years ago. He was seventeen,' Maisie said, still not quite ready to descend the stairs and walk past Sid's reeking piss.

'I'm sorry,' Fred said. 'What happened?' His tone was kinder.

Sid let out a deep, pained sigh. 'He just died. No fuckin' reason, no fuckin' reason at all.'

Maisie bit her lip. His pain was still so raw even after all these years. It was hard to contemplate. Jason had been such a great kid.

'He could have been a star – isn't that right, Maisie? He had a way with the ball. You shoulda seen him.'

'He was a great player, Sid.' Even though she was angry with him, her heart went out to him. *Who am I to judge you, Sid? I know I'd never get over that kind of loss.*

Fred put out his hand. 'You have to get up now.'

'I can't. Me foot.'

'There's an ambulance on the way,' Tom said, from just behind Maisie.

'Ah, no,' Sid cried.

'Ah, yes,' Tom said. 'Unless you want to die here.'

Sid gulped.

'We'll let them clean him up and we'll take a statement in the hospital,' Tom said.

They heard an ambulance siren pealing in the background. Maisie moved for the first time in what seemed like an eternity. She took each stair slowly and deliberately, and opened the front door. Fred walked the few steps into the hallway and opened the drawer of the old phone table. He pulled out an address book and held it up. As Tom reached Sid on the stairs, he nodded at Fred, who pocketed the book.

'It's time to go, Sid,' Tom said.

Sid said nothing. He didn't speak again until the paramedics had him secured on to a gurney and he was being wheeled out of the house. 'Maisie?'

'Yeah?'

'It wasn't always like this, was it?'

'No. There was a lot of good too.'

'Some really great times,' he said.

She wondered if he even remembered or cared that his son was missing. He didn't seem concerned. He was too preoccupied with feeling sorry for himself. It occurred to her that if he died Rave might be better off.

She watched them load him into the ambulance. Fred had followed her into the garden. So many times he had stood where she was standing, watching paramedics load her into a van. It felt oddly familiar.

'He'll be OK,' he said.

'I don't care. I just want to find those boys.' She was calmer now. If Rave thought he was in danger, she didn't doubt that Jeremy would go with him. Their disappearance finally made sense to her.

'They're going to want to search Jeremy's room.'

'If it helps.'

'How you holding up, Mai?' he asked.

She could feel his desperation to make some kind of meaningful connection with her but she just couldn't give it to him. 'What do you think?' She walked to her car, leaving Fred alone on the grass, staring after her.

Fred

Fred sat in his car smoking a cigarette and waiting for Tom to leave the house. When he finally appeared he was talking on the phone and stalked the Murphys' lawn, giving instructions. Eventually he got in beside Fred and rolled down the window.

'Those things will kill you, Fred.'

'Maybe so.' Fred sniffed.

'Well, the good news is that some kid spotted the boys on the Bohernabreena Road around half ten Sunday night.'

Fred exhaled. 'They're not in the tank.'

'We can't know for sure yet, but it's looking unlikely.'

'Thank God.'

'Linda took a statement but I'm heading over to see the kid myself.'

Fred nodded. 'I think there are some items missing from Rave's room.'

'Oh?'

'I saw CDs but no player.'

'He could have broken it or sold it.'

'No toiletries, not even toothpaste, in that bathroom, and for a kid as clean as Rave that doesn't make sense.'

Fred had walked around the small bathroom. It had smelt of bleach – the bottle, with a cloth and bathroom cleaner, was in a box beside a pale pink bath. He had opened the cabinet above the washbasin. It had contained nothing but an old shaving kit and rose-scented hand cream: the only things that suggested Rave had once had a mother and father living with him. Fred pictured Rave scrubbing the toilet, the bath, the washbasin and maybe even the lino on the floor. It had holes, revealing rotting wood beneath it. That bedroom and the bathroom were clearly

Rave's living quarters. Tom was right: if it was the kid's bathroom, why was there nothing of his in it?

'Wherever he's gone he has his toothbrush,' Tom said. He looked at the photos Fred had taken from around Rave's mirror. Other than the one of Rave and Jeremy, there was one of Rave and Casey, arms around each other's waists. There was one of the lads on a bus: Rave was sitting in the back, legs up on the seat in front; Jeremy was giving a thumbs-up, his face partly concealed by Dave's raised hand; Dave was sitting in front with Mitch, who was leaning forward to avoid Rave's feet and giving the camera the finger, while Jonno was in front of them.

'So these are our boys,' Tom said.

Fred identified each one.

'What was Rave wearing Sunday night?' Tom asked.

Fred consulted his notes. 'A khaki military jacket, black jumper, black jeans and a pair of black hobnail boots.'

'So where is the black leather jacket he's wearing here?' Tom asked, looking at Rave in the photo with his friends. 'And we're missing a denim shirt too.' He pointed at the photo of Rave and Casey.

'There's a basin with some washing powder in it under the bathroom sink so my guess is they're not at a launderette,' Fred said.

'I don't know about Jeremy Bean but this kid had plans to go somewhere,' Tom said, and Fred nodded. *This is good. This is very good.*

The rain had stopped so when the car got stuffy they sat outside on the damp step, waiting for the search team. Fred took out another cigarette and smoked it. Tom's stomach rumbled and he bemoaned the diet his beautiful German girlfriend had put him on.

'My heart bleeds for ya,' Fred said, betraying a hint of bitterness. He had never known Maisie to be so cold. It was gut-wrenching. He was losing her.

Tom looked at his watch. It was midday. 'As of now the kids have been missing approximately forty hours,' he said. 'Maisie called you at what time?'

'I think it was around six a.m.'

'So that means Jeremy was missing for over thirty hours before she noticed.'

'That's not fair. There were circumstances.'

'We've got ourselves two missing boys. We'll need to get consent to publicity, the sooner the better, but that comes with extra scrutiny.'

Fred knew what he was saying. 'Mai can handle it.'

'Can you, though, Fred? You could do with a holiday. I suggest you take one now.'

'We went on a date. We did nothing wrong, Tom.'

'I know, but if it goes pear-shaped you'll need to be on the right side of this, standing by your woman. That's where you belong now.'

'She doesn't want me anywhere near her.'

'She's upset – you know what women are like.'

'I dunno, Tom. I feel responsible. I can't just walk away.' *I promised her I'd find him.*

'Then don't. You can be my unofficial family liaison, get me all the details on friends and relatives, places the boys frequent, any medical conditions they suffer from, financials, everything. I know they're kids but even a post-office account or info on an empty piggy bank will help, and events that may link to their disappearance. I'll interview Sid myself once he's in some kind of shape but it seems to me that Maisie Bean might have a better insight into Rave's life than she gives herself credit for. He may have successfully hidden his current circumstances from her but it's clear she's invested in him.'

'I'll have to talk to Jim first, get his sign-off.'

'I've already spoken to him, Fred. It's sorted.'

Fred sighed. *Of course he'd talk to the boss before he'd talk to me. Fair enough. It's what I'd do.* His friend had presented him with a very real problem and the best possible solution. He'd be an idiot if he fought him on it. 'Thanks,' he said. 'You're a good man, Tom.'

'Tell that to my ex-wife and kids.'

'No one's perfect.'

'Yeah, well, keep that in mind when this turns into a shit-storm.' Tom clapped him on the back.

Fred knew he was right. If the kids weren't found before the case went public, Maisie's life would be turned upside down. The story was too juicy; two photogenic teenage boys missing for a day and a half before anyone noticed. In the photo they looked like butter wouldn't melt in their mouths and would be portrayed as innocents, victims of their working-class backgrounds, Rave's father a junkie, his mother missing, Maisie a single mother, Fred's involvement and, of course, Jeremy's father. *Oh, Jesus, Danny.* His past with Danny Fox always had the potential to bite Fred Brennan in the arse but he could never have conceived of the truth coming out like this, just when he and Maisie had got together.

He needed to explain. He just didn't know how.

Lynn

Lynn had spent much of the 1980s walking her dog Marvin in her local park. It suited her for many reasons. She could let Marvin off the lead, it was close to home, there was always a little action going on, either in the form of teenagers' ham-fisted attempts to seduce one another by the trees or little kids trying to murder each other in the play area, and in the summer there was a small bandstand, which hosted local acts and buskers. They weren't very good but that didn't matter – the worse they played the better she liked it. She watched the seasons come and go in that park and the local kids grow up. Over the years she came to recognize the faces of the regulars, taking time to chat to some – 'Ah, there you are, Sofia! How's that dodgy bowel of yours?' – and avoiding others like the plague. *Geraldine Grey! Keep the head down, Lynn, and say nothing. She loves the smell of her own shite that one.* She was comfortable there. It felt like home.

There was a bench she liked to sit on to watch the world go by while Marvin chased bunnies, stalked birds or hounded children for their snacks. It usually remained free even when the park was busy. Lynn came to think of it as hers. Then one day a heavily pregnant woman was sitting on it. *I don't like the look of this one.* Lynn would have walked on if she hadn't been short of breath. *Bleedin' angina.* She sat down, holding her chest with one hand and digging in her bag with the other.

The stranger seemed alarmed, jumping to her feet quite quickly for a woman the size of a small elephant. 'What can I do for you?' she asked, but poor Lynn was in no position to answer. She just stared at the woman, who was now taking off her shoes. 'There's a phone box just outside the park – I can be there and back in less than five minutes.'

Lynn shook her head as she retrieved her spray. She opened it and squirted it under her tongue. By now the woman was about to race off.

'It's OK,' Lynn said, able to talk again. 'Just angina. I'll be grand.'

'Are you sure?'

'I'm fine. Honestly, no need to sprint anywhere.' She smiled.

The woman plonked herself back on the bench. 'Thank God. I wasn't sure I'd make it on these sausages.' She pointed to her swollen feet.

Lynn looked to the woman's small canvas shoes. 'You know you'll never get them on again?'

'I do.' She sighed. 'I'm Maisie, by the way.'

'Lynn.'

They sat together for a few minutes. Maisie pointed out her son Jeremy and his best friend Rave: they were having a competition to see who could fly higher.

'Poor Jeremy, Rave always wins.' Maisie laughed.

'Why's that?'

'He hates heights,' she said, 'but he'd scale Everest for Rave.'

It was getting late and Lynn needed to go home to put on the dinner for her husband and kids. Maisie got up. 'Kids, let's go.'

'Where, Maisie?' Rave asked.

'We're taking this nice lady home, lovey.'

'Ah, no, you're joking! I'm grand,' Lynn protested. 'Sure I have the dog.'

'Can your dog talk?' Maisie asked.

Lynn grinned. 'No.'

'Can he do CPR?'

'No. Can you?'

'No, but I can talk so I'm still one up on the dog.'

By the time they reached Lynn's front door, they knew they'd be friends for life.

Lynn was six years older than Maisie; she'd had her children young too, although she'd still managed to become a nurse, and her husband actually supported her working. He was a freelance gardener, and when he was employed the kids went to her mother's, and when he wasn't he was the mammy in the house, a really good one at that. When Lynn's heart started to give her trouble in her early thirties, she found out she was going into early menopause. An emergency hysterectomy followed, and after that her world shrank. She left her job and became a full-time mother. Despite her frequent mood swings and a new, stricter regime, her boys grew up in a loving home. Lynn kept her hospital appointments, walked the dog in the park and always had a new hobby to keep her occupied. That was it, until she met Maisie.

Lynn hadn't had time for friends when she'd been working as a full-time nurse, wife and mother so a late close friendship with Maisie came as a lovely surprise. Both women had been 'lost' when they came into one another's lives. The angina made Lynn vulnerable in a way she'd never been before but being there for Maisie empowered her in a small way, and she'd spotted Maisie's predicament within weeks of their first meeting. Lynn had been a nurse long enough to see past flimsy excuses. She confronted her new friend head-on.

'Don't lie to me and I won't judge you. I'll just be there and when you're ready, and I hope some day you will be, you'll leave that toerag and I'll be cheering you on. If me ticker's not misbehaving I might even do a dance.'

'I wish I could leave,' Maisie'd said, and that was how she'd confirmed she was being beaten. She never talked about it; she never gave Lynn any details. Even lying in a hospital bed she never said how it had started, why it happened or what she went through. She didn't even complain about the pain. She and Lynn just talked around it. Lynn understood that if they were to remain friends Maisie would have to deal with her marriage in her way, not Lynn's. It was hard to stay quiet, sometimes almost impossible, but she did her best. With each attack, it became harder on Lynn not to interrogate her friend, not to mull over every detail, not to scream that Maisie was crazy and should dump him. She bit her tongue because if Danny suspected she knew what went on behind closed doors he'd make their friendship unworkable. He was the kind of man who pointed out to his wife what needed doing in the house when Lynn came to visit. He would take over the hosting duties while 'the missus' finished bathing the baby, ran down to the shops for some coffee or handled a screaming toddler. He liked to show off and any audience would do.

Lynn had soon put a stop to that. *I'm not here to spend time with you, dickhead.* She would speak to the top of his head, pretend she was hard of hearing and call him 'son', which annoyed him, although he played nice. *If you can act I can act too.* It became a game of sorts. Eventually he took the hint and left when she arrived, but until then she put in a solid performance every time.

'Sorry, son, what was that you said?'

'I said, how are you?' he shouted.

'Oh, my ma's long dead, love.'

'No. I said, HOW ARE YOU?'

She'd look at him and nod. 'Yes.'

'Fuckin' mad auld one,' he'd mumble.

The more stupid he thought Lynn was, the less of a threat she became, and finally Maisie had a friendship her husband tolerated – after all, what harm could the simpleton do? Lynn and Maisie used to laugh about it as soon as the front door closed behind him.

'I should have been an actress, Maisie.'

'Well, you certainly deserve an Oscar.'

Lynn still knew most of the staff in the local hospital so when Maisie was brought in one of the girls would let her know. They'd also chart Danny's visits and call her when he'd just left so she'd never run into him there. *Better he doesn't know that I know what's going on.*

'When the time is right, you'll know,' Lynn said once, when she was visiting Maisie after an 'incident'. He had only fractured her wrist that time so it wouldn't be then. She didn't follow up with *I hope it's not too fuckin' late.* But she thought that a lot. *Come on, love, get the fuck out of there.* She got her friends to give Maisie the leaflets on safe-houses and refuges – she even spoke to Fred behind her friend's back about what could be done – but everyone agreed that Maisie had to make the decision on her own.

Ordinarily Lynn would have walked away from a friendship with someone so determined to stay in a bad situation but there was something about Maisie. She couldn't be doing with self-destructive people. People who gave out about their terrible lives but never changed them bored her. *Either put up and shut up or get out. Easy.* Maise didn't give out and she would leave, Lynn was sure of it. It was just a matter of time. She was there to witness Maisie growing stronger, when she found her voice and her feet and finally walked away. She was proud that, no matter what challenges they faced, their friendship had become deeper with every passing year.

Maisie supported Lynn, encouraged her and made her feel good about herself. She taught Lynn how to apply her make-up, and even when she had little or no money she'd find a way to buy the latest creams for menopausal skin. Maisie always seemed more excited about them than Lynn did but she was grateful, especially when she saw and felt the results. Maisie cut and styled Lynn's hair, and helped her shop for clothes when her waist thickened and her belly bulged.

Maisie never panicked when Lynn had an angina attack: she'd just reach for her medication, spray it under her tongue and keep chatting as though nothing out of the ordinary was happening. When Maisie moved in with her mother, Bridie joined the gang and for a while it was good fun, all three ladies together, laughing and lunching in Jingles. It was Lynn who spotted the first signs of Bridie's dementia. She was heartsick saying it, but it needed to be investigated. And it was Lynn who comforted Maisie and Bridie upon hearing the diagnosis.

'I knew a man with dementia once,' Bridie said tearfully. 'We always said he'd be better off dead.'

'Bridie, things have moved on from then. We'll take care of you and you'll be fine,' Lynn said firmly.

Maisie had been in shock – her world had literally imploded. 'It won't break you, Ma.'

'But it will, Maisie. I can feel it come upon me, like fog descending on the sea. Everything disappears under it.'

'Ah, come on, will ya stop, the pair of yous?' Lynn said, choked. 'You are loved, Bridie, and you will be cared for.'

'I don't want that.'

'Tough,' Lynn said.

Lynn was always there when Maisie needed her and she always knew what to say to make her feel better, but now she was at a loss. She was doing her best to put on a happy face but she was no fool. Jeremy would never willingly put his mother through such torment, no matter how much he cared for that friend of his. If Jeremy wasn't in touch, it was for a very good reason. She tried not to think about all the horrors that could have befallen him. She was becoming more frightened by the world they lived in with each day that passed, and Jeremy's disappearance was threatening to tip her over the edge. She closed her eyes and told herself to calm down. *He hasn't been kidnapped by some sex fiend or driven off a cliff or left for dead in a ravine, especially as there are no ravines in Tallaght, so just calm down.* Lynn felt as though she was made of crumbling rock: she was slowly wearing away. Lynn had her perfect husband and her two grown boys, all of whom would do anything for her. Despite her ill health, Lynn knew she was lucky and her friend was not. It made hoping that much more difficult.

She'd left Maisie's just a few hours ago, and Bridie was sleeping soundly in the other room, but she wanted to talk to her friend. She picked up the phone, then realized she hadn't a clue what to say, so she sat with it in her hand practising her opening line, until she dared to dial the number.

Maisie

On the opposite side of the village, Maisie sat on the floor of her hallway watching the phone, which was in its charger. She couldn't afford for the battery to run low. She thought about what she'd seen at Sid's place and she was more angry than afraid. Angry with herself for not seeing how distressed Rave was, angry with Jeremy for not telling her, angry with Sid for being a fuckin' waster, angry with Carina Murphy for walking out on her family. She was angry with Valerie, too, for lying to her. This morning she'd been in shock, and all she could see was the terror in Valerie's eyes, but now, sitting on those stairs for hours on end, waiting for just one sign that her son was safe, she was boiling mad. *If you'd told me he wasn't in school yesterday I could have done something so much sooner. If anything happens to him, how will I ever forgive you?* The only phone call she'd received all afternoon was from Fred to tell her about the photos they planned to use for publicity.

'So how does it work?' she'd asked.

'We get the pictures out there, alert the local and national media that we're looking for two boys and take it from there. We'll talk more when I get back to your place later.'

'You're coming here?'

'For the search.'

'Oh, yes.'

'It's Tom's case, Mai, but I'm going to liaise between you and the police, if that's all right with you.'

'But you are the police.'

'This is the best way for me to do my job right now, Mai.'

'I don't know what that means.'

'It means I'll be there to ask and answer any questions. I'll be there to look out for your interests, to make sure nothing is forgotten and to be there when you make a statement.'

She fell silent, allowing everything to sink in.

'Mai?'

'Yes?'

'Is that all right with you?'

'OK,' was all she could bring herself to say. She hung up before he spoke again. She couldn't bear it, because although she was angry with everyone around her, mostly she was angry with Fred. If he hadn't asked her out and if she hadn't accepted, she would have raised the alarm two days earlier.

She hadn't moved from the spot in more than two hours. She didn't eat, she didn't drink, she just waited for the phone to ring. She was bug-eyed from staring at it. When it finally rang, she was in such a daze that she started. As she stood up she realized her legs were dead and she had pins and needles in her feet. She hopped across the floor and grabbed the receiver. 'Hello?'

'Any news?' Lynn said, and Maisie felt like crying.

'No.'

'I'll keep your mother as long as you want,' she said. 'I'll feed her tea and bring her back when she's good and tired. The last thing you need is Bridie kickin' off.'

Maisie was deeply grateful. She wasn't able for her mother, not now. 'Thanks, Lynn, you're a life-saver.'

'I'd better let you get back to staring at the phone.'

'How did you know?'

'Sure what else would you be doing? Look, I'm not going to say it'll all be OK because I don't know, but I'll say this. Do not lose it.'

'I won't.'

'Losing it never helps.'

'I know.'

'I love ya, Maisie.'

'Love you, Lynn.'

'I'll take good care of Bridie.'

'I know you will.'

'And you take good care of you.'

'I promise.' Maisie hung the phone carefully on the charger. She sat on the floor again, her back against the wall, and waited for change. It was five o'clock: Jeremy and Rave had been missing for forty-three hours. *I am losing it, Lynn. I'm trying not to but I am.*

After some time, Maisie stood up, picked up the phone, opened the front door and walked into the garden to stand in the rain. She needed oxygen and she needed to think. Bad things just kept happening to her and to her family. Danny, dementia, and now this. *Why? What have we done to deserve it?* Maybe she was cursed or had done something bad in a previous life or was simply born under an unlucky star . . . or maybe it was simpler than that: maybe things went pear-shaped for Maisie and her family because she was weak. *I didn't even want to go on the stupid date.* She wondered what Lynn would do in this situation. She'd steel herself and maybe play a game of Patience. Maisie had never been any good at Patience.

She noticed the curtains twitch in number thirty-four. Then she looked over at thirty-six and thirty-eight. There was movement in every window. *Nosy neighbours. They'd all have heard by now.* She walked across to number thirty-four and rapped on the door.

Leslie O'Shea answered it almost immediately, as though she'd been standing behind it. 'Howya, Maisie.'

'You heard?' Maisie said.

Leslie nodded and tilted her head to the side sympathetically. 'Tony in the garage mentioned it – his young one filled him in at lunchtime.'

'Did you see him that night?'

'Ah, no, sorry, Maisie. I was at a party New Year's Eve. I was bleedin' floored, took to me bed around seven.'

'Did anyone else in the house see him?'

'Well, it's only me here till the kids come home. Peter is down the country tonight.'

'Will you ask them?'

'I will.'

'Thanks.' Maisie moved off.

'I used to see him and that dark long-haired young fella come and go from his bedroom window all the time, though,' Leslie said.

Maisie turned back. 'You did?'

'Ah, teenagers, they're mad yokes – you never really know what they're at, little bastards.' She chuckled.

It's not funny.

'It's a storm in a teacup. You wait and see, they'll be home before you know it.'

'Thanks.'

She knocked on every door on the street. Those who weren't at work or in the pub said they hadn't seen the boys but they'd keep their eye out and come to her with any information. Maisie finished at Vera Malone's.

'I was wonderin' when you'd get to me,' she said.

'Do you know anything?' Maisie said.

'I know you're going to drown if you don't get out of the poxy rain.'

'About Jeremy, Vera.'

'Well, I know lots about Jeremy, Maisie, but it doesn't include his current co-ordinates.' Vera's dog was rubbing himself against her left leg.

'Well, if you hear anything . . .'

'I'll bang on your door.'

'Thanks.' Jake took a step out into the rain, shook himself and backed into the house.

Maisie started to walk down the path.

'He's a good kid, Maisie,' Vera called after her. 'I really hope he's all right. I'm praying for them.'

Maisie stopped dead and turned to face her. Vera was the first person not to shy away from the possible truth. *Something bad has happened to these children. Nothing else makes any sense.* The two women stood opposite each other, one in the warmth of her home, the other exposed in the rain. They were silent. It wasn't necessary to speak. Vera just allowed Maisie to feel what she was feeling without pretence, false cheer or silly sentiment. Jake barked, drawing Vera's eye to the right of Maisie's head. Maisie turned and followed her gaze to a police car pulling up outside her house. She watched two lads in uniform get out; the third, the driver, was on the phone. 'I have to go.'

'Mind yourself, Maisie.' Vera closed the door.

Soaked to the skin, teeth chattering, Maisie greeted the men. 'In here.' She pointed to the open door.

'You'll catch your death, missus,' one of the lads said.

She didn't respond, just led them inside.

Tom pulled up in a separate car just as Maisie was coming out of her son's room. She waited for him at the front door.

'Hello again,' he said. 'Fred around?'

'Not yet.'

'You need to get in a shower.' Maisie saw that she was standing in a pool of water in the hallway. 'The last thing you need to do is catch pneumonia.' Her hair was stringy and soaking: when she put her hands through it the rainwater ran down her back.

'I didn't touch anything,' she said, nodding towards the men coming and going from her son's bedroom.

'Good. Safe to say no calls?'

'No calls.' She realized she was holding the phone: she'd taken it across the road. *I don't remember picking it up. Oh, Jesus, it's soaked. I've broken it!* She shook it wildly, until Tom took it from her. He wiped it on his jacket and turned it on. She heard the dialling tone and relaxed.

'Why don't I keep it for a while?' he suggested. 'You go and have that shower.'

She went into her bedroom in a daze. The coppers in her house reminded her of the bad old days when she had been just another victim, degraded, bleeding, swollen, broken. Today she was fine, upright, talking, not a mark in sight, but this was far more crippling. *Where are you, love?* She sat on the end of her bed, listening to the strange men walking and talking in the small bungalow. She couldn't quite hear what they were saying. *Even if he ran off with Rave, he would have called by now. I might not know him the way I thought I did but I know him well. Whatever dragon you have to slay, love, please slay it and come home to me.* Silent tears streamed down her face as she waited for the men to leave.

Valerie

Valerie stepped out into the rain just as Fred pulled into the school car park. She turned to Noleen. 'That's him again.'

Noleen gawked at the huge hairy man pulling up to the kerb. 'Jesus, he looks like he belongs in a bleedin' national park.'

'That's what I said.'

'Well, you were right.'

'I'd better go,' Valerie said.

'Call me if you want to talk.'

'I don't.'

'Nah, of course you don't. That would be normal. Won't stop me askin', though, will it?' She threw her bag on her back and walked on. 'Maybe I'll wanna talk – maybe I'll call you,' Noleen shouted.

'OK. Whatever.' Valerie was glad Noleen was her friend. 'Thanks,' she shouted, to Noleen's back. Noleen just raised her middle finger high in the air, making Valerie smile. She walked over to the car and bent down next to the driver's window.

Fred rolled it down. 'Get in.'

'Are you my chauffeur now?'

'If ya like,' he said, as she walked in front of the car, streaking her finger through the rainwater on the bonnet. He rolled up his window as she got into the passenger seat.

'Any word?' she said.

'No.'

'Shite.'

He put the car into gear and drove past her fellow students talking in the car park. It was obvious Valerie was the topic of conversation. 'They haven't shut their mouths all day. It's like Jeremy and Rave goin' missing is the best thing that's ever happened,' she said.

'Yeah, well, people talk – it's what they do.'

'They shouldn't. They should shut their mouths. It's none of their business anyway.'

'What about you?'

'What about me?'

'Is that why you covered for Jeremy last night, because you keep your mouth shut?'

She bit her lip. 'I suppose Ma wants me arrested.'

He laughed. 'She hasn't mentioned it.'

'Worse again. When she stews on something it's always bad.'

'So?' he said.

'I thought I was doin' him a favour. Ma gets hysterical over the smallest things. You can't tell her anything without her having a bleedin' eppo.'

'Eppo?'

'Epileptic fit.'

'Oh. I see.' He thought for a minute. 'She's not really epileptic, is she?'

'Are you sure you're a detective?'

'Positive.'

'It's just a sayin'. It means me ma loses it if everything's not perfect.' She cased 'perfect' in air quotes.

'Is that why Jeremy never mentioned Rave's da was on the gear?'

'Yeah. Ma would have called the social, which is bleedin' rich if you think about it.'

'She does her best.'

'Whatever.'

'What about Jeremy? Does he keep a lot from your ma?'

'If he does, he keeps it from me too.'

'I ordered food,' he said, changing tack. 'Do you like black bean chicken with mushrooms?'

'It's me favourite.'

'Mine too.' He pulled into a parking space. 'Do you want anything else while I'm in there? Spring rolls, Coca-Cola, one of them weird fried ice-cream desserts they do?'

'No.'

'Sure? OK, giz a shout if you need anything.' He slammed the door and ran into the takeaway. Valerie watched him lumber through the door of the shop. Her stomach ached, her head and eyeballs hurt. She was exhausted but sleep was beyond her. She wanted to cry but she couldn't. Her insides felt dry and dusty, her tongue tasted of sand, she was desiccating and it hurt. She had spent most of her day thinking about where her brother would go, what he was thinking and whether he'd given her some clues that she'd either been too dumb or self-involved to pick up on. She'd replayed Sunday night over and over again in her head. *Why did I cause a fuss? Why did I go to my room? Did something happen when I was there? Did he try to tell me something? 'You don't want to be like me.' That's what he said. What did I say to him? What was the last thing I said? I don't know. I can't remember. Why can't I remember? Where is he? Where are you, Jeremy? Why shouldn't I want to be like you? What pissed you off? Jesus Christ, would you ever come home to us. Me heart is breaking, Jeremy. I'm really scared now.*

She stared at the takeaway window. Fred was handing money to the man behind the counter. He grabbed the bag of food and turned towards her. He smiled kindly and winked at her as he emerged through the glass door and headed for the car. Her chest heaved and she closed her eyes to hide in the dry, dusty darkness.

I need you to stop being nice to me. I need you to bring Jeremy home. Then, if possible, I need you to fuck off and leave us alone. Sorry, Fred, I just wanna go back to the way it was.

They were turning into Cypress Road when Fred asked Valerie about Rave's mother. 'Did you know her?'

'I was a kid,' Valerie said.

'Do you know who her friends were?'

'Nah, sorry. Why? Do you think Jeremy and Rave have gone looking for her?'

'Maybe.'

'I heard she was a Moonie.'

'Where did you hear that?'

'Everyone.'

'Right.'

'Which means it's probably shite talk.'

He smiled. 'You may be right, but if necessary we'll find her.'

'What about my da? Are you going to find him if necessary?'

Valerie fixed her eyes on Fred, but all she could see was her father's face. Her heart raced. Her palms were sweaty.

He tugged at his beard with one hand. 'Only if it's the last resort.'

Last resort? What will that even look like? 'This is really shit, isn't it?' she said quietly.

'Yeah, it is.'

When Fred and Valerie arrived home, Valerie realized her mother was in the shower – she could hear the water running in the bathroom. Then she saw strange men leaving her brother's bedroom. They walked around the house as if they belonged there. She felt an immediate pain in her stomach. So many men in her house and not one of them Jeremy. *I don't like this.* She could have cried but she held her resolve. *No tears in front of strangers – well, anybody really, but especially not strangers.* 'What are they doing here?'

'Just trying to find anything that could lead us to the boys.'

'Well, they're not under the bleedin' bed!' she shouted at the men. She often replaced crying with shouting. Her back straightened, her hands balled into fists. She was ready to do battle. *They don't belong here. They have no right to go through his things. That's Jeremy's room.*

Fred handed her the bag of food. 'I'll make sure they don't mess anything up. Go on into the kitchen and help yourself to some of this. You must be starvin'.

All of a sudden Valerie felt weak and lightheaded. She had eaten little or nothing all day.

Fred nodded to her. 'It'll be OK. I promise.'

The fight drained out of her. She had steered clear of the school canteen because as soon as she went anywhere near it all eyes were on her, and her ma's packed lunches stuck in her throat even at the best of times. She had hidden in the class-room for most of the day, with Noleen for company. Valerie was the kind of kid who liked to blend into the background and didn't relish the attention she was getting. 'Maybe Jeremy and Rave have been recruited by the CIA,' Noleen said.

'The CIA is in America.'

'So?'

'So they don't recruit Irish people, especially two Irish teenage thicks.'

'How do you explain the IRA, then?'

'They're terrorists. What have they got to do with the CIA?'

'Just that they're good at being terrorists.'

'Are you on drugs?' Valerie asked.

'Ah, you know what I mean.'

'No, I don't.'

'Just that if the lads in the IRA are good at all that terrorist stuff maybe the CIA think they could be just as good as agents.'

'But Jeremy isn't in the IRA.'

'That's true. Or is he? Do we even know?'

'Noleen?'

'Yeah?'

'Shut the fuck up, will ya?'

'OK.'

Now she could smell the black bean chicken with mushrooms in the bag. Her stomach rumbled and her mouth watered. She hadn't even felt hungry till now. She took the bag from him and went into the kitchen, leaving the door open so she could see what was happening in the hallway.

She was still eating when Fred came in to reheat his dinner. A few minutes later he was sitting opposite her at the table. He sniffed his food.

'Can't beat it with a stick, wha'?' He dug in.

'Is Ma all right?' she asked.

'She's still in the shower, I think. Jaysus, she's been in there ages.'

'She does that when she's freaked. She stays there for ages – sometimes it goes cold. I know 'cause when I try the taps it's mad freezin'. Jeremy says cold showers are good for you.'

'Great for the skin.'

'Yeah?'

'So they say, but you wouldn't catch me under a cold shower for love or money.' He shuddered.

She giggled. 'Me neither. It's like torture.'

Valerie liked Fred. She didn't want to but she did. He was easy to be around. He smiled when she talked and not a lot of people did. It was nice. She didn't feel good about liking him, not because it was disloyal: her dad didn't deserve her loyalty. It was just that he was a man trying to invade her home so, as nice as he was, he was still the enemy. *Stay firm, Valerie. Don't let him break you down. Find Jeremy, then go away, Fred, please.* Fred had a newspaper tucked under his left arm while he ate. Valerie spotted her brother's photo. She took the paper from him and opened it. It was a copy of the *Evening Press*. The picture of Jeremy and Rave took pride of place at the top left-hand side of the page and there was a small paragraph asking anyone with information as to their whereabouts to come forward.

'Where did you get that photo?' she asked.

'Rave's house.'

'Jeremy hates having his photo taken. He used to look like a headcase or as if he'd had a stroke in every one. Ma used to get him to relax by making jokes and getting him to say things like "shite" instead of "cheese" but it never worked. Then she told him to give the thumbs-up. Now he does that in every photo. He's still kinda goofy but at least he doesn't look like he needs special care.'

She examined the photo intently as she spoke, staring at her brother's face. 'Rave's a funny one. Everyone thinks he doesn't care about anything but he does.'

'Go on.'

'Someone told him he was cool once so that's how he acts but he's not so cool and I'm not sayin' that to be smart.'

'I know what you mean.'

That was unusual. Most of the time people thought Valerie

was being a bitch when she was just trying to explain how things were.

'Rave's just as scared and messed up as everyone else,' he said.

'Yeah.' She shook her head. 'I was thinking he's a dickhead but, yeah, that's it exactly. I saw him crying once.'

'When was that?'

Valerie usually reacted poorly to questioning but she wanted to talk. Fred would listen to her. Also, it was a distraction from her brother's disappearance and her own feelings of culpability. 'A while ago he was sitting on Jeremy's bed and he was crying. He didn't see me.'

'How come?'

'I was in the wardrobe. I'd been in the room pinching a fiver from Jeremy's shoebox. Grammy gives him loads of money – she thinks I don't know about it. Rave came in the window. He sat on Jeremy's bed and then he cried. He was crying for ages. I thought I was going to suffocate in the wardrobe or, worse, that it would fall over.'

'Did he do anythin' else?'

'No. He just wiped his eyes and left.'

'Where was Jeremy?'

'He was at the dentist. My ma's boss fixes his dodgy back teeth for free.' She finished her meal, got up and put her plate in the sink. 'Is Grammy in Lynn's?' she asked.

'Yeah.'

'Is she stayin' there?' She didn't miss her grandmother much – she certainly didn't miss her freaking out every five minutes – but the place was weird without Jeremy and Grammy. It didn't feel like home.

'I think she's comin' back,' he added.

'OK. Good.'

She left the kitchen without another word and headed for her room. She closed the door behind her, put on Jeremy's Oasis CD, *Definitely Maybe,* and lay on her bed staring at the ceiling. She thought about Jeremy and, in particular, one night they'd spent sharing a bed in their father's mother's house.

Nanna Fox was nothing like their grammy. She was a rather proper woman, who lived in a house full of religious stuff, not just Catholic, all religions, from Jesus dying on the cross to witches' heads, jolly fat men, clothed elephants with earrings and a statue of a woman with four arms. A freakfest, Valerie always called it. Nanna Fox wasn't the warmest of souls but she wasn't mean: she made them their favourite shepherd's pie and always had jelly and ice-cream, chocolate cake and crisps. The house was so completely creepy, though, that it scared the life out of them.

Their grandfather (who demanded to be called 'Grandfather') was a distant, reserved man, whom they only saw at the dinner table. He talked at them rather than to them and spent most of his time locked away in the boxed room he referred to as his office although he did nothing in it except read comics. On the night Valerie remembered most vividly, thirteen-year-old Jeremy had taken one of his grandfather's comics to read in bed. Grandfather had stormed in and grabbed Jeremy's hand so tightly he'd screamed. He had snatched the comic back. 'These are not for children!' he'd shouted.

'Yes, they are,' nine-year-old Valerie had said. 'They're exactly for children.'

'Not these ones,' Grandfather had hissed. 'And don't you ever talk back to me again.'

Valerie had said nothing. She'd cried when he turned off the light, closed the door and left them in the dark. Jeremy had just been reading her the comic to take her mind off the big weird Jesus with a red glowing heart that hung on the opposite wall.

'I'll tell you a story.' Jeremy had put his arm around her.

'Not a scary one.' Valerie had snuggled in to him.

'In this place? Are ya mad?'

'OK.' She closed her eyes.

'It's a story about a boy who was always scared.'

'I thought you said it wasn't a scary story?'

'It's not, I promise.'

'OK.'

'He was always scared of being different.'

'How different?'

'I dunno . . . Like, he liked fish when everyone else liked meat.'

'I like fish.'

'Well, this story isn't about you.'

'Go on.'

'But then one day he met someone exactly the same as him.'

'Like a twin?'

'No, someone who liked the same things as he liked.'

'Like a fisherman?'

'Yeah, exactly.'

'OK.'

'And he didn't feel so weird or stupid any more.'

'But why did he feel weird or stupid in the first place?' she asked.

'I dunno – he just did.'

'That's a shite story.'

'Well, you asked so many questions you put me off.'

'I don't know anyone who doesn't like meat, do you?' she said, and he shook his head.

'No. That's the thing. No matter how hard he tried he just couldn't eat it. He didn't even really want to be around when everyone else was eating.'

'So when he met the fisherman they could just eat fish in peace.'

'Exactly.'

'Maybe they could set up a chipper.'

'Yeah, maybe.'

'And get rich.'

'That would be cool.'

'Yeah,' she said. 'It's still a shite story, though.'

Jeremy laughed, and out of nowhere he hugged her. 'I love you, Shortstuff.'

'I love you too,' she said, before she'd even thought about it, and for a second she felt like crying but mostly she felt really good. They hadn't said those words since then but it didn't matter: Jeremy knew how she felt. *I know I'm a pain but I do love you, Jeremy. Please come home right now. OK?*

She hadn't seen her mother since that morning and she was scared to see her because she'd be angry and she was right to be. *I'm a bad person.* She closed her eyes and tried to sleep but her head was too busy, thoughts whizzing about. They made her jumpy, restless. She felt like running but there was nowhere to run. *If I left, Ma wouldn't even notice.*

It was still early evening and Grammy would be home soon; Lynn would have to bring her back before she got overtired. She was a nightmare when she was overtired. Valerie covered her head with her pillow and waited helplessly for the next bad thing to happen.

Maisie

Maisie heard the knocks on the bathroom door. She tried to ignore them but they only grew louder and more urgent.

'Please, Maisie, it's time to come out,' Fred said. She switched off the shower and stood frozen to the spot, too cold to move. She had once done a meditation course, on Lynn's insistence. Lynn had found it wasn't for her but Maisie had picked it up quite easily. 'Sometimes I meditate without even knowin' it,' she'd said to the impressed instructor. This was one of those times. She had been somewhere else for a while – she wasn't sure how long but the fact that her lips and nails were blue and her skin light yellow told her it was possibly too long. Her limbs actually ached. *Oh, brilliant. I'm frozen. What the hell is wrong with me?*

'Mai, what's goin' on in there?' Fred sounded concerned.

199

'Nothin'. I'm fine.' She tried to stop shivering.

'I want to see you out here in less than one minute or I'm comin' in.'

She knew he meant it. He could probably break down the door with one shoulder. Her husband's taunts raced around her head. *You're nothing, less than nothin'. You're the most useless cunt that ever lived. Why the fuck can't you get anythin' righ'? Why did I marry such a fuckin' less-than-nothin' fuck-up like you? I must have been mad to end up with a fuckin' useless fuck-up like you.* She could hear his voice so clearly. She could see his twisted face, the spit collecting on his lower teeth and lip, his jabbing finger. She tried hard to switch him off but it was almost impossible. *Don't be useless – not now. Think, Maisie. Please. Where could they be?*

She moved slowly and painfully. It took everything she had to step over the edge of the bath, then grab a towel and her dressing-gown. She didn't rub herself down, just wrapped the thick towel around her waist and covered it with her towelling dressing gown. She caught her hair up in a smaller towel and twisted it into a knot, then opened the door.

Fred was clearly relieved. 'There you are, Mai.' He guided her to the bedroom and closed the door behind them. He sat Maisie on the bed. She didn't have the will or energy to do anything else.

'Where is your sock drawer?' he asked.

She gestured with an unsteady hand, then watched him root through it and pull out the thickest socks he could find. He placed them on her feet and then he sat beside her on the end of the bed. 'You need to warm up,' he said. 'Get under the covers for a few minutes.' He helped her into bed, then propped her so that she was sitting up and the duvet was tucked up to her neck. 'I'm going to fill a hot-water bottle and I'll be back to ya. Wait there.'

'Where's Ma? What time is it?' She moved to get out of the bed.

'Stay there.' His hand was in the halt sign she'd seen coppers make while working traffic. 'Lynn's on the way.'

She must have phoned, Maisie thought. *Oh, Jesus, the phone.* 'Where's the phone?' She was suddenly in a blind panic.

'On the kitchen table, fully charged. We can hear it from here – from everywhere in fact. You're not livin' in Buckingham Palace, Mai.' He smiled.

'I'd like to keep it close.'

He left her alone for a few minutes. She started to thaw, gradually regaining enough flexibility to rub herself down, shed her towels and put on a clean nightdress. She looked in the mirror. Her lips were more lilac than the dark purple they had been. *Useless, ugly old bitch. Can't even look after yer own children. What fuckin' good are you?* She returned to her bed moments before Fred reappeared with the hot-water bottle, toast and tea on a tray, the newspaper tucked under his left arm. He put the tray on the end of the bed and handed her the hot-water bottle.

'Thanks.'

He placed the tray on her knees.

'I can't,' she said.

'Six bites.'

She smiled. 'That's what I used to say to Jeremy. Six bites. I was always willing to accept four.'

'I'd be happy with three.'

She eyed the newspaper. 'Is that it?'

'Take a bite and I'll tell you.'

She did as she was told. The toast felt like sand in her mouth. She swallowed.

'Is it all right if I sit?' She nodded. He sat on the edge of the bed facing her and handed her the newspaper.

She looked at the photo of her son and his best friend, both in shorts, Rave's arm slung around Jeremy, a surf board in his other hand, and Jeremy giving his famous thumbs-up. 'They look so happy,' she said.

'Yeah, they do.'

'It's a lovely photo.'

'It is.'

'I can picture them on the beach, sun beating down on them, glistening water, messing with that surf board, having the time of their lives.'

'Me too.'

She read the small paragraph, which said nothing they didn't already know, that the boys had been missing since Sunday. *How could this have happened?* 'Do you know what they took from his room?' she asked.

'No.'

'I let him have his privacy. It's important for a teenage boy.'

'You were right.'

'Maybe I wasn't. Maybe I was a fool.'

'You weren't and you aren't.'

'We'll see.'

'Two more bites.'

'One.'

'Make it a big one and I'll tell you the latest development.'

She took a bite, chewed and swallowed.

'Tom interviewed the young fella who saw the lads by Bridget Burke's pub. Chris Kinsella.'

'Jugs? He's on the football team.'

'That's right.'

'The good news is that the pub has a CCTV camera and, if Jugs is right, the boys will have been captured on it. It will give us a definite time and an indication as to which way they were headed.'

'CCTV – that's something, isn't it?'

'It is. Drink yer tea, love.'

She did as she was told.

Lynn brought Bridie back at eight and she was clearly un-settled, agitated and upset. She cried when Maisie opened the door. 'It's gone,' she said. She couldn't rest or relax. She wanted to find something she'd lost but couldn't remember what it was.

Maisie pulled her mother into her arms. 'It's all right, Ma, I'm here, Maisie's here.'

'It's really gone this time, Maisie.' Bridie hugged her daughter close.

'No,' she soothed. 'We'll find it.' Maisie was crying again. 'We won't stop looking till we do.'

Bridie wiped the tears from Maisie's face. 'OK, love. That would be great. You know how I hate to lose things.'

'I do, Ma.'

Bridie sniffed. 'Don't be upsetting yourself on my account.' She walked into her room.

Lynn hugged Maisie. 'She's been up and down all day.'

'Has she asked for him?' Maisie said.

'No, she's just been talking about when he was a little boy.'

'She knows,' Maisie said, and her insides burned. 'She doesn't know that she knows, but she knows.' *Oh, Ma, I'm so sorry.*

Lynn nodded, and Maisie felt like dissolving into a puddle. *What am I going to do?*

'What else can I do?' Lynn said, taking off her coat and hanging it in the hall.

'You can have a cup of tea.' Fred emerged from the kitchen.

Lynn smiled at him. 'It's nice to see you again, Detective Brennan. That'd be lovely.'

'Fred, please.'

She followed him to the kitchen.

Maisie went into Bridie's bedroom wearing her nightie and the thick socks Fred had insisted she keep on. She helped her over-tired, overwrought mother into bed. It didn't take long. She cried softly, but was compliant. Maisie tucked her in.

'I wish I was somewhere else,' Bridie said.

'Where's that, Ma?'

'Where Jeremy always goes.'

'Where, Ma? Where does he go?' For a moment she dared to dream that maybe Jeremy had told Bridie something he hadn't told her.

'Inside of happy.'

Disappointment hit her like a train.

Maisie sat quietly at the end of her mother's bed, taking just a minute or two to gather her thoughts. By the time she was ready to stand up Bridie was sound asleep.

Later, she said goodbye to Lynn at the front door. 'Thanks for today.'

'I'll be here first thing to pick her up,' Lynn said.

'I really appreciate it.'

'While you were putting her to bed I checked in on Valerie.'

Maisie remained silent.

'This is not her fault, Maisie.'

'I know.'

'You should speak to her.'

'I can't. I'm just too angry, Lynn.'

'She needs her mother.'

'She needs a good . . .' She shook her head. 'I'm sorry. I just don't understand.'

'She's a kid covering for her brother. She didn't know. None of us knew.'

'You're right. I know you are.'

'So you'll talk to her?'

Maisie nodded and sighed. *I'll do my best.* 'Did you see the photo of them in the paper?' She changed the subject.

'I did, handsome boys.'

'Yeah.' Maisie smiled.

'I really want to say it's gonna be all right.'

After several years as a critical-care nurse, Lynn wasn't one for platitudes. After several years of having the shite kicked out of her, Maisie wasn't much for them either. So Lynn was never going to say that everything would be OK. It wasn't OK and it might never be OK for Maisie again because her boy was missing.

'We're in it together, you and me, in sickness and health, good times and bad. You got that?' Lynn said.

'Got it.'

'Right then, I'm off. One last thing.' She paused. 'I'd trade my soul for those boys.'

Maisie could see her biting the inside of her cheek, trying to keep it together, but the tears were welling in her eyes. 'Come here, ya thick,' she said, and they hugged and cried together. Neither spoke. They just held each other in the porch, bawling their eyes out.

Then Lynn disengaged herself, straightened up and wiped her eyes. 'Jaysus, if he comes home tonight we'll feel like awful eejits.'

'I hope so. I'd give anything to feel like an eejit now,' Maisie said. She watched her friend drive away into another rainy night, then stared down the avenue, praying to see her son. *Come on, Jeremy, just walk down the road. Crawl if you have to, just come back to me. Please, son. Please come back to me.*

She took a breath, steeled herself, closed the front door and walked into her daughter's room. Valerie was passed out cold, the radio on, and beside her on the bed was a notepad. Maisie picked it up. She'd written down the updated reports she'd been listening to. Maisie read the descriptions of the boys, what they were wearing, the appeal for witnesses in Valerie's neat handwriting and traced her fingers over their names. Just under it Valerie had written Jeremy's name three times and circled each one, linked them and joined them up to a big question mark: *Where are you, Jeremy?* In the corner of the page she'd sketched a broken heart. Maisie kissed her sleeping daughter on the forehead, placed the notepad back beside her on the bed and sat on the floor, leaning against the wall, watching her child, until Fred escorted her to her bed.

10 p.m. to 11 p.m., 1 January 1995

Jeremy

Rave wove the bike slowly and unsteadily through the village, which was empty except for one or two fellow lost souls making their way around in the rain. He narrowly avoided more than one tree as he left the park. He cycled through two sets of lights, and even though the streets were all but empty, Jeremy was nervous. He sat straight up, facing the onslaught of rain and cold, arms folded tightly across his chest. *It's cool, Jeremy. Stop being such a sap. Just enjoy this. It's an adventure. Dave would sell his ma to be on the back of this bike. Just relax, you asshole.* He couldn't relax, though: something was wrong with his best friend and Jeremy wished he'd say something. The holidays had been tough on Rave. Jeremy had begged him to come to theirs for Christmas Day but he'd refused. 'I'd feel like a thick,' he'd said.

'Why?'

'It's your family, Beany. I just don't wanna be a spare man.'

'But you're not spare in my house,' Jeremy said.

'That's nice of you to say.'

'It's the truth. We all love you, man.'

'Shut up.'

'We do.'

'I'm a big boy, Beany. I can take care of myself, all right?'

Whenever Rave said 'all right' at the end of a sentence it meant the conversation was over.

'All right,' Jeremy said, even though it wasn't. He'd seen the state Rave's da was in. He'd sneaked over to the house when Rave was with Casey after his friend had come to school with a black eye and a split lip. He'd made up a stupid excuse but Jeremy was no fool. He knew his friend was lying. He knew his da had hurt him and it made him so angry he walked around to the back of the school and kicked a wall. He'd really hurt the nail on his big toe so he'd cried a little before he went back inside. *He thinks no one's watchin', but I am. The auld fella needs to know he won't get away with it. I won't let him.* He decided to go to the house and face him but only when Deirdre agreed to walk him to the corner of the road as moral support.

'I'll wait here,' she'd said, sitting on a wall a few doors down. 'Good luck.'

Moments later, Jeremy was standing on the path in front of Rave's house. He gathered himself, then opened the gate. *What am I doing?* He didn't notice the state of the garden: his eyes were fixed on the front-room window. Sid was standing there, staring straight out at him. He was gaunt, bony, creepy and, more than that, he was black and blue. Jeremy stopped in his tracks, waiting for Sid to acknowledge him but he didn't. He just stared, his glassy eyes focused on something in the middle distance. He reminded Jeremy of his grammy: he was there but not really there. He almost turned and ran but he didn't. *Rave needs me to step up.* He banged on the door and Sid came in his own time. When he opened it, he kept it tight. Despite that, the place reeked enough for Jeremy to take an immediate step back.

'Ah, how are you, Mr Murphy?' He couldn't bear to look at him, so he kept his eyes on the ground at his feet.

'I'm fuckin' brilliant, thanks for askin'.' Sid started to close the door but Jeremy was holding it open.

'I was wondering if everything was OK here.' His voice was shaking. *What I am I bleedin' doing?*

'What do ya mean?' Sid asked, and suddenly he was engaged.

'Rave's pretty beat up. I'm worried about him.'

'Well, don't. He can take care of himself,' Sid said.

'No, he can't. He's a kid,' Jeremy said. 'He needs you.'

'Go away, Jeremy.'

Sid moved to close the door but Jeremy stuck his foot in it, the one with the dodgy nail. 'No,' he shouted. His temper was rising. He was shaking and he tried his best to hold it together but when he spoke his voice shook too. 'I won't.'

Sid laughed. 'Are ya sure it isn't Rave should be looking after you?'

Jeremy wanted to punch his already black and blue face but his legs felt weak and Sid was closing the door on his nail. *Oh, God, that hurts.* But he wasn't going anywhere. Instead he called on every ounce of strength he had in him and pushed open the door. Sid fell back a little. 'You don't hit him again.'

'What?'

'You don't hit him, ever again. Do you hear me?'

Sid laughed. 'Oh, I hear you. Are we finished now?'

'You're supposed to take care of him,' Jeremy said, and tears sprang into his eyes. 'You're his da.' *How can you be so mean?* He looked at Sid, taking in his ravaged, tortured face.

Sid's mouth opened and he let out a sigh. He bowed his head a little and bored his thumb and index fingers into his deep-set eyes. When he released his fingers and met Jeremy's eye, tears spilled down his dirty cheeks. Jeremy tried not to cry but he couldn't help it.

'I know that. Don't you think I know it? I tried me best. I just can't do it.' He crumbled.

'I'm sorry.' Jeremy's anger was gone now, and all that was left was a well of sadness.

'Me too,' Sid said. 'You tell him that.' Jeremy started to walk down the path. 'Jeremy?'

Jeremy turned to face him. 'Yeah?'

'Do ya have a few quid? I've got no food in the house.'

Jeremy had a fiver for chips for himself and Deirdre. He looked at the man standing in front of him with his hand out. 'It's just a fiver.' He knew full well it wouldn't be spent on food but he was unable to say no.

'You're a good boy.' Sid took it from him and slammed the door.

After that, whenever Jeremy cooked, he cooked extra for Rave. He kept a lunchbox in his room and filled it with Rave's portion, then dropped it into Rave's bag or locker the next day. Mostly Rave didn't mention it. He just ate the food and pretended he didn't notice when Jeremy retrieved the empty lunchbox. Sometimes Jeremy would drop a few quid into his bag too. Whatever he could spare. It wasn't much but it was better than nothing. Every now and then Rave would smile at him. 'You're the best mate in the world,' he'd say, and Jeremy would light up inside. He always left his window open so that Rave had a place to escape to. One night, a week later, Jeremy woke up to find Rave in the sleeping bag he'd stashed under the bed. After that, whenever things got too much at home, Rave would come through the window and sleep on the floor next to him.

They only really talked about Rave's predicament once. Rave appeared before Jeremy had fallen asleep. He'd been up and studying for a Christmas history test and his head was too much a muddle of history facts and Deirdre's words to sleep. He tried to focus on history but Deirdre kept pushing herself into his mind. Something she'd said ate away at him. She'd said it the night he'd confronted Rave's da. He'd been berating himself for giving Sid the money.

'I'm a thick.'

'You're not.'

'Please, please, never tell Rave.'

'It's between you and me, Beany.'

'Thanks.'

She had kissed him on the mouth, a quick kiss, not one of those slimy, soft ones that dragged on. She drew away and smiled at him so he pulled her close and hugged her tight. *I do love you, Deirdre.*

'You're not like other boys,' she'd whispered into his ear.

She'd meant it as a compliment but he'd felt sick. He'd been reliving those five words ever since. *You're not like other boys.*

Does she suspect anything? If she does I'll lose everyone. I'll be alone. Dave had told them a story months before about two poofters who were caught kissing by a gang of lads down some back alley and they'd run for it. One had got away but the other wasn't fast enough. Dave made a joke about the bloke wishing he'd worn a pair of runners instead of his ma's high heels. The others had laughed, even Rave, but Jeremy didn't find it funny. The men had beaten and kicked the man, called him names and told him he'd come from Hell. They'd decided that it was their job to send him back to where he'd come from. They had tied his feet to the back of their truck and dragged him for miles.

Jeremy had felt paralysed by that story while his best friends had laughed, then moved on to fighting talk about football. *I don't understand. They tore him apart.* He'd had nightmares about it since, and when he was stressed it invaded his waking thoughts. *How painful was it? How long did it take him to die? What were his last thoughts? Did he beg? Who did he think about? Was it just too violent for words or thought?* It took a while for Jeremy to forgive the lads for laughing that night, especially Rave, but, then, they didn't understand and they never would.

That night, Jeremy sat up when Rave hauled himself through the window.

'Oh, sorry, do you want me to go?' He seemed surprised that Jeremy was still awake, as though he'd been waiting for him to fall asleep.

'No! Are ya mad? Course not.'

'OK.' Rave pulled out the sleeping bag and shook it. He took off his jacket, then his top and jeans. Even though it was dark, Jeremy turned and faced the other way while his friend undressed. Rave slipped into the sleeping bag. They lay in silence for a little while.

'You OK?' Jeremy said eventually.

'Good.'

'Hungry?'

'No. I ate that shepherd's pie you left me. You're getting better, Beany. It was almost edible.'

Jeremy laughed. 'Cheers.'

'I know you spoke to me da,' Rave said, after a minute or two. Jeremy's heart threatened to stop. 'It's OK, I know why you did it, but don't go back there again. All right?'

'I won't.'

'I'm trustin' you, Beany.'

'I promise.'

'And you'll never tell anyone what you saw?'

Crap. I told Deirdre, but his da didn't know Deirdre was there. 'I won't say a word.' *From here on in. It's not a lie.*

Now Jeremy wished they were lying in his warm, dry bedroom. It had taken them for ever to get up the road, Rave zigzagging this way and that, and when he hit the second parked car, waving to Jugs Kinsella, Jeremy had had enough. 'Keep yer eye on the road, will ya?' He jumped off the bike.

'Shite, sorry, lost me bearings.'

'I'm going home.' He turned to walk away.

'Ah, come on, man. Sorry. I'll get me act together.'

'Nah, I need to go, man. I can't leave me grammy and Valerie on their own. It's not cool.'

Rave got off the bike and followed him. 'We'll walk a bit. I'm soberin' up – please.'

Jeremy stopped in his tracks. Rave was pleading with him. He never pleaded with anyone. He hated letting his best friend down.

'I need you,' Rave said.

Shite anyways. 'OK, but we're not walking. I'll do the cycling.'

'My bike is your bike.' Rave slapped him on the back. Jeremy put his hand on the saddle. Rave let it go.

'This is stupid,' Jeremy said.

'It's not, I swear.'

'It's freezing.'

'It's life.'

'You're pissed.'

'Please, Beany. Please come with me.'

Jeremy looked across the road. He saw Jugs Kinsella's ma's car pull out of Bridget Burke's pub car park. *Lucky bastard. Off to a warm bed.* Jeremy's feet were frozen. He fixed his schoolbag on his back. 'All right,' he said.

'Cool.'

Jeremy stepped on to the bike. Rave sat on the saddle. 'Where are we goin'?'

'Right up Bohernabreena Road,' Rave said.

Jeremy took off, Rave waving his arms in the air and singing, 'Here we go, here we go, here we go . . .' He cycled fast to get where he was going and to warm himself, Rave still singing into his back. He cycled until Rave shouted, 'Here!' when they reached the gates to the reservoir.

'You're jokin', right?' Jeremy imagined himself telling Deirdre about this madness tomorrow. *She's gonna have something to say about it.*

'Not jokin'. Come on, driver, let's go,' Rave said.

The gates were open even though Jeremy was hoping they'd be locked. *Shite, what are they open for? It's dangerous around here. I've a good mind to write a letter of complaint.* He followed the narrow track beside the rushing water. His heart raced and he wanted desperately to get off the bike. 'Why don't we walk this bit?' he shouted back to Rave.

'What?' Rave said.

'Let's walk it!'

Rave leaned to the side to hear him.

Don't lean! It's slippy as fuck – don't lean, you nutter!

'Is Beany scared?' Rave laughed, grabbed Jeremy from behind and shook him so that they wobbled. For a second it felt like they were slipping towards the water. Instinct took over: Jeremy gripped the handlebars, straightened the bike and forged on through the muck and undergrowth. Rave held on for a few seconds too long and Jeremy could feel his heart beating against his back, the weight and warmth of his body. He gulped. He felt Rave's hands move towards his chest, his breath on his neck. *Oh, God.* When his friend pulled back, the cold wind whipped between them.

'I don't feel well,' Rave said. Jeremy stopped the bike just as they hit the reservoir bridge. Rave slipped off the saddle and stumbled a little. 'I think I overdid it, Beany. Feelin' dizzy.'

'What can I do?'

'Just give us a minute.' Rave sat on the ground, leaning against the bars of the bridge. Jeremy wasn't used to seeing him so compromised. *He was fine when the lads left.*

'Sit with me for a minute, Beany.'

'It's soaking.'

'It's not too bad.'

Jeremy sat down gingerly, his back against the rusty bars. They felt gaping, unsafe. The water was a good drop down but he still felt too close to it. 'Did you take something?' he asked Rave.

'No. I swear. I never would. The booze just hit me all of a sudden.'

'OK.'

'And I'm tired.'

Rave did look tired, Jeremy thought – in fact, he looked exhausted. His eyes were hollow, his face gaunt.

'Been one of those days,' Rave said, arching his neck to look up at the night sky. It was dense, cloudy, no stars, just darkness and the threat of more rain. He leaned against the bars on the bridge, slowly filling his lungs with oxygen.

'You OK now?' Jeremy said.

'I feel better.' He slapped Jeremy's biceps, then kept his hand there, steadying himself.

Jeremy felt tightness, slight tingling and mild dizziness. He wanted to reach out and grab Rave's hand but he fought the instinct with every fibre of his being. 'We need to move.'

'OK, but not on the bike,' Rave said.

'Where are we goin'?'

'Told you, it's a surprise.' Rave looked towards the bushes. 'Stash it in there.'

Jeremy sighed. 'Fine.' He wheeled the bike down to the bushes. Rave was still sitting on the ground, gazing into the sky. 'It feels better looking up than looking down, doesn't it?'

'Are you sure you didn't take anything?'

'Never. Never ever.'

Jeremy pushed the bike into the leaves and bushes as best he could.

'You'll find it here, right?'

Rave looked over. 'A fuckin' blind man could find it.' He laughed.

Jeremy joined his friend on the bridge. 'So, which way?'

Rave pointed up the side of the mountain that swept down to the reservoir. 'Up there.'

'No way! We'll slip and fall.'

'No, we won't.'

'It's been rainin' for three days straight – there's a bleedin' landslide waitin' to happen.'

'It's grand.'

'We can't see where we're going.'

'If you're scared hold on to me.' He set off.

Jeremy stared at the muddy, uneven ground ahead. *Ah, shite.*

Before they'd even got off the bridge the rain had started to fall. Rave turned to Jeremy and laughed. It was good to see he was feeling better but still this was lunacy. 'We're going to die here,' Jeremy said, at the foot of the hill.

'We've got to die somewhere, Beany.' Rave took the first slippery step, turned to Jeremy and held out his hand. Jeremy grasped it and Rave hauled him up. 'No turning back now, Beany.'

WEDNESDAY, 4 JANUARY 1995

Chapter Seven

'Patience'
Guns N' Roses, 1989

Fred

IT WAS A ROUGH NIGHT. Fred put Maisie to bed around ten p.m.
'You should go,' she said to him.

'I'll just wait until you're asleep.'

'You should go,' she repeated.

'OK.' He handed her a sedative.

'I can't take that.'

'You need sleep, if you're to be any good tomorrow.'

'But my ma . . .'

'They're light. If she needs you, you'll wake.'

She trusted him, but he was lying. She'd be out for at least five hours. *I'm sorry, love, but you're a zombie and we need you back.*

He lay on the sofa, closed his eyes and was asleep in seconds. He woke several hours later, after three a.m., to hear Bridie shuffling and mumbling. It was impossible to sleep with her on the prowl. He contemplated going to see if there was something he could do for her but he knew better. She had it in her head that he had done something bad and he had, but if pushed he'd do it again without hesitation. *Don't you remember why*

I did it? Don't you remember asking for my help? There was a time when Bridie had trusted him and they had been allies. She'd forgotten that. When she looked at him now, she saw a dangerous man. Every shuffling step she took was a little knife in his heart. *Just go back to bed, old woman. It's not right you wandering.* He couldn't approach her without all hell breaking loose, and the last thing he wanted was to frighten her. All he could do was sit up and listen to her lest she fell or attempted to break out.

He wondered what Tom had taken from the house. *Two boxes.* Tom had been cagey, a little less forthcoming than Fred had expected. Linda would fill him in. He made a mental note to call her first thing. Outside the job he'd been friendly with her and her husband for many years. They were members of the same golf club and played together at least once a month. Linda wasn't like any other woman he knew: she was a powerhouse, a woman of few words and, some would say, limited vocabulary, but she was loyal, trustworthy, and knew when to break a ridiculous rule. Besides, there was a fellowship among golfers that transcended the bonds of mere co-workers.

He sat up and considered putting the TV on but, again, it might disturb the restless Bridie. He thought about the first time he and Bridie had really talked. They had been in the hospital after that last terrible beating, while Maisie was in surgery. Bridie was worried her child would die. She was in the family room with a set of rosary beads in her hands. She was twisting them but she wasn't praying. She was far too distracted for that.

He'd gone to her and introduced himself. 'We got her here as quick as we could.'

'Have you got him?'

'We have.'

'Will it even matter?'

'He'll be charged, with Maisie's help.' He sat down beside her.

'He's been knocking lumps out of her for years.'

'I know.'

'She pretends it's not happening so I pretend it's not happening, and look where all this pretending has got us.' She closed her eyes and a tear wound down her cheek.

'She's strong.'

'Her father was a soldier. He saw and probably did things that no man should see or do but he was gentle and kind to us. She probably doesn't remember that, though. She was so small when he died.'

'It's not your fault.'

'He wouldn't have insisted she marry that animal.'

'I'm sure you didn't know.'

'It never even dawned on me. I must be a very stupid woman.'

'I doubt that.'

'All I ever wanted for her was a kind man.'

Fred said nothing. There was nothing he could say.

'Will he do time for this?'

'I hope so.'

'But you're not sure.'

'Domestic violence is difficult.'

'Shouldn't be.'

'No, it shouldn't.'

'If Maisie survives this, she's comin' home with me, her and the kiddies. I'm not takin' no for an answer.'

'Good. Don't.'

'I'll keep her safe,' she said.

'And I'll help.' He gave her his card.

She'd smiled at him. 'You're the one Lynn calls the fuzzy knight.'

He'd laughed, rubbing his hand over his beard.

Bridie must have seen some goodness in him. She would never have used the card he'd given her if she hadn't. She'd have plenty of time for Fred Brennan if she hadn't lost her mind.

He heard Maisie stir and get up at three thirty. He strained to listen as she talked gently to her mother, guiding her back to her room. He wanted to help but his hands were tied so instead he just sat in the dark and waited. It wasn't in his nature to do so and it only encouraged him to feel even sorrier for himself. He hated to be maudlin, but he wanted more from life: a family, warmth, love. He wanted someone to take care of and to be taken care of. It wasn't too late. Maisie saying yes and that magical evening they'd spent together had meant anything was possible, but in an instant everything had changed. Instead of the fantasy life he had conjured in his head her boy was missing and she was shattering in front of him all over again. *How many times must I watch you suffer, Mai?* He lay down, finally closing his eyes. *Please don't hate me, Mai. I'm doing me best, please.*

He dropped off for a few minutes but woke when Maisie came into the sitting room. She was carrying a blanket and laid it over him, tucking the edges in around his body. He opened his eyes and they stared at one another for a moment or two before she slipped away.

His phone rang at eight, just as the people in the house were stirring.

'It's Tom. There's been a development.' He sounded subdued.

Fred sat up. 'What?'

'The boys are front-page news this morning.'

'But that's good, right?'

'Fred, the papers have an idea about the boys.'

'What idea would that be?'

'That they may be in a relationship.'

'What the hell? What the fuck is goin' on?' He shot to his feet.

'We found some gay porn in Jeremy's room. It looks like one of the lads left the box unattended for a few minutes.'

'Gay porn?' Fred repeated, pacing the sitting-room floor.

'Yeah.'

'What do you mean it was unattended?' Fred asked. He was still trying to get his head around the notion that the boys were gay. *The photo in the newspaper, they were naked from the waist up, arms around one another. That's gonna look bad now.*

'One of the search team put it in the boot. It was raining and he was trying to hurry. He thought there was no one around so he didn't close it when he went in to grab the other box. It couldn't have been unattended longer than a few minutes.'

'So you're telling me one of the neighbours spotted the porn and called the fuckin' press?'

'It looks like it.'

'Christ almighty, Tom. Christ al-fuckin'-mighty.'

'It shouldn't have happened.'

'What are the papers sayin'?'

'Well, it's just one so far, but you can be sure the others will pick up on it. They're sayin' the boys are missing since Sunday night and they're not putting forward the notion that they've run off together but it's insinuated. They're asking them to come home. They've added details of a gay helpline.'

'Jesus.'

'Look, it's not the end of the world. At least they're on the front page now. If they're out there we'll find them.'

'I'm not even gonna dignify the idea with—'

'The thing is, it's a strong theory.'

'Ah, come on.'

'The kid is gay, Fred.'

'Because of some porn? He could have found that God knows where.'

'Kids don't keep gay porn unless they're gay.'

'Bollocks. He has a girlfriend.'

'Fred, listen to me. If the lads have run off to be together it's the best possible scenario with the best possible outcome. But we'll follow any and all leads until we find them.'

'You're not going to make the papers retract?'

'That would not be helpful at this juncture.'

'Christ.'

'You need to prepare Maisie.'

'And how am I supposed to do that?' Fred said angrily.

'I'm sorry, Fred. I'll keep you posted.'

'You do that.' Fred hung up. He could hear Maisie moving around, taking care of her mother and talking to Valerie. The kettle was on. Toast popped up. His stomach growled.

He sat for a few moments wondering how in the world he was supposed to break this news to Maisie but also keenly aware that time was running out: the vultures would descend soon enough. The house phone started to ring. *Oh, shite.* He ran into the kitchen in time to hear Valerie's urgent 'Jeremy?' He saw her face change. 'What?'

'Put down the phone, love.'

'What did you just say?' Her face changed colour.

'Valerie, put the phone down!' he shouted.

Maisie, still in her dressing-gown, looked at him with raised eyebrows. Bridie was sitting at the table. She was dressed but her hair was a mess. 'Where's Jeremy?' she piped up.

'What the bleedin' hell? Who do you think you are?' Valerie said into the receiver.

'Give me the phone, Valerie.' Fred held out his hand, his voice still raised.

'Yeah, well, you can go and get fu—'

Fred grabbed the phone and hung it up. Valerie, Maisie and Bridie all stared at him, waiting for answers. 'The papers are running a story about the boys. They're saying that they're . . .' He was scrambling for the right word. 'Homosexual' sounded so technical.

'Faggots,' Valerie said. 'They're sayin' they're faggots.' Tears welled in her eyes.

The last bit of colour drained from Maisie's face. She found a seat and sat down. 'Why would they say that?' she asked, in a hoarse whisper.

Bridie put her hand on her daughter's shoulder and gripped it firmly. 'They're liars and liars lie, isn't that right?' she said to the room.

Fred didn't know if Bridie really understood what was going on. She seemed too calm.

'Jeremy's a good boy.' She got up and walked into the sitting room.

No one followed her. Instead Valerie and Maisie waited for an explanation. Fred took a chair beside Maisie. 'Sit down, Valerie.'

Maisie put a hand on his arm. 'Fred, please explain what the hell is going on.'

She was hanging on for dear life, he thought. He placed his hand on hers.

'All right, Mai, I'll try.' And he started talking.

Bridie

Bridie stared at the television. She wasn't sure what she was looking at but it didn't matter. She was singing the chorus of 'We'll Meet Again' in her head over and over, and suddenly she was back in time, waiting for Arthur to come home. *When the war is over we'll have kids. I'd like five. Three boys and two girls. I couldn't be doing with a small family. Lots of noise and love and laughter, that's what I want.* She was smiling to herself when Fred came in and sat down beside her. *I'd like a big old bus to drive them around and we'll go to the sea every weekend. Oh, and we'll have a small boat to go fishing in and I'll teach them all to swim. Learning to swim is very important when you live on a small island.* Bridie's Arthur couldn't swim. *I'll teach him too. You can't not know how to swim.*

'Bridie?'

'Yes, love?' she said to Fred, while at the same time looking through him, seeing only the images in her mind.

'Can I have a word with you?'

'Is it about Arthur?'

'No. It's about me.'

'Who are you?'

'I'm the man who cares about your daughter.'

She laughed. 'I don't have children, not yet but someday.'

'Bridie, it's me, Fred Brennan.'

She stared at him, good and hard, but she didn't recognize him.

'I'm sorry,' he said gently. 'I just wanted you to know that I'm very sorry and I'm begging you not to say anything, not yet.' Then he walked away. She heard the front door close and watched him step into the rain.

'I wonder does he know my Arthur,' she said to her reflection in the window.

Maisie

The reporters appeared in Tallaght village in dribs and drabs over the course of the day. By ten o'clock there were a few newspaper journalists knocking on doors on Cypress Road. Lynn stayed with Maisie in the house. Fred didn't want her left alone. It meant that Bridie stayed, too, but she remained quiet in the sitting room, watching her *Blockbusters* tape. Valerie wanted to go to school but Maisie put her foot down.

The newspaper was on the counter. Lynn brought it with her when she arrived. Maisie stared at it. The photo was beautiful: two fresh-faced boys, joyful best friends so full of life, smiling for the camera. The words below made the photo tawdry. The article didn't say the boys were gay: it just laid out the facts. Two boys go missing. A stash of gay porn found. If anyone has seen these boys together, call the helplines set up and that other helpline for gays in case they're reading the article and need to reach out. The mind of the reader did everything else. *They're friends. They're best friends. There's no harm in that. They've known each other since they were babies, for God's sake. This is just a misunderstanding. It's all just . . . What is it? What is this?* Maisie could feel a headache coming on.

'They'll never want to come home now,' she said. 'I can just hear jaws rattling. The whole village will be laughin' at them.'

'Let it,' Lynn said.

'He's a sixteen-year-old boy! How is he supposed to deal with this?'

'Things blow over.'

'Where is he, Lynn?'

'I wish I knew.'

When Fred had sat her down and told her what had happened, she'd found it difficult to absorb so much information. She needed a minute. *It's a big mistake. That porn is not my Jeremy's.* She had no doubt about that. The thing that really played on her mind was a neighbour's betrayal. *Who would do that? Which of them would be so callous and hurtful? Who would be so incredibly bloody nosy, mean-minded and selfish?*

Fred couldn't answer her. All he could say was that it might actually help find the boys. 'Isn't that what matters, Mai?'

'Of course it is, but the truth also matters. My son's good name matters.'

Fred needed to run some errands. He didn't say what they were but she knew they had something to do with her son. He whispered to Lynn before he walked into the sitting room to see Bridie and closed the door. Maisie asked her friend what he'd said.

'That it's going to get worse.'

'How much worse?'

'They're going to drag up every little dirty secret Jeremy has.'

Maisie felt her breath leave her body. 'He's just a boy.' *He doesn't have any dirty secrets.*

'I'll make us a nice cup of tea,' Lynn said.

Maisie heard the front door close. Fred had finally left the house and it was a relief. 'I need to think,' she said, and walked into the sitting room. She sat on the sofa holding hands with her mother, who seemed mesmerized by the quiz show she'd watched so many times before.

Valerie

Valerie didn't last long in her room. *Screw this.* She opened her window and hopped out, crossed to Vera's, then walked to the back of her house so that she could climb over Vera's fence to avoid the few journalists and nosy sods in the street. Vera was putting her washing out when Valerie appeared. 'You escaping?' Vera said.

'Yeah.'

'I've chocolate fudge cake in the fridge.'

'I'm not tellin' you anything.'

'I'm not asking.'

'Is it double chocolate?'

'It is.'

'That's me favourite.'

'I've got ice-cream as well. Raspberry ripple.'

'I prefer mint chocolate but I like raspberry ripple too.'

'Well, then . . .' Vera said, and walked into the house with an empty basket. Valerie followed and sat at her kitchen table while Vera put together a plate of cake and ice-cream. Jake was under the table, snoring.

'He likes a sleep mid-morning,' Vera said, referring to her dog. She put the plate in front of Valerie and handed her a spoon.

'Thanks.'

Vera sat. 'It's a wonder he doesn't wake up with the smell of that cake. He loves chocolate cake.'

'But that could kill him,' Valerie said.

'It hasn't yet.'

Valerie spotted the newspaper with her brother's face on the front. She turned away from it, looking out into Vera's back garden. 'Why do you put washing out when it's raining?'

'It's not raining now.'

'But it will be soon enough.'

'And then I'll take the clothes in.'

'But they won't be dry.'

'They'll be aired, though.'

'What's aired?'

'It's nature's freshener.'

'Ma uses Lenor.'

'That's good too.'

'Did you read it?' Valerie indicated the newspaper.

'I did.'

Valerie dug into her cake and ice-cream. 'Ma and Grammy say they're liars, just so you know,' she said, between mouthfuls.

'The press gets things upside down all the time.' Vera curled her lip.

'Like when?'

'Like always.'

'Give me an example.'

'Ah, I can't think on the the spot like that but I'm tellin' you.'

'Some neighbour ratted him out.'

'What do you mean?'

'They saw some porn in a box in the back of the coppers' car and told the press.'

'Well, the whole road was watchin' that car last night.'

'Did you see anything?' Valerie asked.

'Couldn't find me glasses. Only had me readers on and they're no good for spying.'

'Maybe Jeremy's friends planted the porn for a joke. They do shite like that all the time.'

'Valerie Bean, watch your mouth.'

'Sorry, but they do. Dave O'Loughlin thinks he's some sort of comedian. I bet he did it or Mitch – he can get his hands on anything. They probably got a great laugh out of it.'

'At least it's not raining,' Vera said, glancing out at her washing.

'Yeah,' Valerie said. 'I hate the rain.'

'Where my Sebastian lives, it never rains.'

'Really?'

'Well, almost never.'

'Will he ever come home?' Valerie said.

'He's thirty-four, settled with a wife and kids, so I suppose not.'

'Sorry.'

'Don't be. He never did fit in over here.'

'Why's that?'

'I don't know.' She thought about it for a moment. 'I suppose just because you're born in a place it doesn't mean you belong there.'

'Everybody's gonna say that Jeremy's a fudge-packer,' Valerie said quietly.

'They won't call him that, young lady.'

'Gay, homo, queer, fruit, mattress-muncher, poofter, it's all the same. If Jeremy's not dead he'll kill himself now.'

'Of course he's not dead and don't say that.'

'It's true.'

'Look, Valerie, there'll be enough people linin' up to point the finger and call your brother names. I don't want to hear that you're one of them.'

Valerie thought about that for a minute. 'Father Moss says being a fudge— I mean a gay is a crime against God.'

'That's only if you act on it,' Vera said.

'And if you do?'

'Well, then it's up to God.'

'If that's the case Jeremy's screwed.'

'Why's that?'

'Well, if Jeremy was looking at pictures of fellas doing the bold thing it wasn't so he could say his prayers, was it?'

Vera didn't have an answer. She pursed her lips, kicked off her slippers and rubbed the dog's back with her feet.

'God sends people to Hell,' Valerie said.

'He also sends them to Heaven.'

'So are you saying there's a homo section in Heaven?'

'I'm saying we don't know. It's in God's hands.'

'He's not one anyways. He has a girlfriend.'

'So there's nothing to worry about.'

But Valerie *was* worried. She kept thinking about what Jeremy had said to her on Sunday night. *You don't know me, Valerie.*

Valerie was only halfway through her cake and ice-cream when they both heard a frantic Maisie screaming her name. 'Oh, shite,' she said.

'You know your ma goes mad when you swear. God knows I hear her losing it all the time through these thin walls.'

'Sorry.'

Valerie followed Vera to the door. Maisie was on her front lawn, pacing and hollering, and a photographer was taking snaps. A pregnant woman and a man were vying for an interview.

'Just a few words, Mrs Bean.'

'It's been three days now, what would you like to say to the boys?'

'Valerie! Valerie Bean, where are you?'

She was walking back and forth, like a caged tiger. Lynn was trying her best to keep hold of her but she was too distraught.

'Valerie!'

'I'm here, Ma'sie,' Valerie said, from Vera's door.

Maisie whirled round. 'I told you to stay inside!' she screamed, in front of all the strangers and the neighbours who were in their gardens: Jim Buckley, with his arms crossed; Leslie O'Shea, in her porch on the phone; the Ryans sitting on plastic furniture in their driveway. They were all watching the show. Mortified, Valerie moved in behind Vera.

'Get over here now.' Maisie pointed at the ground beside her.

'Maisie, calm down,' Lynn said.

'I won't. Valerie, I asked you to do one simple thing!' she shouted. 'Just stay indoors! How hard is that?'

Valerie disappeared completely behind Vera.

'She's fine, Maisie,' Vera said. 'She's just upset, like you.'

The two journalists stood as close as decency would allow, their tape recorders held high and pressed to record. Maisie stared at them, then at her neighbours, all watching her life fall apart as though it was some kind of entertainment. 'Go away!' she shouted at the press people. 'There's nothing for you here.' But they didn't move. 'Get the hose,' she muttered to Lynn.

'What?'

'Get the hose.'

'Seriously?'

'Get the fuckin' hose, Lynn.'

'Right.' She turned to Bridie standing in the doorway. 'Let's get the hose.'

Then Maisie focused on her neighbours. She pushed past the press and into the middle of the road so she could address them all. 'And yous, I know what one of yous did. I know that these vultures are saying terrible things about my son because of one of you. Why would you do that? My child's never been anything but nice to yous. He helped you cut your grass, Leslie O'Shea, that summer you broke your ankle and that useless bastard you married was too busy sunning himself. All summer he tended those fuckin' begonias of yours and he wouldn't take a penny from you. And you, Jim Buckley, he joined that stupid karate class of yours and got his friends involved even though he hated it, just to give you a dig-out and get the classes goin'. As for yous,' she said, pointing to the Ryans, 'remember when Livie locked you out in the fuckin' snow, Malcolm? It was only a month ago. Jeremy brought you to ours and asked if you could sleep on the sofa. I told him no. I didn't want a strange man in my house, not with my mother the way she is, but he insisted. "Ah, Ma, we can't leave him. It wouldn't be right."' She was crying now. 'You know why he did all those things? Because he's kind and he's caring and he's a hell of a lot better than all of yous. So enjoy the show, yis disloyal fuckers.'

Lynn emerged with the hose and handed it to Maisie. 'Are you sure about this?'

'Never been surer of anything in me life.'

'That one is pregnant.'

'So she'll be pregnant and wet.' Maisie turned the hose on and directed it at the gathering, dispersing them instantly. They ran in different directions protecting their cameras. Some tore down the road, others hid behind the cars.

Valerie emerged from behind Vera's skirt. 'That was cool.'

Maisie walked up to her daughter and put out her hand. Valerie took it.

'Sorry I shouted,' Maisie said.

'Sorry I left.'

'It's OK, Buttons.'

Maisie hadn't called her 'Buttons' in a long time. It made Valerie smile. 'Thanks for the cake, Vera,' she said.

'You're welcome, Valerie.' Vera made her way back to her front door.

'Let's get you two inside,' Lynn said, and ushered the Beans into their house.

Fred

The station was quiet and, except for Linda standing behind the desk, deserted.

'Tom's following up a lead he found in the Murphy household.'

He sat in the swing chair beside her. 'Oh?'

'He visited Sid Murphy. It turns out the ma sends a Christmas card every year.' She showed Fred the card. 'Get a load of this.'

The card was a simple line drawing of a baby in a crib. Inside was written, *Dear Son, wishing you a holy Christmas, Mother.*

'Jesus.' He turned it over. It was signed on the back by a Wexford artist.

'Sure these could be sold nationwide.'

'Nah, we checked. He sells the cards at local Christmas fairs. It's a start.'

'Any news on Sid?'

'His leg has to come off.'

'Christ.'

'He's more upset that the press are calling his son a poofter than he is about the leg.'

Fred was tugging at his beard, lost in thought. 'Valerie mentioned that the rumour around the village is that Carina Murphy joined the Moonies, so maybe we should check into any and all local communities.'

'Will do.' She wrote it down. 'How's Maisie?'

'There's a part of me thinks I should step away. I might be doing more harm than good.'

'Nonsense. She needs you now more than ever.'

'I don't think she sees it that way, Linda. It's all too much.'

'Well, whether she sees it that way or not, she needs you. You're her liaison. Suck it up.'

He laughed. 'Fair enough.'

She slapped his thigh. 'Come on, I'll show you the CCTV footage.'

They sat together and watched the tape of the boys on the Bohernabreena Road just opposite Bridget Burke's pub. Jeremy had a bag on his back but Rave didn't.

'Rave's schoolbag was missing,' Fred said. 'So where is it? And his clothes. Where would he stash them on a rainy night? That backpack is half empty.' He pointed to the screen.

'The lads are combin' the graveyard and the mountains as we speak. The phones have been hoppin', half the village has volunteered their assistance and we've got a huge search party organized to cover the entire area.'

'Really? They don't all think the lads have fucked off to some queer island in Greece?' Fred said bitterly.

'People want to help regardless.'

'A mother should never have to hear personal information about her son like that, Linda.'

'Preachin' to the converted.'

He stood up. 'I should let you get back to work.' *Where to now? What do I do?* He didn't know. He was lost. Maisie didn't want him in the house, and he didn't want to be in her way, not when there wasn't anything to do or say.

'Go home, get some sleep, then wash yourself and bring that woman out to the search. Let her see how many people she has pulling for her.'

Good idea. 'Thanks Linda.'

A little later, Fred entered his empty house and walked heavily up the creaky stairs to the bedroom that had once been his mother's. He sat on his super-king-sized bed, which took up much of the space, and for the first time since he'd laid his dead fiancée to rest he wept like a baby.

Maisie

After fielding twenty-five calls in a row, Maisie's oldest friend was losing her mind. 'I can't live like this, Maisie!' Lynn was breaking into a sweat. 'It's like a form of torture. Ringing, ringing, ringing! I can't bleedin' think.'

'Take it off the hook.' If Jeremy tried to call, he wouldn't get through, but the police had given a choice of phone numbers he could use. He was all over the press. If he wanted to make contact he'd find a way. *It's going to be OK.*

Maisie dressed herself and sat with Valerie at the kitchen table, while Lynn settled Bridie down for her sleep. The radio was on, and as a song ended, the news came on. Maisie reached over and turned up the volume. 'In local news, two boys, Jeremy Bean and John Rave Murphy, both sixteen, have been missing since Sunday night. Jeremy is five foot seven, with curly sandy hair and brown eyes. He was wearing a long-sleeved black shirt, denim jeans, a blue rain jacket and white runners. John is six foot one, with black hair and grey eyes. He was wearing black jeans, a black jumper, a khaki military-style jacket and black hobnail boots. They were last seen on New Year's Day on the Bohernabreena Road on a black Dynatech 405ti bike at approximately ten fifteen p.m. If anyone has any information on the whereabouts of the boys, please contact the Tallaght garda station. Any information gathered will be treated as confidential. The gardaí have decided to search the areas around Bohernabreena, including the graveyard, the mountain area around Kilbride and the reservoir. All volunteers are welcome. The search begins at Bridget Burke's pub at two o'clock, and the gardaí advise all volunteers to bring their wet gear. The rain may have stopped but the search areas are considered treacherous.'

'At least they didn't say they were fruits,' Valerie said.

'That's because they're not,' Maisie said sternly. 'And don't call your brother a fruit. People deserve respect, no matter what they are. I have nothing against the gays and neither should you. But my son is not gay. That's it, end of discussion.'

'OK, Ma'sie.'

They heard Lynn going into the bathroom.

'Are we just gonna sit here, Ma'sie?'

'No. We bloody well are not.' She stood up and grabbed her keys. 'Come on.'

'I have to go, Lynn,' Maisie shouted, through the closed bathroom door.

'Where?'

'To look for Jeremy. Take care of my mother, will you?' She grabbed her and Valerie's coats from the rack and two pairs of wellies.

'Ah, wait!'

'We won't be long, Lynn.'

The journalists waiting by the door gathered around them as soon as they left the sanctuary of the porch. Maisie pushed through, saying, 'No comment,' just as Fred had told her to.

The neighbours were still watching from their gardens. She made her way to her car, Valerie close behind.

'Did you know your son was gay, Mrs Bean? Do you think it's a factor in his disappearance?'

Just keep calm and say nothing.

'Is Jeremy's father aware of his disappearance?'

Maisie's heart threatened to stop. Her fingers loosened and the keys slipped to the ground. *Danny Fox. I can't cope with Danny Fox.* Clamouring voices vying for attention. Strangers asking questions Maisie couldn't or wasn't prepared to answer. The front door seemed miles away. The car door was straight ahead and locked. *The keys, the keys, where are the stupid keys?* Maisie bent over to search the muddy ground for them and her inquisitors descended on her.

'Get off her, yis leeches!' Valerie shouted, and pushed the man closest. Maisie continued scrabbling for the keys in the wet grass and mud while her youngest stood guard, pushing random strangers away from her.

Suddenly Fred's face appeared through the throng, his strong arms coming around her and hauling her up. 'Let's go,' he barked. He led her and Valerie away, shutting them into his car. He leaned over Maisie's knees and rooted in the glovebox, then presented her with some tissues. 'Here.'

She took them and wiped her knees and hands, as best she could. They were halfway down the road before anyone spoke.

'Where are we going?' Maisie asked.

'To join the search,' he said. 'Isn't that where you were headed?'

'Yes. Thank you.' She was glad he was there.

'Right, then.'

'Ma'sie soaked the journos at the door and gave out shite to the neighbours,' Valerie said, with great pride.

'Did she? Whatever happened to "no comment"?'

'She said that too.'

'Well, that's OK, then.' He winked at Valerie.

He's so good with her, Maisie thought. *Much better than I am.* Danny Fox's voice spoke in her head calling her terrible, vicious, hurtful names, and concluded, *It's your fault, Maisie. It's all your fault.*

'Any news?' Maisie asked, in a bid to silence Danny.

'Nothing yet, Mai, but people are rallyin' and that's good.'

'I want Jeremy's stuff back,' she said.

'You'll get it in good time.'

She was silent for the rest of the journey, looking out of the window at the changed world. *Different but the same*, she thought, as they drove past familiar shops and faces.

The car park was full of people, all walking around in raingear. There were plenty of guards, too, standing around holding walkie-talkies, a few journalists and a TV crew. Two guards created a line between them and the volunteers. Tom was in the centre of the crowd, speaking through a megaphone.

'Can anyone who has a mobile phone with them stand to the left and hold it up, please?'

About twenty of the eighty-strong assembly held up mobile phones and moved to the left.

'Good. Now put this number in your phones.' He called it out. 'Do not dial that number unless you find something relating to the missing boys.' He repeated the number again slowly, while the men and women with phones eagerly keyed it in.

'I want yous to get into teams of five, with either a guard or a volunteer with a mobile phone. We'll assign yous a search area, and after that you walk your area. You stay together and if you find something pertinent you phone it in. Are we clear?'

A few people mumbled something.

'Are we clear?'

The crowd shouted, 'Yes.'

'Grand. Find a team and form a line over there.' He waved towards a guard sitting at one of the pub's outdoor wooden picnic tables.

Tom caught Maisie's eye and made his way over to her. 'The

response has been strong,' he said, gesturing at the volunteers.

'Well, the story is juicy enough to bring out the best and worst of us,' Maisie said.

'I'm sorry about that, Maisie.'

'Me too.'

'I see you've got your rain gear on,' he said.

'We need to help.'

'Good. We've cleared the graveyard, but there's still some of the mountain to cover and the reservoir.'

'And after that?'

'Let's start with the obvious and move on from there.'

'OK.' She spotted Deirdre, Casey and Mel Calley in the crowd, standing close to Jeremy's friends, Dave, Mitch and Jonno. 'Excuse me,' she said to Tom, and walked over to the group.

They saw her coming and even though Jonno Lynch looked like he was going to make a break for it, they didn't move, staring at her, like deer caught in headlights.

Deirdre

'Hi, Deirdre,' Maisie said.

Deirdre nearly died. *Jesus, what am I gonna say?* 'Hi, Mrs Bean.'

'There's six of you and only four of us,' Maisie said, pointing towards Fred and Valerie. 'Why don't you search with us?'

Deirdre's face fell. 'Ah, no, it's OK, Mrs Bean.'

'Please,' Maisie said.

Deirdre looked at Casey and Mel. Casey cast her eyes to the ground. Mel shrugged her shoulders. 'OK.' Deirdre followed Maisie, leaving her friends behind.

Deirdre had been crying all morning. Her father had broken the news about Jeremy and Rave over breakfast. 'I don't want to upset you, love, but I can't have you going into school without telling you.'

Her mother was mortified 'It's not right,' she kept saying.

Deirdre didn't believe them until her dad showed her the newspaper. 'He's not gay, Da.' But even as she said it, something inside her clicked, and every question she'd ever had was answered, every doubt validated. She left the room crying and lay on her bed with her head buried in her pillow. *You can't be, Jeremy. You said you loved me. I asked you. I said if you didn't want me you had to tell me, and you said you did. 'I love you.' That's what you said. I trusted you.*

'Deirdre? Are you all right, love?' her mother asked, through the locked door.

She could hear her father out there beside her mother. 'Ask her if she's been careful with that young fella.'

'I will not. She's not doing anything with him,' her mother hissed.

'He could be carrying something.'

'Don't be so ignorant, for God's sake.'

'Don't be so ignorant? Them gay fellas are dropping like flies.'

'Get down those stairs before I lay hands on you. They're only kids, you stupid man.'

Deirdre didn't leave the room until her dad had gone to work, and even then she ran out of the door before her mother could give her a few quid for her lunch.

At school that day, Principal Young announced during lunch hour that the fifth year and Leaving Cert classes could take a half-day to join the search for their classmates. There was a stampede to the front door. Dave, Mitch, Jonno, Deirdre, Mel and Casey were left sitting around a table in the canteen.

'You goin'?' Dave was the first to speak.

'Of course,' Jonno said. Mitch nodded in assent.

'I'm going,' Casey said. It was the first thing she'd said all morning. Casey had a tendency to bite people's heads off when she was in a bad mood and she was definitely in a bad mood. She had a face like thunder. She didn't eat. She just sat there, giving the evil eye to every kid who dared look her way.

'Me too,' Deirdre said.

Mel's mouth was full of chips so she raised her hand. 'I'm in,' she said, as soon as she'd swallowed them.

'Rave's gonna be seriously pissed off about this gay thing, I'll tell ya that,' Mitch said.

'So is Jeremy.' Tears stung Deirdre's eyes. She didn't know why she'd said it. Who was she protecting? *Me, Jeremy or both of us?* Was he gay? It was all so confusing.

'Yeah, of course, but Rave has a worse temper,' Mitch said.

'It's bullshit, isn't it?' Jonno said.

'Of course it is,' Mitch told him.

'What do you think Beany was doing with the porn, then?' Jonno wondered.

'It wasn't his,' Deirdre said, out of nowhere, and Casey stared straight at her, boring a hole in her with her eyes.

'What?' Dave said, and all of the faces turned to her.

'We found it in a bush and I told him to get rid of it in case little kids saw it.' She was telling the truth: that was what had happened.

'So why'd he keep it?' Dave said.

'He was probably waiting for the bin collection. I don't know.' She was blurring the truth now. They had found the porn but it was months ago. *He kept it in his room.*

'Thank Christ for that. I was beginning to think I was the only non-fudge-packer in the whole of Tallaght,' Dave said.

'I knew it! I just knew it!' Casey exclaimed. 'Rave should sue those newspapers. Bastards.'

Now, walking alongside Maisie, Deirdre felt nervous. She wasn't a fool: she knew why Maisie had asked her on to her team, but words failed her. They walked in silence, a little way behind the policeman and Valerie, as they turned up on to the mountain track ahead.

'I haven't seen you for a while, Deirdre,' Maisie said.

'Just busy with school, Mrs Bean.' Deirdre always called Maisie 'Mrs Bean'. 'Ms Bean' sounded so weird.

'But you and Jeremy, you're still together.'

'The porn wasn't his,' she blurted out, and even before she'd explained, Maisie let out the greatest sigh of relief.

'Oh, thank God,' she mumbled, as though the world was suddenly a brighter place.

But he is gay. He's gay. He's so gay. If I wasn't so worried I'd fuckin' hate you, Jeremy. In fact I do. I hate you, Deirdre thought, but she didn't say anything. Instead she explained the find and said he was making sure little kids didn't see it.

Maisie smiled. 'That sounds like him.' She gave Deirdre a hug. 'Thank you, love. That's a huge relief.'

'Did you hear that, Fred?' Maisie called, to the copper who had talked to them at the school.

'I did, Mai. He's a good boy.'

'Of course he is.' She smiled. 'He's the best.'

'Jesus, Ma'sie, calm down,' Valerie said. 'They're still missing.'

Fred's phone rang and he came to a stop to answer. She and Maisie hurried up to join him where he was standing.

'Right, thanks, Tom. We'll see you up there,' he said, looking sombre.

'What, Fred? What is it?' Maisie asked, the moment he hung up.

'They found the bike.'

'Where?'

'The reservoir.'

Maisie gulped. 'And the boys?'

He shook his head. 'We're calling in the Sub-aqua Unit.'

Deirdre covered her mouth. She could picture the night sky, the tumbling rain, the muck and mud, one boy slipping, the other holding on tight, them both falling in, being dragged by the current, deeper down into the darkness. 'No! No way! Jeremy would never go near the reservoir. He's always been

240

nervous of it. He hated it up there,' Deirdre said, through tears. 'He said it was eerie, especially when it rained.'

Maisie was silent, clearly stunned. Valerie grabbed her mother's hand.

Deirdre felt sick, like she actually wanted to vomit. She covered her mouth with her hand and tried not to cry too loudly.

'Well, you can call in who you like, but he's not there, Fred.' Maisie's voice was high-pitched, verging on hysterical.

'Let's just make sure, Mai.'

Deirdre, Maisie and Valerie followed him to the reservoir. Valerie was silent but Deirdre couldn't help the sobs rising out of her. Maisie put an arm around her, holding her close. 'Don't you fret, Deirdre. They're not down there. I'd know. A mother would know.'

A crowd had gathered at the reservoir. The guards had cordoned off a large area and people were being warned to step back. As they made their way past, they were acutely aware that they were being watched: every word, every movement, every reaction was being monitored, digested and logged. More press descended. Men were setting up cameras, photographers were taking long-distance shots of the cordoned-off reservoir. Reporters were hassling the guards assigned to keep them out. One of the older guards raised the tape, allowing Deirdre, Maisie, Valerie and Fred to pass. Fred escorted them to Tom, who was standing by some men in black rubber suits.

'Where's the bike, Tom?' Maisie said. The policeman pointed to some bushes. 'Are you sure it's Rave's?'

'Certain.'

'Why?'

'There's some marks on the frame that match marks we spotted on the CCTV footage.'

'And you could see it that clearly?'

'Yes, but we also confirmed it with the boys' friends.' He waved to where Mitch, Jonno, Dave, Casey and Mel were huddled together at the foot of the mountain.

Deirdre wished she was with them. *I don't belong here, with his family.*

'He's not in there. I'd know if he was, Tom.' Maisie gestured to the dark water.

Deirdre looked at the rusty bridge, the mountains sloping down to meet the path and at the large expanse of seemingly still deep water. Then her attention was drawn to the gushing noise behind her where the lake fell away, its water cascading to everywhere and nowhere.

The search-and-rescue helicopter came into view and hovered over them, the Dublin coast guard's boat visible from the bridge.

Fred ushered them away. 'Let's get you ladies into the car and turn on the heat.'

'You want to sit with us, Deirdre?' Maisie asked.

'I'll go to me mates if that's OK with you, Mrs Bean.'

'Of course it is, love. Of course it is . . . Thank you, Deirdre.' Maisie drew her in and hugged her tightly. 'They're not in there, Deirdre. We'll get them home.'

Uncomfortable, Deirdre walked away. *I don't know what she's thanking me for. I'm a lying sack of shit. Your son's a homo and I'm a fool. As for you, Jeremy Bean, I really hope you're not in there but that doesn't mean if I see you again I won't kick the shite out of ya.*

She joined her friends and they made their way up the mountain to a spot that offered shelter and a good vantage-point.

'Casey was interviewed by RTÉ. She told them the lads weren't gay and that she was Rave's girlfriend. She mentioned you too. She told them they were all wrong and she wanted them to make it right. She said she loved Rave and asked him to come home. It was cool,' Mel gushed.

'That's great.' Deirdre felt numb. *Maybe Rave will come back to Casey but me and Jeremy are done.* Her heart ached.

Once they'd found the perfect spot, they sat on their school-bags and watched the press, the guards, the sub-aqua team, the boats and helicopters.

'It's like something off the telly,' Jonno said.

'They're not in there,' Dave said. 'They're more likely to find Jimmy Hoffa riding Shergar or Amelia Earhart down there.' Nobody laughed.

Casey started to cry and Deirdre put an arm round her. Mel handed out cigarettes to anyone who wanted one.

Nobody really talked, save for the odd thing about needing to go to the loo or offering chewing gum, a smoke or a piece of chocolate. When a few hours had passed and the crowd below was dispersing, Jonno looked at his watch. It was well past his teatime. His ma would be having a fit but he just sat back, relaxed, as though he didn't care.

'So we're staying,' Dave said, and Deirdre nodded. *I'm not going anywhere. I might hate you but I love you too, Jeremy. You're me best friend, you stupid bastard.* They all settled in, snuggled together, keeping warm, watching the searchlights skim the water and men like seals appear from and disappear into the deep darkness, against the sound of a low-flying helicopter and the whirr of the coast guard's engine. It didn't matter that they were cold and hungry. It didn't matter that they knew in their hearts there was no way their friends were in a watery grave. They stayed until the last man was out of the water and the last light had been turned off.

Chapter Eight

'Today'
The Smashing Pumpkins, 1993

Maisie

MAISIE, BRIDIE, LYNN, FRED and Valerie sat in front of the TV with pizza on their laps, waiting for the news.

'This is a treat,' Bridie said. 'I didn't think I'd like pizza, Lynn, but then Jeremy talked me into pepperoni and it's great. He likes the one with pineapple on it but I can't get me head around that. Where is Jeremy, Maisie?'

'We don't know, Ma. Remember?' Maisie said, and everyone waited for Bridie to absorb the information.

'Oh.' Bridie's eyes welled. 'He's gone off and left us.'

'But we'll find him,' Maisie said. 'Just like we talked about.'

'He'll be on the news now.' Bridie focused on the TV, clearly trying her best to keep up.

'That's right, Ma.'

'I never thought I'd see the day that our Jeremy was on the news,' Bridie said.

'We'll get him back, Ma, I promise you. We will.' Maisie was adamant and Bridie seemed to relax.

As she had sat in Fred's car, watching men search for her son's dead body, Maisie had reached a big decision: she would be positive. *He's not in there. He's so not in there. In fact, if that reservoir was the last place left to be on earth he'd be on Jupiter. A mother knows.* It didn't matter that her skin crawled, her stomach twisted and her heart ached. It didn't matter that every inch of her screamed, 'Oh, no, oh, no, oh, no,' over and over. None of that mattered because they hadn't found any bodies: the boys weren't in that lake. She was determined to wear a smile and whistle a happy tune – despite the deep dread that spread like an infection from her mind into her heart and the very pit of her stomach – because no news was good news. She decided to choose hope. Maisie was good at making decisions like that. When she had been a battered wife, she had decided to cope, to stand tall, to endure, to protect her children, to carry on regardless and, despite all the odds, that was exactly what she'd done. So, sitting in the front seat of Fred's car, she had decided that everything was going to work out. That was Maisie's decision and it was final.

'Does anyone else want another slice before that big lump eats all the pizza?' Bridie said, pointing to Fred, who was angling a large slice to fit into his mouth.

Valerie laughed.

'That's Fred, Ma,' Maisie remonstrated, 'and he's far from a big lump. He's helping us to find Jeremy so please have some respect.'

'Well, there's a cheek in me own house. I didn't see that comin', Lynn,' Bridie said.

Maisie sighed and shook her head. She wasn't in the frame of mind for Bridie's bad behaviour.

'Eat your pizza, Bridie,' Lynn said.

'You're all snotty tonight!'

Lynn raised a finger. 'Enough.'

Bridie bit her lip and sat back in her chair. 'My house,' she mumbled. 'Bought and paid for, thank you very much.'

Fred was quiet, and Maisie was worried about him. *I know*

I've been off with you, and I know you're doing your best. If only you hadn't asked me out. If only we hadn't slept together. Maybe then I could look myself in the mirror without wanting to punch myself in the face. It's all my fault but I'm trying, Fred. I really am.

The news came on and everyone fell silent. Jeremy and Rave were mentioned in the headlines, but then the newsreader launched into a story about Bill Clinton signing a North American Free Trade Agreement.

'Who cares about that?' Valerie said.

'No one, love,' Bridie said.

Maisie couldn't have cared less about Bill Clinton. She only cared about her son. Now his smiling face, alongside Rave's, filled the screen and her heart skipped a beat. *Hello, son. There you are, love.* The newsreader spoke about how long they had been missing, what they were wearing, the bike and how it had been found earlier that day by the reservoir, but all Maisie heard was her son's voice: 'Remember, Grammy, Jeremy Bean loves you.' The woman spoke of the fears that the boys were in the water, how many hours the search had gone on, and Maisie closed her eyes: she saw his bright smile and his thumbs-up.

The woman handed over to a reporter on the site. He was standing against a stark, dark background, only a few people around, most of them police. He described the feelings of the local community, how difficult the search had been and how it had started on foot earlier that day. Then the report cut to an overhead view of the reservoir. She could see Jeremy's friends and Deirdre standing on the hill. *All your friends are waitin' for you, love.*

Now Casey was looking into the camera's lens: 'Rave, I miss you. I love you. Come home.'

Then it was back to the studio. 'Emotions running very high there.'

'Yes, indeed,' the reporter continued. 'It's been an exceptionally trying day for all concerned, not least the mother of Jeremy Bean, who seemed incredibly unhappy with what she saw as press intrusion earlier today.'

Maisie's heart sank. 'Oh, please, don't show it.'

'They can't, Ma'sie. They didn't record it,' Valerie said.

'Thank God.'

'They still think we're knackers, though. It says so in the evening papers.'

It was true: the reporters had presented the plight of the missing boys and their family circumstances with a jaundiced eye. They reported on Rave's junkie father, mentioned that the boys had been missing for more than thirty hours before it was reported. Even Maisie's injuries at the hands of her husband had become part of the story. So, too, had the fact that both boys were brought up in one-parent families and that Maisie worked two jobs.

'They wrote about us like we're scum,' she'd said to Fred earlier.

'They don't know you. They don't live your life. It's easy to judge. It's easy to look down on people, Mai. It's easier than being decent about others and honest about ourselves. It's just the way it is.'

'I know.' She was used to people judging her, looking down on her, pitying and despising her, distancing themselves from her, but that was local judgement. This was national. *Everything is going to be OK. I've decided.*

The reporter moved on: 'Of course, following the press report earlier this morning, rumour has been rife about the nature of the relationship between the two boys and if that relationship has anything to do with their disappearance. The sub-aqua unit and the coast guard will be back at the reservoir at first light, but in the meantime the guards have asked us to urge anyone with any information on the whereabouts of these boys to get in touch. Back to the studio.'

The room was silent. Bridie started to cry. 'He's not in the reservoir, Maisie. If he was in there he'd be drowned. He'd be dead, Maisie. Our boy would be gone.'

Maisie got up and knelt on the floor in front of her. 'They're only checking, Ma. But I know they're not in there. You know why? Because when I close my eyes I can't see him there. Can you, Ma?'

'No,' Bridie said. 'No, I can't.'

'We're pretty good at pretending, Ma, you and me, aren't we?' Maisie said.

'We are, love.'

'But I'm not pretending when I say I know our boy is not in the reservoir. I promise, Ma.'

'But it's bad, love, isn't it?'

'Do you remember when Jeremy was only seven and we went to the zoo, and Valerie was still in the pram?'

Bridie nodded slowly.

'Jeremy ran off to see the monkeys and when we got there he was nowhere in sight. Do ya remember?'

'We ran all over the place. Me heart was crossways.'

'And that nice security guard helped us. We walked everywhere, screaming Jeremy's name. I was crying and Valerie was crying.'

'And I was cryin',' Bridie said.

'And then he woke up under a bench – do ya remember, Ma? He was too hot so he cooled off under a bench and fell asleep. Rolled up in a ball . . .'

'. . . somewhere inside of happy,' Bridie finished, a smile spreading over her face. 'Still, I nearly brained him, the fright he gave us.'

'But do you remember how happy we were when we found him?'

'We were thrilled, Maisie.'

'Hold on to that feeling, Ma.'

'All right, love. I will.'

'He's coming home. I've decided.'

'Good girl.'

Maisie kissed her mother's cheek and stood up. 'Who's for a cup of tea?'

Fred

Fred sat on the outside step finishing a cigarette. He pulled out his mobile phone and made a call to Linda, then lit another. 'Sorry to call so late.'

'You're grand.'

'Any news?'

'Well, your tip paid off. Carina Murphy is currently residing in some hippie religious sect that goes by the name of the Collective just outside Gorey.'

'I've heard of them. They're more Catholic than the pope.'

'And they like growing vegetables, singing, dancing and making jam and, get this, she's called Marianne now. The local lads recognized her photo and paid her a visit. I'm sorry to say that Marianne hasn't seen her son since she left for the commune and she doesn't seem in the slightest bit concerned for his safety.'

'Christ.'

'Some people shouldn't be allowed have kids.'

'Anything else?'

'Not before I left the station, but Tom was still workin' when I left.'

'Thanks . . . Just do me a favour and keep me up to date – I don't want Tom thinking I'm stepping on his toes.'

At that moment he spotted Danny Fox walking towards him. He nearly dropped the phone.

'Will do. Good night, Fred.'

Danny was heavier than he had been the last time they were together. He walked with a pronounced limp and Fred wasn't sure if it was real or just exaggerated for his benefit. He still wore that stupid half-arsed moustache but it was grey, as was

249

his once dark hair. He was still handsome but his weather-beaten face and nicotine-stained teeth and hands had aged him prematurely. He could have passed for fifty.

As Danny approached, Fred widened his stance, ready to do battle.

'Well, it all makes sense now. Livin' here long, are ya?'

'I don't live here.'

Danny eyed him. 'Can I speak to my wife or are you gonna guard the door all night?'

'She's not your wife.'

'Yeah, Inspector Clouseau, she fuckin' is and she will be for as long as she's breathin'.'

He had a point: divorce wasn't legal – Maisie was stuck with him even if it was in name only. Fred took a step closer to him. He towered over Danny, who stumbled back. 'You want to dance with me again, Danny?' Fred said.

'Didn't think ya were up for a twirl without your trusty bat.' He was trying to play the hard man but he was nervous. He would have been insane not to be.

'Oh, I am,' Fred said. 'Any time, any place. How's that leg of yours?'

'I could take your job any time I want,' Danny said. 'I could tell them what you did.'

'What I did?' Fred laughed, but it wasn't funny. *You could take more than my job. I'd do time for what I did to you.* 'That's mad. Why would I do anything to you?'

'That's what I couldn't work out till just now.'

Fred's heart was racing, but he was careful to maintain his cool. 'I thought we agreed that you wouldn't come back to Dublin ever.'

'In case ya hadn't noticed, me son is missin' and even you aren't gonna stop me being here so ya can threaten me all ya fuckin' like. Now, I want to talk to my wife.'

'Stay there. I'll get her.'

'You do that,' Danny said, clearly attempting to regain his

composure but his voice was shaking.

'Step into this house and you'll lose that leg.' Fred pointed to his good one. Danny took another step back.

Maisie was standing at the kitchen counter, her head in her hands, listening to the radio. She looked up to greet him as he came through the door.

'I think if I keep listening maybe the newscaster will tell us something we don't know. Stupid.' She laughed.

'Mai?'

'Yes?'

'Danny's outside.'

If I haven't lost her already I'm gonna lose her now. He moved closer to catch her if her knees gave way.

Maisie

Maisie's face collapsed, her breath quickened, and she held her chest with her left hand. Fred helped her sit down. Tears stung her eyes. Every inch of her wanted to run. *Run, run, run.* She had escaped. He was gone. She'd never wanted to look upon that snarling face again. *Can't, can't, I just can't.*

'Maisie?' Fred said. 'What can I do for you?'

He was so kind and so honourable. She broke down and wept on his shoulder. 'I'm sorry! I'm so sorry I was mean, Fred.'

'Ah, now, stop,' he said. 'Stop right there. You're going through hell, Mai, you've nothing to be sorry for.'

She held on to him tight. *Please, please, please don't leave me alone with him.* Every hurtful thing Danny had ever said or did rolled around her head, so much so it threatened to explode. A searing pain sliced through her left eye. After all this time he could still physically hurt her.

'You don't have to do this. I can send him away,' Fred said.

But Maisie knew she'd have to face him sometime, and she'd sure as hell rather do it when Fred was there. She knew he wouldn't take no for an answer. *Valerie! Oh, no. Valerie.* She had to gain control and get on top of the situation. She needed to delve deeply into her last reserve of strength. She rose up from the chair. 'OK.'

'I'm here.'

'Oh, God.'

'Mai, it'll be all right.'

'I just need a minute.' Seeing Danny would be like seeing a ghost. She needed to prepare herself. 'I'd hoped he was dead,' she said circling the kitchen. 'It seemed like the only explanation. One day he's here terrorizing me, telling me I wouldn't be allowed to live without him, and the next he's gone. I thought he must be dead. I even thought his da might have killed him and maybe he was under his ma's patio or under that fuckin' bird-shit Virgin Mary shrine she has in her garden. I *hoped* he was dead.' She was speaking quickly, and with every word her pace increased until she was almost jogging.

Fred grabbed her and held her still. 'He's not gonna hurt you, Mai. You're not alone.'

'The thing about Danny is he'll do what he wants.'

'I have this under control.'

'I don't want Valerie seein' him.' *I can't let her see him, not like this. She's not ready.*

'I agree.'

She sighed. *Just breathe.* Fred let her go and she moved to the kitchen door. 'She's in her room, Fred. Please make sure she stays there.'

'I will.'

She walked to the front door slowly, carefully, as though she was moving across treacherous ground. She could feel Fred behind her, propelling her forward. She knew he was standing guard at Valerie's room. She put her hand on the lock and turned it. She felt the cold air hit her face and did her best to ignore the pain in her eye as she stood facing Danny for a long three seconds. She took in his weight gain, the second chin he'd developed since they'd last seen one another. His grey hair was alarming. It aged him significantly, as did the stupid moustache, which had never suited him in the first place.

'Long time,' he said, looking her up and down.

'Not long enough.'

'Yeah, well, ya went and lost me son so that's on you.'

'What do you want, Danny?'

'To find me son, even if he is a fuckin' fruit. Thanks for that by the way.'

'He's not—'

'Livin' with two women, what d'ya expect?'

She gulped.

'It was only a matter of time before it all fell apart, wasn't it, Maisie?'

'Good luck with your search.' She moved to close the door.

'Don't you fuckin' dare,' he growled. 'I want to see my little girl.'

'No.'

'You don't say no to me.'

'Yes, I do. No. No. No. No. No.' She could see the curtains twitching. She was grateful the last of the journalists had gone home. They would have had a field day with this: *Wife-beater Comes Home to Settle Scores in the Driveway*. Or maybe they'd paint him as the victim: *Concerned Father Returns to Find Missing Boy: Door Slammed in His Face*.

'I'm comin' back tomorrow and I will see her.'

'I'll make a decision with her tomorrow.'

'Don't test me.'

'Test you?' Something inside her snapped. 'How dare you come to my home and make demands of me? I don't owe you anything. You don't own me. I am my own person. You don't get to talk to me like that. I've moved on, Danny Fox. Maybe I was nothing once but now you're nothing. *Don't test me.* Who do you think you are?' She stepped outside and faced him down, staring him right in the eye, her fists balled, her head, ears and face on fire. 'I'll take a fuckin' hatchet to you, Danny.

I will! I swear it! It's been a long time and I'm not scared of you any more.' She was lying: she was terrified. Her pulse was racing so fast she feared she'd pop a vein.

'Ya should be,' he said, but she wasn't convinced. They were toe to toe. She was pushing forward and he was the one on the back foot.

'Don't you ever walk up to my door again,' she said, in a voice she didn't even recognize.

'I have a right to see Valerie.'

She pushed him backwards down the path and on to the roadway. 'We'll see about that, Danny.'

'If you ever speak to me like—'

He was now standing on the side of the road but she'd turned her back on him and was already walking up the pathway. He'd lost his power over her and in that moment they both knew it. Her pulse slowed. *Nah, you're not gonna do anything. We're done here.*

'Tomorrow, Maisie.' He pointed his finger at her as he used to do, except this time the finger wasn't stuck in her face. This time there was distance and it was more than a pathway: a deep gulf had formed between them. There was no going back.

She watched him walk away, noticing his pronounced limp for the first time. *What happened? Did you get a taste of your own medicine, Danny?*

When he was out of sight she sank to the step. She was shaken but she'd held her nerve. She hugged herself tight and felt freer from him now than she ever had. The pain in her eye was gone. If her son wasn't missing it might have been the best moment of her life. Now it was too cold to stay outside and, anyway, she was on show. She'd figured half the road weren't in front of their televisions that night: they were watching her house, the comings and goings. One of her neighbours could be speaking to the press even as she sat on her step. She stood up and brushed herself down, then went inside.

Fred was still on guard outside Valerie's room. Grateful, she smiled at him.

'You OK, Mai?'

'No,' she said. 'But I'm still standing and that's something.'

'There's something I need to tell you and then I'm going home,' he said. She knew instantly that whatever it was she wouldn't like it. *What now? I don't know if I can take much more.* She followed him back into the kitchen. The house was quiet. Lynn had left an hour earlier to make dinner for her husband; her mother and child were sleeping. It was late. It had been a long day.

He sat opposite her at the kitchen table. 'Do you remember the last time Danny came around here?' he asked.

As if she could forget. 'He put a brick through the window and told me he could just stroll in and kill me anytime. I believed him.'

'Do you remember what you said to your mother that night?'

At first she couldn't. It had been a long time ago and she wondered why he was bringing it up.

'You said you'd have to go back to him. Do you remember?'

She nodded. *Yes, of course.* 'I thought if I didn't go back we'd all be dead. Then he disappeared.'

'I know, Mai.'

'I know you know.'

'No. I mean, I know what he did, I know what was said and I know what he was capable of. Your ma called me the very next morning. She told me everything and she asked for my help. And I know why he disappeared.'

Maisie couldn't believe her ears. 'What did you do?'

Fred didn't look her in the eye. 'I frightened him.'

'What did you do to him, Fred?' she said, with growing unease.

'I followed him from the pub one night. I hit him on the back of the head, knocked him out and put him in the boot of his

car. I drove him to the Dublin Mountains, Maisie. I made him
dig a grave.'

'Jesus Christ almighty.'

'For two hours I made him think he was gonna die. He made
a run for it. I caught him and I had a bat. I beat him so badly I
broke his leg in two places.'

Impossible. Fred is gentle. Danny is the animal.

'I drove the car and stopped about a mile from the hospital.
I opened the boot, and before I walked away, I warned him
that if he ever mentioned my name or if he ever went near
you again I had a grave waiting for him in the Dublin Mountains.'

She felt sick.

'I'm not proud, Maisie. It was the worst thing I've ever done.
I know it was wrong. I crossed a line that I can't uncross but
I'm sorry and I promise you I'm not that man. I swear to you.'
He was begging her but she couldn't take it in. *He broke his
leg in two places. He made him dig his own grave.* Fred tried
to reach for her hand but she pulled away. *Oh, no. Another
violent man.*

Fred

Fred saw the fear in her face. He didn't move a muscle. He
knew she felt threatened. He remained seated, even when she
put herself in the corner. Instead he closed his eyes and pictured
himself standing over Danny, the bat coming down on his leg.
He saw it twist and heard it shatter, then Danny's agonized
screams.

'The second it happened I felt sick, Mai.'

It was his biggest regret and he needed her to understand
that. He had acted the hard man on that porch step with
Danny but it was all a lie. He hated himself for that beating.
Years later it still haunted him. He had nightmares about it.

'You made him dig a grave,' she said quietly.

'I just intended to frighten him but in the end I frightened both of us.'

She shook her head in utter disbelief. 'And Ma knew?'

'For a minute I was a hero, but then she rang the hospital and discovered the damage. She was still grateful but she was weary. Who could blame her?'

'She's scared of you,' Maisie said, and her voice quivered.

'It made me change how I looked at meself. It's my one regret in life, and yet if he was ever a threat to you, I'd go up that mountain and I'd do it again.' He wasn't being macho, he was being honest. That's the thing that worried him most: that if he had to he'd do it again.

'I need you to leave.'

'Mai, please.' He stood up, and as he did, she reared back. He stayed where he was with both hands in the air. 'I'm no threat to you. Jesus, Mai, I'd do anything for you.'

'Go home, Fred.'

His heart burned a hole in his chest. 'I'm so sorry,' he said.

'Get out.' She looked scared and angry, bitter and so very sad. 'Get out,' she roared, tears spilling from her eyes. '"Never trust a man with a beard. He's a man with something to hide" – that's what my mother has always said and she was right.'

'That's it, Mai. That's the worst of me. There's no more. Please.'

'Do I have to call the police?' Her words stung as surely as if she'd slapped him across his face.

'OK. I'll go.'

She stayed in the corner of the room, and as he passed her, she didn't move a muscle. When he was in the hallway he heard her sobs. He wanted to run to her and make everything all right. He wanted to wrap his arms around her and save her, like he'd always saved her, but this time he'd be saving her from himself, and even Fred Brennan couldn't do that.

11 p.m. to midnight, 1 January 1995

Jeremy

It was still raining but not as heavily. The clouds were dissipating and it was dark, except for the moon, whose light was mostly concealed by trees. Jeremy felt as if he was following Rave into the mouth of a monster. He stalled. The wind was like cold breath sending shivers down his back. The leaves, heavy with rain, splattered his face and neck, as Rave beat back clawing branches to form a path through unfamiliar dangerous ground. When he didn't feel Jeremy close he turned to find him. 'Come on.'

'Where the hell are we going, Rave?' Jeremy shouted.

'It's cool. Come on.'

Rave continued to ascend. Jeremy caught up and followed as closely as he could, hunkering low behind his friend. *This is madness. I shouldn't be here. I hate this place – it freaks me out. It's always freaked me out. He knows that!*

As they moved forward the night sky became more obscured by denser woods. *I can't see me feet!* He could feel the undergrowth pulling and tugging at him, trying to trip him up. Every step became harder, the incline steeper. *This is not gonna end well. I just want my bed.* Then, all of a sudden, the ground flattened out and Rave was running through tall trees, past dense, prickly bushes. 'Come on,' he shouted, and Jeremy ran to keep up, afraid that if he didn't he would truly be lost in the woods.

'Rave!' He couldn't see him. 'Rave!' He could feel his pulse beat in his neck. *That's not good.*

When he finally made it into the clearing, Rave was standing there, head back, arms raised, like Sly Stallone in *Rocky*. They were on a tiny stamp of rock but the white moon hung directly over it, as if it was shining just for them. It was blinding at first, but when his eyes became accustomed to the brightness, he moved forward and reached out his hand. 'That's mad,' he said. 'It's like I can almost touch it.'

'Cool, isn't it?' Rave said, and walked to what appeared to be an edge. 'And over there.' He pointed. Jeremy was feeling a little lightheaded so he stayed rooted to the spot, but when he followed Rave's eye-line he could see city lights for miles.

'Welcome to my Dublin.' Rave laughed.

'Wow. How did you know about this?'

'I've been coming up here for months.'

'On your own? Why?'

'Just mooching, following trails, seeing where they'd take me.'

'All alone?' Jeremy said.

'What are you worried about, Beany? D'you think this place is haunted? Wha-ha-ha-ha!'

'Less worried about ghosts than about bumping into the gangs or the IRA burying their dead.'

Rave considered it. 'That's a very good point. Still, there'll be no burying or murdering done tonight. Nobody likes to work in bad weather.' Again, he raised his arms, threw his head back and looked straight at the moon. 'Tonight this place is ours.'

'Only because no one else is mental enough to be up here.'

'You don't like it?' Rave seemed disappointed.

'I do, it's deadly but I'm freezing to death here.'

'Let's fix that.' Rave walked on.

'Oh, come on!' Jeremy said, running up behind him.

'Being up here is like living in space, Beany.'

'It's late, Rave.'

'It's not far.'

'What's not far?'

'Salvation.' Rave slapped Jeremy on the back and grinned.

'Well, don't run off like a bleedin' billy goat again.' Jeremy was worrying about getting down from the mountain.

Rave put an arm around his shoulders. 'We'll do the last bit together.'

His arm felt heavy and good. *Don't sink into him. Don't sink into him. Oh, Jesus, is that a hard-on? Now? In the poxy rain and cold? Why can't you just be normal?* 'Get off,' he said, and playfully pushed Rave away.

For a second, Rave seemed hurt. 'I don't have fleas.'

'As if.' Jeremy grabbed his friend roughly around the shoulders, then shoved him away. Rave smiled.

If only you knew.

'You're getting stronger, Beany.'

I wish.

They walked on. The path was narrow and Jeremy could feel branches sweep close to his face but the ground was more even, as though it was an actual pathway. Rave walked ahead, Jeremy close behind. It was pitch dark again but dry, the trees either side forming a canopy over the boys.

'So, you and Casey did it?' Jeremy said. *That will take my horn down.*

'Yeah. So?' Rave said.

'So you didn't tell me.'

'I don't tell you everything.'

'Clearly.' Jeremy removed a stray twig from his mouth.

'Why? Do ya not believe me?' Rave said.

'Course I do.'

'So what's the problem?'

'No problem.'

'You should do Deirdre. It's great.'

'Shut up.'

Rave laughed. 'According to Casey, she's gagging for it.'

'Seriously, Rave, shut up.'

'I'm only saying.'

'Yeah, well, don't say.'

'What's crawled up your arse?' Rave said.

'Anything could have in this bleedin' jungle.'

Rave laughed. 'We're nearly there, I promise.'

They walked on in silence. Jeremy had no idea what was waiting for him, and although he was fascinated, mostly he worried about getting home. *Ma will be home before me. I'm dead. I'm so dead.* Suddenly Rave was running.

'You promised you wouldn't run!' Jeremy shouted. When Jeremy emerged from the dense wood into another small clearing, Rave had stopped, his hands on his hips. This time, instead of the moon being the focus, it was a small broken-down wooden cabin. Rave walked up to its rickety door, took a key out of his pocket and opened the padlock.

'What's this?' Jeremy said.

'Home, sweet home.' Rave pushed open the door.

Jeremy stood on the threshold, his mouth wide open.

'Come in.' Rave took a lighter out of his pocket and lit a few candles resting on a wooden shelf, then a bigger, fatter one in the centre of a large table by the window.

It was a tiny room with a small, antiquated wood-burning stove. To the right, a sleeping bag and a pillow lay on the floor and a big wooden bench stood against the window. Hooks had been screwed into the wall, with rusty tools on them, and it was dotted with long nails sticking out. Rave's clothes hung from a line he'd made with old nylon rope. He kept a pair of boots and runners tucked neatly side by side underneath. Jeremy closed the door behind him and took it all in.

'I think the nails were used to hang animal heads – you know, like game hunters. It definitely belonged to a hunter,' Rave said.

'Or a psychopath,' Jeremy said.

'Either way he's not coming back. I put that lock on it over the summer. No one's been here. It's all mine.'

In the corner there was a case with Rave's toiletries and underwear in it. The clothing was folded neatly, the toothpaste, mouthwash, soap and sprays stored in separate clear plastic bags. There was a black plastic brush in the corner opposite.

His stereo was on the floor near the sleeping bag and beside that there was a stack of books, CDs and a stash of batteries to last a year.

'Jesus,' Jeremy said. 'You're serious!'

Rave smiled. 'I can do it up. There's even running water over there.' He pointed to a tap. He had placed a plastic basin beneath it and beside that he stored cleaning products. The place was old and tired but it was as clean as Rave could possibly make it. *He must have scrubbed it for weeks*, Jeremy thought. He could smell furniture polish. Rave had polished every single surface over and over again. The smell was ingrained in the wood. 'It's good, isn't it?' Rave said, and he looked to his friend for validation. Jeremy didn't know what to say. He wasn't even sure what he thought. 'Yeah, it's deadly.'

'Come on, I'll make a fire,' Rave said, grabbing some firelighters from beside the stove and pulling out his lighter again. 'Sit down.' He pointed to the sleeping bag. 'Make yourself at home.'

'This is totally nuts but OK.'

Rave laughed. 'Take the bag off your back and let's get some of those sandwiches out. I'm starving.'

Jeremy did as he was told. *Do not get another hard-on, Jeremy Bean. I am warning you. Just be cool. Super-cool. Can you be super-cool for once in your life, please?*

When the fire was lit, the room warmed up quickly, even though there was a hole in a corner of one of the windows. Rave had shoved a sock into it, then taped newspaper over it on both sides.

'I'll get around to fixing that.' He sat beside Jeremy on the sleeping bag. Jeremy handed him a sandwich from the backpack.

'Any vodka with that?' Rave asked.

'Haven't you had enough?'

'Come on, man, I'm sober now.'

'Well, we still have to scale down bleedin' Everest to get home.'

'I know you're freaked, and you want to go home to mind your grammy because you're Mr Reliable, but just one drink to celebrate.'

Jeremy relented and handed him a small half-full bottle of vodka.

'Grab yourself a bottle. Let's do a toast.'

Jeremy took another bottle from the bag. Rave raised his and Jeremy reciprocated.

'To my new gaff and to us,' Rave said, and they clinked bottles. Rave slugged; Jeremy sipped. Rave picked up half the sandwich. 'Here, share it.' Jeremy took a bite and Rave grinned.

Jeremy looked around at the candles flickering, the stove burning, and through the recently cleaned window he admired the full moon and the city lights. He was sitting beside his best friend with a cheese and ham sandwich in one hand, the vodka in the other. Even strait-laced, follow-the-rules, don't-disturb-the-peace Jeremy Bean had to admit this was cool. He looked to Rave, who was even more handsome in candlelight. *It's perfect.* 'Very cool.' He relaxed a little more and Rave punched him playfully.

'Fuckin' A it's cool.' He leaned over to his stereo and pulled a CD from the pile. 'How do you feel about a little *Unforgettable Fire*?'

'Old school. I like it.' *Old school! What did you say that for? What's wrong with you? You sound like a head case. This is starting to feel like a date. My head is melted. Don't relax. Do not relax.* Rave sat down beside him, brushing up against him. *Keep it together, Jeremy, keep it together!*

They sat eating the sandwich and every now and then Rave took a slug of vodka until the bottle was empty.

'This is just between you and me,' Rave said.

'Why?'

'I tell the lads about it, soon everyone will know and it'll be over.'

'What about Casey?'

'No. This is just for us, Beany.' Jeremy's heart skipped a beat. 'Our secret. Yeah?'

'Yeah,' Jeremy agreed. His voice was so hoarse he wasn't sure that Rave had heard him, so he nodded vigorously.

'It's going to be great,' Rave said. 'It's only going to be good from here on in. I'm gonna paint the place, get rid of those nails and stick some posters up. In the spring and summer this place is gonna be a dream.'

'It could be really cool.' Jeremy found himself getting excited.

'We've a year and a half left in school, Beany. I can do a year and a half here easy.'

'And then what?' Jeremy said. He worried about school ending. He worried that being Rave's best friend was the best thing that would ever happen to him. He feared that once school was over and the world opened up he would lose him. He could say goodbye to the others, even Deirdre, but he couldn't imagine his world without Rave.

'I dunno. London maybe?'

'Doing what?' *What about me? Where am I going to be?*

'Anything. Casey's da says there's loads of work on the buildings.'

'I can't see you as a builder.' That seemed so bleak, not like Rave at all. *It has to be better than that.*

'We could work on the boats, like you said.'

Jeremy's heart danced in his chest. *It's gonna be OK.* 'Best idea ever,' he said, and laughed.

'But I'll be the captain,' Rave added.

'No way. I'm the captain.'

'We'll both be captain and we'll sail around the world in one of those luxury cruisers, livin' the life.'

Jeremy closed his eyes and saw them on a beautiful boat on dazzling water under a bright blue sky. 'OK, let's do that. Let's find out what we need to do that. I'll study my balls off, man. I'll do whatever it takes.'

Rave grabbed Jeremy's bottle and drank from it. 'We'll talk to the careers guidance counsellor tomorrow.'

'That's what we'll do.' He really hoped that Rave wasn't drunk again, or messing with him, or just high on the polish fumes of his new home. *I could see myself doing that, I really could – and with Rave, Jesus, that would be amazing.*

Rave jumped up. 'Excuse me, Beany, I need a wee.'

'Where are ya gonna go?' Jeremy glanced around the room.

'Out there, among nature.' Rave walked out of the door and closed it tight after him, leaving Jeremy alone to savour their secret hideaway. *This is cool. It's so cool.* He leaned back against the wall. With the Edge's guitar in his ears and the city lights in his eyes, he was warm, cosy and hopeful. For a second he allowed himself to imagine the future with his best mate, as they travelled the world together, sailing on crystal blue seas. *Someone has to do it, why not us?* He'd be captain and Rave would be the engineer, or Rave could be captain if he really wanted and Jeremy could be the cook. *I'd be happy doing anything as long as we're together.* He imagined exploring exotic countries – he could almost feel the warm sun on his back and the sea air filling his lungs. His great-grandfather had been a fisherman. The sea was in his blood. It made sense. It was possible.

He could see himself on the deck of the boat, Rave at his side, sailing away from Ireland towards somewhere bigger, better, somewhere he could be who he really was and Rave would understand. The world would open his eyes and he'd accept Jeremy. Rave wouldn't be afraid of him. Jeremy might even find love and he'd get over his crush and they'd be best friends for ever. It was a dream but it could happen if he focused, worked hard enough and wanted it badly enough. *Why not?* He lay down on the sleeping bag. For just one second he pictured Rave lying beside him: he was putting his hand through Rave's hair, sweeping it behind his ear, looking into his handsome face and his grey eyes and kissing him, deep and long and—

Oh, Jesus . . . I told you not to relax. Get down! He slapped his dick and pushed it, holding it down. It bulged against his hand. *Oh, God, please, just go!* He felt that horrible fit-to-burst sensation and considered running out into the cold night and having a wank in the wild. *He'll never see. I'll say it's my stomach. Oh, God, what if there's something out there? That's all I need, something to chomp off me knob. Maybe that would be for the best.* Jeremy placed the rucksack on his crotch and leaned heavily on it. He heard the rain hammer on the roof before he looked up from his lap and saw it pour from the sky.

'Oh, no.'

Rave ran in and slammed the door. He was soaked. 'Holy shit. It's mental out there.' He pushed his wet hair back from his face and tucked it behind his ear, just as Jeremy had done in his fantasy. *You're killing me, you're actually killing me.* He went to the line and grabbed a clean towel. Jeremy looked away as his friend stripped down to his jocks. He felt sick and his hands trembled, even though he was holding on to the rucksack as tightly as he could.

'Beany, we might have to stay here till morning,' Rave said, wrapping himself in the towel. He moved over to the fire and warmed his hands over it.

'I can't,' Jeremy said.

'We have no choice. There's no way we'll make it down safely in that weather.' Rave sat down beside his friend.

'I need to go,' Jeremy said.

'You're not going anywhere till this rain stops.'

Jeremy looked out over the soaking city. The rain battered the roof with such ferocity that Rave had to turn up the music. *He's right. Oh, God almighty. I'll have to stay here.*

Rave laughed. 'Cheer up, Beany. You look like I just killed a kitten. We'll sneak back first thing in the morning. What's the worst that can happen?'

Oh, I don't know, I might just start crying, and if I do, I'll never stop or, worse, I could just break down and tell you I love you, I've always loved you. I always will. 'Nothing,' Jeremy said. 'It'll be fine.'

Rave smiled. 'Best night ever.'

THURSDAY,
5 JANUARY 1995

Chapter Nine

'Outshined'
Soundgarden, 1991

Maisie

FOR JEREMY'S THIRTEENTH BIRTHDAY Maisie paid a magician to entertain the kids. It was her first children's-party hire: he sounded like such an accomplished and nice man on the phone, and his price was so reasonable it meant she could go all out on the food.

It was a huge mistake. The Amazing Antony was a retired bank manager who knew exactly four card tricks, used a child's magic set his wife had bought him for Christmas, and his balloon animals consisted of a snake, a snail and something he referred to as a dog but looked more like a chair. He wore a pressed suit under his red cape, and a purple pointed hat that looked less fairy-tale wizard than Ku Klux Klan. It was disconcerting but he seemed genuinely excited to be there, and it was obvious he really wanted the kids to have a good time.

'Are you ready for the show of your lives, kids?' he said, seating them in a row in front of him.

'Yeah,' Valerie and Bridie shouted. No one else answered him. Maisie clapped a little too enthusiastically to conceal her nerves.

'What kinds of tricks would you like to see, kids?' he said.

'You disappearing,' Dave responded. The only boy who didn't laugh was Jeremy.

'Oh, that's a really hard one,' he said.

'Not really,' Dave said. 'The door is just behind you.' The boys laughed again. Dave was on a roll.

'Oh, yes, very good.' He was looking flustered. 'Now, how about a card trick?'

Maisie felt her stomach twist. She wasn't sure whom she felt sorrier for, the Amazing Antony or poor Jeremy, who had turned red-faced while his eyes filled with tears. When the Amazing Antony dropped the deck of cards, Jeremy stormed out of the living room and slammed his bedroom door. The magic act was going nowhere so the lads took the opportunity to pile into the sitting room and turn on the TV. Her boy was crying freely in his room when she knocked.

'It's going terrible, Ma.'

'I'm so sorry, love. I blew it big-time.' She put her hands up in the air.

'I just want them to go home.'

'They can't go now. Your grammy's been baking all morning and she's still at it.'

'They're watching TV, Ma.'

'That's not so bad.'

'It's *Murder She Wrote*.' He could hear it as clear as day from the living room.

'Oh, right.'

Maisie sat on the bed beside him. She didn't try to hug him. He was too upset for that.

'I'm thirteen! What were ya thinking?'

'I don't know. I forget you're growing up.'

'I'm a man now, Ma.'

'Don't get ahead of yourself, son.'

'I'm not a baby, though.'

'I'm sorry.'

'Dave is going to make fun of me for the rest of me life. Even Jonno's ma wouldn't hire a mental case like yer man.'

He was right. She knew he was. She needed to salvage it with no time or budget. She racked her brain. They were too old for traditional games but she'd read an article that had made her laugh a few weeks previously on her break in the dental surgery. A female journalist had bemoaned the childish ways of her boyfriend. The article was entitled, 'When the Boy Becomes a Man . . . Maybe Never'. Her boyfriend was twenty-eight, and his favourite occupation was to compete with his mates doing the most ridiculous things. She had listed every inane and insane thing they had done and rated it. 'I have an idea.'

'What is it?'

'An eating contest.'

'What?'

'There will be three rounds. The first one is to determine how many crackers you can eat in a minute.'

'Easy.'

'You'd think so, but it's really hard, trust me.'

'OK.' He wasn't sure.

'The second is drinking raw eggs.'

'Ugh.'

'I know.'

'I like it. Go on.'

'The third is who can eat the hottest chilli in the world.'

'Do we have the hottest chilli in the world, Ma?'

'No, but it's really hot.'

'OK.' He didn't sound convinced.

'Wanna try it?' she asked hopefully.

'OK.'

Maisie raided the press and fridge, then sat the boys around the table. She explained the rules and waited for a reaction.

'Sounds pretty simple,' Mitch said.

'OK, then, Mitch, you go first.' Maisie said.

'Grand.'

'When I press this timer, you start. Eat as many crackers as you can in a minute.' She pressed the buzzer and Mitch took off like a champion. The first two went down fairly easily, but after that he was coughing and spluttering yet he kept shoving them in. The boys were laughing as he choked.

'. . . five, six, seven . . .'

'Water!' he gasped. The lads counted as he valiantly struggled on, their excitement growing and their voices louder.

'. . . eight, nine, ten . . .'

'No water,' she said, and the lads clapped.

'Ah, man.' He nearly choked, sending the lads into fits of giggles.

'. . . eleven, twelve . . .'

He kept going, the lads shouting him on, his mouth so full he couldn't close it.

'Thirteen!'

He was trying his very best to jam in the fourteenth when the buzzer went.

'Stop!' Maisie called, as referee.

The lads cheered and Rave whistled. Bridie gave Mitch a glass of water.

'Good work, son,' she said, as he spat the guts of fourteen crackers into the sink.

Rave managed eleven, Jeremy nine and Jonno didn't get past five. Dave got to twelve just as the buzzer went. He was gutted. Mitch celebrated by punching himself in the gut. 'Bring it on!' He did a victory lap of the kitchen table. 'Next!' he shouted.

The raw-egg challenge made Jonno and Jeremy gag so much their lips didn't even touch the glass. The more they gagged the louder the lads laughed. Dave managed to drink three raw eggs before he threw in the towel. 'I can't. I just can't.' Mitch drank four, then brought up the lot. The lads loved that. Rave managed five without breaking a sweat and won hands down.

The final challenge was the one that Maisie really built up.

She put on her Marigold gloves for effect and held up a Scotch Bonnet chilli. 'This chilli could burn the eye out of a tiger. It's so hot it could stop an elephant's heart. This chilli could change your lives, boys, and not for the better.'

'Jesus!' Jonno whispered.

'Cool,' Mitch said.

'Are you ready to do this?'

They nodded.

'I can't hear you.'

'Yes! Yes! Come on, yes!' Mitch shouted. 'Let's do it.'

The lads laughed nervously.

She cut the chilli slowly, deliberately and with great flair. They all sat head to head around the table, focused on Maisie and her deadly chilli. Bridie leaned in with a fresh tray of muffins, filling the boys' noses with the scent of chocolate.

'I saw a man cry an ocean and jump into a lake after eatin' one of those. He was a wild man after that,' Bridie said.

'This is serious. This is the big one. So, who's brave enough to go first?' Maisie said.

'It's not a case of brave enough, Maisie, it's a case of mental enough,' Rave said, and everyone turned to Mitch.

'Count me in,' he said.

She winked at him. 'Good man.' She placed the piece of chilli on a plate and handed it to him. She took off the glove and shook his hand. 'Just in case. It's been nice knowing you, Mitch.'

'You too, Ms Bean.' He gulped, cracked his fingers and stretched his neck.

'You ready?' Rave whispered.

'I'm ready. Give us the glove, Ms Bean.'

She handed it to him and he put it on. Then he picked up the chilli and popped it into his mouth. The lads leaned in. Maisie crossed her fingers behind her back, hoping that the chilli was a hot one. For a second or two he seemed perfectly fine. 'Easy!' Then his face went flaming red and he started to gasp. 'Me lips! Me lips! I can't feel me lips! Water, water!' He was holding his mouth and running around the table, like his arse was on fire. The other boys thought it was hysterical. Dave was laughing so hard he was slapping himself.

'Oh, no, seriously, me tongue! Oh, me tongue!'

Jeremy was crying with laughter.

No one else tried the chilli. They didn't have to: Maisie had triumphed.

After that the boys sat around the table eating pizza, muffins, sweets and birthday cake, reliving every moment of the previous hour's entertainment. Mitch couldn't taste any of it, which made everything taste all the sweeter for his friends.

'Best laugh ever,' Dave said, as he was leaving.

'Your ma is seriously cool,' Rave said, and Mitch agreed.

That night Maisie tucked Valerie into bed. 'Look, Ma'sie, it's Rover the chair.' She was showing Maisie her balloon animal.

'Did ya like the Amazing Antony?'

'No, but he was really nice.'

Maisie kissed her daughter goodnight and met her son in the hallway. 'Did you have a nice birthday?'

'Best birthday ever, Ma.'

'Good.' She sighed a happy sigh.

He walked to his room, and just before he went in, he said, 'Best ma ever.'

She was so happy she felt like weeping. 'You'd better not forget it.'

Maisie woke up on a tear-soaked pillow, thinking about that day. She got up, put on her dressing-gown and a pair of socks, instead of slippers, glanced in the mirror, tugged a brush through her unruly hair, and walked to the kitchen.

There, she found Tom with Valerie.

'Morning, Maisie.' Tom raised his mug of tea in a salute.

'Oh, God! Sorry,' she said. 'I didn't know we had company.' Thank God she'd brushed her hair. It was something.

'We have some good news, Maisie.' Tom was grinning.

'You've found them?' Hope flooded through her.

'No, but we will. Rave used his bank card last night in Blessington.'

'Are you sure it was him?'

'We caught him on camera.'

'Was Jeremy there?'

'The cameras only pick up the person using the machine.'

'OK.'

'If he needed money it was to buy something so we're canvassing all the local shops today. I'm heading down there myself. In the meantime I think it's time for an appeal. Are you comfortable with making one on camera?'

'Whatever it takes.'

'Good.'

She sat down on the chair. 'This is good news.'

'It means they're not in the reservoir,' Valerie said.

Tom put his tea down and met Maisie's eye. 'It means Rave isn't in the reservoir. It's unlikely that Jeremy is, but until we get an official sighting, we're going to keep looking, albeit on a scaled-down basis.'

'OK, but Rave would never leave him.' Maisie smiled. 'He's not in the reservoir.' She paused. 'It's not good news. It's brilliant news.'

'I'll schedule the appeal for four o'clock. That gives the TV and radio stations plenty of time to package it for the six o'clock news.'

'Fine. Great. Whatever you need.'

He walked around the counter and sat in the chair beside Maisie, facing her. 'I spoke with your husband at the station last night.'

'Oh.'

'Look, Fred has filled me in a little on why you pair separated but, Maisie, you should know he wants to be part of the appeal.'

'No. No way. He'll drive Jeremy away.'

'My dad is here?' Valerie said.

Maisie's heart dropped into her stomach. She turned to her daughter so quickly that, for a second, she thought she'd pulled a muscle. 'I'm sorry, love, I was going to tell you.'

'When?'

'This morning, first thing.'

'Well, thanks! Thanks a lot!' she shouted, and ran out of the room.

'I'm sorry, that was clumsy of me,' Tom said.

'It's not your fault. I should have told her last night. I was just preoccupied.' The fight with Fred flooded back to her.

'Fine, we'll let him attend but keep him off the podium. Don't worry, Maisie, he'll be managed. Speaking of which, where is Fred?' He checked his watch and started to leave. Maisie followed him into the hall. 'Ask him to talk you through the press conference, OK?' His hand was already on the door.

'Who is appealing to Rave?'

'I'm afraid it'll be just you and me, Maisie.'

'What about Sid? Surely he's well enough now.'

'He's in surgery today, having the leg off.'

'Oh, God.'

'There's no way he's going anywhere, and the mother has made her feelings on the subject very clear. Marianne doesn't have any children.' He opened the door and waved. 'I'll see you at the press conference.'

He was halfway down the path when she shouted after him, 'Who's Marianne?'

'Fred will fill you in.' He was in his car and gone before she could ask anything else.

Valerie

Valerie wouldn't talk to her mother. She sat on her bed and faced the wall. Maisie took the time to clear up the mess in her younger child's room. 'I'm sorry,' she said, picking up dirty clothes from the floor.

'You're not sorry. You're only sorry you were caught.'

'That's what I say to you.'

'Yeah, well . . .'

Maisie sat down, hugging Valerie's dirty socks. 'Valerie, you're not angry at me. You're angry because your da is back and you don't know how to handle it. I don't know how either.'

Valerie's eyes filled and her lip trembled. She just couldn't push down her emotion no matter how hard she tried. 'I just want Jeremy home and him gone and things to be like they were.'

'Me too,' Maisie said.

'I don't want to see him, Ma.' She was lying: she did want to see him and she felt really guilty about that. *He really hurt me, Ma. He really hurt Jeremy, too, but what if he's changed? What if he's sorry and he wants to make it up to us? What if he's lonely and nobody cares about him?*

'It's your choice, Valerie.'

'Jeremy says he's evil – he says if he shaved off his hair he'd have "666" written on his head – but I don't think he ever did anything bad to me, did he, Ma?'

'No, love.'

'I still don't want to see him. Jeremy would go mad if I did.'

'But this is not about what Jeremy wants, love. This is about you.'

Valerie sighed. 'I don't remember him, not really. I don't even know who he is, Ma.'

'Valerie, if you do want to see him you can, and no one will blame you or fight with you. He's your da and you're entitled to meet him.'

Valerie could see that hadn't been easy for her mother to say, and it wasn't easy for her to admit her true feelings. Tears streamed down her face. 'Maybe just to say hello.'

'OK, love.'

Maisie was uncomfortable, Valerie could tell, but she smiled anyway. 'Ma, will you be there?'

'I won't leave you alone for a second.' She squeezed Valerie's hand.

'And maybe Fred could come too.'

'We can ask him.' Maisie dropped her gaze to the floor.

'Doesn't mean I want him movin' in or anything.'

'Understood.' She stood up. 'OK?'

Valerie wiped her nose with her hand. 'I don't love me da. I never could. I just . . . I dunno . . .'

'You don't need to explain, love.' Maisie hugged her daughter. 'I love you. I don't say it enough so I'm gonna say it more. I promise.'

'I love you, too, Ma, even though you're a pain in the . . . swiss.'

Maisie laughed. 'Thanks.'

'Notice how I didn't say "arse"?' Valerie said.

'I did, and I was very impressed.'

'I'm gonna do better, Ma,' Valerie said. 'I'm gonna try.'

Maisie kissed her cheek. 'You're my baby.' She left the room.

Valerie lay down on her bed and closed her eyes. She tried to imagine what it would be like to stand in front of her father but all she felt was anxiety. She tried to picture him but, as hard as she tried, she couldn't conjure up a clear face. She had seen photos years ago, before her mother had burned them all, and she had a fuzzy recollection of the man in the flesh, but she'd been a toddler when he'd vanished. She wondered if she'd recognize him. *Does he look even a little like me?* He certainly wouldn't recognize her. She could have walked past him on a deserted street and he wouldn't have known her. She wondered how she'd feel when she met him. Maybe she'd be revolted, like her grammy. Or angry, like Jeremy. Or even terrified, like her mother. Or, worse, maybe she'd be happy. Her stomach somersaulted.

The thing that set Valerie apart from the other Beans was that she had loved him. She'd once thought he was the best thing in the whole wide world. She remembered the warm feeling she'd had when he'd laughed at her and ruffled her hair. She remembered him lifting her high and swinging her around while she screamed, 'More, Daddy, more!' She remembered travelling around the streets of Tallaght on his shoulders. She'd liked the view from up there and the feeling of his strong arms wrapped around her legs holding them tight to his chest. All the bad stuff was just a fog and second-hand scary stories told by Jeremy.

She didn't know if she really wanted to see him or not. She might not go through with it. She was scared but she was also curious. She just wasn't sure in what measure. There were things about her that she didn't see in Jeremy, her mother or Grammy. She wondered if she'd see any similarities between herself and him, and if she did, would it mean she was a bad person? Jeremy said there was nothing good in her dad, and although her mother had never said anything like that, she had never mentioned anything good about him either. *What if we're the same?* She couldn't remember his voice. *I wonder what he sounds like? What if I love him all over again? What if I think he's the greatest thing ever? What happens then? Will he hurt me like he hurt Jeremy? And what about Jeremy?* She thought about Jeremy for a long time and what he'd say. *He'd hate this. So you shouldn't have fucked off, Jeremy.* He'd tell her she had no business being around her da. *So come on home if you care so much.* She felt like bursting into tears, running a marathon, jumping the Great Wall of China, flying to the moon and curling into a ball, hiding in the darkest, deepest hole and burrowing to the centre of the earth all at once. She wanted to shout and, at the same time, be very, very quiet. She wanted to be still and jump up and down.

It was all too much so she walked around her room in circles, bit her nails down to the quick, and when her thumb refused to stop bleeding, she finally let go and cried till her jaw ached, her eyes burned and her head throbbed.

Enough, Valerie.

When she heard her grammy going to the toilet, she left her room and called, 'Are ya all right, Grammy?'

'Ah, I'm grand, Jeremy love,' Bridie said, from the bathroom.

Valerie leaned on the door, and when it became obvious that Bridie was in there for the long haul, she joined her mother in her grandmother's room. Valerie helped pick out Grammy's outfit, and Maisie offered to show her how to do her hair just the way she liked it.

Bridie was cooperative while they helped her dress and it was almost like the good old days before her mind had begun to erode. Now she was sitting on the chair in front of her dresser mirror, looking at herself. 'I like this white blouse,' she said to Valerie.

'That's why I picked it.' Valerie pulled a pale pink cardigan from its hanger in the wardrobe and threaded her grandmother's arms into it. Then Maisie blow-dried Grammy's hair, and instructed Valerie on how to put up a bun.

'She learned that from an air hostess called Trixie,' Bridie said. 'Trixie was her name – you couldn't make it up.'

'No, Ma, I learned how to do it in the hairdressing school. I taught Trixie how to do it when she got the air-hostess job, remember?'

'Oh, yeah,' Bridie said, 'but "Trixie"! I mean, why would you do that to a child?'

Valerie laughed. 'It's not as bad as calling a kid "Assumpta" or "Jacinta".'

'Ah, I like "Jacinta",' Bridie said.

'Or "Bridie". Sorry, Grammy.'

'Ah, no, love, that's fair. "Bridie" is a desperate name. Me mother's mother was Bridie and she didn't even like her that much. She probably picked it because she was too cheap to buy a baby name book.'

'I don't think they had them back then,' Maisie said.

Valerie laughed. 'In the stone age.'

'Ha-ha! You can laugh now, Valerie Bean, but it passes in a

flash, this life of ours. You'll blink and twenty years will have gone by and the world will have changed and I'll be pushing up daisies.'

'Ah, don't say that, Ma.'

'Why not? It's true. I don't mind, love. Rather that than sit there dribbling.' Her eyes swam with tears but she smiled anyway. 'Quick is the best.'

Maisie allowed Valerie to secure Grammy's bun. 'Good job,' Maisie said.

Grammy smiled. 'Ah, lovely, you've got your ma's way with hair. You're a very good girl, Valerie.' She held her granddaughter's cheeks and leaned forward to kiss her forehead.

Grammy looked like her old self, pretty and light, and for the first time that day, Valerie felt happy. Despite the sadness, fear and apprehension, the insane crying and stubby sore fingers, it had turned into a nice morning.

Maisie

Lynn arrived after eleven, complaining about being delayed at the GP. Maisie could hear her, bustling about the kitchen helping Bridie make tea, while she spoke to Lorraine at the dental surgery about needing some more time off.

'Of course, anything you need, Maisie. It's terrible, awful, I mean the things they're sayin'. We want you to know we're all behind you one hundred per cent. You're a lovely ma, a great ma and, well . . . that's it. Sorry. We miss you.'

'Thanks, Lorraine.' She said goodbye and walked into the hallway with the phone in her hand. Lynn was frying something and Maisie could smell bacon.

'This will put meat on your bones, Valerie Bean.'

'I'm starving, Lynn.'

'Good girl. Set the table, and, Bridie Bean, stay away from the fridge. No cheese for you today.'

Maisie went to the front door and opened it. The clouds had

lifted, revealing a white and silver sky. She sat on the step and studied the phone. Then she pulled the card with Fred's number from the pocket of her trousers and reviewed it. He had done something terrible, inconceivable. *He did it for me and for my kids. I got to be free of Danny. I have a life. My kids are happy – at least, they were . . . When I get you home, Jeremy Bean, I'm going to kill you.* Fred had always been kind to her. He had protected her from Danny, and even Valerie had asked for him to be there when she met Danny. Maisie needed him on this day of all days . . . but even though he had done what he did for her, he had still done it.

She dialled his number. He picked up after two rings.

'Detective Brennan here?'

'It's Maisie.'

'Mai.' He sounded relieved.

'Rave took money out in Blessington last night.'

'I know – Linda called. It's positive news.'

'There's a press conference on later. I need to prepare for it.'

'Would you like me to ask one of the other lads to come?'

'Valerie was hoping you'd be there.'

'Valerie?'

'She's seeing her father today. He's coming.'

'He's not making the appeal – Jeremy will run a mile if he sees him.'

'No, he'll just be there in the background.'

'OK.'

'So will you come back, just for today?'

'Just for today?'

'Yeah.'

'I'm already here, Mai.'

She looked up to see him stepping out of his car halfway down the street.

She was gazing at her feet when he sat beside her. 'You were outside the whole time?'

'No. I had one of the lads watch the house last night. I

took over at seven. Not taking any chances with Danny Fox back.'

'He's no threat to us any more, Fred.'

'I'm no threat either, Mai, I promise ya that.'

'I believe you, I do. I just can't get me head around—' At that point she looked up and saw Fred's clean-shaven face. 'Jesus.' Her hands automatically covered her mouth. 'You're so white.'

'That's the look I was going for.' Without the whiskers concealing it, he had a wide, brilliant smile.

'You look ten years younger.'

'Well, I feel a hundred years old.' His eyes were sad.

'You shaved because of what I said.'

'"Never trust a man with a beard"? I shaved all right, but not because of some stupid saying.'

'It's not stupid.'

'Right. Well, not because of that.'

'What, then?'

'I was still grieving Joy back when I did that to Danny. I couldn't save her but I thought I could try to save you. I crossed a line, no doubt about it. I went to counselling. I made a mistake but I made peace with it. It's not who I am. I won't be defined by it.' He stood up and faced her. 'This is me, Mai. You get what you see, so if you can't move past that night, I'll accept it, and as soon as we find Jeremy I'll move on.' He pushed open the door. 'Now, if you'll excuse me, I smell a fry.'

He left her sitting on the step, thinking about what he'd said, and despite everything that was going on Maisie Bean found herself smiling.

When Maisie finally made it into the kitchen, Lynn and Fred were hovering over a map.

'If the boys are in Blessington and they ditched the bike, they either thumbed a lift or walked there. If they thumbed a lift, surely that person would have come forward by now, and if they stashed the bike and walked from the Bohernabreena

Road, the shortest route is at least eleven miles, which would take approximately three and half to four hours, maybe more with the weather conditions, and the question is why?'

'Maybe there's a girl,' Lynn said. She was studiously ignoring any implication that Jeremy was gay.

'Even if there is, why didn't they cycle rather than walking?'

'Maybe they did take a lift and the person left the country the next morning,' Lynn said.

'Maybe.' He sighed. 'Maybe something else . . .'

Maisie used the moment to divert the conversation. 'How long would it take to drive to Gorey from here?'

'Not long, depending on which part.'

'The part where Carina Murphy lives.'

'Now, Mai . . .'

She held her hands up. 'I know what you're going to say, Fred, but please hear me out.'

He crossed his arms over his chest.

'Rave deserves to have a parent at that conference, asking him to come home.'

'I know he does, but it's not possible.'

'Everything is possible. I just want to talk to her. Five minutes.'

'I don't know . . .'

'She's not the fuckin' Queen of Sheba, Fred. She's a mother who has abandoned her son once already and now she's doing it again when he needs her most, except this time she's being supported.'

He rubbed his new chin, sniffed and pulled at his nose. 'Right then, five minutes.'

'I'll get my coat.'

Lynn agreed to watch over Bridie, who was happy, having disappeared into the TV.

Maisie found Valerie in her room. 'Fred and I are going for a drive if you're up for it?'

'You're going to find Rave's ma?'

Maisie nodded.

'Is she a Moonie?'

'I don't know what she is, love.'

'Nah, thanks. Noleen brought over some homework. I think I'll just get stuck into that.'

'Good girl.'

'Noleen said that everyone is sayin' nice things about us and the press have a cheek.'

'They're just doing their jobs.'

'They're saying we're scumbags, Ma.'

'They're not.'

'They might as well be.'

'It doesn't matter. We know what we are.'

'Yeah,' Valerie said. 'What's that?'

'We're just people doing our best under the circumstances, love. Nobody's perfect.'

'Even Jeremy?' Valerie said.

'Even Jeremy,' Maisie admitted.

'Have a nice drive, Ma.' Valerie returned to her studies.

Maisie had her reasons for wanting Carina Murphy to step up to the plate. She didn't know what the boys were doing in Blessington or why they were doing it, and instead of driving herself mad, thinking in circles, guessing and wondering, she was focused on getting them back, and Carina was the key. She knew that if Rave was watching the conference and Carina pleaded with him to come home, he would. She knew this because Rave had stayed in her house and in Jeremy's room on and off for two years after his mother had abandoned him. She had comforted him when he'd cried himself to sleep, she'd fed him and put clothes on his back when Sid hadn't the will to get out of bed, long before he'd taken to heroin. She'd talked to Rave and shown him how to clean a house because he'd wanted to know. He wasn't a cook but scrubbing gave him great satisfaction and a general sense of wellbeing.

They had been close. He would tell Maisie things he wouldn't tell anyone else, little secrets about his daddy sleeping all day or how cold it sometimes got in the house. 'It's all right, though, Maisie. I keep me coat on and stay under me duvet.'

Back then, she had knocked on Sid's door more times than she could count, giving him lectures about caring for his son and paying for his heating when she could barely afford her own. She'd talked to him for hours, trying to get him to fight for himself and his child. He wasn't a person who suffered from depression, he was just lonely and miserable, lazy, selfish and sad. He grieved terribly for the son he'd lost while ignoring the son he had.

When Rave was twelve he'd arrived after school one day at Maisie's house with Jeremy. She hadn't seen him for a few days and he looked awful. 'Rave, you're a little yellow. Are you OK, lovey?'

'I dunno.'

'Will ya tell me what's wrong, lovey? Try to explain.'

'I think I'm dyin'.'

'Why's that, lovey?'

'I'm burnin', then I'm cold, then I'm burnin' again. I keep getting sick and me . . .'

'And what, love?'

'Me wee smells desperate, Maisie.'

The whites of his eyes were yellow. She took him to the doctor that afternoon and he confirmed the child had jaundice. Rest, lots of water and good healthy food should cure it. Maisie kept Rave for the week: he took Jeremy's bed and Jeremy was happy to sleep on the floor. When Jeremy was in school she'd bring Rave books and set him up on the sofa in the sitting room. Bridie cooked him vitamin-rich food and slipped him a bar of chocolate when Maisie pretended she wasn't looking. During that time, Rave revealed a lot about himself and one of the things he talked about was his longing to see his mother.

'I like your perfume, Maisie.'

'It's just soap, lovey.'

'It's lovely.'

'Thanks.'

'My ma used to smell nice. She probably still does.'

'What did she smell of?'

'Flowers, and she had soft hands. And long nails.'

'You miss her.'

'Me da says I shouldn't. He says she's not worth missin', but I do. Someday I'm gonna find her and tell her that everything's OK, 'cause I know she had a good reason to leave.'

'She was very sad after your brother died,' Maisie said.

'Yeah, and when I'm sad I like to be alone,' Rave said. 'I'm probably like her that way.'

'Well, I'm sure you'll see her again, lovey.'

'Yeah, 'cause she loves me.' He smiled. 'You know how I know?'

She shook her head.

''Cause she sends me birthday cards all the time and that means something, doesn't it, Maisie?' he said.

'Yes, lovey, definitely.' She left him to watch TV, went into her bedroom and had a little cry.

It had been four years, and a lot had changed since then, but she knew that Rave still loved his mammy even if she didn't love him.

Fred kept the radio on in the car. The news bulletins were updated with the information that Rave had withdrawn money at the cash machine in Blessington. Anyone who had seen the boys was urged to contact the guards. The clouds slowly rolled in and it was cold but still dry and fresh. It was nice sitting in the passenger seat watching the world go by.

'Thanks for this, Fred,' she said.

'No need to thank me.'

'There is.' She felt freer around him than she had in days and no longer under some sort of obligation, or promise. He'd said what he'd had to say. She could take him or leave him. It felt

289

like a fresh start. For the first time in their relationship they were equals. He wasn't perfect but neither was she.

He turned off the radio and glanced at her. 'I need you to prepare yourself to be disappointed.'

'I've had a lifetime to prepare for that.'

'Very good. *Touché.*' He sounded as if he felt unburdened too. Maybe it was his confession, or maybe the loss of his beard.

'I knew her once,' Maisie said. 'We were even friends for a while.'

'I didn't know that.'

Maisie and Carina had not been natural companions. They were thrown together because of proximity and the undeniably close bond between their children. Carina was the opposite to Maisie in many ways. She was well educated and studying to be a naturopath when nobody knew what a naturopath was. Maisie still wasn't sure. Rave had inherited his mother's looks: she had the same grey eyes and dark hair. Maisie had felt like a peasant standing next to Carina, and Carina had liked that a little too much for them to be true friends.

Back then, Sid had worked in the city. He managed an independent bookshop and loved his job. He had encouraged Rave and Jeremy in their love of reading. Rave's elder brother, Jason, had lived his life outdoors, playing on a pitch or digging up the garden so his mother could plant flowers or spuds or whatever caught her fancy, but Rave had spent most of his childhood reading in his room or Jeremy's. Sid would bring his son two books every week. He'd read one, pass it to Jeremy and read the second. By the time he had finished it, his dad had brought home two more, and the process would start again. They'd spend hours talking about the stories and fantasizing about being the great characters they'd read about. The bookshop had gone into liquidation a year before Jason died. Sid had had to take a job as manager in a local supermarket and resented every day he spent there until they'd fired him eighteen months after his son's death. Carina had left him two months later. She had written letters for everyone close to her – her parents, two brothers, her husband and Rave.

Maisie had read Rave's soon after Carina had gone: Sid had crumpled it into her hand. She remembered it clearly, even now.

My dearest son,
I'm leaving because I have to. Where I'm going you can't follow and I don't want you to. I wish you luck in life and love, and hope that you make good choices. You are the captain of your own ship. You decide who and what you want to be. Nobody else does that for you. I'm sorry if I've let you down as a mother. I cannot change who I am, any more than you can change who you are. All we can do is make our sacrifices, offer up our pain and suffering, and hope it's enough to save us. Remember that. God is watching and waiting for us all. He took Jason early but you and I may live to a good old age. After the curtain falls, depending on God's judgement, I hope that we will see one another again.
Goodbye for this life,
Yours,
Mother XXX

It was the strangest letter Maisie had ever read. She read it and reread it, trying to make sense of it. Carina had always been a strange woman: she'd said things that were sometimes uncomfortable, at others downright rude, but Maisie would rather spend time with a bitch than a bore any day, and Carina Murphy could put Danny Fox in his box faster than any other man or woman on the planet. For that reason alone, Maisie had liked her – until she'd walked out on her son. That was unforgivable.

'Do you think you can appeal to her inner fuzzy?' Fred said.

'The woman doesn't have an inner fuzzy.'

'Then why?'

'I just need to be able to look Rave in the eye and say I tried. I want him to know that someone, even if it's just Maisie Bean, cares about him.'

Fred pulled over.

'What are you doin'?'

'I'm stopping the car to tell you something.'

'It'd better not be bad news.'

'You're an amazing woman, Maisie Bean. You have no idea how special you are and it needs to be said. So I've said it. It's done.'

'Ah, would you ever—'

'Done, I said.' He raised his hand to stop whatever she was about to say, then put the car into gear and took off. Neither of them said anything else, but if he'd looked to the right, he'd have seen that she was grinning.

The commune hid behind two enormous metal gates with the words 'Private Property' written on them in red paint. They sat in the car looking at the mountain of steel between them and the woman who now called herself Marianne. There was no intercom system. Even though they couldn't see what lay behind the gates, the line of tall trees that seemed to go on for a mile behind them indicated that knocking was not an option. They waited. Twenty minutes later the gates opened and they began to drive through.

A man with a shaved head and a white beard jumped out of the car the gates had opened for. 'Can't you read? You're not invited here.'

Fred rolled down the window. 'We're looking for Carina Murphy or Marianne.'

'Marianne has made it clear she doesn't want visitors.'

'I didn't ask what she wanted.' Fred showed his badge.

After much discussion they were taken to a small but pretty log cabin. Carina was sitting on the deck wearing her signature black and wrapped up in an expensive oversized cardigan. Her hair was as grey as her eyes but, rather than ageing her, made her even more beautiful and dramatic. She stood when she saw them and smiled enigmatically. *Maybe she is the Queen of Sheba after all.*

'Hello, Maisie. How lovely to see you.' She put out her hand to shake.

Caught off guard, Maisie took it. *Balls, I shouldn't have done that. She's a horrible person.*

'And you must be Detective Brennan.' She pointed to seats on the deck, signalling that they weren't welcome inside her tiny home. She offered them tea but they declined. She sat facing them, curling her legs beneath her. 'So, what can I do for you?'

'Well, that's a stupid question,' Maisie said. 'You know what you can do for me – well, not for me, for your own son.'

'And what's that?' Carina said.

'You can help us find him.'

'Nonsense! And even if it weren't nonsense, did it ever occur to you that he doesn't want to be found?'

'He's sixteen years old, Carina.'

'It's Marianne, and age is just a number, Maisie.'

'That's rubbish and you know it.'

'My neighbour Vincent.' She pointed behind Maisie, who turned to see another log cabin nestled among some trees in the near distance. 'He's eighty-five years old, fit as a flea, works all day, never misses evening prayer and he knows how to enjoy himself. On the other hand my seventeen-year-old son died of a massive heart attack in the middle of a field. When I say that age is just a number, I mean it.'

Maisie laughed. 'You and Sid can trade on the dead-son thing all you want. Sid can kill himself and you can live in a tin can, for all I care, but don't try to sell me your psycho-bullshit about age and whatever other shite you've been telling yourself all these years. You have a boy who is alive. He still loves you and misses you and needs you. You should want to be there for him, not just now but until you die. That's what being a mother is.'

'I'd forgotten how much you bang on, Maisie.'

Fred stood up but Maisie grabbed his hand and pulled him back into his chair.

'You can look down on me, Carina – be my guest, the whole fuckin' country's doing that – but the only thing that matters is bringing my son home and I'll move fuckin' hell and high water to do it.'

'Do you talk to God with that dirty mouth, Maisie?'

'Oh, I do – and you know what I say to him? I tell Him if Heaven is reserved for pious, cruel, selfish, heartless arseholes like you, He can keep it.'

'Always such a beautiful way with words, Maisie. Are we done now?' Carina said.

Maisie wasn't done: she was there to plead Rave's case. 'Please,' she said. 'Please, Carina or Marianne or whoever you are now, please, I am begging you to just come to the press conference and tell your son that you love him and ask him to come home.'

'And then?'

'What do you mean?'

'Move back into that hellhole with Sid the junkie? Make lunches and pack schoolbags? Is that what you want?'

Maisie was so taken aback that she almost cried. She remembered Rave's words: 'I know she loves me. She's always sendin' me birthday cards.'

'I want you to love him. He's lovely. He's kind and sweet and really smart, and he looks just like you.'

Carina's carefully constructed façade cracked. Tears crept into her eyes.

Is that some human emotion?

She bowed her head. 'He sounds like a nice boy, Maisie, and I wish him well. You should know that me staying here and dedicating my life to prayer is the best thing I can do for my son.' When she looked up she was smiling and her hands were knotted in a prayerful pose.

Maisie looked at Fred, who shook his head. 'OK, I tried. I'm done. Let's go.' They stood up. Carina remained in her chair. 'Prayer doesn't feed, clothe or keep him warm. It doesn't love him or protect him, but you keep praying because you're right about one thing. He is better off without you.'

Carina didn't respond.

They walked back to the car together, breathing in the fresh air, surrounded by tall trees, wild flowers and creatures, all the while listening to scratching and scurrying on the ground and birds singing far above them.

'I don't know about you, Fred, but the countryside brings me out in a rash.'

He laughed. 'Let's get you home. I'm sorry it didn't pan out.'

'Don't be. We tried and that's good enough.'

In the car on the way home Fred caught Maisie smiling to herself. 'What's put that frown upside down?'

'I used to think Carina Murphy was so much better than me. What a joke. I don't give a shite what anyone thinks.'

'That's the spirit.'

'And I'll tell you something else. When we get those boys back, Rave is coming to live with me.'

Fred chuckled. 'The more the merrier.'

Maisie felt so sure she was getting her boys back that she daydreamed about it all the way home.

Chapter Ten

'Nothing Else Matters'
Metallica, 1992

Bridie

Lynn was telling Maisie, Fred and Valerie to go, some-thing about a conference. 'It's time, I'll take care of Bridie.'

Maisie hugged her friend. 'You're saving my life.' She kissed her mother. 'Do I look all right Ma?'

'Lovely.' She meant it. *You're lovely, Maisie. You always were, you always will be.* Bridie wasn't exactly sure where Maisie was going but she knew she was going there to find Jeremy. *My boy, me best boy. Remember, Jeremy, Grammy loves you.* She wasn't happy about being left behind. *I want to find him too. I should be looking for him. I shouldn't be sitting here with What's-her-name.* She wasn't happy Fred was going either. At least, when she really thought about it now, she knew he was the man who helped Maisie. *So why does he make me nervous?*

Lynn led Bridie into the sitting room. *I'm sick of this place.* Lynn followed her back into the kitchen. *And here. Have I nowhere else to go?*

'It's going to be all right, Bridie,' Lynn said to her.

'It was all right – it was even good for a while – but times change and good turns bad and there's nothing we can do about it, no control. You think you have some but you don't, love.'

'I know things look bleak but they'll get better again. We just have to get up and over this mountain. Then it'll be blue skies and green pastures.'

'Things are never gonna be the same again.' Tears rolled down her face. 'I don't know much, love, but I know that.' *Where's everyone gone? Why did they leave me?*

'Things always change, Bridie. That's life.'

'But it was so good for a while.' After that, Bridie didn't speak.

Lynn tried to talk her into an episode of *Blockbusters* but she wasn't interested. She asked her if she'd like a nap but Bridie felt too agitated to sleep. She made tea and offered her cake and even her favourite cheese, but she wasn't hungry. She just wanted to sit in her armchair, rocking to and fro.

Then Bridie remembered something that set her nerves on edge. She'd heard Maisie talk to Valerie about Danny. *He's back. He's here. They're with him now. No wonder our beautiful boy ran from us.* Bridie turned to the window. The press were clearing up and leaving, and she decided that, before she forgot, it was time she did the same.

Lynn

Lynn took her eye off Bridie for less than three minutes to have a wee. She knew it was less than three minutes because she had timed herself many times. She was never one for dawdling in the bathroom. She described herself as a slash-and-go kinda girl. In, out, wash your hands, dry them on a towel or your own clothes – never those dryers, they're useless – pat yourself down and the job was done.

Whenever she'd timed herself over the years it had always taken less than three minutes. She had been spurred on to time herself by incidents in which she had been made to wait ages by other inconsiderate, selfish women who seemed to enjoy whiling away their time on public toilets while making other people wait. It was one of the reasons Lynn had stopped travelling, going out to pubs and unfamiliar coffee shops or restaurants. In Jingles she knew where she was. There were two toilets and never enough people in the shop to warrant a big queue.

Lynn's life had become smaller and smaller over the years. The changes and limitations she had set herself had been implemented so slowly that they were imperceptible to others, but the two days she'd spent in Maisie's house and away from the comfort of her own surroundings were taking their toll. She had a routine at home, she knew exactly where she was and, more to the point, she knew what to do there. If she had been minding Bridie at hers she would have had more control. She was sure of it. Bridie'd be in bed, asleep, and she could rest her weary heart and bones. She wasn't sure why or how she exerted more control in her own home but she did. Lynn was queen of her castle and everyone knew it, even poor, demented Bridie. She missed it. She longed for it. It was all she could do to keep from bolting through the door. *Tomorrow she's coming back to mine. I can't be having this, no matter what the circumstances.* Now she walked into the sitting room but Bridie wasn't there.

She didn't panic initially, just opened the double doors to the kitchen, but when Bridie wasn't there her heart flipped. *Oh, don't do that.*

'Bridie!' she said, moving towards Bridie's room. 'Bridie?'

Bridie wasn't there. She wasn't in Maisie's room, Jeremy's or Valerie's. She wasn't in the hall, she wasn't in the back garden and she wasn't out front. Lynn looked around frantically. *Jesus Christ, it's the Bermuda Triangle here. Will people ever stop fuckin' disappearing?* Bridie's coat was missing. She had left and taken her coat. It was a black trench coat she'd had since the sixties. It was faded in places and the seam had given way but she loved it. It always hung in pride of place on the rack by the door and it was gone. *Oh, no. Oh, God, no.* Lynn grabbed her coat and her bag, then raced to her car, heart in mouth, brain screaming. She put her key into the ignition and started the engine, rolling down the window so she could shout a description to everyone she met along the road. *Please, please, please don't do this to me, Bridie.* She couldn't have gone far. *Three minutes. Less than three minutes.*

There weren't many people on the street. It started to drizzle again and it was so cold that she was lucky she didn't have to de-ice the car. She called out to a few kids on the corner. They hadn't seen an old woman in a black trench coat. She shouted to a man on a bike. He hadn't either. She signalled to a man beside her at traffic lights. He was no wiser. *Where in Christ are ya, Bridie?*

She had to pull over. She had no choice: her head was swimming and her heart palpitating. She felt dizzy and nauseous. She had no clue where to look or what to do. *Circle around again? Call the guards? Go back to the house?* She got out of the car and vomited on the side of the road. She grabbed her spray from her bag and squirted under her tongue. *I'm not able for this.* She waited until the black spots ceased to jog around her eyeballs and started the car again. *I've lost Bridie. It was less than three minutes and I've lost Bridie.*

She drove around for another twenty minutes. She went back to the house and called her. As she came back out on to the street Vera was pulling into her driveway. Jake was waiting for her with his paws on the bay window, barking happily, twirling and spinning, chasing his tail with excitement. Lynn ran over, breathless, but before she could get a word out, Vera was talking at her. She pointed to the window and the dog doing his celebration dance. 'That dog is the dumbest animal God ever created but how could you not love the bones of him? The big eejit,' she said, taking her shopping out of the back.

'Vera, please tell me you've seen Bridie!' Lynn panted.

Vera dropped her shopping. 'You've lost Bridie?'

Lynn nodded. 'I lost Bridie. I took me eye off her for less than three minutes.'

'How long ago?'

Lynn looked at her watch. 'Forty-five minutes.'

'Jesus, and you're sure it was less than three minutes?'

'Three minutes and no more.'

'Well, wherever she went she didn't walk. This is a cul-de-sac, there's only one way out and Bridie wasn't a sprinter even back in the good old days. So the question is, who'd she get a lift with and where were they going?'

Lynn remembered the last of the journalists packing up just before she went to the toilet. 'Oh, God, she's gone to the press conference!'

'Well, then, I'd get on over there.'

'I could kiss you, Vera.'

'I wouldn't thank you for it.' Vera chuckled. 'Now, go on.'

'I owe you.' Lynn ran back to the car.

Lynn arrived at the press conference just as it was starting. The school hall had a stage and that was where they'd set up the long trestle table and covered it with a white cotton cloth. Two chairs were placed at the centre of it, with microphones positioned in front of them. There was one bottle of water and two glasses and behind, projected on the white wall, the now familiar large picture of the two boys. The rest of the room was filled with foldaway chairs and there wasn't a spare seat. She glanced around feverishly, hoping to see Bridie. Guards in uniform milled about, cameramen fixed up their tripods, journalists chatted among themselves and others talked into cameras with lights on against a background of shuffling movement. As Lynn took it all in, the walls began to close on her, her breath shortened and she felt the familiar shocking pain. She must have looked ill because a woman appeared from nowhere and offered her a seat.

'Thank you,' Lynn said, fumbling for her spray.

'You're Bridie's friend,' the woman said.

'You know Bridie?'

'She came here with me.'

'Oh, God, you're one of the journalists who was packing up outside, aren't you?'

The woman smiled and held out her hand. 'I'm Joan.'

Lynn shook it. 'And Bridie?'

'She's fine. She's with her daughter.'

'Thank God,' Lynn said. 'Thank you, dear Lord on high, thank you, thank you, thank you.'

'Are you all right?'

'No, but I will be.' She took a hit from her spray.

'She's a nice lady,' Joan said.

'She is,' Lynn said.

'How long has she been sick?'

'A few years.'

'My grandmother had dementia.'

'I'm sorry for that.'

'Maisie has a lot on her plate.'

'Look, Joan, thank you for the chair and thank you for minding Bridie but I'm not talking to you.'

'I understand,' Joan said.

'And, truth be told, I think the press have been absolute bastards. They paint a picture of those boys as though they're degenerate and they have no love in their lives. Well, they do. It comes from Maisie and that old woman who sat in your car.'

'I can see why you'd think that and you're right.'

'Really?' Lynn hadn't expected that.

Joan handed Lynn her card. 'I write for the *Tallaght Echo*. I've spent the last few days talking to everyone and anyone who actually knows Maisie, Jeremy, Bridie and Valerie Bean, and they sound like pretty good people to me. I'd like to reflect that when the madness dies down and the rest of the pack has moved on. I'd like to give Maisie a voice. It's the least she deserves under the circumstances.'

'Oh, right . . . Well, that's lovely. Thank you.' Lynn was taken slightly aback. She looked at the card – 'Joan Wilde', printed in fancy lettering, with a mobile number. *That's posh for a local newspaper.* 'I'll pass this on when it's appropriate, if it ever is,' she said.

'I'm happy with that.'

'And if she ever forgives me for losing her mother.'

'She will,' Joan said.

The room was so packed that steam was rising. *I just have to get out of here.* There were too many people and it was so noisy. Her head felt as if it was in a vice and her heart was threatening to explode but she couldn't leave until she had confirmed that Bridie was safe and she'd spoken to Maisie. She saw Fred talking with another man and made her way to him. Trying to move through the crowd was harder than punching under water. He saw her before she reached him and came to meet her. 'She's fine,' he said, referring to Bridie.

'I took my eye off her for less than three minutes.'

'Lynn, she's fine.'

'Where is she?'

'In a classroom with Maisie and Valerie.'

'Can I see them? Please?'

'Of course,' he said. He put his arm around her and led her away from the crowd into the cool, wide, empty corridor. Finally she could breathe again.

Maisie

Maisie was anxious. Earlier that afternoon she had stood in front of her wardrobe at a loss as to what to wear. She didn't want to look stupid or cheap. She couldn't afford to have people looking down on her because if they did they would look down on her son and be less likely to help. *I'm not the low-life you think I am.* She had showered, washed her hair and blow-dried it so that the curls sat properly on her head. She had put on make-up and painted her nails. *This is too important to just sit there snivelling.* She wanted Jeremy to see that she'd made an effort. It would mean something to him.

She had picked out a pretty dress for Valerie. It was white with splashy red roses on it so she'd matched it with a red cardigan, black tights and black patent shoes.

'I look like a thick.'

'You look beautiful.'

Valerie didn't argue: she was too nervous. 'Do you think I should curl me hair like yours, Ma?'

'Your hair is perfect as it is.' Maisie had smoothed down her daughter's straight brown hair.

'Do ya think me da will know me, Ma?' she'd whispered.

'I do.' Her stomach twisted some more.

Bridie had been quiet, but after Valerie had left the room she'd sidled up to Maisie. 'Maisie, Danny Fox is Valerie's da.'

'Yes, Ma.'

'I don't understand, Maisie.'

'He's come to help find Jeremy.'

'He won't help, Maisie. He won't help at all.' Bridie's trembling hands flitted up to cover her mouth.

Maisie took her mother's hands in hers and held them tight. 'Ma, please. I'm doing my best.'

'I'm sorry for you then.' Bridie had pulled away, walked into her room and slammed the door.

Now it made sense that Bridie had followed her to the press conference: she would never allow them to face Danny alone. *God love you, Ma, you're still doing your best, even if you've no idea what you're fuckin' doing here.*

Bridie was sitting at a desk, staring into space, whatever sense she arrived with now lost. Danny was in the classroom next door and Valerie was like a hen on a hot griddle. She was walking around the room picking things up, dropping them, then walking some more.

'There you are, Ma,' Maisie said.

'You look so beautiful, Maisie.'

'Thanks, Ma.'

'I don't want you marrying him.'

'What?'

'I know you're pregnant, Maisie, but I don't like him. He's not right for you, love.'

'You're pregnant?' Valerie said.

'No, love. Grammy's just confused.'

'Some people are incapable of causing anything but pain,' Bridie said.

'Is she saying Da's one of those people?' Valerie said, on the verge of tears again.

'Ma . . .'

'I'm sorry, love.' Bridie ignored her daughter's interjection.

'I just want to see him,' Valerie implored.

'It's just not right,' Bridie said to Maisie, ignoring Valerie completely.

'Grammy, will you stop being mental for five minutes, please?' Valerie said, walking up to her grandmother. 'Please? Because I just need to know.'

'Know what, love?' Bridie said, to the girl standing in front of her.

'That I'll be OK, Grammy.' Valerie's voice was laced with pain.

Bridie looked at her granddaughter and, for a second, the light returned to her eyes. She smiled at Valerie. 'You are OK, love. You're more than OK. You're brilliant.'

'That's not what you and my ma say all the time.'

'What?' Maisie said. 'Of course we do, love.' She stood up. 'We think you're the funniest, smartest kid we've ever known.'

'No, ya don't.'

'Valerie Bean, I know that sometimes I'm harsh on ya but that's only because you shine so bright that sometimes you can blind people.'

'That doesn't make any sense, Ma.'

Maisie walked over to her and sat on the table, putting her feet on the chair. 'You think of things and see things that other people never do. You put things together in your head quicker than anyone else in the room and say how you feel. You always have an opinion and you're not afraid of anything. While you're a kid, sometimes I need to hold you back a little, but when you're older and you really know yourself, there will be no stopping you. You're special, Valerie Bean.' Maisie was crying and ruining her make-up.

'I agree with the lady,' Bridie murmured.

Valerie hugged her mother. 'Do you really think so, Ma?' she whispered into her mother's ear.

'I really do love you, and I'm so sorry you didn't know that.'

Valerie and Maisie were hugging when Fred entered with Lynn.

'I know you,' Bridie said to Lynn. She was pleased to see her.

'"I know you," she says! You've nearly given me two fuckin' heart attacks!' Lynn shouted.

'There's no need to raise your voice, love,' Bridie grumbled.

'I'm so sorry, Maisie.'

Maisie pulled away from Valerie, kissing her on the top of her head. 'It's fine. I was more worried about you.'

'It was less than three minutes.'

'I know.' Maisie hugged her old friend, then drew away and pulled out a mirror from her handbag. There were only a few minutes to go before she was on. 'How do I look?' she asked, as she fixed her make-up.

'Beautiful,' Valerie said.

Fred put out his arm and she linked it. 'Showtime.'

She felt wobbly going up the stairs. Her mouth was dry and her stomach gurgled. *Please don't explode on the stage.*

Tom was waiting there. He sat her on the chair to the left of him. There was a minute or two of sound and light checking and then, with a nod from a stranger, they were ready to go.

He had briefed her earlier on what to say. He wanted her to

keep it short and sweet and to stick to the programme. We miss you. We love you. You're not in trouble. Come home. She'd got it. She knew what to do, but when the lights beamed down on her and Tom started talking she forgot everything.

He spoke, and it was as though she was listening through a wall. She could hear him but his voice seemed muffled and she couldn't quite make out what he was saying until he looked at her.

'Maisie?'

'Yes?'

'It's time to make your statement.'

'OK.' She looked out into the packed room at the lights and the crowd. Her throat felt like it was swelling, her eyes burned, her guts blazed. She coughed in an attempt to clear her airway. She sipped from her glass of water to try to unstick her lips and loosen her tongue from the roof of her mouth.

'Ah, my name is Maisie Bean. I'm Jeremy Bean's mother. I love him.' *Let's get that right off the bat.* 'He and my daughter Valerie are the loves of my life. I want him home and safe, and I want him to know he's not in trouble.' *What am I talking around him for? Look down the lens, Maisie, talk to your son.* 'You're not in trouble, son. I don't know why ya left and I don't care. Whatever it is, we can deal with it together. Your grammy's here. She's in the back with Valerie and she misses ya, love. She keeps looking for you behind the sofa, under the table – she's even mentioned the attic a few times.'

Maisie laughed softly, then refocused and allowed the audience just the tiniest glimpse of her pain. 'She's desperate to see you, Jeremy. We all are. Valerie's here too, love. I said that, though, didn't I? Please, son, it's time to come home now. OK?' She was emotional but holding it together. *Don't let them see you cry, Maisie.* She looked at Tom, who nodded to her and redirected her to the words on a small screen in front of her.

'If someone else is involved and he's being held for some reason, with his friend, please let them go. And, Rave, your daddy is sorry he couldn't be here. He's in hospital but he's fine, he'll be OK. He loves you. He wants ya home. I love you too. I've known you since before you could walk. You've been my son's best friend his entire life, together through thick and thin. We love you, Rave. The Beans want ya home. Do you hear me, lovey? Come home. If there is anyone out there who can help us, please, just do it. Help us. Thank you.'

Tom handed Maisie a tissue. She blew her nose and looked to the side of the stage, where Fred was waiting for Tom to give him the nod. As soon as he did, Fred walked on stage and whisked Maisie away. Tom turned to the press. 'Any questions?'

The room erupted.

When Maisie hit the school corridor, she bumped into Principal Young. She felt embarrassed: her make-up was ruined and she was clinging to Fred for dear life. The statement had opened a wound that needed time to close. She wasn't ready to face the world yet.

Principal Young stopped and put her hand out to shake Maisie's. 'Jeremy is lucky to have you, as is Rave.'

That's the first time she hasn't given out to me. Maisie shook her hand in a blur and walked on. They were almost at the classroom door when Danny emerged into the corridor, closely followed by his parents and a guard in uniform. 'So I don't get to say my piece?' he said to Fred and Maisie. He pointed to the guard. 'This man says it's over.'

'It is.' Maisie exhaled long and deep. She was too drained to deal with Danny.

'He's my son.'

Fred stepped closer to him. 'And we've decided that it's better for him if it's just his mother who makes the appeal.'

'And who is "we"?' Danny said, squaring off and acting the brave man in the spotlight.

'Calm down, Daniel,' his father said.

'We want him home, Danny. He sees you and he's gone.' Maisie was aware that Valerie was only a door away.

307

'Because of the poison you put in his ear all these years,' he spat.

'No. Because you beat me half to death, and when he tried to stop you, you broke his arm,' she said quietly. She didn't want Valerie meeting him when he was riled. *Tom said he'd be managed. This isn't managed.*

'That was a fuckin' accident and you know it. I never meant to hurt my boy.'

She knew he was telling the truth. She could see that it still hurt him.

'OK, Danny, whatever. You win.' She needed him to cool down: his daughter was waiting to meet him. *This isn't going to work. What was I thinking? Stupid woman.*

Suddenly Danny was looking past her to where Valerie was standing in the hallway. 'Valerie?' he said. Maisie hadn't seen that look on his face for a long time. Any stranger passing them by could mistake him for a devoted father, reunited with his little girl. 'Valerie, it's me, your daddy.' She was frozen to the spot. 'You look so beautiful, love, just like I imagined.' He began to walk towards her. Joy replaced pain, bitterness and anger. He was looking at his beautiful little girl.

Oh, God, oh, God, oh, God. Maisie smiled at Valerie as re-assuringly as she could. 'You can say hello, love, it's OK.'

Valerie looked from her mother to her father and took a step in his direction. Maisie's stomach lurched. *This is a bad idea. Jesus Christ, what was I thinking?* It nearly killed her not to grab her daughter's hand and make a run for it. Fred stood solidly beside her. *It's OK. Fred's here. It's OK. Just relax. Calm down.* She mustered a grin for her daughter while holding her breath.

Valerie

Valerie stared at her father. He was older but if she'd seen him on the street she would have recognized him in an instant. *He's my da*. She had so many questions and so much to say but one question was at the very top of the list. 'Can I ask you something?'

'Anything,' he said and he looked so happy.

'Why did you hurt my ma?' *Maybe if he could tell us, we could sort it.*

His face fell and she could see that she'd hurt him. She didn't want to.

'It wasn't like that.' He stumbled as he spoke.

'What was it like?' she asked, not because she was being smart but because she really wanted to know. He looked from her to Nanna Fox, who refused to meet his eyes, and then to his father, who just shrugged at him. He straightened up and faced his daughter.

'Everyone has their side of the story, Valerie.'

She nodded. *That's why I'm bleedin' askin'.*

'Jeremy said you put Ma's blood on the walls. Did ya, Da?'

He looked like he was going to cry. She didn't mean for that to happen. She didn't want him to cry, she just wanted him to make sense of what he had done. *Please, Da, I know you're good. I know you are.* Danny's face burned as he turned to face Maisie. 'You're such a bitch,' he hissed. 'You're such a stupid, lying, ugly bitch. You did this.' He pointed at his daughter. 'She was the only one, Maisie, the only one who . . . You couldn't even let *her* love me, could you?'

Fred stepped forward but Maisie held him back.

'That's enough of that now, Danny.' The guard stepped in.

'Enough. You don't know the half of it. I should never have married that slut in the first place. Coldest fuckin' fish I ever met.'

'That is quite enough, Daniel. You did this. You think the world owes you something? Well, it doesn't. You get what you give in this life,' Nanna Fox said.

Valerie looked around to all the adults standing there. No one spoke, no one moved. Her da looked like he'd lost something.

'Fuck you, Ma. No wonder I married her. Anything to get away from the two of yous.'

Even though he was behaving badly, Valerie thought her da had a point. Her grandparents were freaks.

'I've had enough,' said Grandfather and walked away.

'I think you should stay in a hotel tonight, Daniel.' Nanna Fox followed her husband out of the door, leaving Danny with the guard.

'You must be fuckin' thrilled,' he said to Maisie. Valerie quickly assessed her mother. She wasn't thrilled at all. She had tears in her eyes.

'Bitch.' Danny spat the word out.

He was hateful and mean and everything Jeremy had said he was. Valerie didn't feel like crying: she just felt sad. *Sorry, Jeremy*. At least now she knew. She could let go and cry about that later. Valerie looked to her mother. 'I'd like to go home now, Ma,' and her mother reached out her hand.

Maisie

With Valerie safe in her grasp, Maisie turned to walk away.

'Did you hear what I said, Maisie? Coldest fuckin' fish I ever met – but, then, you'd know all about that, Fred, wouldn't ya?'

The date-rape flew into her mind. She felt him pull at her underwear and push her head against the wall. She tasted the bile rising from her stomach and pictured him shoving himself into her, the stupid bag of chips going cold in her hand. She blinked it away. *Don't go back there, Maisie. He can't touch you now.* She came back into the moment in time to hear Fred address Danny calmly and coolly.

'We have a little girl here, Danny, and she doesn't need to listen to that kind of talk.'

Danny stepped back a little. He nodded, acknowledging Fred was right, but he hadn't finished. He had a point to make and

310

he wasn't leaving till he'd made it. 'Marrying you was the biggest mistake I ever made, Maisie.'

'You're right. We should never have married, Danny.' She was tempted to tell him what he was, to name what he had done to her all those years ago, but her daughter was standing there, trembling. She squeezed Valerie's hand. 'You should go back to where you came from, Danny. There's nothing for you here.'

'You cheeky bitch,' he spat, and stepped forward. The guard moved in front of him.

Valerie tugged at her mother's hand but Maisie had had enough of Danny's mouth. Her temper rose, just as it had all those times when she'd forgotten to be afraid and her big mouth had landed her a slap or worse. 'You don't know the half of it, mate,' she said, mocking him. 'Remember that expensive special tea you liked so much?'

He looked at her blankly but of course he remembered. He'd thought drinking Earl Grey made him seem a little more sophisticated then everyone else.

'That was a mix of ordinary tea and my piss.'

His face fell. 'You did not.'

'Every time you hit me or knocked me to the ground, every kick, pinch, burn or scrape, I pissed in your tea, Danny. You've drunk more piss in your day than a survivalist.'

Valerie looked up at her mother, wide-eyed, and Fred laughed to himself. Danny didn't know what to say or do. He was speechless.

Fred stepped up to him. 'Time to go, Danny.' He left no room for argument.

Danny sneered at them but he looked small and weak and broken. He walked away in the company of the guard. He was a bitter, broken man. *You've only got yourself to blame, Danny.*

When they went back into the classroom, Bridie was asleep at the desk, Lynn waiting patiently beside her.

'You OK?' she said.

'You heard.'

'I think the deaf would have heard that.'

'Ma, I don't think I wanna see him again for a long time,' Valerie said softly.

'That's a good decision.' Maisie wrapped her daughter in her arms.

'Can we go home now, Ma'sie?'

'Yes. It's time to go home.'

Lynn roused Bridie, and as the family walked out together, Fred leaned close to Maisie. 'So you pissed in the man's tea,' he whispered.

Heat rose to Maisie's face. 'More times than I can count.'

'And I'm the sick one.' He smiled at her and laughed to himself.

Tom met them in the car park with more news. 'Rave was spotted in the supermarket and the post office in Blessington – the lads have him on CCTV buying writing paper, envelopes, stamps, some food, cleaning products and air freshener.'

'And Jeremy?'

'Still no sighting.'

'Well, they're together, they have to be,' Maisie said.

'We're still canvassing. We're getting closer, Maisie. Just hang in there.'

They drove home in silence. There was nothing to do but wait.

Later that night, Maisie was tucking Valerie into her bed like she had done when she was small.

'Is Fred staying here tonight?'

'No, love, he'll be going home.'

'What if me da comes back?'

'He won't.'

'But what if he does?'

'Do you want Fred to stay, love?'

'Maybe just till we're sure Da's gone.'

'OK, I'll ask him.'

'He's nice, Ma. He is. Things are changin', Ma.'

'They are, love.'

'When Jeremy comes home I'm gonna be nicer to him.'

'Why's that?'

'Because he gets sad a lot.'

'We all get sad, love.'

'Yeah, but not like Jeremy.'

Maisie nodded. 'OK.'

'And I'm gonna work harder in school.'

'Now you're just playing with me.'

'Honestly, Ma, me teachers are always saying that I'd be great if I just applied meself so I'll apply meself and see what happens.'

'If you don't stop I'll keel over. Next you'll tell me you want to be like that girl who won Young Scientist of the Year.'

'Fannyfeet's sister, Debs?' Valerie said.

'Fannyfeet?' Maisie was half afraid to ask.

'He came out of his ma feet first.'

'Oh.'

'Nah, Debs has really changed, Ma. Her biggest ambition now is to have a brown baby.'

Maisie laughed. 'Goodnight, Valerie Bean. Your mammy loves you,' she said, just like Jeremy used to say to their grammy.

'Night, Ma'sie.'

Maisie closed the door and headed into Jeremy's room. She sat on his bed and stroked his bedclothes. She lay on his pillow and inhaled his scent. She closed her eyes and imagined him walking through the door. He was so close she could almost feel him.

Bridie

Bridie was ready for bed, wearing her favourite nightie and wrapped up in her dressing-gown. She had her head in the fridge when Fred walked into the kitchen. 'Oh, sorry,' he said. 'I'll wait till you're done.'

She took her head out of the fridge and gazed at him, chewing. She motioned him to sit down. He sat. She could see he was being cautious with her, didn't want to upset her. She sat down opposite him.

'I forget things,' she said.

'I know, Bridie.'

'Some things I remember. Then they go again.'

'It's OK.'

'I know what you did. I remember. You really hurt Danny.'

'Yes, I did.'

'The thing I really forgot was how much of an eejit he was.'

Fred laughed a little.

'It's no excuse.'

'I know.'

'But hearing him talk to my girls like that tonight, well, I'm glad he's gone and you're the reason he's gone.'

'Thank you for saying so.'

'It's no excuse.'

'I know.'

'Good,' she said. 'Now I'd better go before I start poppin' off. I'm still a lady, Fred Brennan.'

'You are, Bridie.'

Maisie had appeared in the doorway. 'Come on, Ma, I'll take you to bed.'

'Don't let me be mean to that man.' Bridie waved at Fred.

'I won't, Ma,' Maisie said, holding her mother close to her as they walked down the corridor.

'I prefer him without that auld hair on his face. Never trust a man with hair on his face, Maisie.'

'I won't, Ma,' she said, as she tucked her mother in.

'Don't leave me alone, Maisie. I'll be gone again soon.'

Maisie lay down beside her mother. 'Shush,' she said. 'We're here together right now. That's all that matters.'

'Time moves differently now, Maisie, doesn't it?'

'Yes, Ma.' She allowed a tear to fall. 'It does.'

They cried together before Bridie fell asleep in her daughter's arms.

Midnight to 1 a.m., 2 January 1995

Rave

Rave liked to pee outside. He especially liked peeing under a dark sky. There was something quite comforting about the darkness.

Having refused Beany's invitation to Christmas dinner, he'd spent Christmas Day alone in his room, with cold food and wrapped cake that his friend had boxed up in his schoolbag and the gift of two books to keep him occupied. Beany thought of everything: that was why Rave couldn't live without him. He took care of him. The books were John Grisham's *The Firm* and Rick Moody's *The Ice Storm*. Rave spent the day picking at the food, drinking a six-pack and reading both books from cover to cover. He fell asleep after midnight, energized, refocused, his imagination bursting with ideas. *I'm never going to be here again. It all changes now.* He had a plan. He just needed to act on it.

Then this morning happened. His da had been out of it for days. Rave rarely went down to the ground floor any more, only when he needed to use the front door and then it was when the house was still. When his dad was on the prowl he'd just use his window or sometimes watch him through the sitting-room window and wait for him to sleep before he let himself in. Other times when he was too tired to wait or too hungry to climb he'd just let himself into Beany's. Sometimes he'd come and go before Beany even knew he'd been there.

Aside from that one fight they'd had, Rave's da wasn't violent. He was a whining, nauseating mess, and Rave couldn't bear to be anywhere near him. Before heroin, he had been a quiet, injured man. Even before his seventeen-year-old son had died on a football pitch and his wife had lost the will to go on, he had been a glass-half-empty kind of man. Eternally doomed, nothing ever went right for Sid Murphy. He was a loser, with a loser's attitude. Rave swore he'd never be like his da: he'd be the exact opposite – he'd make things happen. He'd take control of his life and be a winner. This morning he was sneaking out of the house when he heard the strangest gurgling sound. It wasn't right so he walked into the sitting room where his da pretty much lived. He was out cold on the sofa, foam coming from his mouth.

'Oh, shite! Da! Da! Da!' He shook his father. Sid still didn't move. 'Fuck.' He went to the public phone that his da had installed when the phone company cut off their home phone, the year before. He scrabbled in his pocket for coins as he picked up the receiver. There was no dialling tone. He panicked and pressed some buttons, then noticed that the cord was loose. In frustration he beat the phone with the receiver. 'Come on!' The cord fell out of the wall.

He went back into the room and pulled his comatose father into a sitting position. 'Da,' he said. 'Wake up.' He slapped him a few times but Sid's head just rolled and Rave didn't know what to do. 'Da? Da? Are you dying, Da? Please, Da, look at me? Are you dying?' He was becoming desperate, pulling his skinny auld fella around the room. 'Da, for fuck sake, wake up, will ya?' He was crying and he didn't know why because he'd probably be better off without his da. 'Come on, Da! You're my da! Come on, will ya?' He was holding him up and dancing him around the room when he tripped over a shoe on the floor and dropped his father. 'Oh, shite! Sorry.'

Miraculously his da stirred. 'What the fuck?' Sid said, eyes still closed, wiping the foam from his mouth with his sleeve.

When Rave realized his father wasn't going to die he stepped over him and slipped out of the room without a sound. He could hear Sid mumbling: 'Bleedin' floor . . . Still, there's nowhere to fall from here.' He chuckled to himself.

Rave heard him try to get up. He pinned himself against

the hall wall and listened for a minute or two to make sure he didn't drop dead as soon as he moved. When he heard Sid shuffling about, looking for a roll-up, a lighter or maybe some gear, Rave walked outside and quietly shut the door. After spending Christmas week ferrying his stuff up the mountain he had decided in that moment that it was time. *No more.*

Rave Murphy had taken control of his future and now, standing under a dark sky, it felt good.

The moon was swamped by dark, heavy clouds that slowly swirled above him, and when the skies opened, he basked under the bitter cold shower, treating it as a baptism of sorts, until the night rumbled ominously. In seconds he zipped up his fly and ran back to the hut and Jeremy as lightning lit the sky.

Jeremy

The rain continued to beat down, and even though it was icy cold outside, the cabin became hot and stuffy. Jeremy felt uncomfortable: it was becoming harder to breathe easily.

'We can go outside if you need air, Beany,' Rave said.

'I'll be OK,' he said. 'I just need to walk around for a minute.' He stood up and Rave moved over on the sleeping bag and leaned up against the wall. Jeremy peered at the protruding nails. 'Did you see the heads?' he asked, referring to the animal heads Rave had spoken of.

'They were gone, but I'm sure they were there because there was a chunk of fur on one of the nails.'

'Jesus,' Jeremy said. 'That's cruel.'

'It's nature.'

'Well, everyone knows that nature is cruel,' he said, with a degree of bitterness. He wasn't sure what to do. He didn't want to sit too close to Rave again because he couldn't take another boner, but when he stood up in the confined space Rave's eyes followed him and he felt like he was on display. He turned to the pile of books. 'What are you reading?'

'*1984.*'

'Good?'

'Deadly. It's about a world where they can punish you for thought crimes and individualism.'

'Sounds intense.'

'It is. It's good, though, 'cause against a background of a war-ravaged world there are still people willing to rebel against a system that doesn't care about people, only power.'

'Cool.'

'Except it's not looking good for the hero right now.'

'Why not?'

'He's endured months of extreme torture but now, when it really counts, he's too scared to do what's right.'

'What's the right thing to do?'

'I dunno . . . Hold firm, not turn into an obedient slave like the rest of them . . . but they've pitted him against his greatest fear.'

'Jesus.'

'So he has a choice. He can let them turn his brain back into mush or get eaten by rats.'

'There's no good option in that,' Jeremy said.

'No.'

'So what does he choose?'

'Haven't got that far yet. I'll give it to you when I'm done.'

'Nice one.'

'Are ya gonna sit down?' Rave said.

Jeremy gulped. 'Yeah.' He had no choice. *Just sit down and focus on the wall.*

He sat on the sleeping bag beside his friend.

'Are you tired, Beany?'

'Nah.' He glanced around. Where would he lie down? Not next to Rave. He eyed a space near the makeshift wardrobe. He could just lie on the floor over there and use his backpack as a pillow. *It'll be fine.* But it wasn't fine, it was impossible.

Rave

Rave could see his best friend was uncomfortable. He'd noticed it happening a lot lately. Sometimes the tension between them got so intense it was frightening, and that was when Jeremy disappeared on him. He just wanted to hang out with his friend in his new home but Jeremy was pacing the room like a caged animal. Like he didn't want to be anywhere near Rave. Like he was terrified if he didn't keep moving Rave would do something to him. *I'm not a bleedin' animal.* He knew Jeremy had been freaked when he'd knocked on his door and seen his da so roughed up. *It was self-defence, I swear.* Jeremy didn't support any kind of violence. *Did you think I should just take it from him?* Maybe that was why he was always on edge. He hadn't failed to notice Jeremy's reaction when he'd spoken about having sex with Casey earlier and it had bothered him. What had Casey said to Deirdre? What had Deirdre said to Jeremy? Maybe he'd known Rave was lying and that the sex had been pretty terrible. Maybe Casey had squealed about just how pathetic their attempt was. Maybe Jeremy was secretly laughing at him. *Nah, he wouldn't.* Jeremy hadn't asked one question. He hadn't laughed or messed or engaged. He hadn't even said, 'Congratulations.' Maybe if he had, Rave could have been honest with him . . . but Jeremy never made it easy. Maybe he suspected Rave wasn't who he pretended to be and just didn't want to know.

The wind was whistling through the small hole in the window filled with now sodden newspaper. Every now and then the hut seemed to heave, groaning and creaking.

'I like it,' Rave said. 'It's like it's talking to me.'

'It's saying, "Get out! This kip isn't safe,"' Jeremy said, and they laughed.

Rave saw him relax a little. 'Where d'you think we'll be in ten years?'

'On our boat,' Jeremy said.

Rave grinned. *I wish I could fast forward.* 'My da will be dead soon. He might even be dead now with any luck.'

'Don't say that.'

'I'm not going into care. I've saved a few quid in the bank, getaway money, like. It's not much but I can definitely afford the boat to England.'

Jeremy looked as if he was about to cry, and the fact that he cared so much settled Rave's nerves.

'Things will work out. You've got this place now.'

'It only works if Da's alive and the social aren't busybodying into me life. If he dies I'm still a minor.'

'He's not going to die.'

'It's a miracle he's not dead already.'

'You're obsessing.'

'I'm being realistic.'

'So you'll move in with us.'

'Your ma has enough to deal with.'

'She loves you, Rave.'

Rave thought about his da foaming at the mouth, then pictured Maisie and remembered her kindness. Out of nowhere an ocean of sadness swept through him and his tears fell like rain.

'Sorry.' Jeremy sounded a little panicked.

Rave was embarrassed. He hated people seeing him cry. 'Sorry,' he said, 'something in me eye.' He could barely get the words out, he was crying so hard.

'Are you OK?'

'I'm grand.' He wasn't grand. He was never grand. He just told himself and everyone else that he was. He figured if he said it enough times he'd believe it. Rave had a role to play and he took it seriously. He was the handsome one, the cool one, the guy everyone wanted to impress. Despite his shitty life, his mates still wanted to be him. It was a role he'd been playing for as long as he could remember. If he was enigmatic, charming and magnetic, the girls liked him and the guys wanted to be like him, and it didn't matter that his ma couldn't love him or that his da was killing himself to escape. All that mattered was the world he created, a world in which, even if he was a freak and was incapable of being loved, he still mattered.

Rave had always known there was something wrong with him, and before he could put it into words his mother had told him exactly what it was. Rave's first vivid memory had been laid down when he'd inherited his older brother's *Star Wars* figurines. He played with them night and day and it was always the same game. Luke and Han Solo lived together. Chewbacca was their pet and Princess Leia was their cleaner. His mother insisted he change the game. 'That's not how it works, John,' she'd said.

'But why?'

'Because boys don't live together.'

'But why?'

'Because they don't. Leia belongs with Han Solo and Luke can visit.'

When she caught him rubbing the Han Solo doll against the Luke doll she lost her mind. 'Don't you ever do that again, you dirty boy,' she said, as she slapped the legs off him. The next morning he woke up and the dolls were gone. He knew better than to ask for them back. That was his first lesson in shame. He was six. *Dirty boy.* The first time he saw Jeremy naked he was eight and Maisie had made them strip down to wash after they'd spent the afternoon mud fighting with four-year-old Valerie in the back garden. She made all three of them stand in the bath and sprayed the hose on them. Valerie was trying to pick the watery mud up between her fingers and throw it at Jeremy, who was laughing and holding on to the wall, and all Rave could do was cup himself with both hands hoping he didn't rise up because he couldn't take his eyes off the curve of Jeremy's bum, the small of his back, his dick, his arms.

Maisie didn't notice him looking. He was careful that she didn't: he didn't want her to see him the way his mother did. He was lucky she was too busy trying to shower the muck off the walls and ceiling as well as the kids. It scared him. He wanted to go home and hide. He prayed a lot before his mother left. Then one day she was gone. She didn't say goodbye, and deep down Rave had always known why.

When he was thirteen he found a book on sexual awareness, and there was a chapter called 'Preventing Embarrassment', which taught him how to conceal erections. It cited good-fitting underwear, dark jeans and long T-shirts as working really well. It told him not to be embarrassed: it was natural. He should relax, keep calm and think of something else. Of course, his erections weren't natural because they weren't for girls, but he knew exactly what could bring an erection down in a second: his mother. All he had to do was picture her telling him he was a dirty boy and he lost it instantly. That was helpful. He tried his best to stop looking at Jeremy in that way and it was easier when Jeremy went through an awkward phase. At the time Rave had had a full-on crush on Tim Daly, who played Joe Hackett in the American comedy *Wings*. The first time he saw the show he was twelve, alone, and wanked himself into a stupor.

That love affair lasted two years. It was around then that he started to hear the words 'homo', 'poofter', 'fudge-packer', 'queer', 'mattress-muncher', 'faggot', 'fruit' and 'fairy'. They were always spoken with distaste, always used to put someone down, to suggest they were weak, wrong, less than everyone else, shit, nothing, useless, broken, animal, evil and hell-bound. There were words for girls, too, although he noticed that they tended to be attributed according to the girl's looks. The ugly ones were 'dykes', the good-looking ones 'lesbos', and the lads reckoned they just needed a good seeing-to. If a girl turned a fella down it was perfectly acceptable to spit, 'Dyke!' They were ugly, vicious words, used about people his peers could never understand. Those words described how they really felt about him without knowing it. The only one who didn't use that language was Beany. It became another reason to love him.

The rest of Rave's friends and family's small acts of hate,

intolerance and discrimination ate away at his soul. He saw homophobia play out on-screen in movies and in music, where 'fag' was an acceptable casual insult and where gay-bashing was just a fact of life. He was even condemned by the Church, the very place that purported to welcome all. He saw it even in good people, like Maisie: she would lower her voice and make a face when anything to do with homosexuals came up. *God love them, it's a terrible life.* He knew if anyone else discovered who he really was they'd leave, just like his mother, and he wasn't going to let that happen again.

Casey saved him. She was the perfect girlfriend – she fitted the picture his friends had of him and she didn't just look the part: he appreciated how beautiful she was. He didn't necessarily fancy her but she didn't nauseate him. When he kissed her he could close his eyes and see Tim Daly or Christian Slater in *True Romance* or the guy from the Diet Coke adverts. When he touched her he imagined touching one of them. When she touched him, he closed his eyes and, with each stroke, she moved further and further away and the man in his head moved closer and closer.

He had been angry with himself after the bad-sex incident. Not just angry, disappointed. If he couldn't get his act together, if she left him, he worried that, with another girl, he might not be able to go through with it. Rave was terrified all the time, terrified his mother was right about him, terrified his da would die on him, terrified he'd be found out. Mostly he was terrified that he'd end up completely and utterly alone. Every minute of every new day brought new and difficult obstacles and he was just so tired of it all. He wanted everything to freeze in that moment so that it was just him and Beany hanging out in a log cabin surrounded by wind and rain and U2 playing on the stereo. Beany looked lovely in the candlelight: he admired his lean body, handsome face and wild, sandy hair. He wondered what it would be like to touch him. He wanted to so badly but he never would. He couldn't or wouldn't risk it.

Once when he was sleeping on Jeremy's floor, his friend had woken with a nightmare. He was distressed and said that sometimes he felt as if he couldn't breathe. When Rave had tried to comfort him he'd turned away and said he could never understand. It was strange because Rave was so practised in holding his breath he could have lived under water, but how could Jeremy have known that?

He'd wished he could tell him, right now in that moment, even as it passed.

Jeremy

When Rave was all cried out he wiped his eyes with his knuckles. 'Sorry,' he said again. 'Don't tell anyone.'

'I won't.' Jeremy meant it. Of course he wouldn't say anything. He just wished he could make everything all right. *Why does life have to be so unfair?*

'You think I'm a tosser, right?' Rave said.

'For crying?'

'Yeah.'

'Don't be stupid. I cry all the time.'

'Yeah?' Rave seemed relieved.

'Yeah.'

'Why?'

Jeremy could tell he really wanted to know but what could he say? *Because I'm in love with you and it makes me sick.* 'Dunno.'

'Has to be for a reason,' Rave pushed.

Just open up. Give him something, say anything . . .

'Just life.' Jeremy panicked. *I can't do this.* Rave was staring at him as though he needed something from him. *I don't know what to say.*

'Tell me something, Beany. If you're sad, give me a fuckin' reason.' Rave sounded frustrated, angry even.

Jeremy felt like running. He jumped up – he needed some

space. It was so hot in the cabin that he felt like his skin was on fire. Rave stood up and followed him. Jeremy put himself into the corner, like he always did when they were alone.

'What's wrong?' Rave said, moving forward. 'Why can't you just relax?'

'Sorry.' He couldn't look Rave in the eye.

'Just look at me.'

'I can't.'

'Why not?'

Rave was standing there in a long T-shirt and boxer shorts. Jeremy could see the contour of his chest and arms. His strong legs were on show. There was only a thin piece of fabric between Jeremy and Rave's dick. He needed to get out of there but the relentless rain kept battering the roof, like an endless drumroll.

'Just back off, Rave, please.'

Rave grew angry. 'I'm not gonna do anything to you.'

'I just need some space.'

'From me.'

'Please, Rave.'

'Why?'

'I can't say.' *How did we get here?*

'I'm asking why. Tell me,' Rave said, as though he was afraid of something.

'It's not about you!' Jeremy shouted. 'Not everything is about you.'

He was crying now and Rave stepped back. 'I'm sorry.' He seemed relieved, but curious too.

Jeremy was so raw and so scared he just didn't know what to do.

Rave

Jeremy was sobbing, bent over in a heap. Rave had never seen him cry like that, not even when he was injured on the play-

ing field or after his father had disappeared. He was convuls-
ing, exuding the kind of pain and loneliness that Rave knew
all too well. He didn't think, he just took Jeremy in his arms
and hugged him tight the way he longed to be hugged. 'It's OK,
Beany. Whatever it is, it's OK.'

'It's not OK,' Jeremy whispered, as he wept on his best
friend's shoulder. 'It's never gonna be OK.'

'Why, Beany?'

'Because I love you.' Jeremy broke down in grinding sobs.

Rave pulled away and looked at him, his beautiful face
awash with tears, and Jeremy stared into his best friend's grey
eyes and Rave's lips parted and Jeremy leaned in and they
kissed, at first a soft, gentle kiss, which became more urgent
until they were both holding each other by the back of the
hair pushing into one another and it felt, good, right, natural,
and such a relief. It was the best kiss Rave had ever had. Their
hands searched and found each other's backs and chests, arms,
and then Jeremy touched Rave, there in that place, and he just
needed a second, he wasn't ready for it, and in his head his
mother's voice shouted the words, *'Dirty boy, homo, poofter,
faggot, fruit, fudge-packer!'*

He reacted without thinking. He pushed Jeremy off him with
as much force as he could muster, turned away and fixed himself. He couldn't bear it. It was all too sudden and too much.
'No. We can't do this,' he said, keeping his back to Jeremy, and
Jeremy didn't argue, he didn't say a word, so he must have felt
the same. 'I'm sorry,' Rave said, when he'd gathered himself
together. *I'll make it up to you. It was just such a shock.* He
turned back to see his friend against the wall, half leaning and
half hanging.

'Jeremy?'

Something was off and he couldn't work out why so he
moved closer. Jeremy's eyes were wide open, his mouth agape
and on closer inspection he saw blood pouring down his neck
and shoulders.

'Jeremy?'

Jeremy's stare was fixed. He didn't move a muscle. He was there in the room but as soon as Rave looked into his friend's eyes he knew he was gone.

The nail was long and thick and must have been inside his skull, deep in his brain, because even the weight of his body didn't bring him to the floor. He was like one of those animal heads stuck to the wall.

'Jeremy!' Rave shouted. 'Jeremy!' He shook him but he didn't respond. He remained perfectly still, lost in his first real kiss, frozen there.

'Jeremy – I didn't mean it, Jeremy. Please, I didn't mean it. I'm begging you. Wake up,' he said, over and over again, hopelessly and desperately, but Jeremy wasn't asleep: no one sleeps with their eyes wide open. *I need to get him down. I need to pull him off the nail. If I do that I can do CPR. I can bring him back. People come back all the time.*

'You have to trust me. I can save you, Jeremy.'

He grabbed his friend's head and pulled as hard as he could, so hard that Jeremy came off the nail with such force that Rave ended up on the floor with Jeremy on top of him. He scrambled to get up. He covered the streaming hole in Jeremy's head with his hand.

'Oh, no, no . . . Oh, God, Jeremy.'

He turned him over and started pounding on his chest.

'Jeremy, Jeremy, Jeremy. It's OK. It's OK. I've got you. Just breathe, in and out, in and out. Come on, man, you and me, we know how hard it is to just breathe but we do it. We do it all the time.' He couldn't see through his tears. His nose was streaming and he kept wiping his face with his bloody hand so that he was masked in Jeremy's blood. When he realized there was nothing he could do, he groaned, like a wounded animal.

'Jeremy, I'm so sorry.' He took his friend in his arms, hugging and rocking him. 'I love you. I love you, Jeremy. I've always loved you. I'm so sorry.' He stayed there, hugging and rocking his best friend, until the small hours, then curled Jeremy into a ball and covered him with the sleeping bag.

Rave stayed there beside him for four days and nights until he finally worked out the best thing to do.

4 January 1995

Dear Maisie,

It all happened so fast. We were there and then he was gone and I'm so sorry. It's my fault. I wanted to be normal. I fought my feelings with everything I had in me but I have loved him since I can remember and it killed me because I knew it was wrong. But then all of a sudden he loved me back and it was a miracle, Maisie, like a bolt from the blue. It was the best moment of my entire life. I felt exhilarated, happy, free, content, normal, and I know he felt the same just in that moment. But when the voices that haunt me filled my head I pushed him, Maisie. I didn't mean to hurt him. I'd never hurt him. I just wanted some space to stop, to think, to take a little time. It was all so sudden and so much, I thought my head and heart would burst if I didn't step back, so I pushed him. There was a nail on the wall. He must have lost his footing and fallen against it. He didn't feel anything. I promise. I tried to save him. I did everything I could but he wouldn't come back. He couldn't come back and it's all my fault.

I'm going to say goodbye now. I'm going to post this and then I'm going to go. I can't be here without him. Even if I could, I can't live with myself now so I'm going to join him, wherever he is. That's where I want to be.

I've drawn a map of how to find the hut. He's wrapped up in my sleeping bag. Nothing can touch him here. When I knew he was gone I rolled him into a ball. I wanted him to be somewhere inside of happy, Maisie. I know that's what he'd want. You were always so kind to me. You don't deserve this. I wish I could change it. I wish I could turn back time and do everything differently. I wish . . .

I loved him. I'm so grateful to you and I'm so, so sorry. I hope you get over it. I hope you don't run off somewhere or become a junkie like my parents because Valerie needs you.

Love, Rave

PS I'm in the reservoir if anyone is looking for me.

FRIDAY,
6 JANUARY 1995

Chapter Eleven

'Creep'
Radiohead, 1992

Dave

Dave's alarm went off at five thirty. He slapped it off and turned over with a groan. He cursed Rave for suggesting he bond with Jonno. But once he was awake, training with Jonno was more fun than he'd ever admit. He was standing at the gate by five fifty. It was freezing so he wore a jacket under his granddad's big coat. Jonno finally came running, just after six. Dave was so cold he cycled around in circles trying to keep warm. Jonno was decked out in just a woolly hat and a tracksuit but he'd already run from home and he continued to jog on when Dave broke his circle and cycled towards him.

'Are you right?' Dave said.

'Good.'

'Let's go, then.' Dave pressed the button on his da's stopwatch. 'Let's break some records.'

Jonno started running, through the gates and along the narrow tree-lined rocky road that led to the reservoir and past the trickling stream that threatened to leak into his runners. He ran past the few pretty houses, two snarling guard dogs and a man exiting his driveway transporting a boat. The air was crisp. Except for the possible loss of a few digits to frostbite it was just how he liked it. Jonno looked good. Even the break over Christmas hadn't diminished his form.

'How am I doing?'

'Pissing along. Come on! Focus! Stay the course.'

Jonno nodded and picked up the pace. Every time Dave thought Jonno had shown him all he had, he went into another gear. It was impressive. Dave was lagging behind: he found it hard to keep up. Jonno had wings. Dave's coat was dragging him down and one of his gears kept sticking. Jonno glanced back at him as they reached the reservoir.

'Just keep going, man! Don't slow down!' Dave shouted.

Jonno nodded and ran on. He was near the bridge when he slowed to a stop. Dave couldn't see what was impeding him. He worried that he'd pulled a muscle. *It'll take me all bleedin' day to get him home.* He made his way to the bridge as quickly as his stupid broken gears would allow. When he got there, Jonno was hanging over the railings. *He's puking, grand, he'll get over that.* But then Jonno turned to face him and the horror on his face told a different story.

Dave got off the bike and walked forward, just as Jonno stepped back, another figure beyond him in the gloom. Dave struggled to accept the reality of what he was seeing. It took a millisecond to adjust. It was definitely a boy holding onto the railings of the bridge and it was clear he was going to jump. *Rave? Rave? Is that you?*

Jonno was facing him now and shouting at him but the blood rushing from his chest to his head was deafening. Dave needed a minute. *Rave? What are ya doing, man? What are you hanging off the fuckin' bridge at low tide for? It's freezing.*

'Dave!' Jonno shouted. He was in Dave's face. 'Snap out of it.'

'Rave?' Dave said.

Rave's arms were threaded through the iron bars and his heels barely fitted on the edge. He looked like Jesus, if Jesus had been hanging from a bridge instead of nailed to a cross. He was blue with cold, he'd lost weight and a patch of his black hair had turned white at the roots. His fingers and arms were blue so even if he'd wanted to hold on he probably couldn't for much longer. Dave couldn't take it in.

'Rave.' Jonno leaned over the railings. 'It's me, Jonno. Howya doin', man?'

'Don't fuckin' ask him that. It's very fuckin' clear how he's doing,' Dave said, finally finding his voice.

'Shut up, Dave,' Jonno said. 'Rave, can you hear me?'

'I can hear you.' Rave kept his eyes on the water.

'Oh, good.' Jonno sighed. 'Why don't I help you?'

'You touch me and I'll jump.'

Dave dropped the bike with a thud.

Jonno jumped. 'Jesus Christ, Dave, be fuckin' careful!'

'Sorry.' Dave meant it. He felt really terribly, horribly sorry.

Jonno turned back to Rave. 'I need you to tell me what I can do to help.'

'Nothing.'

'Everybody's been looking for you. It's been mad, hasn't it, Dave?'

Dave nodded, even though Rave was facing the water and couldn't see him. 'The police and the press and Jeremy's ma.'

'Maisie was looking for me?'

Dave saw a little light switch on in him. 'She went on the telly and told you she loved ya. She wanted yis home.'

Rave's eyes filled. 'I wrote her a letter. She'll get it tomorrow.'

'Why did you do that?' Jonno said.

'I needed to explain.'

'Why don't I go and get some help?'

'It's too late, Jonno.'

'No, it's not!' Jonno said, in a panic. 'You just hang on – all right, man?'

'No. Can't.'

'You can – you are! Look at you.'

'It's too late.'

'I could get Maisie,' Jonno said and Rave gulped. 'It's better to say things in person.'

Rave thought about that and nodded. 'You're right.'

Thank God, Dave thought. *Nice one, Jonno*. Dave really didn't know what was going on. What did Rave need to say to Maisie? What was he doing on the bridge? Where was Jeremy?

'OK, good. Hang on while I get her. Dave is gonna stay here with you,' Jonno said, in a calm voice.

'I am in me hole!' Dave almost screeched. *No way! I can't, I can't, I can't!*

'Give me a second,' Jonno told Rave. He walked over to Dave and grabbed him by his coat collar. 'I am faster than you. I am cycling to one of those swish little houses and I'm gonna phone Maisie. You are going to keep Rave company. Do not say anything that will encourage him to jump. Understand?'

'No.' Dave's eyes were wild. 'I can't be trusted. I'm a fuckin' prick, remember.' He was crying all of a sudden. 'I'll say something and he'll fuckin' jump. Please. I'll go. I'll do it. I'll cycle this fuckin' broken bike or I'll run as fast as I can. Don't make me stay. If you leave him, he's as good as dead.' Dave was sure about that, surer than he'd ever been about anything in his life. The best thing he could do for his friend was leave. *Please, Rave, please don't do this to me.*

Jonno relaxed his grip. 'You'll be OK. Just be cool.' Clearly he wasn't taking no for an answer. He picked up the bike and started to cycle away. He was halfway down the bridge when the gears jammed. Dave watched as he jumped off and ran faster than he'd ever seen him run before.

Dave's mind raced. He moved over to Rave with his hands up. 'I come in peace.'

Rave didn't move a muscle. Dave wondered if he was iced to the bridge. On closer inspection Rave's top lip was purple, his bottom lip was blue. 'Hiya,' Dave said, when he was so close he could have touched Rave. He didn't respond.

'Jonno's just gone to get Ms Bean. He shouldn't be too long.'

Rave just stared into the water.

'Jesus, it's fuckin' cold, isn't it? Me gonads have shrivelled to the size of beach balls.'

Rave didn't laugh.

'Get it? They're so big, they shrivel down to the size of beach balls.'

Rave looked tired. He was gaunt and bony. His hair was freaky-looking. Dave was truly terrified. Rave's arms must really hurt, and when he swayed slightly it looked like he was going to fall. 'Oh, Jesus. Hang on – hang on, for fuck sake!'

Rave looked like he was ready to go. 'Tell Maisie I'm sorry.'

'No fuckin' way!' Dave screamed at his friend.

'Just do it, Dave.'

'No.' Dave was crying again. 'No, I won't. I'll tell her you said she could fuck herself. That's what I'll say because if you jump now that's what you're doing. You're saying yis can all go and fuck yourselves and it's not right – it's not right at all.'

Rave looked at him. Finally he had Rave's attention and he was determined not to mess up.

'Please, please, Rave, please don't do it. I know something bad has happened. I know it has, but you doing this is not right. I love you, man. Right? We all do and whatever happens we always will.'

'You don't know what I've done.' Rave's voice cracked.

'I don't fuckin' care,' Dave said. 'I swear I don't. We're in this together, brothers in arms. Don't let me down.'

'I can't, Dave,' Rave said. 'I just can't. I'm sorry.'

For one gut-wrenching moment Dave thought he was going to let go.

'No, no, no, please, man! Please don't turn me into the prick who let Rave die. I can't live with that.' He actually got on his knees and begged, 'Please, please, Rave, don't leave me, Jesus, please don't leave me.'

It must have struck a chord because Rave clung on tighter. 'OK. I'm sorry, Dave.'

'Me too.' Dave was bawling like a baby now. 'Sorry for everything. I love you, man. I love you, man. I really fuckin' love you.'

Dave took off his grandfather's coat and covered Rave with it, then wrapped his arms around him and held on as tight as he could. 'I've got you, Rave.'

He held on to his best friend and together, in silence, they waited. He didn't know how long had passed when he heard the car and turned to see Jonno getting out and running, a man and a woman following as quickly as they could.

'He's tired,' Dave said to them. 'He's really tired.'

'She's coming, Rave. She's on her way,' Jonno said.

The man who had allowed Jonno to use his phone stood back with his wife in his arms, both dumbstruck. There was nothing they could say.

Dave didn't move a muscle while Jonno told Rave to hang on and promised that Maisie would be coming any minute now. 'How long does it take to drive from Cypress Road to the reservoir, Dave?' Jonno asked.

'About ten minutes,' Dave said.

'With a copper driving?'

'About five.'

'We're three minutes in already, then. Two minutes, man. OK?' Jonno said, and Rave nodded. 'Just two more minutes.'

Just two more minutes, Dave thought. *Hold on, don't let go, keep him safe.* He was freezing, his hands and arms ached, but even if Maisie Bean took a month to get there, Dave O'Loughlin was not letting go.

Maisie

Maisie woke up to the sound of a crow cawing at just after five thirty-five. She was still dressed and on Jeremy's bed. She sat

340

up and oriented herself. Bridie hadn't walked the hall or if she had Maisie hadn't heard her. She got up to check. The hallway was empty. Bridie was sound asleep in bed. She exhaled. *OK.* She walked into the sitting room. Fred was lying on the sofa, wide awake and staring at the ceiling.

'You stayed.' She was happy to see him.

'Sorry, Mai, I fell asleep.'

'Don't apologize.' She sat cross-legged on the floor beside him. 'It's been an exceptionally weird week.'

'You can say that again.'

'I'm going to get him home, Fred.' *She knew it, she just knew it.*

Fred sat up and rubbed his face with both hands. 'I believe you.'

She took his hand in hers and kissed it. 'I don't think I've thanked you yet.'

'Not necessary.'

'Thank you,' she said. 'Thank you, Fred. Thanks for saving us all those years ago and thanks for being here now and saving us all over again.'

'Is that what I'm doing, Mai?'

'Yeah. It is.'

'Well, no matter what, I'll keep on doing that.'

She stood up and brushed herself down. 'Coffee?'

Fred didn't get a chance to respond because the phone rang, stealing her attention. She ran to the hallway and picked it up, but before she could say hello she heard Jonno Lynch, half hysterical and crying down the phone.

'Mrs Bean, help! It's Rave.'

'Where?'

'On the bridge at the reservoir.'

'What about Jeremy?'

'He's going to jump, Mrs Bean.'

'Who? Jeremy?'

'No, Rave. He wants you. He'll only talk to you.'

Fred was now standing in front of her and she saw her horror reflected in his face. 'I'll be there,' she said, and dropped the phone.

'Mai?'

Rave was on the bridge threatening to end his life and Jeremy was nowhere to be seen. She switched to autopilot. 'We need to go.' She couldn't leave without waking Valerie to ensure she watched over Bridie, but then she couldn't leave Valerie to wonder what was going on. So instead she woke her mother and child, put slippers and coats on them and sat them in the car.

Everyone was silent. Bridie was nodding off, not sure what was happening and too groggy to engage. Valerie was stone-faced. Fred drove through Tallaght village faster than the speed of sound. Maisie gripped her seat when they turned a sharp corner on what felt like two wheels. It was the longest and shortest car ride Maisie Bean had ever had.

Maisie saw the man and woman standing back on the bridge first, then spotted the boys: Jonno hovering and Dave hanging on to Rave for dear life. She was out of the car before Fred had switched off the engine. Valerie was staring at the scene, clearly in terror.

'Stay here,' she heard herself say, and her daughter nodded.

Maisie and Fred ran onto the bridge together. Maisie was already crying. Rave was a trembling broken wreck. The sight of him took her breath away. She felt Fred's arms around her, keeping her upright. She couldn't think, she could only act.

'Rave, Rave lovey, it's Maisie.'

'Maisie?'

Jonno stood back and she moved towards Rave. She was so close she could touch him. He was a bag of bones and wild looking.

'Let me go, Dave.'

'No fuckin' way.'

'I need to speak to Maisie alone.' Rave started to struggle.

'It's OK, calm down. It's all right, son, just relax,' Fred said, and then he nodded at Dave. 'Let him go. He's staying here with us, aren't ya, Rave?'

Rave nodded. Dave let go gently, moving off slowly to join Jonno. Fred stood back, leaving Maisie and Rave alone. Police and ambulance sirens rang out in the near distance.

'Rave, lovey, what's going on?' Her voice shook. She hugged herself tightly, afraid that if she let go she'd turn into liquid. Her knees were knocking but somehow she remained upright.

'I wrote you a letter. I posted it yesterday.' He was staring straight ahead.

'Why's that, Rave?' *Oh God please no. Please, please no.*

'I wanted to say I'm sorry and I didn't mean it. I really didn't mean it.'

Rave was crying and Maisie was crying, too, because she knew her son was dead. She'd known he was dead the second she'd heard that Rave was alone on the bridge. 'It's OK, love,' she said, but it wasn't. A hot pain ripped right through her. *Jeremy? Oh, my son, my heart, my soul, my sweet baby boy.*

'It's not, though, Maisie. He's gone.'

'I know, lovey. I know he is.' She was nodding, barely holding herself together.

'I did it, Maisie. I killed him. I didn't mean it.'

She wanted to scream and punch a wall. She wanted to roar and shout and blow the world apart but the child clinging to the bridge was not the focus of her rage. Even in that agonizing moment, she recognized the boy's pain and helplessness, still loved him. How could she not? 'Course you didn't.' She reached out and touched him, placing her hand on his bony arm.

'But I pushed him – I pushed him off. One minute he was alive and the next he just wasn't and I didn't mean it.'

Maisie's entire body ached. Her insides burned, her heart tore and her mind screamed. 'Jeremy,' she said. 'Oh, Jeremy.'

'He didn't suffer, Maisie. He didn't. I promise you that.'

Rave released his grip but she grabbed him before he could unwind his arms fully. She hung on to him, much like Dave before her, and held him close.

'Maisie, what are you doing? Let me go.'

'Can't.'

'Please, Maisie, please let me go.'

'Can't.'

'Please.'

'No. I won't let you go, lovey.' Suddenly Fred was there holding on to Maisie, holding on to Rave. Guards and ambulance men were racing onto the bridge towards the boy and the woman crying an ocean in one another's arms.

Epilogue

Maisie Bean Brennan Signing Off

Maisie looked around the packed room and it was silent, except for some nose-blowing and a young girl, who was crying loudly. Two hundred young faces were staring up at her, waiting for more.

'I know what yous all are thinking, that it can't be the end of the story, right? But it was. At least, it was the end of Jeremy's story.' She took a sip of water and the students waited to hear what she had really come to say.

'Jeremy's death was a terrible accident but that accident was caused because of people like some of you and people like me. People who call something gay if they think it's stupid or describe someone as gay if they think they're weak. People like the one I used to be, who felt sorry for gay people because it's no life, but it's only ever no life because of people who are sorry, like I was. Nobody should ever be made to feel like a second-class citizen because of their sex or sexuality. There's nothing to fear from gay people. The fear comes from the way society views and treats them. That's where the pain lies. That's where the hell and horror reside.'

Another girl blew her nose and coughed.

'Rave and Jeremy loved one another, and that kiss should have been the best first kiss ever, like one of those fairy tales or rom coms.' She laughed a little. 'Did I get that right? A rom com?'

A girl in the front row nodded.

'It should have been epic, but fear, judgement and shame got in the way. Rave spent four days alone in a cabin with his dead best friend. He didn't want to leave him alone, you see. It was three days before he came up with the plan to join him in death. Then he walked to Blessington on an empty stomach, bought some paper and a pen and wrote me a letter. He drew a little map so that we could find Jeremy and bury him. Then he bought a sandwich, a bag of crisps, some furniture polish and a can of air freshener. He ate the food to give him enough strength to get back to Jeremy, then cleaned up and sprayed the air so that when we found him he wouldn't smell like Rave's da.' Her voice broke. It was the first time Maisie had allowed herself to cry in front of the students.

'I'm sorry.' She collected herself. 'I'd like to read you the letter now, if you'll indulge me.'

When she was done, she looked at the sad streaming faces, nodding and sniffing and waiting. Lynn was staring up at her, crying her eyes out and holding John's hand, squeezing it and clasping it tight to her chest. He just smiled and nodded.

John pushed his white hair from his face, then wiped a tear from his eye. He hadn't been called Rave in a long time but when Maisie looked at the handsome man sitting in front of her she still saw the broken boy on the bridge. Lynn leaned over and gave him a kiss, dropping her knitting on the floor. Dave picked it up and handed it to her. Still by his friend's side, still hanging on.

Maisie turned to see Fred standing at the side of the stage and smiling proudly. Valerie was leaning on him, giving her the thumbs-up, and behind her stood Maisie's nineteen-year-old son, Arthur. He'd never met his brother. In a sad twist of fate Arthur had been conceived the night after Jeremy died. Arthur had kept his ma and Valerie alive all those years ago. He had bound Maisie and Fred together for ever and he had brought a smile to Bridie Bean's face, even when she was completely gone.

She died the day after Arthur's first birthday in a nice nursing home that specialized in the care of Alzheimer's patients. She didn't know who anyone was, but she still spoke of and to Jeremy right up to the end.

Maisie turned back to her audience. 'A lovely lady called Joan Wilde helped me and Rave – I should say John now he's grown-up – and their friends write this book about what happened, what we learned and how it changed us.' She pointed into the crowd. 'Deirdre Mahony, Casey Shaw, Jonno Lynch, Mitch Carberry, Dave O'Loughlin, can you all stand up, please?' They did so, and the crowd clapped fiercely.

'And now I want to introduce to you John Rave Murphy.'

John stood up slowly and leaned on his best friend, Dave. He was emotional, scared and still, after all those years, deeply sad, but he was all right, better than all right: he was a fighter, a survivor. He overcame everything and he was a success. Maisie was proud of him. She knew Jeremy would have been proud too. When Jeremy's friends were seated again and the applause had died down, Maisie finished with the simple truth.

'It was just an accident, a terrible, stupid, avoidable accident. The real tragedy is how we all made those boys feel: the shame, guilt, pain and hatred we instilled in them. I wish I could have been the mother I am now back then, but I wasn't, and that's OK because I've changed. I've grown. I've educated myself, and that's all I ask of you. Some of you probably don't need to read this book – some of you are already there – but for the others, the ones who have grown up in houses where sexuality is an issue or being gay is something to be condemned, I hope today has lit a spark in you. I hope it's given you a different perspective. Finally, for those of you who are hiding who you really are, I want to say that you are entitled to love. All you've got to do is be who you are, go out there and find it. Thank you.'

The crowd stood as they applauded and laughter bubbled up in her chest. *Maisie Bean Brennan, who do you think you are?*

'Thank you.' She took one last look around the room, then

nodded at John, Dave and Lynn. *Time to go.* John was already navigating Lynn out of the noisy room before it all got too much for her.

She walked to the side of the stage and into the arms of her family. 'How'd I do?'

'You were amazing, Ma'sie,' Valerie said.

'I'm so fuckin' proud I could burst.' That was Fred.

'What about you, Arthur?'

'You rock, Ma'sie. You made me wish I was gay.'

'Cheeky git.'

'Right. Let's get the others and celebrate kicking off your ma's lecture tour in spectacular fashion. Ma'sie's a real poshie now,' Fred said, ruffling his son's hair.

Arthur playfully pushed him away. 'All right, Da! This hair doesn't just happen on its own.'

On the way out, a young man stopped Maisie. 'That was really incredible.'

'Thanks.'

He was shy, nervous, a little unsteady in himself, even. 'Would you mind if I talked to you for a few minutes? It's about what I am.'

'I'd love that, son.' And Maisie Bean Brennan smiled.

Acknowledgements

Two people helped to make this book happen. They believed in the story from the very start. They supported me when illness meant delays and tight deadlines, without saying one negative word. They helped shape this book. So to my agent Sheila Crowley and my Transworld editor Harriet Bourton go my heartfelt thanks. Sheila joked that we're a Dream Team, and I like to think she's right. Sheila, you are fierce, fabulous, honest and driven, and I'm so grateful for your representation. Harriet, every note makes perfect sense, you make me laugh, you know exactly what lane I'm supposed to be in and you always elevate the work. I couldn't ask for more. Ladies, my heart is full.

A huge thank-you to my copy-editor Hazel Orme for her invaluable work on all seven of my novels.

To my entire family: I love you and thank you for everything.

To my friends: you make life better. Thanks especially to Enda Barron and Eimear O'Rourke for providing invaluable insight and local knowledge.

Anna McPartlin is a novelist and scriptwriter. Her previous incarnation as a stand-up comedian left an indelible mark. She describes herself as a slave to the joke and finds humour and humanity in even the darkest situations. Anna lives in Wicklow with her husband and animals. *The Last Days of Rabbit Hayes*, Anna's previous novel, was a Richard & Judy selected title and a top-ten bestseller in the UK and Ireland.